BARBARIAN INCURSION

BARBARIAN INCURSION

SAPIENS BOOK 1

Persimmon

Podium

Podium

BARBARIAN
INCURSION

CHAPTER ONE

Dorea stood at the edge of the great white cliff that towered over her family's ranch, her eyes fixed on the vast expanse of the sea.

The salty scent of the ocean filled her nostrils, and she felt the wind whipping through her hair as she gazed at the horizon.

In the distance, the air shimmered and vibrated, creating distortions that made it seem as if the world was a rock under the full might of the summer sun.

She had heard tales of Nature's Wrath, the catastrophic events that reshaped lands, and the lives of everyone who resided there. Seeing one approaching with her own eyes was something else entirely.

As she looked out at the approaching storm, she couldn't help but feel a sense of unease. The world was a harsh place, and it often reminded its denizens of it, but this seemed like a trial of the worst kind.

Even at this distance, she could make out grand arches of lightning flashing between the gales and the wall of water falling from the dark sky.

She knew well that this was both a curse and a blessing, seeing how the village's shaman ensured every kid knew of their duty.

They would have to withstand Nature's Wrath outside the shelter built for the adults and babies to prove their worthiness to the Mother and hope she would bless them in return.

Dorea also knew that the chances of them all surviving were slim, but since they were supposed to be drugged to the gills by the time the storm made landfall, she knew there was no chance of them helping each other.

All her hard work in setting up the new habitat for the moas would be for nothing. Her father had already explained how, for all their preparations, they would need to readily bend to Mother Earth's whims to make sure not to break.

Attempting to save worthless things such as those could spell their doom.

Dorea's thoughts drifted to the village of the Ubags, whom her tribe had traded with for centuries. An earthquake had destroyed her ancestors' village and claimed a good ten percent of its population.

However, that was nothing compared to being buried alive underneath a mountain. Not a single survivor was found after days of searching, and her people could only come to the conclusion that the entire village hidden in the mountain of the Ubag people had simply ceased to exist.

The aftershocks that continued for weeks convinced everyone of the wisdom of relocating to a calmer land, so the long journey to the coast of Loisos began.

As Dorea watched the storm approaching, she knew that her tribe had chosen these lands for a reason: the climate was mild, even the winter season was not too harsh, and they were away from any kind of fault lines. But even with all their preparations, they would need to be ready to face whatever Mother Nature had in store for them.

Small, muddy feet pounded the sodden ground, doing their very best to convey all the annoyance and rage at being forced into the shelter against their will.

Her sister, Lia, was pouting full blast, desperately hoping that someone would recognize her as a "big girl" and therefore ready to face the upcoming Trial, but Dorea's mind was elsewhere.

Her rucksack was stuffed to the brim with everything she could think of as being helpful and some things that might not be, but one could never be too careful.

"It's not fair! You know that I'm much better than Jonah at basically everything, I should be out there with you, and he should be inside!" the little blonde yelled with as much outrage as she could.

Dorea turned toward her, an exhausted smile on her lips. However worried she was, she still forced herself to not dismiss her sister. She knew very well what kind of opportunity this was and that the dangers must have seemed all too easy to ignore.

"You are definitely braver than Jonah, and if I could, I would have you with me over anyone else, but no one under thirteen has ever managed to successfully receive the Mother's Gift," she tried to placate. "Besides that, considering that the full might of the storm is still half a day away and the winds have managed to send flying every piece of laundry in the valley, I wouldn't bet on them not picking you up and launching you into the sea."

Lia was obviously not appeased, as logic was complicated for a nine-year-old tomboy hell-bent on adventure. However, she recognized her big sister's tone and knew she wouldn't find an ally in her. Dorea being her very last resort, she let out a frustrated scream and ran out the door, likely to pester their father in a last-ditch attempt.

Dorea would usually follow her to try and calm her down, but today was not a typical day, and her mind was entirely focused on surviving the future hours. A mixture of dread and excitement pooled in her belly that resembled the sensation of falling.

She looked out of her window toward the sea, where she could see the still-growing storm, and imagined it being filled with a malevolence that only came with sapience, a will determined to wipe her and everyone she had ever known out with prejudice.

Surviving the Wrath would come with many boons. It would mean a better life for the whole village, considering that they were down to just one Gifted and still were doing much better than they would without.

The blond girl actively returned her focus to her preparations, knowing that she would never spend much time thinking about the minutiae of governance and wealth if she weren't trying to distract herself from the impending Trial.

"Dorea!" came the shout from downstairs, her father's powerful voice jolting her into action.

"Coming!" she yelled back, putting her favorite pendant in the bag that would go with her family to the shelter.

As much as she would love to cling to her grandmother's gift during this trying time, she would never forgive herself if she lost it, which was likely to happen when undergoing the Trial and not in her full mental capacity.

She gave one last long look at her room, knowing that if she ever came back here, she would be very different from what she was now.

Dorea launched herself into her father's waiting arms, breathing in his scent, and relished being comforted like when she was little and had just had a nightmare.

"We really need to get going, dearest," he rumbled, breathing in her scent one last time before reluctantly releasing her from his arms.

"We need to go get your mother; she sprinted to the shaman as soon as the bell started ringing to help him prepare, so she'll be there to walk you through the ceremony."

"Yeah, I think I'm ready now, Dad, thanks," Dorea replied, knowing that delaying any more would just give her cold feet.

She ruffled her sister's hair one last time and picked up her two rucksacks, ready to leave her family's home for what could be the last time.

Her eyes roved over the wooden furniture and leather decorations; they stopped over her chair in the dining area, the kitchen where she helped her mother make many meals, and the fireplace where she listened to her father's stories during more normal storms.

She tried her best to ingrain every detail of her home in her mind, suddenly struck with a feeling that even if she returned here, things would never be the same.

A small hand gently closed around hers, returning her to the present, and she turned to see her sister's worried gaze, a frown starting to form.

"Everything is going to be all right, Lia," she comforted and started walking toward the open door where her father awaited them.

The thunk of the door closing felt much louder than usual, but she strode ahead with her head held high.

"The moas are all accounted for and have enough food in their cave to last a few days. The anoas are likewise settled in the smaller cave northeast of the moas," her father started, rambling as she knew he did when trying to take their minds away from something.

"We really couldn't keep them together; those damn birds would have definitely tried to eat some, no matter how much food we left them."

They slowly made their way on the path leading them out of their ranch and into the unimaginatively named Whitecliff. As her father kept going on about the preparations they had made in hopes of salvaging something after the Mother's Wrath had struck them, she found comfort in the rumble of his voice and the knowledge that she had done all she could to prepare for something that no one was ever ready for.

"The crops are done for, of course, so we'll all have to pitch in a bit after everything to help the farmers out, but there is a reason why we all have to set some food aside in the village storage, so it shouldn't impact our personal stores too much."

"And by then, Dorea will be Gifted for sure, so she'll be able to hunt some big animal for everyone to eat," piped up Lia, apparently over her worry for her sister's safety or desire to participate in the coming Trial. "She'll be super strong and much better than that stupid Jonah!"

Dorea smiled in gratitude for the unwavering trust the little blonde put in her and amusement at how she still wasn't over the baker's boy being included in the ceremony while she was not.

She gave Lia a look. "I'm sure everyone who passes the Trial will do their best to help the village recover from the Wrath."

The only reply was a tongue sticking out, which caused their father to chuckle. "I have all the faith in the world in Dorea's ability to make it and that she'll be a great help, but she will have to take some time to get comfortable with her Gift before we can send her out to the wilds to hunt."

The trust in his voice warmed her heart, and she took courage in his certainty that she would make it.

The time passed quickly, and soon enough, they were standing in front of the shaman's house, a sight she was almost as familiar with as her own home, considering how her mother spent quite a few days helping to prepare poultices and care for the now elderly man.

Dorea spotted the shaggy white mane of hair that belonged to Voggo, the owner of the house, in the middle of a group of teenagers and young adults and braced herself for the last time before turning to her family with a smile.

Her father gave her an encouraging nod, and she received a tremulous grin from Lia.

There was no need to say anything more, so she simply joined the crowd of forty or so others who would attempt to survive the coming Trial to gain incredible power.

A hand snaked out of the mass to grab her wrist and pulled her toward a brunette. "You finally made it! I was starting to think that you would get cold feet."

Dorea rolled her eyes at the jab, not taking the words seriously. "You know that between the preparations we needed to make and the walk here, I'd be the last one, Beth."

Her friend smiled mischievously. "And your mother, the shaman's assistant, would never allow you to skip on it."

The blonde merely inclined her head, conceding the point and focusing on the entrance to the house, where a woman was bustling out, arms filled with a cauldron that contained a sloshing silvery liquid.

A thick curtain of golden hair partially covered her face, and her eyes were fixed on the kids, looking for someone specific.

As soon as she noticed Dorea, a small smile bloomed on her face, and she relaxed her shoulders, releasing a tension that had been invisible until that moment.

She moved toward the shaman, offering no more acknowledgment to her daughter or her friend, who were left standing at the back of the group.

Dorea watched as her mother began to help old Voggo with the preparations, setting the cauldron down in front of him and producing various herb pastes for him to mix into it.

Everyone quieted down, mesmerized by the skillful motions and starting to finally realize that they were a stone's throw away from changing their lives entirely or, in the case of the more unfortunate ones, ending them.

Beth's hand tightly gripped her own, in both a show of support and a request of it. Their hands were clammy, and she would have usually made a joke out of it, but at the moment, she couldn't help but be grateful for her dearest friend's presence.

Dorea did her best to focus on the preparations and not slide back into worrying about the near future, knowing there was nothing else to do. The Mother had decided to test them, and their lives would never be the same.

The elderly shaman chanted for a short while under his breath, the words too soft for her to make out, and the concoction glowed momentarily before settling.

It's time. Please, Mother, protect us.

"Children, form a line and get prepared to drink your portion; I don't want to hear any complaining about taste or texture!" Voggo shouted, his voice easily heard in the silence. "This is necessary unless you want to end up like an enhanced beast, unable to fully control your power."

His aged eyes roved over the forming line, nodding once the first boy, Rupert, one of three sons of farmer Brock who would undergo the Trial that day, had stepped up before him.

The shaman dipped a smaller bowl that her mother had handed to him in the cauldron and scooped up a portion of the silvery liquid into it. "Drink up."

Dorea watched the tall boy take the bowl and drink it in one go, obviously trying his best not to make a face.

It's definitely not gonna be as good as Mom's berry tea or apple juice.

The line moved quickly, and no one seemed to have second thoughts, so it was her turn faster than anticipated.

It's just mushrooms and grass, nothing weird at all. Just gulp it down in one go, she told herself, and psyched up. Dorea gulped the strangely viscous brew with one last look at her mother, who remained impassive save for a slight softening of her eyes.

It was almost bearable, beyond a grassy, muddy aftertaste.

She quickly returned to the crowd of young people and located one of her other friends.

Jonah was somewhat androgynous and could be mistaken for a girl at a distance, but he had a heart of gold, and Dorea had always considered him a dear friend.

He was obviously trying his best not to show how much he was affected by the situation, but it wasn't very successful, considering how he was hugging himself.

"'Lo there, Jonah, everything good?" She wrapped her arm around his shoulders, causing him to jolt and turn red.

The dusting of color on his pale cheeks made him look even more like a blushing maiden.

He really is as pretty as a girl, huh.

"Y-yeah, of course," he replied, nervously tugging at one of the blond locks of hair that curled around his ear.

Dorea gave him a small smile, trying to convey some reassurance. "Don't worry, we'll make it through this. We're strong."

He nodded, but she could see the worry in his eyes. She squeezed his shoulder before returning her attention to the front, where Voggo gave a final speech.

"Children, the Mother's Wrath is almost upon us, and we all need to go into the shelter, but our hearts and souls will be with you during this Trial. Some of you will come out of the other side more powerful than you can imagine. Others . . ." he trailed off, his voice somber.

Dorea felt a shiver run down her spine. She knew the risks, but she also knew the rewards. She took a deep breath, trying to calm her nerves.

Voggo continued. "But know this: no matter what happens, you will have the support of your fellow villagers. We will all be rooting for you."

With those words, he gestured toward the hill she had stood on just a while before. "Now, go. Face the Trial and come back victorious."

The teenagers and young adults moved as one and started trudging their way out of the village and toward the cliff, each one determined to come out the other side.

Their families shouted their last farewells before entering the shaman's house and climbing down into the shelter that every village built in case the Mother decided to visit her Wrath upon them.

"I guess this really is it, isn't it?" asked Beth, capturing her hand again.

"I suppose so. There really isn't much more to do. The brew should start working in an hour or so, and soon the storm will be upon us," replied Dorea.

"Maybe we'll all make it?" Jonah questioned, biting his lip, his big green eyes hopeful.

"I'm sure the Mother will make sure everyone will be fine," Dorea replied, trying to reassure him, but her gaze soon returned to the approaching storm.

The seas were starting to churn, and the clouds looked even angrier, lightning cracking more frequently and the distant booms of thunder coming closer and closer.

The procession soon arrived at the cliff's edge, and everyone started looking for a place to sit down.

History has shown that it didn't matter where you sat, what you brought, or even if you wanted it. Even if you didn't drink the potion made to open your soul to the Mother, you would undergo the Trial, and your chances were not affected by any little detail.

Well, if you don't drink it, you'll still have the chance of gaining magic, but Voggo made it very clear that the chances of survival are much lower.

Dorea sat on a flat white rock close to her friends and looked at the horizon, both scared and hopeful about the future.

CHAPTER TWO

The stone she was sitting on wasn't exactly comfortable, but Dorea's attention was fixed upon the approaching Wrath. It was an almost uniform wall of dark clouds where purple lightning crackled and illuminated the world for seconds at a time. The rain seemed much thicker than any other storm she had ever seen, and though she couldn't feel the winds yet, Dorea could easily imagine them being powerful as well.

The only description of an active Wrath she knew of was that of the earthquake her tribe had survived so many years ago that had forced them to relocate to the coast.

There, her grandmother had gained her earth magic, which she used to great success in her life, becoming the village headwoman for quite some time.

Considering it was an event so terrible that the whole tribe still barely speaks of it decades afterward, I'm not sure that everyone here is aware enough of the very real danger we are in.

Besides Jonah, who was always worried about everything, most others were almost excited about the coming Trial.

I get that gaining the ability to do magic is cool, I really do, but it seems to be the only thing they can think about. I bet they didn't even pack half of what I did.

"Dorea, do you feel ready for the Trial?" Jonah asked nervously, shifting his weight around.

Dorea turned around to face him, her blue eyes meeting his own. "We've always known there was a possibility of it happening to us," she said with a calmness she wasn't sure she felt. "Now we just have to trust Voggo's potion and the Mother's mercy."

"But what if we fail?" He trembled, twisting his hands.

Dorea placed a hand on his shoulder, her touch comforting. "Failure is not an option," she said firmly. "We have done all we could and just have to trust that it will be enough. When it's over, we'll be able to do so much more for our people."

The boy hesitated, his eyes peering at her from beneath thick lashes. "But what about the consequences of becoming Gifted? What if we're not ready for the responsibility that comes with it?"

Dorea nodded thoughtfully, her brow furrowed in deep concentration. "That's a valid concern," she said, her voice soft and empathetic.

"But we can't let fear hold us back. We have to face whatever comes our way and be willing to learn from our mistakes. And as for the responsibility, we'll have each other to rely on. We'll be stronger together."

Jonah looked down at the waters below, his heart heavy with doubt. "I know you're right. I just can't help but think about how our lives will change if we succeed. We'll have so much power, which comes with many expectations."

"But that means we'll be able to do so much more!" Another arm snaked around Jonah's shoulders, and their attention turned to Beth, who had evidently been paying attention to the conversation.

"The Wrath is going to change everything, no matter what we would like to happen," the girl continued, sharing her concerns.

"And think of what the tribes nearby would do to us if we were the weakest one simply because we didn't have enough Gifted to protect ourselves," she added, straying the line between teasing and genuine concern.

"At the very least, the Heidels to the south are unlikely to become more belligerent, but the Northern Mountains tribes could very easily start getting some ideas," Dorea shared, not liking the idea very much but knowing, thanks to her parents' discussions that the other Sapiens tribes in the vicinity, the Northern Mountains tribes, were led by bellicose men, who'd take any opportunity to raid those they deemed weaker.

"That's not particularly reassuring," interjected Jonah with a half-smile, showing that he wasn't offended by their lack of tact.

"Well, as my mom always says, a problem you know about is a problem you can resolve," responded Dorea. "If we know to expect trouble from the north, we can concentrate our attention there and not waste resources elsewhere."

"Eddie said that the hunters will start patrols around the village as soon as the Wrath has passed." Beth's cousin, Eddie, was one of the hunters who brought back meat in leaner times and, more importantly, culled the beast population in fatter ones, when the herds could become dangerous for the entirety of the village.

Jonah breathed out slowly. "I guess it is reassuring that there are plans already in motion to make sure everything goes well." He turned to face the churning waters in the distance. "At least what we can control is well in hand."

"Mom said that this new version of the potion we drank is much better than what they had the last time a Trial visited our tribe," Dorea comforted, giving one last pat to the boy's shoulder before turning back to watch Nature's Wrath approaching.

"Thanks, that helps a bit," Jonah replied, smiling without as much insecurity as before at both girls before falling quiet in contemplation.

I'm happy that he's feeling better. I know that no preparation is enough, but doing something is better than nothing, she thought as she removed her rucksack from her shoulders and placed it in front of her, pulling on the strings that tied its opening shut.

Her brain shut down for a couple of seconds, struggling to process what her eyes were telling her.

In front of her was quite obviously the wrong bag. In her haste, she had to have switched the two identical rucksacks. She brought the one filled with her favorite clothes and accessories instead of the one with all the survival items she had accumulated over the years of "adventuring."

Her shoulders slumped dramatically, and she clenched her hands around the straps for a couple of seconds before glancing up at the storm and forcefully exhaling through her nose.

This sucks, this really, really sucks.

She pulled out her grandmother's necklace and tied it around her neck, deciding that if she had to risk losing it, at the very least, she could wear it one last time.

Dorea unclenched her hands and closed the bag, putting it back on her shoulders.

I know that no preparation is ever enough to survive Nature's Wrath, but I really thought I had done something to help.

She shook her head, deciding it wasn't worth losing her mind over, considering how the wind was slowly picking up.

To her left, Jonah and Beth were focused on the storm, and she didn't want to bother them with something so inconsequential.

It's not like it actually matters; get over it, Dorea.

She turned to her right, where a much taller boy than Jonah sat. Rupert was the first to drink Voggo's potion and, as far as she could remember, had always been the village's most courageous and adventurous kid.

Her eyes followed one dark lock of hair that almost touched his eyebrow, down his straight nose, and stopped at his plump lips.

He's grown a lot this last year, huh.

He was always the tallest boy in the group, but his shoulders had filled in quite nicely, and he had lost most of his baby fat, leaving behind a chiseled jaw and noticeable cheekbones.

So focused was she on her examination that she didn't realize she was openly staring, so when his mouth opened, she was startled out of her focus. "You know, my lips are as soft as they look," he whispered, winking.

Dorea almost jumped, blushing red down her neck and stammered back, "I-I wasn't staring at you; I was just thinking about the Trial!"

"I'm sure that's true, dear Dora," was the cheeky reply, complete with a big stretch of his arms that pulled up his shirt and revealed a flash of his abs.

Her eyes followed the slip of skin for a second before she realized she had betrayed herself once again and forcefully looked up to see Rupert openly chuckling.

She shook her head and turned toward her friends, hoping nobody had seen her. Jonah appeared to be lost in thought, not paying attention to anything, but Beth was smirking at her, eyes twinkling with merriment.

Dorea decided to cut her losses and faced the approaching storm, committed to not think about her embarrassment anymore.

Surely with the Trial and all, they won't remember this moment, will they? she asked herself, not sounding very convincing.

Her attention was drawn away from her spiraling thoughts by a strange feeling of heaviness that came with every breath.

The air itself seemed to be thickening with power as she had known it would once the Wrath had come close enough.

In the past, this sensation would have been the only warning that something more than a typical weather event was coming, but the presence of shamans served as a much earlier warning.

I'm not entirely sure about how they do all they do, but Mom assured me that shamans worth their salt are capable enough to sense when Mother Nature is moving.

That had not always been the case, but these last few decades had seen an increase in the capabilities of shamans alongside the frequency of the Wraths being visited upon the lands.

According to her mom, the world produced more mana than it used to, thus causing both humans and beasts to change alongside it. Some people thought it was the Mother's will, while others, like her father, believed that it was a natural, cyclical process.

It used to be once every three or four generations per region, but now we have them every two or so. I'm sure I heard some hunters say that the Mother is preparing us for something, but I have no clue what it could be.

It seemed to her a bit of a reach to think that they could interpret their Goddess's reasonings when the shaman, whose job mainly was to connect the tribe to her will, wasn't saying it was so, but she supposed there could be some truth to their thoughts.

Father said that we can't know if the coming of the Wraths is even Mother Nature's will or if she just gives us the tools to survive them and rebuild.

She supposed that since other tribes had different beliefs, they would necessarily have different explanations for how the world worked. Still, she had never met anyone outside her village beyond the seasonal merchants, and they were more interested in selling their wares than discussing philosophy.

The only people that regularly met with outsiders were the scouts, who patrolled their territory and saw other villages' equivalents, but she had never had the opportunity to ask.

Dorea soon decided that getting lost in the theological debate wasn't particularly useful at the moment.

The wind was really starting to pick up, and she could even begin to feel tiny raindrops hitting her, though the bulk of the storm still wasn't close to making landfall.

The potion her mother and Voggo had prepared was the fruit of many generations of Trial and error. It was meant to open their spirits to the Mother's influence and prevent them from going insane at the influx of power. According to her mom, the shaman was confident that the casualty rate this time would be much lower than her grandmother's generation's near-split chance.

The old man had been obsessed all his life with perfecting the concoction to such a degree that no one would die unnecessarily or, worse, have to be put down after going mad because of the power going rampant through their bodies.

Apparently, every tribe had some variation of it, and they all produced slightly different effects. Still, their shaman had become Gifted after surviving a close encounter with a Mana Geyser, a type of localized Wrath that granted weaker, nonelemental powers.

That meant he did not develop powerful offensive abilities, but his skill at perceiving mana flows was second to none.

Their specific potion was supposedly meant to grant them greater control and prevent most accidents during the Trial. Still, considering that it had never been used outside of the tests Voggo had run, Dorea wasn't sure how anyone could know its full effects.

Nevertheless, she had to put her trust in her mother and the elderly man who was like a grandfather to her.

Not like I have any other choice, do I?

As she sat there, facing the incoming storm, she could feel something start to change. It crept up slowly, beginning in her hands and numbing them down, only to reach her neck and heat it up. Dorea started sweating, feeling present but, at the same time, not at all.

It's starting.

That was her last fully coherent thought, and she looked up to her friends to see them as confused as she felt, some staring at their hands like they had never seen them, while others, like Jonah, laughed hysterically at a blade of grass.

It seemed to her that the potency of the brew had been somewhat understated, but by that point, her mental process had stopped being made of singular thoughts and had expanded to the feeling of time passing by.

It was a very peculiar experience; Dorea had never considered how time itself was both a donut and a long, uninterrupted line that stretched beyond her sight.

Days seemed to pass as she contemplated the concept of time being edible, and she felt as if she had made a great discovery, so she tried to turn to her friends to tell them, only to be distracted by an equally important situation.

The grass below her feet seemed to melt into a sticky mess that she could feel cling to the bottom of her sandals whilst the storm was suddenly not far away. The winds had become hotter than the summer sun, and her sweat started to collect as a halo around her.

Dorea tried to see through the thick curtain of vapor that surrounded her but recoiled in shock when a single gigantic eye stared back at her, seeming to peer into the depths of her being.

She was paralyzed in terror, feeling smaller than she ever had and knowing in a primitive part of her brain that she needed to make sure not to arouse the thing's attention.

Whatever it was, it passed by quickly, seeming not particularly interested in her. She followed its wake with her sight, somehow disconnected from her eyes which she could feel were still closed.

It was a gigantic beast, larger than the mountains to the north, but it moved so fast and bright that she couldn't make out the shape. It felt oddly disproportionate as if something that wouldn't be capable of moving in the waking world.

Barely recovered from the fright, she was shocked to look down at herself and not be able to see her body at all. She didn't even feel her eyes moving while shifting her vision, but she could still do so.

Around her, beams of light started to flash into existence, seemingly striking things at random. The residue of their path slowly coalesced into one single cloud, getting bigger and bigger and starting to flow toward a direction she didn't know things could move into, becoming a suspended stream of lights.

Dorea wondered for a moment how it would feel to bathe in it before deciding that she didn't want to find out. Something told her she wouldn't be able to return from it.

Parallel streams came into being in the distance all around her, intertwining to form great light currents before separating again. It had beauty beyond words, as if her mind was not adequately equipped to describe such a thing.

She could feel the winds, the real ones, whipping around her and knew that the Wrath had made landfall, even though she had no control over her body to try and interpret the signals it was giving her.

Though her sense of touch had become muted, she could still hear her heartbeat, even over the pounding of the rain. Her tastebuds were filled with different flavors, somehow shifting from sour apples to spicy peppers, but her mouth still felt firmly shut.

The streams of lights started pulsating, disorienting her even further and distracting her from the sensation of heat around her neck.

In the far distance, she could still see the creature that had frightened her earlier. Her feelings, however, became increasingly muted as the lights continued pulsing.

Somehow, she vividly remembered brushing her family's moas that very morning, the feathers soft on her fingers. The memory was so clear that she was half-convinced she was still there, and everything that had happened since was a dream.

The sky stole her attention as it seemed to become a mess of colors, shifting quickly as if an undecided toddler were in front of his favorite toys. A pattern began to emerge from the medley of colors, but Dorea could not yet discern it.

As the world around her kept shifting, the feeling of her body becoming more distant, she felt the heat from before still very much present, somehow having managed to affect her even in these conditions. She couldn't sweat, but she was sure she should have been.

The streams of light recaptured her attention as they seemed to end their spectacle, finally coalescing into three separate gigantic ones.

Dorea could tell that they were bigger than they should have been and somehow denser as well. They all moved toward the sky, feeding the forming shapes and turning them into something more well defined.

As she looked up, her mind hurting from everything she witnessed, the heat started to build up again.

CHAPTER THREE

The building heat started coalescing around her neck, her grandmother's pendant feeling as if it threatened to burn her.

"I'm sorry, Mr. Pendant. I didn't mean to bring you here," she tried to say, desperate to convince the inanimate object not to harm her, unable to move her hands or feet as they had become entangled in the sticky purple grass.

Her mind was in shambles, fluttering around any little thing that caught its attention. The heat was uncomfortable, but she seemed unable to do much about it, so she turned to explore the changes happening around her.

Distant flashes of purple light and geometric patterns became more common as if building up to something.

Suddenly, her attention was stolen by a fractal appearing in the sky. The repeating shapes had somehow taken the spot of the storm, and her mind began to fry at the sight. She couldn't comprehend what she was seeing, but she felt something in her both yearn for it and be repelled by it.

As the heat kept building, her very self threatened with nonexistence, Dorea felt a tiny piece of what she saw be revealed to her, understanding with emotions and feeling things she had no frame of reference to put into words.

Still, it was too much, and she was scared she would be subsumed by the weight of the world pressing upon her.

Desperation made her look around, no longer afraid of whatever was lurking in the colors. She turned without moving any muscle, her attention captured by a scene happening outside herself, but it felt as if it was inside her mind.

Rupert, the boy she had been speaking with just a few minutes before, was shifting in colors like a bird trying to attract a mate.

It didn't make any sense to her how she could tell that he was doing it wrong, that getting that much attention was very bad, but she knew it all the same and so she tried to shout at him, but her mouth refused to open.

She had no idea how he had managed such control over his own form but knew this was not the place to experiment.

The thing that had just passed by may be the only inhabitant of this dream-like space, but it could very well not be, and Dorea really didn't want to find out if the others would be as disinterested in her as it had been.

He was trying to swim toward the streams of light, apparently having decided it was the way to receive their powers, or maybe simply out of curiosity.

Whatever his intention was, Dorea would never know.

Suddenly, the heat she could still feel that threatened to scorch her multiplied, her entire world becoming light, and Dorea felt deep in her bones that *something* was looking at them, a thing greater than anything she had ever known.

Whatever this *thing* was, it was much greater than the earlier encounter. Its mere existence threatened her own with the weight of its attention.

Dorea knew they needed to get away from *it*, frustrated beyond words by her inability to do so. The halo surrounding her flared up, blinding and disrupting her sight, saving her mind from collapsing.

In what could have been a second or a year, Rupert vanished, turned into light in front of her mind's eye.

He was simply gone; no trace of him remained.

The heat kept building up, reaching a crescendo that made her scream without her mouth.

Then, the thing shifted its attention elsewhere, and Dorea was again whole. The pieces of her that had been fractured in that terrifying encounter returned to her and were reforged thanks to the excessive temperature that surrounded her.

The terrifying energy surrounding her had been twisted by the *thing* and made unrecognizable from what it once was. Most of it was dispersed into the ether, but bits and pieces stuck to her, slipping between the gaps that had formed and were now coming back together.

Knowing without the need to be told that allowing such an influence inside of herself would be a monumentally bad idea, Dorea focused on trying to expose the corrupted energy to the incredible heat that surrounded her.

She shifted around, moving without a body or senses to orient herself, desperate to remove the taint she could feel probing the cracks in her soul.

Luckily, whatever was causing the heat wanted it gone just as much as she did because it became much more focused on specific places, no longer in the form of a halo.

For a while, there was a struggle between the two forces, the heat trying its best to burn away the corrupted energy while the latter desperately clung to her soul.

Dorea tried her best to push what little energy she had available to her to the aid of the heat, as it seemed to be acting in her favor.

Suddenly, it seemed as if both had expended all their power, and with one last flash, they vanished, leaving her with gaps in her form that started to absorb her surroundings in an attempt to become whole once again.

The energy available at this point was neither the *thing's* corrupted mana nor the streams she had observed earlier, but something less defined.

Dorea, desperate not to return to her body with gaps in her soul, did her best to grab on to it and pull it toward herself.

Slowly, oh so slowly, it started to move in her direction, but it didn't seem to do much more other than aimlessly circulate around her.

Through the haze of her thoughts, Dorea realized that she needed to focus on the little power available to her and use it to coax the surrounding energy.

While she worked on exerting her limited control over her soul, the mana around her kept shifting, transitioning from a formless state toward a more elementally charged one. Dorea could feel it behaving more like a fluid, subject to invisible currents and lightning streaks.

Instinctively, she knew that letting it change entirely would render it unusable for her purposes, so she redoubled her efforts to absorb it to fill her broken soul.

Though her thoughts were muddled, something within her knew how to do what needed to be done, and finally, Dorea managed to plug the cracks with what she was sure was the storm's power.

She pulled in as much power as possible, as it seemed that her soul could take it without swelling into something else.

She drank deeply from the power surrounding her, using it to seal the cracks where the corrupted energy had tried to slither in and more, feeling something in her rejoice at the largesse.

Dorea knew that she had gone so far from the normal process of passing a Trial that most of her preconceptions wouldn't apply anymore, but she had no other choice beyond becoming things she didn't want to think about.

Still, the storm's power was becoming hers, and she wouldn't give it up now that she knew just how much more one could be.

Even though it felt a bit sacrilegious, taking what should have been given to her by the Mother as a reward for passing the Trial, Dorea very much preferred it to going around as a shell of herself, never entirely whole as she knew she would be had she not repaired her soul.

With her soul reforged, Dorea felt a sense of relief wash over her. Had she been able to, she would have slumped, but she contented herself with not being in danger of becoming an abomination anymore.

I suppose that will have to do, she thought sarcastically, startling herself with her ability to have a coherent thought.

It seems that whatever I did, I did away with most of the confusion that comes from drinking the potion.

She turned her attention to her form, now better able to distinguish it. The properties she had observed in the energy were now evident in her soul, though she guessed it wouldn't usually be that easy to see.

This is so freaky.

The knowledge that she had changed something fundamental about herself didn't scare her much, having been ready for it to happen even in the best-case scenario. However, the way her most intimate place had been influenced by everything that had happened to her was still a bit much.

Dorea felt more present now, still not in her own body but at the very least capable of logical reasoning. *I haven't processed everything that happened, but I shouldn't have survived.*

Her grandmother's pendant had saved her, first from the eye's attention and then . . .

Dorea recoiled from the thought, feeling as if she would get much worse than a headache if she tried to remember what had transpired fully.

That felt horrible! My head is too small for the thought it was trying to have. This is the weirdest feeling ever!

Wary of provoking whatever effect had caused such discomfort, Dorea returned to her previous exploration of her changed soul.

There's not much that seems to require my immediate intervention.

She felt a new power course through her, separate from the flavors she had just experienced and wholly her own. Her attempts at integrating it into her soul seemed at least somewhat successful.

There are better places to experiment in.

She thought the memory of whatever had befallen Rupert made her unwilling to attempt anything in case it attracted any attention.

And so, she focused on herself, trying to connect back to her body and finally end the Trial.

Considering my thoughts are no longer scrambled, I should be able to get out of here.

Dorea decided that an excellent way to do so would be to try and apply Voggo's teachings about finding oneself.

It's probably not the exact intended use, but it should still apply here, right?

She pictured her body in her mind's eye, from her blond hair to the growing bust and widening hips; she tried to place every mole in its exact spot, concentrating on the feeling of opening and closing her hands and curling her feet.

Her mind usually tended to wander, not liking being forced on a single task for too long, but desperation and sheer grit worked wonders. Slowly, she regained feeling in her limbs, able to tell that the grass was tickling her feet.

The air started to rush back into her lungs, breaking whatever spell had taken her into the dreamlike world and finally waking her up.

The sun shone upon her brow, tickling her nose and making her sneeze. The air felt crisp, untainted and more alive than she had ever felt. Half her left leg was in a puddle, the water embracing her like a long-lost lover.

Dorea opened her eyes to see a painfully ordinary and incredibly changed world. Birds were chirping, the sun was shining, and the sea was calm. Beyond that, she could feel a phantom extension toward all the puddles around her, the air she was breathing, and, weirdly enough, the buzzing in her own head.

It took her a few seconds to conclude that there was no audible buzzing; it was simply her brain trying to tell her that she had control over something inside it. Wary of messing herself up, Dorea decided to leave testing her newfound powers for later.

Looking around herself, she saw the bodies of her friends and companions and was initially alarmed, but the same weird feeling that connected her to the air told her that they were alive.

I can feel the air they are breathing as it enters them.

It felt surreal. She was momentarily worried that she was still in that indefinite place the potion had brought her to, but this felt too real.

I definitely didn't have this much control in the dream. I suppose I could be in a different one, but that kind of thinking is not very productive.

Jonah's face was scrunched up as if frozen in an argument. Beth was relaxed, dreaming of something peaceful. She turned around, curious to see Rupert's sleeping expression, only to find an empty depression in the grass.

She stared at the spot for a while, all her senses, newfound and old, telling her that nobody was there, but her conscious mind refused to bridge the gap between what had happened in the dream and what was in front of her.

Dorea stood up, pushing away from the white rock she was propped against and shuffled toward the place that should have contained her friend's resting body.

Her right hand reached forward, trembling in a desperate hope that maybe something else was going on. Perhaps he was just invisible to her eyes. It found nothing but empty air, just like her new sense had told her it would.

Abruptly, she twisted around, straightening and moving with purpose around the cliff.

Maybe he was thrown around by the storm! It would be weirder if he didn't move at all.

As she stalked around the other kids' bodies, absently noting that more than just Rupert were missing, dread started to build up. Everybody had known that some of them wouldn't make it—no one had ever heard of a whole group surviving the Trial—but they had all hoped that they would make it together, be it Voggo's potion or their sheer grit.

It then started to sink in that what she had seen was not just a dream. *Maybe they woke up before me and had already left,* she desperately thought.

Dorea ran to the cliff's edge, hoping to see someone on the beach below, only to find it empty. Again, she quickly moved toward the path that brought her back to the village, just to see it mostly intact but entirely empty.

I can still see the storm moving toward the hinterland. It's too early for them to be already up and back in the village. No one has even gotten out of the shelter yet.

Weakness filling her limbs, Dorea collapsed on her knees, tears streaking down her face as she finally realized that some of the kids she had grown up with, the boy she had a crush on and who had teased her for it not too long ago, were simply gone.

She wept for their loss, curling in on herself as the emotions crashed through her.

It was not the first she had encountered death—their lives were not that lofty—but it usually happened to the elders or the hunters who ventured too deep into the forest. It should not have happened to kids her own age, barely beginning to live their own lives.

And so, Dorea mourned, looking back up to the sky to stare at the retreating Wrath, feeling something take shape within herself. A resolve to find a reason and meaning for her friends' deaths.

Because there has to be a reason. I refuse to believe that it's just how the world works!

CHAPTER FOUR

After Dorea mourned the loss of her friends, or at least began to process it, she gathered herself and walked back to the cliff.

By her count, thirty out of the forty-one that had partaken in the Trial had survived. Almost three-quarters had managed to make it. According to the stories Voggo had told them, this was virtually unheard of. Half of the participants becoming Gifted would have been a reason for celebration in her grandmother's generation.

I still can't help but feel horribly bitter about all this. I know that this is excellent news for the village, but we still lost eleven people. It's just too much.

Rustling to her left broke her out of her contemplations and made her happy to see her friends start to wake up. She had entertained the idea of shaking them awake for a second before remembering the shaman's stern warning not to, as that could mess up their new Gifts' assimilation process.

Jonah was surprisingly the first to wake up, and from what she was feeling through her new mana sense, he was already experimenting by moving the air around himself.

Without bothering to call out, Dorea sprinted through the distance and launched herself at him, causing them both to tumble in the grass.

His sputtering and confused expression finally broke her out of her mood, and bright laughter rang out. "We're alive!" she shouted at him, uncaring of personal boundaries.

"D-Dorea, please get off," was the weak response. "I'm glad to be still in one piece myself, but at least let me get up from the grass," Jonah pleaded.

Dorea grinned toothily at the boy, feeling happiness bubble up as she finally realized she had actually made it. She had been so focused on specific parts of the Trial that she hadn't even allowed herself to feel relieved to have survived it.

"Are you feeling okay?" she asked Jonah, patting him down to ensure nothing was out of place.

"You should have asked that before throwing me around like a doll," he sputtered, batting her hands away with a blush.

Suddenly, they were engulfed in a tight hug, thin but surprisingly strong arms tightening around their necks and bringing them together.

"I can't believe we made it!" Beth exclaimed, threatening to suffocate them with her show of affection.

"Release! Please release!" Jonah begged, apparently being squeezed too hard.

They were both let go, fully turning around to face a sunny smile that lacked any guile. Or so one would have thought had they not known the brunette.

Dorea returned the smile, too happy to think more deeply about it. The relief she felt at having come out of the Trial with her best friends was too much to contain, and she reached back toward Beth for another hug.

"Yeah, I can't believe it either," Dorea said, finally releasing the other girl. "It's almost like a . . ." *dream*, she thought, the mood suddenly plummeting again as she remembered what she had witnessed in the hazy world she had just gotten out of.

Noticing the shift in her expression, her friends turned more serious, the smiles slipping away from their faces.

"How many have we lost?" questioned Beth, already turning toward the others to see with her own eyes.

"Eleven," replied Jonah, eyes closed in concentration. "I can't feel eleven people at all unless they already left?" he finished with a questioning tone, head tilted toward Dorea.

"To the best of my understanding, I was the first to wake up, and no one else has left before me."

A moment of silence passed as they all contemplated the consequence of such a loss. "I suppose that this is a decent rate of survival," interjected Beth with a quiet voice, evidently not feeling it much herself.

The two blonds nodded in agreement, intellectually knowing that this was a good day but not up for much rejoicing about it.

Dorea took a deep breath, trying to shake off the melancholy that had settled over her. "We should see if the others have woken up."

Jonah jumped to it. "Let's do that, yeah," he said and was soon followed by the two girls.

As they approached the others, what her senses had been telling her for a while revealed itself to her eyes, where Rupert had settled before the Trial stood another boy.

Thick brown hair fell over his brow, covering his eyes. He was kneeling by the flattened grass where someone had obviously sat not too long ago.

As she came closer, Dorea recognized him as Thomas, Rupert's younger brother. He was shorter and stockier, but the resemblance was evident in his facial features. They were twisted in grief, fat tears falling through his lashes.

Dorea kneeled alongside him and gathered him in her arms. He went with it, not responding verbally but leaning on her shoulder.

She let him sob for a few minutes, caressing his hair in an effort to comfort him. After a while, Thomas stopped shaking and breathed deeply through his nose with his eyes closed, trying to regain his composure.

She let him, staying silent as she had been instructed by her mother if someone needed to vent their grief. It was somewhat uncomfortable, how they had been taught how to deal with the possible coming of Nature's Wrath, but no amount of preparation felt like it was enough now that she had been through it.

"Thank you," the boy mumbled, slowly gathering himself and standing up. Dorea watched him give one last look at the place where his older brother had vanished and turn around, stepping toward another boy that was just then waking up.

It was Mark, his other older brother and the last of the farmer's sons. He looked so much like Rupert that Dorea quickly turned, the wound still too fresh.

All around her, people were waking up and either falling into despair at the loss of someone or shouting in happiness at having passed the Trial.

She ignored Mark's shout of anguish, not feeling ready to think more deeply about what she had witnessed.

Stomach twisting in a knot, Dorea made the rounds, checking in with everyone. She knew everyone, though not to the level of calling them all friends. The age disparity between a fourteen-year-old and a twenty-year-old person was not exactly conducive to making friends.

Mark the Blue, called so because of the slightly bluish tint of his hair and to distinguish him from the other four Marks that lived in the village, was twenty-one. He was at the cutoff for taking the Trial, and had it happened a few months later, Voggo wouldn't have allowed him to participate.

He was a member of the village scouts, a group that ensured no one intruded on their lands and acted as information gatherers on the herds' movements.

At the moment, he was making lightning dance between his fingers, enthralled by his new power.

He's the oldest here; he'll probably soon become one of the lead scouts considering the sheer gap between Gifted and non. If we just don't overhaul Whitecliff's systems.

Considering the new power dynamics, their little society was about to change completely. It was not like anyone would attempt a hostile takeover as it sometimes happened after a Trial, Dorea knew, but things were naturally going to be different.

Voggo has taught us that power gravitates toward those who have power. The strongest Gifted will inevitably have a greater voice in how things are run.

It was not necessarily a bad thing in her mind. Their life wasn't lacking, but it was still very monotonous. The shake-up would only make things more interesting.

If Voggo knew what I thought, he'd clip me around the ears for thinking that young people can solve every problem.

Dorea smiled fondly. The old man was a cantankerous sort, but he had led the tribe as its only Gifted for more than two decades and allowed them to live in peace.

It was not uncommon for people to gain powers and suddenly start having dreams of conquest. *In fact, I bet that gathering information on how the surrounding tribes are moving will be his first priority after ensuring the village is still livable.*

Whilst she was thinking, the others had started to gather. Their grief was not gone, but they all knew there would be time for it later. They needed to trek back to the village and alert everyone else that the Wrath had passed.

The mighty storm was still visible in the distance, purple lightning arches visible even from where they stood.

More than one person looked at it with a complicated expression, both angry and thankful for the Gifts it had provided.

Others were experimenting with their new powers; from what she could see, the majority had water or wind magic. Only a couple had lightning sparking around them.

I suppose I'll have to face the fact that I can feel connections to all three elements soon, huh?

Dorea had a feeling that what she had gone through in the dream should have killed her. Whatever she had met, she had had no way of protecting herself from them, and the only thing that had saved her was the pendant still hanging around her neck.

It felt cold and inert to the touch, like a perfectly ordinary object, but she knew very well that it was not.

I really need to talk with Mom and Dad when we finally get some privacy. They have not been telling me everything about Grandma.

What happened in the dream also changed how her Gift was given to her; that much was clear.

I have never heard of anyone with control over more than one element.

Dorea closed her eyes and tried to make the air around herself move like she was feeling a few of the others do, but it felt sluggish. It was like she was waving her hands in a useless attempt at making the air move while the others had great fans aiding them. She could create a weak breeze with a lot of effort, but it was nothing compared to the manipulation she saw the others manage.

Frustrated, she switched to trying to move the water in a puddle nearby. It didn't go much better; the most she could get was for it to rise from the ground slowly, the ball of water trembling as if threatening to escape her control.

Almost dreading the result, she raised her hand, concentrating on the feeling of buzzing that came from her brain. She tried to replicate it between her fingers, imagining an arc flashing, the lightning coiling.

Her efforts were rewarded with a lackluster spark, more like the effort of two rocks striking each other than like the streaks of light she could see Mark the Blue playing with.

It seems like I'm not the special little snowflake I thought I was.

Her mood souring, Dorea decided to revisit the problem later.

"Hey guys, I know we are all very proven after going through all that, but we really need to start heading to the village." She decided to get moving to avoid thinking too deeply about it. "We should let everyone know that the storm has passed."

Everyone seemed to startle at her words, apparently not having thought about how their families would still be in the shelter waiting for them to come and tell them that it was safe to come out.

Slowly, people got up from the grass and started to move toward the trail that would lead them back to the village. Dorea walked forward at the head of the line and was quickly reached by her two best friends.

The trek back to Whitecliff was done in quiet contemplation as they all observed the damage wrought by the storm. While the landscape was quite devastated, their homes were mostly intact. Dorea knew that this was only possible because, at the time of the founding, their tribe was full of earth mages, who had survived the terrible earthquake that had destroyed their previous village.

They, alongside the few metal mages they had, had dedicated themselves to building houses that would stand the trial of both time and Nature's Wrath. The few buildings in bad condition were those made after the last earth mage died almost two decades ago.

That did not mean, however, that there would not be work to do. The infrastructure may still be standing, but from where they were walking, it was pretty noticeable how all their fields and pastures were mostly gone. There had been no time to pull in a harvest, the warning coming far too late for such a thing.

And even if we managed to save most of the livestock, I'll be surprised if we can keep them all alive in the next few days. Dorea twisted her lips in thought. *Far more likely, we'll have to butcher them and share their meat with everyone to make up for the absence of crops.*

Her dreams of going on an expedition in the forest to hunt megafauna were quickly dying as she seriously doubted that she'd be able to do much more than ruffle a therium's hair.

I will have to experiment a bit more once I have some time to myself. I refuse to believe that is all I'm capable of.

The village was coming closer, and the excitement to see their families was warring with the sadness of having to share their losses with them.

Though everyone knew to be prepared for the eventuality, it was a different thing for it to actually happen.

The last few hundred feet felt more like a walk to the headsman axe than a homecoming of triumphant heroes. Dorea could only hope that Voggo had been preparing the parents of those who underwent the Trial for the real chance of never seeing their children again.

They stopped in front of the shaman's house, where, only a few hours before, they had received the potion that would allow them to survive the Trial in such high numbers.

It felt bittersweet, being there once again, and a solemn mood fell over the crowd of youngsters.

After a moment of silent contemplation, Dorea entered Voggo's place and went directly to the middle of his living area, where a stone slab covered the shelter where the villagers had taken refuge.

Concentrating on her control over the air, Dorea attempted to make her words louder and direct the sound below.

"The Wrath has passed. You can come out now," she tried to convey.

It took her a while, more than she would have liked, but the subtle manipulation came more successfully than her earlier attempts.

At least I have a little finesse. I'll have to work with that.

Movement from below her roused her from her contemplation, and she stepped back to allow the people below to push the slab away from the entrance.

Voggo was the first to step through, shouldering aside Tom, the blacksmith who had apparently been chosen to move the heavy stone. He looked at her up and down, smiling briefly in relief before schooling his expression, and ventured outside to see the situation.

Shortly thereafter, the villagers started to stream outside; elderly and kids, men and women, all greeted her with a smile of congratulations before hurrying out to see if their relatives had made it.

Almost last, her parents and sister walked out of the shelter, their worried expressions melting immediately at seeing her.

Dorea found herself engulfed in her parents' arms; her little sister's coming around her midriff. She would have customarily protested, but at that moment, she could only breathe in the familiar scents and relax for the first time since the news that Nature's Wrath was coming had broken.

And if a few tears slipped from her eyes, well, no one was there to notice such a thing.

Buried in her father's chest, her mother's hands caressing her hair, and her sister's arms tight around her, Dorea felt finally at peace.

After a few minutes of emotionally charged silence, they started to unwind from each other.

Lilian, her mother, caressed her cheek with great tenderness whilst her father spoke with misty eyes, "We knew you would make it, dearest. We are incredibly proud of you."

Dorea smiled brightly, her heart full of love.

"I had no doubt!" came from Lia, and though the tear tracks and red eyes betrayed her, Dorea chose not to mention it.

Together, they exited the shaman's house and walked to where Voggo was holding court. The old man had wasted no time noting what power every new Gifted had gained and was apparently already giving them orders.

A group containing Beth was moving toward the fields, apparently chosen for their water magic. *I bet they will have to drain the excess water and try to save as many crops as possible.*

Noticing them, Voggo motioned for them to join him. "Dorea, what kind of magic can you use?"

"I can use all three elements of the storm," she replied to astonished faces. "But I seem to be more focused on finesse than raw power," she added, a bit embarrassed.

The look in the old man's eyes told her he was quite surprised, but he quickly gathered himself. "We'll have to test that later; help your parents put the ranch back together for now. We'll need the meat."

His apparent nonchalance seemed to convince everyone that her situation was not too weird, for which she was grateful.

She nodded at him to show that she understood the subtext and joined her family as they returned home.

CHAPTER FIVE

The walk back to their ranch was mainly done in silence. Her sister and mother occupied Dorea's hands while her father walked slightly ahead.

It was quite obvious that something devastating had just passed through, considering the broken pieces of wood that lay around what had once been a shed that sat to their right. This scene was repeated quite often. Everything that had been built after the last earth mage died was gone.

It looks weird how some things are practically untouched while others are broken beyond repair.

It looked to her like, had it been a more normal storm, though of equal intensity, the village would have survived mostly unscathed.

Of course, had anyone outside the ages thirteen to twenty-one tried to stay outside Voggo's protections, they would have risked mana deviation. It is apparently a horrible way to die.

She shuddered at the thought, drawing comfort from the way her mother squeezed her hand.

Well, the kids are usually fine, but leaving them outside while all the adults hide in the shelter would have been pretty stupid.

She recognized Mr. Todd's house, her father's friend who mostly dealt in mining and resource acquisition. Unlike most others, he had wanted to build himself a bigger residence and had, over the years, expanded the place he inherited into something more luxurious.

It was now almost entirely gone. Most of the stone was still near the house, but it would take quite some time to remake it into something livable.

Luckily, it seemed that the original building was still there. It would be a tight fit, considering he had four very young children and a wife, but they would have a roof over their heads and be protected from the elements.

Her father sighed at the sight, shaking his head. He was probably considering how to chip in to help his friend rebuild.

While it may sound foolish to build things beyond what we already know can withstand everything, people still want to move out of their families' homes.

Dorea recalled her parents talking about this a few weeks before when there had been a spring squall. Her mother had wondered whether it was foolish to dedicate so much time to creating something that they knew wouldn't last that long, while her father thought that it was better to develop the skills needed to do so and not rely on the hope of their village gaining new earth mages soon.

It seemed, in retrospect, that they were both correct. *You can't just wait for the Mother to give you the solutions for all your problems, but that doesn't mean that doing things you know will not work is a good idea.*

Now things were going to change, obviously. While they didn't have any new earth or metal mages, the ability to use water and wind would make construction quite a bit easier.

Some of the older buildings that had been abandoned would need refurbishing, while the newer ones would require a heavier hand.

There is going to be a steep learning curve for everyone in the next few months, but I'm sure we'll make it.

While she was busy contemplating such things, they had gotten close enough to their house to begin making out the damage.

The main building was mostly fine, with the storm just hitting the porch. That would require some work in the following weeks, but Dorea was sure her father would be able to do it primarily by himself. He had been the one who built it, after all.

The bigger problem was the barn. Its foundation had held, luckily, but the ceiling had been scooped out entirely. It looked like a giant had simply grabbed and taken off with it. It was nowhere in sight, to her bafflement.

I suppose that such strong winds could have carried it high up.

She considered, thankful for her new instinctive understanding of the mechanics with which air moved.

If the roof stayed together and acted as a kite, it could have been carried for quite a distance.

That would require more work, and she would need to help or, more likely, use her powers to help. As athletic as she was, it would not be efficient to let a fourteen-year-old girl move construction material.

What worried her the most was whether the animals had survived the storm unscathed. Also, there was a very real chance that one of them had become an enhanced beast and would need to be put down.

She was dreading that option, seeing how she could not fling lightning at much of anything at the moment. She would still have to take a look after Voggo's visit, but maybe she should bring a spear with her. And her father.

It's not like beasts immediately become super powerful after getting enhanced; they still have the same growth curve as humans. She tried to calm herself down.

They walked through the broken remains of the fence that delineated their property, and Dorea started slowly pulling the water away from their path.

A dramatic gasp interrupted her concentration. "That's amazing, Dora!" Lia shouted. The little girl's eyes were round and large as she looked at the wobbling water in the air.

She noticed proud smiles on her parents' faces and redoubled her efforts at clearing their path from the detestable puddles.

Slowly and with great effort, she managed to dry out the last bit of dirt, and the way was finally clear.

"Good job, dearest." Her father's warm hand on her head sent a warm feeling of accomplishment through her.

Their house was in disrepair, and they needed to rebuild much of their property and check on the animals before talking with the shaman about the weirdness of her powers and then lending aid to the others who needed it. Still, Dorea didn't feel afraid of the future. She had passed the Trial and was together with her family. They would make it.

A knock woke Dorea up from the doze she had fallen into, the late afternoon sun showing that she had slept for a few hours.

"Come in!" came the call from the kitchen, where Lilian had corralled Lia into helping her start clearing up the mess it had become.

Most furniture was fine, but there was dust everywhere, and things had been thrown around a bit, so she had immediately set on making their home livable again.

Dorea had been afforded some mercy thanks to having just undergone the Trial. *I don't expect it to last much longer.*

The door opened, and through it stepped in the village's shaman. While he was not a common fixture around the house, he was seen often enough. He was, after all, her mother's mentor and had been a friend of her grandmother's.

"I know you are all tired and have work to do, so I'll try not to take up too much of your time." He sat on the chair opposite her.

"What is it that you wanted to talk about?" asked her father as he cleaned his hands from the soot they had gathered with a rag.

Voggo stayed silent for a while, his aged blue eyes taking her in.

"Did you mean it when you said that you could control all three of the storm's elements?" he finally asked her.

Instead of replying, Dorea chose to demonstrate. She raised her hands and, concentrating, managed to call upon a burst of wind first, a tiny spark next, and levitate the water in the bucket her father had been using next.

It was not the overwhelming display of might she had been hoping to be capable of, but it served the point.

The shaman's eyes briefly glowed a bright blue before he nodded to himself, apparently satisfied with her little show.

"I didn't doubt you, little Dora, but I had to make sure you weren't mistaken," he sighed. "What you have here is a rare type of Gift that our tribe's records only speak of in vague sentences."

Apparently noticing how little his words had satisfied them, he kept going, "As far as I can tell, since you can control them so cleanly and without any discord in your mana signature, it's a perfectly natural Gift. It looked to require more effort than I expected, but that is likely compensation for the sheer range you have at your disposal."

That's mostly what I suspected, though it doesn't really account for everything that happened in the dream . . .

Shaking her head to refocus, Dorea asked, "Does that mean I'll always be weaker than the others? Am I really the only one that can use more than one element?"

"I wouldn't say you'll necessarily be weaker than the others. Everyone starts at basically the same point, but their degree of growth is based upon many factors," he chuckled, trying to assuage her fears.

"You'll likely need to put more effort than the others into your training if you want to be on their level, and you'll have to truly dedicate your life to it to have any hope of becoming a powerhouse, but having three elements at your disposal will easily make up for it." He addressed her first question, rubbing his beard in thought.

"As for you being the only one to use more than one element, I didn't say so. It is true that we only have sparse records of such a thing, but powers are very much still a mystery, even to one such as me who studied them for his whole life."

"Does it mean she should keep it under wraps?" asked her father, worried for her safety.

"Beyond her already having announced it," responded her mother with a long-suffering look. "It doesn't seem likely that anyone will raise a fuss over it, especially since Voggo made a point to diffuse its weirdness," she finished with a grateful look toward her mentor.

"I'm relieved to see that it was a much simpler case than I expected," responded Voggo, apparently satisfied with what he had found.

"And what did you expect to see?" asked Dorea, suddenly very curious.

The old man gestured vaguely with his hands. "There are many types of Gifts, and some require more monitoring than others."

He stopped the deluge of questions that his words had induced with a weathered hand, amused eyes telling her that he was doing it on purpose.

"I did what I came here to do and am happy that everything is well. Now it's time for me to take my leave. Both you and I have much work left to do."

Without caring for her curiosity, he nodded to her parents, smiled in the direction her sister was hiding in to better overhear them, and left.

Dorea raced after him, unwilling to let him give her the slip after hinting at such exciting information.

"You'll learn more in the next few weeks, little Dora. I'll hold some lessons for all new Gifted to explain your roles in the tribe and to go more in-depth about how the world works." These were his parting words as he waved his right hand carelessly goodbye while walking away.

Though Dorea would have very much liked having the opportunity to catch up with the old shaman and ask all the questions he had denied her the answers to, and maybe a few things more, her mother was very unamused with her laziness and immediately set her and her father to check on the livestock.

They still had at least an hour of full sunlight left, and wasting it by lazing around to ponder the mysteries of mana and Gifts was not an acceptable way to go, apparently.

And so, Dorea armed herself with a hunting spear that had once belonged to her grandfather and, alongside her father, also armored as best as he could, started the trek toward the caves they had hidden the animals in, in the hopes that they would survive the Wrath and not massacre each other.

This little expedition would be so much easier if I could blast anything that moved wrong with lightning. She grumbled.

"Now, we don't know that anything happened to them. The caves should be deep enough for them to have avoided the Wrath entirely, but you never know," Dodro spoke, going over the protocol the tribe had developed to deal with the livestock in such situations. "A couple of the younger animals may have become enhanced; as you know, they are likely to be rampaging. Do not think of them as the animals you knew. An enhanced beast that lost control of its power is impossible to control."

Dorea nodded along. Considering the bond she had with them, it would be unfortunate if they had to put down any animal.

We slaughter and eat them when they age enough, which is just part of Nature. If we have to kill a young one who went mad, that would just suck.

As they planned what to do, they approached the first of the two caves where she hid the animals.

Loud bellows could be heard from the anoas' cave. They hurried inside, hoping to avert a disaster.

It was immediately apparent that more than one of the horned beasts had become enhanced, but things had gone differently than expected.

The corpses of three juvenile anoas were thrown to the back of the cave, gored to death by the herd's alpha. It stood proudly, though drenched in water and careful not to put too much weight on its left leg.

"Mimi!" yelled Dorea, forgetting that she should do a sweep to make sure that no other animal had become enhanced. The anoa turned toward them at the sound of her voice and bellowed a greeting, slowly trotting toward her.

"Dorea! Stop immediately!" yelled her father.

Reluctantly, she slowed her approach and took her time observing the animals to ensure nothing would attack them. On the left side of the herd, another juvenile anoa stood shakily. His sparking wet fur told her that he, too, had gained powers but had apparently managed to retain his mind.

The pieces of the puzzle were slowly coming together. *It is likely that one tried to face the other enhanced ones but was overwhelmed, and Mimi intervened in his favor. We're lucky they were not particularly powerful.*

She shared her thoughts out loud, and her father nodded thoughtfully. "It's good to see that Mimi can still protect the herd."

He patted the leader, showing appreciation for his hard work and checking for injuries. "It seems to me that he took some blows but he'll survive. He was lucky that their water magic was pretty weak."

Dorea scratched the spot between his horns that she knew he loved, smiling faintly.

"What are we gonna do about the other enhanced one?"

Dodro rubbed his chin in thought, considering the animal. "He seems to be in control for now, and as far as I know, if he was gonna lose it, he would have already." Then he motioned toward Mimi, who was clearly enjoying the scritches. "And if anything happens, Mimi should be more than enough to deal with him. Let's go check on the moas, and if there is nothing too crazy going on there, we can bring these guys back down. They'll have to stay outside for a few days while we rebuild the enclosures, but they'll be fine."

Dorea gestured toward the three carcasses of the crazed anoas. "Can we use those?"

"We should be good to eat those. As far as I know, there is nothing different between them and a normally enhanced beast that the hunters would bring back to eat occasionally."

Satisfied with his response, Dorea gave one last pat to Mimi and walked with her father back outside and toward the larger cave that held the moas.

The birds are always going to be more problematic. They are ornery enough on a daily basis; I don't want to think about what a crazed enhanced one is like.

As they entered the cave, sounds of combat could be heard, so they hurried their pace.

They burst upon the scene ready to fight, Dodro with his shield held high and spear prepared to skewer anything that moved wrong.

It was immediately evident that in this cave, things had gone differently. The bodies of five moas were strewn around the rocky floor, while three more were injured enough to lie down and keep away from the fighting, which was an indicator of how bad things were, considering how combative the birds usually were.

An obviously enhanced moa was batting around most of the flight, creating gusts of wind by moving his wings and sending his opponents flying.

His maddened screeches were enough for them to understand that he was too far gone, and Dorea braced herself for her first fight as a Gifted.

She had been worrying about what she might be able to do with her weak powers, and so had developed a simple plan.

Since she could not quickly gather much water, she would do so in advance and bring it along. The wind was out as she seriously doubted it would not just be wrenched from her control by the crazed moa, and lightning would serve its purpose in just a bit.

With a grunt of effort, she threw the large ball of water she had gathered during their trek to the caves, and it splashed against the moa, sending it to the ground. Not giving it time to recover, she sent a series of electric sparks its way, shocking it enough that the remaining moas could tear into it, killing it quickly.

"Well, I suppose that anticlimactic is better than anyone getting hurt," commented her father with a bemused expression.

"I guess that's it," she added, smiling at the adrenaline rush.

CHAPTER SIX

The excitement of the evening over, Dorea and Dodro quickly settled the two groups of animals into makeshift enclosures. They set down some of the broken pieces of wood to create a division and trusted that the beasts would be too tired to make much of a fuss about it.

They kept a wary eye on the enhanced anoa, but he seemed content to keep to himself. Mimi, the alpha, made the rounds, checking that every member of his herd was safe and comfortable before settling down himself.

They took that as a sign that things would hold until the following day and returned to the house.

While they were outside, Lilian and Lia managed to give the building a semblance of order. Most of the dust was gone, and the decorations were back in place.

They were greeted by the tired duo, the mother putting the finishing touches to dinner while the daughter set the table.

The little girl's feet were dragging, and it was obvious that the day's exhaustion was finally catching up with her.

Dorea felt pretty tired herself, an ache deeper than she had ever experienced and emotional tiredness threatened to send her to sleep as she sat at the table, but fear of what she would see in her dreams kept her awake.

I've managed to avoid thinking too deeply about what happened, but I can't ignore it forever, however much I'd like to.

Desperate to distract herself, she asked the one question that seemed innocuous enough. "So I accidentally brought Grandma's pendant with me to the Trial, and I'm pretty sure it did something to help me through it. Do you know anything about it?"

The parents looked at each other silently over the table, exchanging a hundred words in a glance.

"You already know that your grandmother was a Gifted, and an earth mage to be more specific," answered her mother, "and she had a passion for tinkering with strange objects like your pendant. It wouldn't surprise me if she did something to it."

It seemed vague to Dorea, but looking at their tired expressions made her hesitate to ask more. *I can grill them further tomorrow. It's not like they are going anywhere. But there is something else to this.*

The moment passed, and her father started listing everything they needed to do the day after. Unfortunately for her, she was assigned to salvage as much of the broken fence as possible, and after she was done with that, she'd need to help him with the barn. If, for a strange reason, she still had some time on her hands, she was to go to the village and offer her services to Voggo in case she could help with anything.

The promised lessons would likely start in a few days or weeks since they needed the time to acclimate to their new senses and powers and rebuild what had been broken.

After dinner was eaten and plates cleaned, Dorea returned to her room, grateful to have one for herself. Their house had been built to host her grandparents and whatever families their children would have, which meant it was quite large.

Unfortunately, her uncle had died young, struck by a winter fever, and it took her grandmother a while before she felt ready to have another child. She had Dorea's mother pretty late in life and no other child, so everything they had went to her family.

Dorea settled in bed, unwilling to go to sleep yet. *It's not like I'm afraid of nightmares; I just want to experiment with my magic for a bit!*

"Try not to break the house from the inside and do what Nature's Wrath couldn't!" Her father's laughing came through the wall.

"I'm not gonna!" she yelled back, slumping into her bed at having been caught.

I wasn't going to do anything dangerous anyway.

Grumbling, she returned to thinking about how to use her powers better.

I know that Voggo said I'm not necessarily weaker than the others if I put work into it, but it sucks that I have to do much more than I should have to. At least I'm the only one who can use all three elements.

Feeling pleased with at least that part, she tried focusing on the senses she had gained since she awakened after the Trial.

It felt like touching a hot pan with a leather glove. You could tell that it was touching something, and if you left it in contact long enough, you could tell that something was hot, but it wasn't a precise feeling.

The weirdness was compounded by the fact that she was getting three different signals. The air in her room was entirely under her control, and she could tell the position of almost everything through it. The plants outside, the buckets of water in the kitchen, the gathering humidity of the night, and the moisture inside her family members gave her another signal, and the buzzing of lightning inside everything with a brain gave her another.

Thankfully, her range was not particularly large, barely twenty feet in radius, so she was spared a headache trying to figure out too many competing feelings.

Still, she knuckled down and tried to parse everything she sensed. It had felt like a passive ability, but it expanded and contracted simultaneously when she focused on it.

The range got a bit larger, and her focus sharpened more. She could sense her parents' room as they got ready for bed, and if she concentrated a bit more, she could tell that her sister, on the other side of their bedroom, was already asleep.

The passive sense was more encompassing, feeding her information about everything that happened in her domain, while the active one was more precise for specific targets.

I'm sure I'll be able to get better with it, but it is already very cool. The world is so different from yesterday.

Getting used to feeling things outside her five senses would likely take a while, but she'd put in the work. She had never been accused of being unmotivated, after all.

Afraid of getting sensory overload, she put her experimenting aside for the moment. She'd get back to it, but at the moment, she was simply too tired to avoid doing something stupid like getting her mind stuck outside her body.

Is that even possible? It sounds scary enough that I don't want to find out.

Turning away from such thoughts, Dorea focused on her elemental control. She tugged on the water she could feel in the plants down below, but it didn't budge. She tried on the bucket, and it moved almost effortlessly.

It seems like even if I can feel it, I'm not necessarily able to use it.

The quantity she could control also changed depending on the distance from herself, and she needed to remind herself of this a couple of times lest she splash some around and face her mother's wrath.

She could form water into vaguely shaped constructs with ease, but trying to add too many details made it much harder.

It's something to work on. I bet it would help my overall control.

Next on the list was air. This element was much easier to control without making a mess, though she guessed it would change once she could pack more of a punch.

She could create a breeze from seemingly no direction and, if she concentrated a bit, could focus it into a stronger gust. *Well, strong is a heavy word. It moved the chair a bit. Better than nothing, I guess.*

Dorea decided to attempt something she knew her mother would disapprove of. She purposefully kept adding more air to a specific spot, hoping to replicate something similar to the water constructs.

I know I probably shouldn't be doing this. But no one else seems to understand how cool it is to suddenly have mystical powers. I have magic!

A slight distortion formed in her sight, indicating that something was happening. Whatever it was, it didn't seem as stable as her previous attempts at manipulating water.

Now, Dorea was usually a decently careful girl. She liked danger as much as any teenager who had just gained supernatural powers but wouldn't normally do anything as reckless as experimenting with her newfound powers in her room in the middle of the night.

But, she was exhausted from the day's events, traumatized from seeing a boy she fancied get atomized by a cosmic entity that she was doing her best to repress, and scared for the future. It was a dangerous cocktail that made her less careful than usual.

Suddenly, the distortion collapsed in on itself before releasing a tremendous bang, sending Dorea flying out of her bed and her room into disarray.

A muffled shout of surprise could be heard from the nearby room, and the sound of feet stamping on the floor quickly came closer.

"What in the hell happened here!" her father yelled, almost ripping the door from its hinges in his haste to open it.

Dorea slowly righted herself, looking quite befuddled with her hair sticking every which way in the middle of all the chaos she created.

"I think, young lady, that that is quite enough for tonight."

Her mother's words froze her as she got up, and she sent a pleading face to her father, who looked at her in annoyance mixed with amusement.

The older woman walked into the room, carefully avoiding the mess, and knelt beside her daughter. She checked her head and body for any severe injury, and when she found none, she smacked the back of Dorea's head.

"I don't even want to attempt to understand what was going on in your mind, but know this: if your room isn't spotless by tomorrow morning, and if you are not ready and willing to help around the ranch without so much as a peep of grumbling, you'll find out with great detail what is going on inside my head, and I can promise it's not going to be pleasant."

Still frozen on the ground, Dorea nodded her head quickly. Lilian smiled at her, kissed her forehead, and walked back out of the room.

Her father gave her one last look before following his wife with a besotted expression. From behind the door peeked little Lia, holding her hands over her mouth to stifle her giggles.

She mouthed a silent, mocking laugh before sprinting back toward her room before her sister could regain her bearings.

Dorea, for her part, felt quite embarrassed at her mistake but was equally excited about the possibilities this brought.

Even when concentrating most of her strength, she could barely move lighter furniture, but the blast caused by whatever she did was enough to send everything in her room into disarray. She wanted to be able to do that at will.

I suppose I should leave further experimentation for tomorrow. After I finish my chores and whatever Mom cooks up to punish me, I'll find a quiet spot to practice some more with it and try lightning out. It probably was not a good idea to try that in here anyway.

It took her some time to give her room some semblance of order. If one didn't know what had happened, it would have been an easy mistake to think the Wrath had gotten inside.

By the time she had finished, it was truly the hour of the wolf, and Dorea was more tired than ever. She laid back on her bed, and the moment she got under the covers and her head touched the pillow, she slipped into sleep.

The morning's light hit her eyes, waking her from the deepest slumber she could remember. Dorea felt both sticky with sweat and dry in her mouth. Her bladder was crying for attention, but she was very glad to have avoided any nightmares.

Getting up from her bed, she concentrated for a couple of seconds and managed to control the sweat stuck to her skin.

She went from limb to limb before cleaning her torso and, finally, her head. *This has to be the best thing ever. It's almost worth it, just for this.*

Quickly going through her routine, she dressed for the day and went downstairs to the bathroom.

As she got out, she saw her mother preparing breakfast for everyone. "Today it's potato and moa hash. Your father has been up since early and has already butchered two of them."

Dorea thanked her and took her place at the table, suddenly ravenous.

"Thanks to working with Voggo for so many years, I know you Gifted eat quite a bit more than anyone else. So dig in, and get the energy you need for all the work you'll be doing today."

The blond girl merely nodded in assent, too focused on her meal and enjoying every bit of it. The potatoes were soft inside with an outer crust thanks to being panfried with rendered moa fat, the meat was soft thanks to a long cook, and the added onions gave it all a decadent sweetness.

Lilian sighed, seeing her daughter was too caught up enjoying her meal to listen properly. Her pride as a cook warred with her desire to be heard, but she decided to let the girl have her moment.

However much she and her husband tried to keep up a confident front, they had been terribly scared of losing their little girl and worried about raising her properly now that she had gained access to magic.

While she wouldn't say that Dorea was a hellion, the girl had always been adventurous and had a weird fascination with getting into scuffles with boys.

While this kind of behavior would typically meet a swift end once time allowed the males to outstrip the females in the physical department, the addition of mystical powers made the field much more equal.

Her own mother had been considered the most powerful person in the tribe for as long as she had been alive, but the woman had been much more serene than her granddaughter.

Lilian wasn't worried that her daughter would misuse her powers, however much she thought that she wasn't off to a good start with her previous experimenting. Still, she couldn't help but worry that her new abilities would enhance the more reckless bits of her personality.

"Once you are done, you need to take a better look at what remains of the fences and start putting them back up. Check up on the animals occasionally as well; your father is also doing it, but you are the only one with powers, and he has told me how useful they were yesterday."

Almost done with her plate, Dorea nodded again, though she was obviously more present this time. Her pace as she shoveled food in her mouth had slowed down, and she was finally starting to enjoy it properly.

Once done, she passed her plate to her mother for washing, ruffled her sister's hair as the girl descended the stairs, and exited the house.

I can probably find and dry most of the wooden fence if it hasn't been sent too far away.

Concentrating on expanding her senses, Dorea quickly found the first few pieces. The ones that were too broken to be useful she discarded in a pile and didn't bother to dry out, while the ones that were good enough she set aside for later work.

I need to survey the land to find all of them, separate them, dry out the useful bits, and finally go back to the house to get some of our emergency nails.

They didn't have enough iron nails to put it all back up. She seriously doubted that the blacksmith would be able to supply them with the ones they needed considering the more pressing issue of rebuilding some of the houses. Still, she was hopeful she could salvage some and put up something decent in a few days if her father started helping once he finished the butchering and the barn.

As Dorea walked through her family's ranch, she absentmindedly drained the mud pits that had formed during the storm. Even though the intensity had been great, the Wrath had been present only for a few hours and simply didn't have the time to alter the landscape too much.

Most of the grass was hidden in the mud, and quite a few trees had been uprooted from the ground, but it was still what she had always known.

The thing that changed the most was her.

CHAPTER SEVEN

The previous few days had been a blur of reconstruction, acclimating to her new powers, and keeping an eye on the animals, especially the new enhanced anoa she had taken to calling Bebe.

He was a cuddly little thing, unaware of his new status in the herd. Whenever Dorea checked on him, he'd run over and rub his snout into her chest, making happy noises if she scratched at the base of his horns.

Mimi, the herd leader, had been a bit nervous initially but had calmed down and started interacting with Bebe. The enhanced anoa still sparked occasionally, but it had lessened with time.

This told Dorea that they would need to be prepared for a surge in beasts that had just gained power and managed to stabilize themselves to start showing up.

She was sure the hunters and scouts had already noticed such, but it was probably better to be safe than sorry, so she decided to drop by the village to relay her speculations to Voggo.

I'll take the occasion to check up on Beth, Jonah, and everyone else. Mom told me they are all fine, but I haven't seen them in a while.

Dorea gave one last pat to Bebe, grateful not to have been shocked this time, and walked back to the house. There, she alerted her father, "I'm going to talk to Voggo about a couple of things, and then I'll check up on my friends. I've already done my chores, so I'll be back before dinner."

Dodro simply waved at her in acknowledgment, busy as he tried to build the barn's roof back up. It would take weeks more for the repairs to be done and likely months before the last scars of the storm were gone, but things were looking up.

The trip to Whitecliff was quick, as she busied herself with trying to identify everything she could feel with her mana sense. It was still quite muffled, but she was making some progress.

Indeed, though the early days of gaining power were known to be of significant growth that would be irreplicable later in life, Dorea was sure that she was getting more out of it than most.

Well, I hope so. I'm working my butt off! I try to incorporate magic into everything I do, and not because I'm lazy, no matter what Mom says!

The fuzziness in her sense was still there, though now she needed less time to be able to identify what she was feeling.

Most of all, her ability to concentrate an element into a greater expression of itself had made leaps. She was now able to replicate the air explosion she had accidentally made the first day in about five seconds, and could do similar things with water and lightning.

Water was the easiest, as she just had to replicate the previous experiment, adding more and more pressure and then releasing it in an omnidirectional wave.

Her next objective was to concentrate the explosion in one direction only, as she was in the splash zone whenever she used it.

It's still progress!

Lightning was the trickier of the three elements. She wasn't familiar with it, and it was much harder to find in nature than water or air.

That didn't discourage her from experimenting with it. Which she now understood to be a somewhat foolish thing to do, but she believed the burn marks on her hands to be punishment enough.

If they don't heal properly, I'll have to ask Mom for help with them, and I know she'll make a big deal out of it.

In the end, what she had come up with was less a condensed ball of electricity and more a violently churning sphere.

Giving it a spin and direction made it more stable, at least for a while, as long as she kept feeding the construct power. The moment she stopped, it would destabilize into arcs that scorched whatever they touched.

It was pretty long-range too, and she managed to send it in the opposite direction most of the time.

I just need some more time to work on it, and it will be a proper spell. We'll see who's weaker than average, then!

Of course, her biggest weakness was that all these showings of power required, at the minimum, five seconds of complete concentration. It was very far from being combat-ready, but it was better than contenting herself with paltry tricks and drying out puddles for a living.

She willfully ignored that until a few days before, she didn't even have a smidge of power and hadn't been worrying about the future so much.

By the time she had extracted herself from her spiraling thoughts about her future, she had made it to the shaman's house.

Dorea knocked on the door and let herself in, already familiar with the building. Inside, her mother was working on some poultice in a well-ventilated room, having returned to work after the worst of the cleanup at their house.

She didn't bother the woman and moved to the back rooms, where Voggo was more likely to be, analyzing some sample or experimenting with a new way of making a potion.

She found him peering at a transparent crystal, engrossed in how the light reflected off it, and muttering to himself.

Well used to his oddities, she tried clearing her throat to get his attention, and when that didn't work, she banged on the door.

That did the trick, and the old man jumped, rushing to carefully put down what he was holding.

"Damnit, girl, there is no need to be so loud!"

Dorea merely looked at him with a deadpan stare, making him fidget a bit.

"Well, what did you want to tell me so much you had to interrupt me for?"

"Were you really busy with something important, or was it something one of the hunters brought back and that captured your attention?" she asked, used to his fascination with baubles of all kinds.

"I don't like the cheek," Voggo harrumphed, "and I'll have you know that I was examining this piece of glass found in the forest by the hunters. It seems like enhanced beasts are getting stronger quite quickly."

Suddenly reminded of why she was here, Dorea relayed her thoughts. "That's actually why I came over. Bebe, our enhanced anoa, is starting to be able to control his lightning, and I thought this could mean that the same was happening to the beasts in the wild."

"It seems like you were correct. You did well in coming to tell me, as it's always better to receive more than one piece of information that confirms your theory."

"Do you think we'll start seeing attacks from enhanced beasts soon?" she asked, worried about what that could mean for the livestock.

"I'd say we have a week at most before they stabilize enough to start ranging outside their previous territory. The old monsters from the previous generation should handle the worst of it, but some spillover is to be expected. I'll need to alert everyone to the possibility and set up patrols with the new Gifted for safety," he responded, mumbling to himself at the end.

Aware that when the old man got like this, it was useless to try and talk with him, she said her goodbyes, getting a distracted wave back, and left the house.

I wonder what kind of power can make glass . . . I thought that required a lot of heat. Our forge only makes a tiny bit for Voggo's use.

As she contemplated what kind of elemental manipulation was the origin of the piece of glass that the shaman was examining, she walked toward the bakery, the spot where she, Jonah, and Beth would usually meet up.

There, she found her two friends already present, sitting on the bench in front of the shop and enjoying a couple of donuts.

"I see how it is!" Dorea exclaimed dramatically, "You have already forgotten about me, led astray by sweets and false promises!"

She swooned toward Beth, twisting her expression into one of exaggerated sorrow.

Jonah rolled his eyes, reaching into the sack on his side and bringing out another for her.

She immediately dropped the act, snatching it from his hands and biting into it with gusto. "Ah! Honey and lavender, my favorite!"

"We know that there would be hell to pay if, somehow, word reached you that we had eaten them without setting one aside for you," chuckled Beth.

"Yeah, we were actually discussing if we should come by the ranch to try and save you," the blond boy teased.

With full cheeks, Dorea replied, "You have no idea! I did one itsy-bitsy experiment in my room the first night and haven't known peace for days!"

Her two friends laughed at her plight, scooting over so as to make enough space for her.

"How have you guys been?" she asked once their laughter had subsided.

"It's been a bit weird. My water magic has been useful, and I've gotten good enough to move a ton of it around. I've been draining mud and holes around the village," explained Beth.

"I'm not really good at sending blasts of wind, but my senses are probably the best, from what I've heard. I can tell if something is moving and roughly its shape from almost four hundred feet by now, and Mark, the scout, told me that he wanted me to start patrolling with them in the coming days." Jonah didn't seem very sure about going into the wild, but for all of his scaredy-cat nature, if he thought something needed to be done, he would do it.

"I was actually just talking about that with Voggo. He thinks that enhanced beasts will start moving around more in about a week and that we'll need to participate in the patrols as protection against them," replied Dorea.

"Are you sure you feel up to it?" asked a worried Beth to Jonah.

"Mark told me that I would only need to use my senses to tell them where stuff is. I wouldn't need to fight anything until I felt ready for it."

The brunette shook her head. "Yes, but you never know what can happen once you are out there."

The boy's plump lips pursed in thought, his eyes lost in the distance as he weighed his options.

"I don't think we have much of a choice here," interjected Dorea. "Individually, we can say no, but if we all did that, the hunters and scouts would be left without any support from a Gifted as they deal with more and more enhanced beasts."

Her words obviously displeased Beth, who shook her head. "The other boys will be all for it. Every one of them wants to go out and fight. Let them do it; there is no need for Jonah to risk himself."

Dorea sighed. "I agree that there is no pressing need for him to be in the wilds, but this is probably the safest time to do so and get used to it. The beasts are the weakest they'll ever be, and the hunters can still deal with them."

"Will you go, then?" asked Beth pointedly, obviously expecting her to say no.

"I will," Dorea said simply.

Jonah's head whipped in her direction. "But it's too dangerous for you!"

"It's dangerous for everyone; why would it be more so for me?" questioned Dorea, confused at his response.

There was a moment of silence as her two friends thought over what to say carefully before Beth spoke up, "We know better than anyone how adventurous and athletic you are, Dory, but maybe you should leave this kind of thing to those whose powers are more suited to it?"

"What?"

The three looked at each other in confusion.

"I'm not super strong, Voggo has already told me that, but I can use three elements and have already practiced a lot!" Dorea replied heatedly.

"We didn't mean to imply that your help wasn't needed, but everyone heard that your manipulation is quite weak," softly rebutted Jonah.

"I'm not weak! I'll show you." Dorea abruptly stood up, concentrating on the air before her; she extended her hand. Her embarrassment and anger were forgotten momentarily, as she had learned that any stray thought could lead to unfortunate consequences.

Nothing happened for a couple of seconds, and Beth was about to speak up before Jonah stopped her, staring intently at a spot ten feet ahead. His eyes widened, and he grabbed the brunette, throwing himself to the ground.

There was a big bang as the condensed air exploded violently, pushing everyone away from the epicenter. It lasted only for half a second, but the new pots that had been put outside the bakery were thrown against the wall, denting. Dorea was sent ass over teakettle, rolling to a stop against the door to the building.

The mess evidently gathered the attention of everyone nearby, who looked out of windows thrown open by the blast.

"What in the hell is going on here?!" thundered a thickly built man who came out of the bakery, hands and apron dirty with flour.

"I'm sorry, Dad!" squeaked Jonah from his place on the ground where he had covered Beth.

"Look! I'm strong!" shouted an unrepentant Dorea, a bright grin firmly affixed on her face.

After taking one long look at the girl, the baker rolled his eyes. He stopped as he saw the mess made by the broken pots and scowled at her. "That's going to come out of your pay once you start earning, girl."

Instead of her being chastised by his words, the blond girl's smile turned smug. "See, he agrees that I should go on patrols."

"I don't think that's what you should focus on, Dory," commented an exasperated Beth, holding her face with her hands.

The blond girl readily agreed with the baker to pay him back once she had made some money from going on patrols, unbothered by the destruction she had caused.

To her, the fact that her friends were so shocked by what she had done meant that her experiments had, at the very least, reduced the gap between her powers and the others.

It seemed weird to her not to play with the mystical powers they had just received as much as possible, but she supposed that not everyone had the same drive as her.

The rest of the day was spent cleaning up the mess she had made with her exhibition and catching up with her friends, enjoying each other's presence without much thought about what the future would bring.

The vast area in front of Voggo's house was once more full of young people, though this time, there would be no potion to drink and definitely no deaths to come. *At least in the near future, I hope.*

The old man had prepared benches for everyone to sit on, and all thirty new Gifted were present to hear his words.

"I have called you all here because it's about time I explained a bit more about how the magic that now resides in your bodies and souls works," he began, his aged voice cutting through the murmurs and silencing everyone.

"You are all aware of the basics, how the powers you now wield are a result of Mother Nature Gifting you with control over the elements of the Wrath you survived. Thus, there is no need to repeat myself again; I'm not here to listen to myself talk, after all."

He took a moment to look everyone in the eyes, holding them to ensure he had their attention before moving to the next.

"Humans are capable of using magic only after being in contact with an extremely powerful source of a specific type and develop that accordingly. The first example of this is the ability to manipulate the raw element, moving an already present source around and perceiving things through it or, a bit more advanced, using a small amount of it to make more through expending a large quantity of mana."

Voggo took a breath, pacing back and forth as he waved his hands around. No one made a peep, too concentrated on not missing anything he said.

Some of this was already explained to us, but he has yet to give a lecture about it the same way he does about mathematics or reading. This is much more interesting!

"Now, all this is part of the major ability called manipulation. It's one of the three main ways of doing magic and the most easily accessible to any new mage. The other two are, as you know, spells, which are derived by manipulating magic into a fractal until it gains enough stability to settle, and, less well known, rituals, which are generally more complex and require long preparations and, at times, reagents."

The old man stopped pacing, bringing his hands forward and closing his eyes. In front of him, a translucent shield started to take form.

Its appearance was like the ones the hunters used in their drills, that of almonds rounded at the top and curving down to a point.

It emitted a bluish light and hovered in front of the shaman, covering him entirely and slowly drifting around him.

Voggo dismissed it with a grunt before turning back toward them.

"This is Mana Shield, a spell I crafted to protect myself. It took me weeks to make it work and many months to perfect it. I had to meditate upon the fractals I remembered during my Trial, and though my experience was much different from yours, I believe it should still work the same."

He sighed, eyes looking into the distance and reminiscing.

"I want every one of you to start working toward a spell by concentrating on making the mana work into a fractal similar enough to what you saw. It will take some time to find its stable point, and be sure to do so away from any home, but in a few weeks, I want everyone to have at least one spell working."

It was obviously a dismissal, as he started to walk toward his house and left them there to ponder the task he had just given them.

I'm sure I can be the first to have one working.

Dorea left quickly, with a smile and a pep in her step.

CHAPTER EIGHT

Voggo's lessons had continued in the same manner for the next few days, with him dumping knowledge on them, showing an example, and then assigning some work.

Luckily, no task came close to the level of difficulty of making their own spell, and everyone remembered enough about the fractals they saw during the Trial to attempt to craft one.

Still, finding a specific effect they could make with their manipulation and turning the mana flow into something stable through the fractal's pattern was much more complex than he had implied.

I wonder if the fact that his element is mana itself makes it easier for him. Or maybe he just wanted to mess with us?

Dorea believed herself closer to achieving a genuine spell than everyone else, thanks to her intense practice in the first few days. That, unfortunately, did not mean that she was there yet.

Her lightning sphere seemed the closest to stabilizing into a valid pattern, but she had lost some of her edge by splitting her focus into all three elements, hoping to blow everyone out of the water with three new spells.

That wasn't very productive. The amount of attention required to even try forcing one's mana into a fractal pattern is insane. Getting it to be stable is still some ways away.

Dorea had lost some of her advantages but had learned some valuable lessons. First of all, don't waste time chasing more than one project simultaneously. Secondly, trying to match the lightning's spin with the fractals she remembered gave the construct a more powerful effect.

As much as Dorea would have liked to have suddenly become the strongest mage in the village, Mark the Blue had already shown everyone how much more mana he had.

The man, and he was a man compared to them, being twenty-one, had managed to blast a boulder that was half as tall as she was into rubble with an almost effortless bolt of lightning.

He was already a scout and was now considered one of the up-and-coming stars of the village.

This had been well received since it was important for every tribesman to know that their Gifted were strong enough to protect them, as both beasts and other tribes were expected to start making moves soon.

Meanwhile, as she exercised her powers in an attempt to craft a spell and sulked at not being the strongest, Dorea had to lend some aid to the reconstruction efforts.

Most of the work on their ranch was thankfully done, and her father had felled a few trees with her help to turn them into wood planks. As he worked through them, smoothing them into something useful for the barn's ceiling and the fence's remaining empty spots, Dorea was tasked by her mother to help around the village.

Finding work that needed to be done didn't take much time. In this case, she just had to ask the first person she saw, Beth's mother, Eloise, and she was suddenly standing in a muddy field, draining the water out of the ground.

Her best friend was there with her, and they made it a competition to see who could clear a field in the shortest time possible.

Beth was quicker at manipulating water and could pull more at once, but Dorea was not without tricks of her own. Initially, she used her wider senses to reach farther into the earth, but she soon learned that she couldn't just pull all the water out of the ground, as that would leave it cracked and lifeless.

Instead, she had started using her air manipulation to ease the burden of floating such quantities of water around, thus surpassing her friend in the amount she could move around.

She still couldn't pull as much as the brunette, but her double use allowed her to keep up.

While her mana pool was only limited by what her soul could produce and hold safely, her ability to manipulate an element was further constrained by her skill. As of that moment, she could only push about a third of her whole mana pool into a single effort, significantly limiting what she could accomplish.

Adding another element, while lowering what she could manage even more for a single one, allowed her to use about half of her mana pool.

It regenerated quickly, though according to Voggo, as they grew in power, it would take longer and longer to refill completely.

Unfortunately, splitting her concentration so much led her to getting a headache rather than winning the competition, but the fields they had been assigned to were clear, and that was enough for her.

Looking for the farmer to tell him they were done, the two girls stumbled upon Mark, Rupert and Thomas's brother.

Seeing him brought back memories of the boy she had fancied, whom she had seen get annihilated by something in the dream.

She still hadn't faced those experiences, thankful for the blurriness from the potion they had drunk, and she wasn't ready to feel everything she knew she would if she thought about it more deeply.

His face was maddeningly similar to Rupert's, different only in the eye color and the eyebrow thickness. It was like looking at your room, knowing somebody had been there and moved something, even if you couldn't pinpoint it exactly, because it felt wrong. He was subtly different enough to tell her it wasn't him but similar enough that it could be him.

The boy looked up and smiled at them. "Hey, girls, all done? Dad told me somebody would come over to help out, but I didn't know it would be you."

Beth took the lead, sensing her hesitation. "Yeah, we cleared the northwestern fields. You should be good to use them now."

Mark smiled in response, coming closer. His eyes searched Dorea's, trying to get her attention. "Hey, Dorea, I heard that you can use all three elements! And you are getting better faster than anybody else!"

She smiled shakily, looking at a spot just to the left of his eyes. "Yeah, you know me, I'm very dedicated."

Sensing her discomfort, Beth moved in. "Everybody's been working hard since Voggo's lessons have started. We really need to get going; we still have to do some work."

The boy shook his head, dismissing her words. "I'm sure they can spare some of Dorea's time. Knowing her, she's been working way too hard. Don't let me stop you if you need to get going, though."

The blond girl's hand closed tightly around her friend's, rooting her in place.

"Maybe I expressed myself incorrectly, but we really need to go now, Mark. Me and Dorea both." Beth's voice had lost its warmth.

The boy's smile slipped away, now looking annoyed. "I think that she's perfectly able to say so herself. Do you really need to leave so soon, Dorea?"

She forced herself to look him in the eyes, shocked to find them of a different color than what she expected. That gave her the strength to speak up. "I'm sorry, Mark, we still have much to do. I need to go."

His lips twisted in disappointment, and a cloud of anger passed by his eyes before he shook his head and plastered a smile on. "We'll have to have a chat the next time, then. It's a promise!"

So saying, he turned around and left them there. The two girls looked at each other in surprise, mouths hanging open.

"That guy! Who does he think he is to talk to us like that!" complained Beth, nose twisting in disgust. "It was obvious you didn't want to spend time with him!"

"Sorry, just looking at him hurt."

The brunette sighed, pulling her closer for a hug. "I know that he looks too much like Rupert. And he's a smarmy ass. I wouldn't leave you alone with him."

Dorea breathed in, drawing strength from her friend's arms. Seeing the boy she had a crush on turning into nothingness was something she hadn't talked about with anyone, and she had no intention of doing so, but she could share a bit of the burden in her heart.

"He even has his voice. When he's not so annoying, it hurts how much he sounds like him!" She laughed wetly.

"Mother, is he! He looks for a victim every once in a while and doesn't let go until he scores. He's gone after Sue and Bethany in the last year alone." Beth chuckled.

Raising her head from her friend's shoulder, Dorea smiled back. She was already feeling a bit better. *It's just been a shock. I have seen him during Voggo's lessons, but there were so many people that I could ignore him.*

Mark had been trying to get her attention for a couple of days already, but she had managed to fake not noticing him so far.

Unfortunately, her luck had run dry, and the confrontation had been forced. *I don't have anything against him. If he just left me alone, I would be happy to forget he exists.*

"It's not so much that he hits on me that annoys me, but that he knows I was talking with his brother. It's not even been a month; the mourning period isn't over!"

Dorea let out her frustrations, anger and sadness mixing into an ugly emotion. Thankfully, Beth was a steady rock upon which she could rest. They had always been like this, the two of them. Assisting each other when necessary and covering the other's butt when needed.

At least I'll always have Beth with me. Nothing's gonna come between us.

The two girls stayed there for a while, hugging and releasing their pent-up emotions. The Trial had been a harrowing experience, however little they could clearly remember, and there hadn't been a moment of release since.

In part, it had been their own fault for not wanting to stop and think about it too much, and the rest was done by the natural human process of blurring and relegating memories of traumatic events to the back of the mind.

Their families had helped where they could, but hadn't been through what they had. The only other person who had an inkling of what it was like to become a Gifted was the old shaman, whose experience had been thoroughly different by his own admission.

It was also challenging to put into words the things she had seen. She just didn't have the vocabulary for it, and it felt even more frustrating to think about it, so she mainly had just let it go.

Seeing Mark, hearing him talk to her in a flirty way, had forcefully reminded her of his brother, and she had frozen up. Thankfully, with Beth there to assist her, they managed to get out of it quite quickly.

Just the thought of him trying to chat me up gives me the shivers. He knows perfectly well that Rupert and I were more than friends, even if nothing happened beyond a couple of kisses.

Unfortunately for the girls, they actually did have some work to do, so they got up and started walking back toward the village, hand in hand.

Voggo's lessons hadn't all been as interesting as the first one, but as the days passed, more and more people started to understand their usefulness.

At first, it had just been social pressure that made sure they weren't skipping any, as the urge to play around and revel in their newfound powers was great, but since they started attending them, everyone had noticed a marked increase in their elemental control.

Small exercises, like holding a specific shape for a set amount of time, and more extraordinary exertions, like dumping as much mana as possible into one use before bed, were slowly starting to show their usefulness.

Dorea had started as the person with the weakest mana pool and the best control. Things which, according to Voggo, were related. As the days passed, her control level had stayed at the top in all three elements, which was quite surprising to the shaman, while her mana pool had gone up a few positions.

Much to her dismay, hard work and dedication couldn't make up the difference their starting point had created.

Still, the fact that I was able to go from dead last to fourth to last means that I can get better. That's all I need to know.

Dorea was willfully ignoring the lack of dedication that the people she had surpassed had demonstrated. She wasn't about to put herself down too.

Already, Mark, the farmer's son who had hit on her, was looking quite smug at being more powerful than her. It didn't matter that Mark the Blue surpassed him by several magnitudes; he was apparently content with just being stronger than her.

With a smug smirk whenever he demonstrated his water manipulation, he immediately looked at her, seeking her eyes. It was both a pathetic show of attention-seeking and a challenge.

She had been tempted several times to toss a lightning sphere at his feet just to see what kind of expression he would make at the show of power.

It grated on Dorea something fierce, having to deal with that kind of behavior, but thanks to Beth's timely interference, they managed to avoid a confrontation. Until it suddenly was inevitable.

That day, they were nearing the end of Voggo's lesson on the kinds of enhanced beasts, and how to deal with them, which touched upon old strategies the tribe had used.

"The way we used to deal with them when we had earth mages was completely different than what we should attempt these days, but we can still take some lessons from those tactics," the elderly shaman explained.

"They'd use their ground sense to pinpoint the location of animals in a radius, and the next mage, located almost at the end of the previous mage's range, would do the same. They had worked out a method to communicate their findings to each other and used this net to safely patrol the lands around the village. Now this obviously is not replicable on a one-to-one scale, but the air mages we have should start trying combinations to put this tactic into place."

As he finished the lecture, Voggo rose from his chair and started walking toward the empty space behind his house they had been using for practice.

He'd hold demonstrations almost daily to show how they had progressed. It had attracted some attention from the villagers in the beginning, but now only a few people stopped to observe.

"We'll start with the air mages. Show me what you've got."

Surprisingly, it was Jonah who moved first. The blond boy walked toward the spot they used. He was strangely confident, which wasn't a bad look on him.

He raised his hands toward the sky and closed his eyes, clenching his teeth. To her senses, pressure started accumulating quickly high up above him.

It didn't feel like a standard air construct because it was heavier and less defined.

He kept feeding it mana for a dozen more seconds before violently throwing his hands down toward the ground.

There was a big *whoomp*, and the area in front of him was flattened. The grass was reduced into a paste, even cracking the ground.

The land shook beneath their feet for several instants as if a gigantic creature had just passed by.

Dorea was even more gobsmacked than the others, as there had been no indication he had been working on something like that.

He hasn't told me anything about it. Why hasn't he talked to me?

Jonah turned to face them with a massive grin, drinking in their expressions of surprise.

"Yes, yes, well done, boy. You managed to crush some grass. Now try to make it into a spell. You won't have so much time when you're out there," cut in Voggo, bringing the enthusiasm down.

Next to her, Beth was smiling proudly toward their friend, welcoming him back with a hug. He woozily acknowledged them, simply too spent to react more.

The rest of the demonstrations weren't as surprising as his. Mark the Blue showed off his lightning bolt, which was more potent by a mile than what Jonah had managed, but he had been ahead of them all since the beginning, and no one was surprised by it.

Mark the farmer took the stage soon after and attempted a complicated manipulation involving simultaneously calling water from different sources to make it a large construct. It took him a while, but he was able to complete it, and riding high off the feeling of accomplishment, he approached Dorea.

"See that? I'd say I'm headed to the top pretty soon. No one else has that kind of control," he spoke to her arrogantly.

It's not even that he looks like his dead brother anymore. I just can't stand him.

"I have seen. It was impressive," she replied coldly.

"Come now, Dorea, you can do better than that. There is no need to be shy with compliments between friends."

Dorea looked around for help, but Beth had moved to the other side to talk with Jonah, and no one else seemed interested in intervening.

"I think we'll have to see whether you are as good as you think you are," she commented, feeling more than a little annoyed at his presumption.

"You don't mean to tell me that you can do better, do you?" He tried smiling patronizingly at her.

"I am sure I can. I'll show you in a second if you are so curious."

"Let's make it a bet then. If you can do something more impressive than what I did, I'll leave you alone. If you can't, you'll have to give me a chance," Mark immediately cut in.

"Fine. Let's do it!" she replied, willing to do anything to get him away from her.

Now I just have to be graced by Mother Nature and manage something I've never come close to.

CHAPTER NINE

I just need to do it. I have attempted casting a complete spell for days and days, and nothing happened. But now it will be different. It has to be.

Dorea's attempts at psyching herself up were not particularly successful, mostly because she didn't believe it was possible to somehow do what she had failed to without changing anything.

Still, she had gotten into this mess and had to dig herself out. The air arrows she had prepared for the demonstration would not be enough to shut Mark up, however proud she was of them.

The only thing she could think of that would make a big enough splash was her experimental spell, Lightning Sphere. If only she could have completed it, it would have been perfect.

I'm so close to it, though. I can feel it's just missing something before it stabilizes enough. The fractal is correct, and I've managed to get enough mana to supply it in one go, but it's not coming together.

The difference between an actual spell and simple manipulation was both minimal and incredibly vast.

To the untrained eye, someone using the water from the sea to make a large wave and crush his target was the same as someone doing it through a spell. The spell would be quicker, and the resulting effect would be more substantial, but nothing earth-shaking.

The true difference stood within the actual workings of one. If a mage tried to manipulate an element, someone with the same affinity could interfere and even try to usurp control from the caster; a complete matrix was both instantaneous and immutable.

The fractal-shaped mana within would reach a level of stability that made it almost impossible to mess with, and its form was forever enshrined in the caster's mind.

Once a mage successfully cast a spell, they would never forget it. It became an intrinsic part of their understanding of magic.

The difficulty was in finding the proper pattern, which was primarily done by blind-testing different variations of what one could remember from their Trial and trying to fully understand it and its effects on the world.

According to Voggo, one cannot cast a spell if they are not intrinsically familiar with its shape and workings. If you do not know how fire can affect the world, you cannot hope to cast a fireball, even if you know the proper fractal.

Dorea stood in place, hesitant to make a fool out of herself but too annoyed and frustrated to care much.

The pattern spun up in her mind's eye, and she went over every effect the Lightning Sphere could have.

She focused on the way it scorched her fingers when she first started her forays in magic, the way the ground would blacken and crack whenever she used it, and the beauty of the lightning arcs.

Nothing seemed to happen, and she could hear people start to whisper.

Desperation crept up, closing her throat and making concentration difficult. As a last ditch to achieve it, she returned to the first thing she had felt with the electricity sense after the Trial.

The buzzing in her mind seemed to increase in loudness, and something finally clicked.

The spell spun up smoothly, guzzling enough mana in an instant to almost send her to her knees, and she manifested the Lightning Sphere in front of her outstretched hand.

It was the size of her head and made up of white-blue arcs of electricity contained within a ball. The humming became suddenly intense, and she let it go, startled.

The spell blasted out of her hand, crossing the distance between her and the log she needed to aim for in a fraction of a second.

As it touched the wooden post, it exploded into a bright storm, engulfing the target and making it impossible to make out. The sound was closer to a saw than to thunder, but it was still loud enough to reverberate through the air.

Her mana sense went haywire, simultaneously telling her that the world was shaking and everything happening was perfectly contained.

It all ended in a few seconds, and the log was revealed to have become charred splinters.

Silence met her ears after the overstimulation, and it was almost as bad.

She turned around to see her friends' reactions. She just managed to glimpse

Beth throwing herself at her, arms slipping around her, and her legs braced for the impact.

It didn't work, and the two girls were sent sprawling on the ground.

"You did it!" the brunette shouted, breaking Dorea out of her daze.

"I did it!" she yelled back.

The mana loss from the spell had disoriented her, and the following sensory overload hadn't helped. However, it didn't matter to her because she had actually done it.

She had been the first to cast a proper spell. No one would be able to gainsay her now.

It doesn't matter if my mana pool is much smaller than all the others. It doesn't matter if I can't manipulate as much of an element as the others. I am the first and only one who can cast a spell.

The euphoria was further heightened by Voggo's enthusiastic clapping. "That's how you do it! Little Dorea went and did it. That's how you cast a spell!"

Surprise and awe were on most people's faces, but she didn't miss the few envious and angry expressions. Mark's face looked like a dried-up prune, given how much he was scrunching, and the sight of it sent her into hysterical laughter.

A rough hand grabbed her, breaking off her bout of hilarity. Voggo picked her up by the armpits, like he did when she was little, and lifted her up.

She stood on unsteady legs, Beth still clinging to her like a limpet.

"You did great, but you need to rest, girl. The Mother knows you expended a lot of mana. You'll be feeling out of sorts for a while, so keep an eye on her, will you?" the shaman grunted, turning to the brunette once it was apparent that she wasn't fully following his words.

Dorea heard him but was suddenly too woozy to assure him of her well-being. She let herself be herded to the side by Beth, who laid her down carefully, took her head, and placed it on her thighs.

The blond girl stayed there for a while, content to bask in her achievement and unwilling to get up and test her balance.

Her friend's fingers carding through her hair helped her remain put.

I really cast a spell. I can still feel it in its entirety whenever I think about it. It's a part of me now.

The space in her mind where the fractals she had received during her trials were, now was also home to the matrix of her Lightning Sphere.

Dorea instinctively knew that she could cast it at a moment's notice. She now understood that the missing part that prevented her from completing it had been her understanding of how electricity worked. Focusing on the buzzing in her head had somehow bridged the gap.

There was still much more to discover, as she had just taken her first step in the lightning magic path, but she had finally truly begun her journey.

They were soon joined by Jonah, who smiled at her brightly. "You were amazing, Dory. I can't believe you were the first to do it!"

His earnest joy at her accomplishment brought her back to the present, and she grinned up at him, making him blush.

The fingers scratching her scalp stopped, and Beth pushed her upright. "I see that you've recovered, Your Laziness."

"I didn't expect it to pull that much mana from me. It drank almost all of it instantly; I thought I didn't have enough." Dorea laughed.

The lesson was already over, but almost everyone was still there, chatting about the demonstration and her casting of Lightning Sphere. Therefore, it was impossible for two of the scouts, dressed as they were for camouflage in the forest, to go unnoticed as they approached Voggo.

Whatever it was that they told him, he wasn't happy about it. His face grew graver with each passing moment as they finished their report. He raised his hand to gather their attention, even though everyone was already looking at him.

"I have received crucial information and need to hold a meeting about it in a few hours. Please inform everyone without exception."

Tribe meetings were a rare occurrence in Whitecliff. Usually, they happened only in case something massive had happened, and there was enough time to share it with everyone.

Usually, either the shaman or the leads of scouts and hunters would deal with whatever the problem was, and people would get informed naturally once there was time to do so.

It wasn't a perfect system, but it worked most of the time, and no one wanted the hassle of having a chief. Voggo did most of the ceremonial and long-term decision-making parts of leadership, and the people with the proper knowledge would decide for their profession.

There was no need for a farmer to have to consult a hunter to choose when to start planting.

Well, according to Mom, Voggo could have easily pushed to be recognized as chief, but he doesn't want to deal with the position. Unfortunately for him, he's the chief in all but name.

Being the only Gifted left in the tribe gave him disproportionate power over the rest. It wasn't uncommon for the new mages to go out into the world and look for a tribe that didn't have any to lead them. The safety that they could provide was unparalleled, after all.

The power dynamics in a region were subject to quick change when Nature's Wrath passed through it, and everyone was expecting things to start happening quickly.

Bets had been made about whether the first problem to crop up would be enhanced beasts or Gifted from other tribes trying to muscle in on their lands.

Considering how troubled Voggo looked, Dorea would have to amend her bet. It looked more likely to be a man-made problem now.

People started to disperse, heading toward their homes to alert their families and neighbors about the meeting. So she said goodbye to her friends and went to do the same, torn between annoyance that her big moment had been stolen and trepidation about what the future would hold.

A few hundred people standing together might not seem much to someone who was used to the crowds of the city-states in the far southeast, but to Dorea it still was an incredible sight.

To her senses, it felt even more impressive. Everyone had a slightly different aura, not to mention the other Gifted, who felt like beacons thanks to their abundance of aspected mana.

The crowd quieted as soon as Voggo became visible, escorted by Ed, the lead hunter, who was a very unassuming man with a deep voice and scarred hands, and Mark, the lead scout, a lithe man who seemed the most nervous of the three.

There was no podium to speak from, like during the festivals, but the shaman didn't need such things to ensure everyone heard him. A blue spark materialized around his throat, and when he opened his mouth, his voice reverberated through the clearing as if he were a giant.

"I'm sure you are all very curious and worried about why I've called the meeting. I'll cut to the chase and say it plainly. Our scouts, led by Mark here"— he gestured toward the blond man—"have completed their latest assessment. It seems like the northern tribes are moving and that they have been raiding their neighbors in the mountains."

Questions started flying, worried conversations broke out, and composure was all around quickly lost.

Instead of immediately breaking the confusion up with his voice, Voggo let it play out for a few minutes, allowing people to vent their anxiety.

"All right, people! We knew this was coming!" he finally shouted, getting everyone's attention back.

"Tomorrow, we'll start patrols with the new Gifted as planned, and together with the scouts, they'll monitor our lands." He gestured toward where the young people were gathered.

"If it were just that, I wouldn't make that big of a deal out of it. The problem is that some of the northerners are apparently winning handily. Our scouts reported at least two villages were left empty, their people and things moved to become part of a bigger tribe."

His stern voice prevented anyone from questioning him again, and it was evident that Voggo wasn't happy with the situation.

"What we think happened is that they got a larger than average number of Gifted, and one of them took control of a specific village. I have met old Jorm, the previous chief of the strongest tribe, and he would not have behaved this way. The fact that they are acting so aggressively makes me think that they don't want to give anyone time to develop their Gifted into a proper defensive force."

This doesn't sound good at all. We'll probably have to fight them soon if they are so thirsty for conquest.

"I want to make it clear that it is not our assessment that they are gonna start coming for us soon, but we definitely are in their strike zone, and considering that both of our tribes are Sapiens, the integration would go more smoothly, making us a preferred target."

Damn, I didn't even think of that. If they are trying to unite the tribes under one banner, going after all the Sapiens first would make sense. There are some more in the mountains, but after them, it'll be us and the Forest ones they go after.

"From what we have managed to piece together by talking with some of the friendlier tribes around, the Wrath has seemingly hit the whole Loisosian coast. It was much bigger than what we expected and have records of," Voggo continued explaining. It was obviously the work of all the scouts, but it would have made no sense to present it piece by piece as they got more information.

The scouts must have been run ragged to quickly get information from the north and south.

"This means that the whole region is about to undergo great change. We can expect the next few years to be exciting," he chuckled. "The fact that the storm awakened three different elements means that we won't be able to develop a single tactic to deal with the enemy Gifted, but it gave us quite the range to defend ourselves with."

He then gestured toward her. "And today, we had our very first spell cast by Dorea! This is a great accomplishment! She cast a beautiful lightning spell in the shortest time I know of. And I expect others to soon start being able to complete their own."

People started clapping, searching for her to congratulate her. There seemed to be an almost desperate relief that one of those tasked to protect the village was better than expected.

This is getting annoying, she thought as she was jostled by all the back-slapping and friendly hugs.

Finally, Voggo reasserted control over the crowd. "All right, people, leave the poor girl alone. We have quite the crop of Gifted, and I'm sure things will go smoothly if everyone does their part!"

Everyone seemed to be reinvigorated after the news. Men and women were nodding determinately, ready to tackle their jobs to help the village.

He really is good at this. He first hit them with the bad news, let them stew on it, and then distracted them successfully. He gave them hope that we were capable of defending them. The old man is wily.

"We will all need to work hard in the following times, but we are ready to tackle anything the world throws at us! Go and do your jobs, people!"

The speech ended quickly, as Voggo wasn't one to keep talking longer than necessary on these occasions, and after one last round of congratulations, Dorea was left alone with her friends.

Before they, too, could leave, Voggo caught her eye and motioned toward his home, where he was headed with Ed and Mark.

Now curious about what the three could possibly want with her, Dorea said her goodbyes and quickly joined them.

CHAPTER TEN

Dorea followed the three men into the house until they entered the room to the back, where she had shared her fears of possible enhanced beast attacks with Voggo.

Though she felt that her reasoning then was still perfectly valid, it seemed naive to have discounted entirely the possibility of a neighboring tribe becoming hostile.

Surprisingly, no one made a play for more power here. Well, maybe some would have had they been stronger. I'm thinking of you, Mark.

The shaman gestured for them to sit as he took his place on his favorite leather-stuffed chair. The small table in the center of the room was filled with a steaming pot and four cups.

Obviously, this meeting had been planned in advance the moment news had been relayed, though Dorea still couldn't guess why she would be involved.

This feels like the kind of meeting only the tribe's leaders should attend. Why am I here?

Ed the hunter took upon himself the task of filling the cups with the tea that had been prepared, the dark red liquid still steaming.

"I'm sure you're asking yourself why you are here, Dorea," the old man began, "and there are multiple reasons. First of all, we need one representative of the new Gifted, and though you are not the most powerful, every one of them respects you. That's the easiest answer."

Dorea took a sip, feeling the warm liquid relax her. *I can appreciate being recognized, but they are not telling me something.*

"And what's the real one?"

"The real one is that we need to start including your group in the decision-making. We have discussed between ourselves who to use as the unofficial leader of the Gifted, and with your earlier demonstration, we believe you to be the one most suited to the position."

She tilted her head. "Well, if you wanted someone exemplary, you could have involved Mark the Blue. He's far more powerful than I."

Voggo and Ed turned toward the other man, waiting for him to answer. "Mark is a good scout and a powerful mage. He's not someone I would ever give a leadership position to, however. He works well when given precise orders and low stakes, but pressure has almost broken him several times."

This was news to her, but Dorea tried to mask her surprise by drinking more tea. It had been oversteeped slightly, becoming bitter, but she didn't mind.

"Others are still stronger than me and more capable of standing up to tough situations," she said leadingly.

"None of those others are as good as you with magic—they simply have more mana, and I have little doubt that you'll catch up to them in that department in a few years," answered Voggo.

The old man stared at her over steepled fingers, his eyes hooded and gaze heavy. "We don't want you to think that you will be responsible for Whitecliff's mages, and we lose nothing by including you in this kind of discussion for a while. It gives us a chance to properly assess you."

Ed the hunter leaned back, chair scraping against the wooden floor. "We feel like you have a lot of potential, and nurturing it now means having a better result later. Also, the Wrath changed everything, and we must go with it or face potential destruction. You are only one of the many changes we are trying to implement."

I guess that makes sense. If I fail to meet their expectations, they can always move on to another Gifted. And I should have expected them to shake things up now that we know that the whole coast was hit by the Wrath.

"I suppose I can understand that. I'll play ball. What's the thing you wanted to discuss with me then?"

The old shaman smiled proudly, eyes crinkling in happiness at her words. "I'm delighted to hear that. You'll be able to learn much by just attending these meetings, and I'm sure you'll give us a fresh perspective on things."

He then reached back toward a cabinet, which he opened, and took out a rolled-up scroll. Ed cleared the table of the tea and made space for him to unroll it.

It turned out to be a map of their surrounding lands, extending north into the mountains, east into the forest, and down south to the large river that ran through the steppe.

To her eyes, it was pretty detailed, being full of marks indicating villages, herds' paths, and dangerous beasts' territories.

"We have several options at the moment," Voggo began, pointing to the spot where their village resided, close to the cliffs. "We can either bunker up, preparing traps and walls to stop invading armies and slow down any beast who tries to wander into our land." He traced the forest's borders to the east and the northern hills. "We can reach out to the northerners and try to make a deal with them"—his finger pointed to the mountain range at the top of the map—"or try to convince the more moderate villages to help each other and weather the coming storm."

All three men looked at her expectantly, apparently curious about her opinion.

"I don't think we'll be able to reach a deal that we could trust to hold with the northerners," Dorea answered the unspoken request. "If they are already on the warpath, they will likely want to keep momentum on their side, and showing weakness now just means becoming a target."

They remained impassive, waiting for her to finish her point, though knowing Voggo, she believed that had she said something foolish, he would have already interrupted her.

"I don't think it's a bad idea to fortify our position, though I wouldn't put all our resources into it. Our wall should protect us from anything trying to sneak in from the south and the east. The northern side is quite a bit more vulnerable, though. Knowing that we could be in a better position to repel any attack but not having it because we trusted our information too much seems foolish to me; no offense meant." She bowed slightly to the scout in apology, getting a negligent wave back.

Dorea took a moment to drink more tea, grateful that the warm liquid soothed her throat. "In the end, I think we should contact the villages we know would be more receptive to cooperation, to at least exchange information, but not rely on it to change things. We need to be strong enough to stand on our own."

There was a beat of silence as the three men observed her and then looked at each other. The first to break it was Ed. "I don't think I agree with everything you've said, but I can't deny that you are a brilliant young lady and would make a fine addition to the village council, though not in any official capacity for a while."

Voggo remained quiet, merely nodding to show approval at his words, and looked at the scout to see if he would have anything to say.

"Yeah, I also think it's a bit naive to think we can take on the northerners on our own, but then again, she doesn't have the information about their numbers that we do. I agree that this is enough to start this little test of yours," he concluded, inclining his head toward the shaman.

The old man waited to see if anyone wanted to add anything, and though

Dorea had many questions, she kept them to herself for the moment, knowing there would be a time for them.

"Well, I'm happy that you two agree with my choice. Dorea is a promising mage beyond just her affinities, and listening to her can only help us out."

His words were meant to signal that their meeting was over, and the two men took it as such, bowing slightly to their unofficial leader and leaving quietly.

I guess they still have work to do, don't they? Can't really spend the day drinking tea and talking with me, especially after the news we got.

As she got up to leave, Voggo stopped her with a raised hand. "Sit back down. We need to talk about something else, and I bet you have more questions to ask. Since now is a good time for me, it's better to get it over with."

A bit offended that her curiosity was considered an annoyance, Dorea dropped back onto her seat. "What else do we need to talk about that we couldn't do so in front of them?"

The shaman's eyes suddenly blazed with arcane light, a sure sign of a spell at work. He inspected her thoroughly, and she felt his gaze piercing her very core.

"Hey, what gives?!"

"It is better than I feared but still somewhat concerning," he answered cryptically. Seeing the outrage forming, he chuckled and explained, "You'll remember how I came by after the Trial, even though the village was very much in need of my time. I had feared your ability to manipulate three elements to be the consequence of a curse, but it turned out not to be so."

"What kind of curse?" she asked worriedly.

"The process of getting one's Gift is very much still a mystery, but we know that sometimes *things* can interfere with it, and the end result can be horrible."

Now very distressed, Dorea thought back at what she could remember of her own Trial and, pushing against the instinct of flinching back at the memory, recalled *something* killing Rupert and trying to interfere with her soul.

She debated for a second not telling the old man about it, but knew she could trust him. "I remember that. There was a *thing* that was alerted to our presence by something Rupert was doing, and it made him vanish into nothingness with just its attention. I think I was saved by my grandmother's pendant."

Her hand automatically removed it from her shirt and showed it to Voggo. His face was grave as he reached for it with a glowing finger.

The moment it touched the amulet, he reared back with a hiss of pain. "To the hells! That thing is definitely strong enough to shield you from a powerful being's sight. It's almost depleted now but has enough in it to smart."

He sucked on his finger, as if he had been burned by fire.

"But I haven't felt anything from it, and I tried every day to push some mana into it! It felt inert like a brick," she replied in shock.

"Your grandmother was a very resourceful woman, little Dorea. You are named after her, and I'm not surprised that she took steps to protect her legacy. She was the most powerful mage we ever had in our tribe, and not a week goes by that I don't curse the necessity of her sacrifice."

That was news to her.

"What sacrifice?! My parents told me that she died from a sickness!" She was almost shouting now and recognized her anger was misplaced. She sat back down, not even realizing she was standing, and bowed her head in apology. "Sorry, I shouldn't have shouted."

"It's fine; I guess it's a bit of a shock. She did die of an illness, they didn't lie to you, but she got sick because she fought a mighty enhanced beast that could turn the very air into poison. It killed everything in its path and went out of its way to destroy any village it found. Doressa, your grandmother, was the only one capable of protecting herself from its gases long enough to actually fight it. She killed it, but it left her weak and fragile."

Dorea sat there in shock, both proud of her and confused at never having been told the story. "But then she's even more of a hero than I thought! Why wouldn't they tell me?"

"It was not a pretty sight," Voggo sighed. "Her decline came fast enough that you could see it as the days went by, but nothing we tried stopped it. She died after we managed to put her to sleep, so at least she didn't suffer in the end. Your parents simply took out the more grisly details; they didn't lie to you."

It took her a while to digest what she had been told, and thankfully Voggo was kind enough to let her have it.

It doesn't change much; I already knew she was considered a great mage, and they told me many times about how wonderful she was. It's just a lot of new information.

"But what about the pendant? How could she have made something like this if she was an earth mage? And if she could, why haven't you done something similar?" Her words came out a bit more biting than she wanted them to, but the shaman ignored her tone.

"I have honestly no idea. It could be that she reached such a level that she tied the earth's protective nature into it through a ritual, or she could have found it somewhere or even taken it from someone." He seemed a bit embarrassed. "I couldn't possibly hope to make something that powerful. I have tried for many years to cook up a new way of giving everyone a better chance at surviving the Trial, and I believe the potions I made to be much better than what we had when your grandmother undertook her own Trial."

His words made sense, and Dorea felt ashamed at having spoken to him so harshly. *He doesn't know everything. I keep forgetting that he's just human, like us. And he did as much as he could to help us.*

"I'm sorry, Voggo; I didn't mean to speak in that tone. I was upset, but that doesn't mean I should have taken it out on you," she apologized, thankful for her father's lessons on taking responsibility for one's errors.

The old man chuckled. "I can see so much of Dodro in you sometimes; it's like you are his female clone."

"I'll take that as a compliment."

He hummed in agreement. "The pendant will likely stay a mystery, as I doubt you want me to crack it open in the fleeting hope that I'll understand its workings."

Dorea clutched it in both hands, stuffing it under her shirt to his laughter.

"I wouldn't do it anyway; it's too good of an artifact to risk it," he explained further, shaking his head at her unconvinced expression.

"I know how much you like tinkering with any weird object you can get your hands on," she accused, only half jokingly.

"That pendant is too valuable to play with, much to my dismay. It will also be advantageous to you in the coming days once you are out there in the wilds running patrols and fighting with beasts."

"And so we get to why you asked me to stay behind. What do you need me for?" she asked.

The old man sat back, fingers drumming on the arm of his chair. "There are two reasons why I kept you here. The first, the most important, was to check up on you. While the pendant can hide your soul from my sight, I can still make out enough to tell that your pattern is slightly different than it should be."

"Different in what way?" she interrupted.

"Well, normal mages have a system overlaying their bodies comparable to your veins, where the mana is the blood. It's not an exact comparison, as it's mostly static and it doesn't have a physical presence, but it's good enough."

Voggo gestured widely toward her chest. "I thought you would have a slightly more complex system representing your three affinities. Instead, everything is hazier than it should be, though it could be because of the pendant, and it seems both intricate and somewhat patchwork."

"Should I take the pendant out to let you see better?" she asked, moving to do so but stopping when he raised his hand.

"I already checked earlier when you gave it to me. The haziness is still there, and while it could mean that it extends its protection for quite a distance, that goes against most of what I know of artifacts. It's more likely something unique to you."

Dorea bit her lip, somewhat worried that she didn't look normal to his sight. *Obviously, it is a consequence of what happened during the Trial, but what does it mean for me?*

"As far as I can tell, it's nothing too dangerous, but we'll have to see. The first few months after gaining your powers are fundamental to stabilizing yourself.

Your future growth depends on it. For now, take note of any weird feelings and come to me immediately if you suspect something's wrong," he reassured her, sensing her distress.

His hand had taken hers and was caressing it gently. His eyes were those of a grandfather looking at his favorite grandchild. *I guess I'll just have to trust him to help me.*

Dorea smiled a bit weakly at him, trying to show her gratefulness.

"The second reason," he began after the moment had passed, "is that I want you to go with the scouts on their expedition to the southern Heidel tribe. We'll need their help, or at least their neutrality, and a show of power might be just what is needed to help them make the right choice."

This time, her smile was much less reserved. "I can do flashy if you need flashy."

Voggo chuckled at her mood switch and patted her hand one last time before shooing her away. "Now go, I still have work to do, and I'm sure your family is waiting for you to celebrate your accomplishment."

Oh yeah, I cast a spell today.

The thought felt a bit weird, considering how much stuff had happened just that day, but Dorea had never been one to say no to a party. *Better if there is something sweet at the end. I'm sure we have enough honey for Mom to whip up something.*

CHAPTER ELEVEN

Her parents had been waiting for her to return home to celebrate. Though neither were mages, they were interested enough in magic to know that to be the first to cast a spell and do it in less than two weeks was quite the accomplishment.

Little Lia didn't need a reason to celebrate her big sister but was more than happy when the honey cake was taken out.

It had been a wonderful evening, and Dorea had done her best to immerse herself in it and not let her swirling thoughts about the day's events distract her.

She had been mostly successful, but her mind betrayed her when it was time to go to sleep.

I'm worried about going on such a critical mission. I haven't even left the village yet! What were they thinking, giving such a responsibility to me?!

Being part of the delegation that would contact the Heidel tribe to the south was both nerve-racking and a source of pride.

She didn't want to mess it up and risk alienating one of their only relatively friendly neighbors, but she was chosen specifically because she was so quick to advance her magic.

The risk between coming off too aggressive and losing a potential ally, and being seen as weak and not worth their time, or worse, easy pickings, was one she would have to balance very carefully.

And I can't even ask them to wait for a couple of weeks to make sure I'm stronger because, at that point, casting spells won't be much to be awed by.

Aware that her thoughts were going nowhere, Dorea decided to just take things as they came and not to bother too much with the idea of failure.

It's gonna be on their head too, since they decided to give me this much responsibility.

* * *

The expedition team met up a day later at the outskirts of the village on the southern side.

Mark, the lead scout, was present, as he would be the one to do the actual negotiating. And hadn't that been a relief.

At least they haven't gone completely insane. If they had also asked me to become a diplomat, I would have just started blasting.

Luckily, it hadn't come to that.

Jonah was there as well, still rubbing the sleep from his eyes. His fluffy hair was sticking out in every direction, and his pack was still on the ground, with things strewn on the grass as the older scouts checked that they had brought the correct provisions.

While he had never been particularly courageous, Dorea was glad to have him with her. The thought of having no one to talk to the whole trip, which should take about two days going and two getting back if everything went well, was too much to bear.

While this was not the first mixed expedition of scouts and Gifted, as Mark the Blue had been going on a few, it was still new enough a thing that everyone was a bit antsy.

No one wants incompetent kids running between their legs while they work, much less ones that can blast them away if they are not careful enough.

There would likely be some tension before everyone got used to each other.

Her mother had told her to expect things to get better only after an enhanced beast got too close, and they killed it without risking anyone.

She's right. We'll have to prove ourselves not to be nuisances.

The luggage inspection was soon over, and everyone gathered before Mark.

"Today, we are not just going on a normal patrol, people! Today we are tasked with securing our southern border for good! I expect a smooth trip down south and for any problem to be handled quickly," he began, his voice raised enough that everyone could hear him clearly.

"We'll be joined by three of our Gifted today, Dorea, who will be our main damage dealer; Jonah, our insurance against sneak attacks; and Tom, who will replenish our storages of water and provide support as needed. They are young, and it's their first expedition, but I expect everyone to treat them well!"

The group consisted of the three mages, Mark, and six other scouts. It was a more numerous patrol than usual, but it was understandable, considering their need to impress the Heidels and the length of the trip.

Also, Voggo wants to make sure we all come back. Losing people now would be a massive blow to morale. And it would just suck.

* * *

The six professional scouts were older than her, being at most in their late twenties, and their air was that of veterans preparing for a difficult mission.

They set off at a decent pace, and Dorea was thankful that none of the less athletic mages had joined them. *It was likely on purpose. No one wants to add a whole day to the trip because Mia or Jack got too tired to walk.*

It felt weird to leave the village behind. She had gone on a few excursions with her friends and father before, but she had never gone so far away and always returned before dark.

"We'll walk through the forest for half a day before we reach the grasslands. The southern side of it is less thick than the eastern part, thankfully," came a voice to her left.

Dorea turned to see one of the older scouts, Eddie, walking beside her. *I need to pay more attention to my senses. Jonah is the one tasked with feeling around for anything that moves, but that doesn't mean I can just space out like this.*

She smiled up at him. "Eddie, right? You are Beth's cousin."

"Yeah, we've met a few times but never really talked, huh?"

"There wasn't much to talk about when I was six and running around the festivals throwing eggs at my friends, and you were sixteen and chasing skirts, I guess." She smiled.

He chuckled embarrassedly, scratching the back of his head.

"I just wanted to make sure you were okay with this." He gestured to the forest surrounding them.

"I'm okay, thanks. It's a bit overwhelming how quickly life has changed since the Trial, but we all have our roles to play, don't we?"

"That's a good point," interrupted a rough voice, "and you have something you should be doing, don't you, Eddie?"

Mark, the lead scout, had apparently decided they had been too relaxed in chatting. Eddie stiffened in response and let out an involuntary "Yes, sir!"

He nodded hastily to her and moved ahead to join the forward party.

"He's actually not on duty right now, but I wonder how long it will take him to remember," the older man chuckled.

He left her standing there with her mouth wide open before she shook her head and laughed to herself. *The man has a sense of humor!*

She was soon joined by Tom, the water mage.

He was a bit older than her, being seventeen, and though they knew each other, he had never seemed particularly interested in getting to know her better.

"Gets kinda repetitive, all this walking in the forest, huh?"

It seems that I'm the designated target to make conversation with today.

"We should be getting out of here in a couple more hours. We have already left what is considered our territory, so things should be getting more interesting from now on." She smiled tightly.

"Man, I hope we don't get attacked by any beast. I'm getting decent at cleaning wounds, but I'm definitely not a healer," he complained.

It's not an easy role, but you volunteered for it. You should have stuck to helping in the fields if you didn't want any responsibility.

"Our path has been scouted in advance. We shouldn't meet anything too strong."

As soon as she said it, she felt Jonah stiffen through her senses. His head snapped to the left, and he called out, "There is something quite big coming our way. It's not moving too fast, but the sheer mass that's moving is crazy."

Everyone snapped to attention, and with a gesture from Mark that she caught only thanks to her senses, one of the scouts moved in that direction. He was quick but made almost no sound.

They all waited in silence for more than five minutes before he returned. "It's a therium. It doesn't seem to be enhanced, thankfully, and if we move quickly, we'll be able to lose it."

Eddie piped up, "If he's moving with any speed, he'll be here long before our scent has gone away. We'll have a twenty-foot-tall beast hounding us all the way if we don't deal with it now."

"It's a therium," cut in another. "They are not exactly known to be quick. We'll probably be able to reach the Heidels and return before it has arrived here."

Dorea looked to Mark, whose brow was furrowed in thought. He turned to Jonah. "How quick is it moving?"

"It's not super fast, but it's huge, so it'll be here in less than five minutes."

Mark looked for confirmation from the scout who had seen the animal, prompting him to speak up, "Four minutes tops. It's a pretty big animal, so if we want to take it down, we must prepare immediately."

"Start setting up the lines. Kids, I need you to stand at the back for this one. Be prepared to intervene if I call out to you; otherwise, don't interfere. It's a good opportunity to show you how we work so that next time you know what to expect," the lead called out.

A bit annoyed at having been sidelined at the first chance of action, Dorea was still excited to see them hunt a live therium.

They were massive beasts that could reach twenty feet in height when they stood up and eight on all four.

Whenever a therium was hunted down, it became an event for the entire village.

Such giant animals could provide a wealth in hide, claws, bones, and meat. It required a dozen men to move, even if it was partially processed at the kill site.

The preparations were done quickly, and rope lines were expertly hidden in the underbrush. Tied around large trees, the mix of animal tendons and plant fibers treated with Voggo's potions was almost invisible.

Though they aren't hunters, they are pretty good at this. I guess that when the opportunity comes, it doesn't really matter what your specific job is.

Hidden in the shrubbery, Dorea observed the men move smoothly into position, bows at the ready. One of them had gone back to the therium to lure it into the proper position, and after a couple more minutes, she started hearing something big coming.

The man was the first to appear and jumped over the ropes, running at a sedate pace. Behind him finally appeared the animal.

The first thing she noticed was the cone-shaped mouth covered by flappy lips. It was running on all fours and was still taller than any adult in the village.

It crashed through the tensed lines of rope, which went taut under the strain. For a second, Dorea thought it would break, considering its sheer bulk.

Luckily, they held, and the animal went tumbling down with a cry.

Immediately, four arrows were shot into it and buried in its flank. Mark and Eddie then stepped in, without giving it time to try and right itself, and plunged their spears into its ribs.

This continued for a while, alternating between shooting it in concentrated bursts and stabbing to bleed it.

The therium fought until its last breath, thrashing around and pushing the arrows deeper into itself.

The end was anticlimactic, as its legs gave out, and they all waited until it stopped breathing.

Finally, Mark gave the signal, and everyone relaxed. They poked it for good measure, sticking a spear in its wound just to make sure, but either the bleeding or the weapons had done it.

"What are we gonna do with it? We can't take it with us, but leaving it here would be such a waste," asked Tom.

Mark gestured to one of the other scouts, who took off at a sprint toward the village. "He'll leave a signal for the next patrol, and they'll take care of it. Hopefully, they won't have to fight off too many animals to get to it, and if they meet with an enhanced beast, they'll just leave it. We have enough meat and parts anyway."

It felt a bit weird to leave the carcass behind. The animal was so large that its slumped form was as tall as Dorea was.

I have been taught since I was little that wasting is a sin. Just letting any animal have at it seems like a crime.

Unfortunately, she had not developed any spell that would be useful in such a situation. While she could stay behind to prevent the smell of it from attracting anything with her air magic, that would mean abandoning the mission she had been given by Voggo.

There is no way any construct I can create right now will last more than a few minutes without me here to keep them going.

She looked sadly at the beast, feeling deep within her that she was doing something wrong, leaving it here, but she couldn't think of anything to solve the quandary.

In the end, they moved out and left it behind. After just a couple more hours of walking, the forest stopped, and they entered the grasslands.

"It extends all the way down to the Kame Desert. Apparently, you can walk for weeks and never get close to its borders," commented Jonah, who had been finally relieved of his role.

The grasslands were still quite dangerous, as many animals called it home, and enhanced beasts would be just as common here as in the forest, but the visibility was much better. Unless snakes started attacking them in droves, seeing something coming shouldn't be a problem.

The scout that had left earlier to send a signal returned in the late evening, just as they were making camp.

Apparently, a patrol had been quite close to his path, and he had managed to alert them. The therium would be well taken care of.

That is such a relief. I just know it would have been the only thing I could think about until we returned.

Jonah bumped her shoulder as he sat beside her, handing over a bowl of stew made of dried meat and mushrooms. It was decently tasty, primarily thanks to the tiny bit of salt and spices they had brought.

Typically, such things are not even considered worth the space they would take, but many possibilities opened up now that we don't need to lug around water.

The sky was the same that she could see from her village, but Dorea still felt homesick, looking at it from an unfamiliar place.

The grasslands stretched beyond the horizon, and Dorea was already getting sick of it. A few streams and small copses of trees had been the only thing to break the monotony of hills and plains covered in green.

Thankfully, the sun was covered by passing clouds, as she hadn't wanted to add a sunburn to the sore feet.

No one ever accused me of laziness, but I'm just not used to this kind of march.

While she had been able to keep her complaining internal, Jonah and Tom had struck up a friendship thanks to their mutual suffering.

"This is some kind of torture; I just haven't figured out why they are subjecting us to it," the water mage muttered.

"Who could possibly choose to live in this place when there is a perfectly good forest around? Even the mountains would be better than this!" responded Jonah, who sounded increasingly enraged.

Dorea rolled her eyes as hard as she could, hoping that they would get the message not to include her in their little pity party.

I'm just as tired as you are, but making everyone's life a living hell because of it is not a good idea.

Conversation with the scouts had been the only break in the monotony, but it had been a couple of hours since anyone had approached the three mages, having apparently reached their quota of complaints they could stomach.

Finally, after another hour of dark mutterings, something distracted Jonah. "I can sense seven men southeast of us, about half a mile away," he called out.

Damn, I can't even make out stuff five hundred feet from me. He's been working hard at this.

Everybody straightened out, leaving behind the tiredness that had fallen over them. They had left the village for this, and while the Heidels were relatively friendly, showing up alongside three Gifted could be taken as aggression.

"Everybody stay silent. I'll talk and try to get an audience with the chief," Mark said firmly. There would be no chance of anyone messing things up if he was the only one to speak.

I'll need to find a moment to show off my spell, but doing it at first contact is a good way of making everyone hostile.

In the distance, they could make out people heading their way. It was still too far to make them out properly, but her senses told her something was up.

I can only feel seven people and identify them thanks to their position, but there is somebody else there that I can't sense at all.

CHAPTER TWELVE

As they got closer, and Dorea could hone her attention better, she started feeling an empty blob where there should have been a person.

Her eyes told her that an elderly woman was walking alongside the seven men, but it was still unclear to her senses.

As the Heidels got near enough, she started being able to make out their features. Their skin was a bit darker than her own but not tanned. It was the pigment itself. Their brows were a bit more pronounced, and their build stockier.

They walk more smoothly than we do. And their center of balance is lower.

After hearing so much about them, she thought it felt weird to finally meet members of another variation of humankind. Mainly because the differences, in this case, were minimal.

Had it been the Ubags, who are much shorter than us, or the Ergasters, who are tall and have broad faces, the differences would stand out more, but these people almost look like us. It's very subtle.

As they waited for the group of Heidels to reach them, they straightened out and formed a line. Mark stood in front of them, ready to start their talks.

Finally, the two groups stood before one another, and Dorea could sense the old woman. Whatever technique she used to mask herself seemed not to work well at short distances.

Or, she slowly weakened it as she got closer to lull us into a sense of false security and can stay completely hidden even this close.

The paranoia wasn't particularly productive, but they were dealing with an older Gifted, which meant she was likely very experienced.

"What do you kids want? Old Voggo sent you to cry for help?" she croaked laughingly.

Old Voggo? Woman, you are at least as old as he is.

"We were sent here to inquire about a possible cooperation between our tribes, Chief Yaomi," Mark responded clearly.

Chief? This old woman? Did she subjugate everyone with her magic?

"I bet you want our cooperation, what with the mess the northerners are making of things," she cackled.

Dorea could feel the surprise of her companions as they shifted uncomfortably. The fact that they knew about it likely meant that scouts had been sent through their territory without them knowing anything about it.

"Hmm? Surprised that I know that much? I've lived long enough to know that you need to keep a finger on the pulse of these things, especially after the whole damn coast got hit by the storm."

Chief Yaomi was apparently much more than the old woman she looked like, and the cunning in her eyes made the hair on the back of Dorea's neck rise.

We can't underestimate her. But we also can't leave here without at least getting a neutrality agreement. If we have to look out on two fronts simultaneously, we'll just weaken ourselves.

"Well, I suppose we should at least hear you out properly. I'm sure old Voggo gave you a few things to entice us." So she started walking back through the route they came from, gesturing for them to follow her.

Her men formed around her without her saying anything, and after a second of delay, where they all looked at Mark for confirmation, they followed.

Though to Dorea it looked the same, the Heidels apparently could orient themselves through the grasslands without much trouble.

After another hour of walking at a moderate pace, as the old woman was either unwilling or unable to sustain a faster one, they arrived at a preprepared clearing.

Logs were spaced around in precisely the necessary numbers, which gave her the certainty that they had been noticed and followed for quite a while before they were approached.

Either that, or they have someone who can divine things with this much clarity, and Voggo told us it is one of the hardest things to do.

Dorea had still been unable to show off her spell, and she was more confident than ever that it was necessary to do so to retake the initiative. Otherwise, they would simply get steamrolled by Chief Yaomi.

It was, however, hard to decide when to do so, as it could be misconstrued as an attempted attack.

The opportunity finally arrived when they got to the clearing. There were animals all around, from frogs close to the small pond to snakes hidden in the grass.

I'm sure anyone, even with the weakest sense, can notice them, but there is something here . . .

Mana sensing was peculiar in that a person could tell where their element was, thus allowing a mage to always know where a living being was as they were all made of tiny bits. Still, one could only tell where their specific one was. Almost no air mage could tell if the lightning was moving, so if a beast was enhanced by a different element, it could pass as normal.

There were exceptions to this rule, of course. Mages unaligned to any like Voggo could always tell if a beast was enhanced but never what their element was.

Still, the fact that a lightning-aligned snake was moving in their direction made Dorea willing to take the chance. Its trace was very faint, denoting a particularly weak specimen.

No one else seemed to have noticed, and whatever the old woman had been doing didn't appear to be electricity-based.

Dorea took a deep breath and concentrated on the spell matrix that resided in her mind, clear as when she first cast it.

It immediately took shape, guzzling uncomfortable amounts of mana, and the crackling sphere took shape.

As it shot toward the snake, she saw the Heidel chief stiffen through the corner of her eye.

The beast didn't even have time to react beyond rearing up as it noticed the lightning mana approaching it.

It exploded on contact, creating the signature cage of electricity as it kept arcing into its target until only its charred remains dropped to the ground.

The attack was over in just a handful of seconds, but the Heidels still managed to fall into formation. They reacted quickly, equipping the shields strapped to their backs and using their spears to form a porcupine wall. In the middle, the chief stood with a raised hand, a fireball already fully assembled and ready to burn them.

"A lightning beast was about to attack!" Dorea called out.

There was a beat of silence before the fireball winked out of existence, and the old woman sighed. "And so you decided it was a good idea to cast a spell when we haven't even started negotiations? You should have alerted us, girl!"

Not one to back down without a fight, Dorea argued, "There was no time. I'm sure you felt the snake, but it managed to conceal its mana until the last second, and it was preparing to do something!"

"I suppose you would have preferred for one of your men to lose a limb instead?" interjected Mark, who had regained his balance.

Yaomi scoffed. "Don't think I can't see your little game. Sending a girl who can cast a spell this soon is a provocation if I've ever seen one."

"Why, is it that weird?" Dorea asked innocently.

The old woman looked at her sharply before throwing her head back in a cackle. "Oh, old Voggo taught you well, girl. What is your name?"

"I'm Dorea, daughter of Dodro and Lilian," she replied proudly.

The smile froze on Yaomi's face. "So some of her progeny are still around, huh?"

She visibly collected herself before turning to her men, who still hadn't left their position. "Enough, you big lugs. We obviously aren't going to fight. Stand down."

Her men didn't protest, evidently used to being treated like that. They smoothly strapped their shields back into place and spears over their shoulders.

They look more professional than us, but considering they are probably their elite warriors, it's not surprising. Since they knew we were coming, we have to assume they wanted to show us their best.

"If we are done measuring our shafts, perhaps we can get to why you are here?" Yaomi asked rhetorically, indicating the preprepared logs with a grandiose gesture.

Her part done, Dorea took her place back with Jonah and Tom. Now it was up to Mark to negotiate; she had given him all the help she could.

I think that went as well as it could. Doing it earlier risked them being too on edge and backfiring on us. I wouldn't know how to deal with that fireball of hers.

"What the hell was that?!" whisper-shouted Jonah.

They were sitting at the back of the rows of cut logs, but that didn't mean they could chat casually, as everybody's attention was focused on the two people at the circle's center.

Tom gave them the stink eye, obviously very involved in the posturing between Mark and Yaomi, and Jonah apologized silently but still lightly kicked her.

Dorea smiled innocently, not wanting to explain the political reasons for her actions.

The boy, too used to her antics, rolled his eyes at her so hard that she thought they would fall off, and huffed in annoyance.

Refocusing on the crucial conversation happening, she caught something concerning.

"And we can't really spare the men to bother too much with you northerners. The tribes to the south have been restless, and I'm worried they'll do something to provoke a response from the Ergasters," Yaomi was saying.

Though it was enough to make Mark pale, he countered, "The Ergasters haven't entered the grasslands in at least two generations. Why would they break the record now?"

"Always fishing for information, huh?" She laughed. "Two generations is long enough for most people to forget things. Long enough for the tribes to try their hand at raiding them and for them to decide to get their revenge."

I know there was a war against the Ergasters when Grandma was young. But I thought that we had stamped them into the ground?

Apparently, the sentiment was shared by the lead scout. "How can they have forgotten how we broke them? It's a miracle they are still around!"

The old woman shook her head in denial. "We defeated them, that is true, but our victory was simply to show them that these lands were not worth killing us all to get. Their resources are great, and we are all no longer tied by a blood pact. Nor do we have the powerhouses we did so many years ago."

Mark jumped on her words. "Then it's an even better reason why we should reestablish ties! We can all hope the Ergasters won't get roused into action, but if they do, we'll rue the day we decided to keep away from each other!"

He's not a bad speaker. He can be pretty convincing when he believes in something. And saying no to that would mean saying that the principles of the old alliance were wrong. Clever.

Yaomi huffed. "Considering how scared you are of the mountain clans, can you really make the promise to come into the battle with us if we were to need it?"

"That's not what I'm asking," Mark countered. "What we want is greater cooperation and exchange of information. There is no need to make promises we all know we wouldn't be able to keep. We just want to minimize the chance of problems arising from the lack of communication."

"Pah! We are not a failing couple who needs to rekindle their love; there is no need to use that kind of language." She smiled. "But I guess I can see what you are getting at. We could extend patrols to the borders of our territories and exchange information at predetermined times. It would be better than nothing, at the very least."

And we are done. Good job, Mark; good job, everyone. That is all we need. Knowing that they are worried about movements to the south, and so can't attack us without leaving themselves open to incursions, and getting their agreement to exchange info is as much as we could hope to get.

The rest of the conversation was over quickly. No one enjoyed wasting time away from their village, and both sides had gotten enough not to feel cheated but given too little to complain.

Dorea was more than happy to head back home, as she could occasionally feel the old woman's gaze on her. While she expected to get some attention, this level of scrutiny wasn't enjoyable.

Who knows what she's plotting. I understand the need to show our strength, but being put on the spot like this is not fun. Not fun at all.

She had been ignoring Jonah's worried gaze for a while now, but he would just have to wait until they were out of there, preferably in the safety of their village, to get an explanation.

Things were finally wrapped up, and they all got up to leave. Dorea looked at the Heidel's chief one last time, meeting her eyes.

Unwilling to show herself cowed by the attention, she didn't break contact. The fire mage smiled crookedly and nodded before leaving, accompanied by her guards.

Somewhat confused but entirely done with the power plays, Dorea quickly joined her group as they returned to their village.

"That went better than I expected," commented Eddie, who had slowed down to join her.

"Did you think it would end up in a fight?"

"Nah, not a fight, but they could have easily rebuffed us, and if we had come across as weak, it would have been a signal for them to pounce," he explained.

"I don't think they would have attacked us, even if we had seemed desperate. The old woman wanted guarantees she wouldn't have to worry about the northern border, so if we were too weak to hold the mountain clans back, she would have been unhappy, but she didn't seem the type to strike us over something like that," Dorea replied.

"You might be right in that they wouldn't attack us, but considering they all but confirmed that they have been going through our territory without announcing themselves, I wouldn't have been able to feel safe." His response was more logical than she expected. Indeed, he would likely have been instructed in political and military matters before becoming a scout as they patrolled the borders and needed such skills.

"I don't think that they necessarily went through our lands. They could have just passed between—" Her words died out in her throat as a massive roar resonated through the grasslands.

Everybody turned around to see a gigantic flames column stretching hundreds of feet into the sky. The air around it visibly vibrated from the heat. It kept going for a dozen more seconds before finally dying down.

Behind, it left charred ground and ash. They would never know what it was aimed at, as nothing remained of it.

The silence it caused was broken by a single "What the hell . . ." that escaped Eddie.

Only one person could have possibly done this, and Dorea was suddenly very sure that her earlier demonstration of power hadn't been as impressive as she had thought it to be.

"That's a message, to be sure," commented Mark. The expedition leader was obviously less surprised than everybody else. In fact, his expression was more resigned than shocked.

"The old hag still has it, it seems."

His words implied that he had known about Yaomi's power before coming here. *Why didn't he tell us we would meet with a damn powerhouse like that?! We would have been much more careful . . . Maybe it's because of that? He didn't want us to appear frightened.*

"That woman," Mark continued, "was once known as the Witch of Immolation for her habit of burning her enemies into ashes."

"Why wouldn't you tell us earlier about her?" asked a still-shocked Ted.

"Because knowing that she could turn us into nothingness if she wanted would have made most of you too scared, and she would have pounced on it. I did you a favor. Though it seems like she took offense to the lack of fear we showed her."

Dorea listened to his words but was still stuck on the show of power they had just witnessed.

Just the amount of mana needed to maintain a fire of that size and intensity is many times what Mark the Blue, the mage with the largest reserves in Whitecliff, has. To just casually throw it around in a spell like that and to be known for it . . . Just how powerful is she?

She could see the sobering realization in her two mage companions' eyes. The gap between them and her was so vast that she couldn't even start comprehending it.

Voggo is nowhere near that strong. It's not just age and experience. She's just a monster.

"That kind of power . . . She could easily raze the village to the ground," Jonah said softly.

Pulling themselves out of their funk took a few minutes, but they started marching again.

The trip back was done quietly, as everyone just wanted it to end.

Thanks to Jonah's air sensing, they quickly dispatched a couple of wolves that had gotten too close for comfort and welcomed the forest like an old friend, more than happy to leave behind the grasslands.

Dinner that night was simple as they set up the crockpot with fresh water and dried meats. Rounds of lookouts were decided upon, and simple conversations were had.

Everyone livened up a bit the next day, and with the eagerness of one coming back home after a long and tiring voyage, they doubled their pace.

Seeing the village's gates in the early afternoon was almost enough to make Dorea cry from relief, and as she passed through them, she finally let go of the dark mood that had taken hold of her. She was home.

CHAPTER THIRTEEN

The village's gates had been a very welcome sight. Days gone from all she had ever known and getting slapped in the face with the disparity of power between her and the Heidel's chief had made her sullen and irritable.

As she passed through the gates, Dorea finally breathed freely again. The worries about the future, the fears about what hid in the forest, and the disappointment of comparing herself to another and finding herself lacking were left outside the gates.

Inside, she could be herself again. She knew very well that her responsibilities would only increase with time, especially since her accomplishment had allowed for a stronger hand during the negotiations. Still, for a little while, she shed all the weight.

"Everyone's free to go. Dorea, I need you to be at Voggo's in a few hours." She caught Mark's words and absentmindedly acknowledged them.

She said her goodbyes to everyone, giving a tight hug to Jonah and whispering a quiet "Later" to him.

I know he's curious, but since I'll have to share everything again with Beth, I'd prefer to do it only once, after I'm rested.

She took off toward her ranch, spurred on by the thought of her bed. The scouts had their ways of making a bedding in the wilds, but a blanket and some leaves did not make for a great rest.

She was sore from all the walking but started sprinting once she saw the fence in the distance.

A head popped up from behind the gate, and her father rose up once he saw it was her. He threw the tools he was using to complete the repairs to the ground and scooped her up in his arms as if she weighed nothing.

The warmth of his embrace and the safety of his arms was enough to release the tight knot of negative emotions she felt in her stomach.

She cried in relief, happy to have come back. She cried to purge herself of the fear that had accompanied her since she had been told she would go on the mission.

Her father simply held her, understanding that the time for an explanation would come later. He rubbed her back, making soothing noises like he did when she was little and had had a nightmare.

It took her a while, but she finally pulled herself together.

"Sorry," she said tremulously.

Tears and snot had dirtied Dodro's shirt, but he shrugged carelessly. "It's a father's duty, don't worry about it.

"Come inside, eat something and rest for a while. You can tell me everything later unless something is particularly urgent?" he ended questioningly.

He ushered her in at her head shake and sat her at the table. He put some berries in a wooden bowl, filled it with yogurt, and drizzled it with honey before placing it in front of her.

"You shouldn't eat anything too heavy if you want to sleep, but at dinner, you'll be able to fill yourself to bursting, considering how much your mother has been cooking to deal with her anxiety," he chuckled.

Dorea laughed along before tucking in. The honey was more of a delicacy than usual for a simple snack like this, but she guessed coming back from her first mission was enough to celebrate.

After she had eaten, she received one last forehead kiss from her father and left to unpack.

Her room was exactly the same as when she left it, but she felt it should have been different to reflect her own change.

Too tired to do anything about it at that moment, she threw her bag on the chair that usually housed her clothes, undressed, and slipped under the covers.

She was out like a light in seconds.

Waking up proved more challenging than usual, as Dorea still felt drained. She stumbled down toward the bathroom and splashed some water from the bucket on her face, hoping to chase away the drowsiness.

It worked well enough, and she dried herself with a linen cloth. Realizing she was still almost naked, she returned to her room and put on some fresh clothes.

Finally, she walked down the stairs to join her family, who had been waiting for her. As soon as they noticed her, her mother and sister ran to give her a hug.

Dorea was peppered with kisses from her worried mother and hugged fiercely by little Lia.

After they allowed her freedom of movement again, she joined them in the living room and sat on her favorite spot on the couch.

"Tell us everything!" demanded Lia, eyes shining in admiration.

I suppose I must look like the victorious adventurer coming back to her.

She began recounting the mission, trying to avoid mentioning anything too brutal. The story of the therium's hunt was well received, as the carcass had been brought back by the group they had alerted, and the whole village had received some meat from it.

The grasslands were deemed "boring" by Lia, as she emphasized its monotony and lack of excitement. The meeting with the Heidels was more of interest to her parents, who leaned forward.

They laughed at her description of Yaomi as a cantankerous hag. "I know your grandmother had met her many years ago. To think she was still alive and well enough to lead her tribe," wondered her father.

"If you knew about her, why didn't you tell me?" Dorea asked curiously. She doubted they had known about the sheer power Yaomi could command, but even a story from long ago could have given her some warning.

"Not many people live that long, Dorea. And certainly, not many remain clearheaded enough to still lead their village. Voggo is an exception, not a rule. Especially because he can cure himself of most ailments that age brings," responded her mother.

I guess I can see it. She called Voggo an old man, but she must not be much younger than him. To think she's still this strong now. In her prime, she must have been a terror.

It was an understatement to say that they were surprised by Yaomi's show of power.

It suddenly became clear to Dorea that she lived in a different world nowadays. Her parents, no matter their willingness and experience with her grandmother, had no real understanding of magic and its consequences besides the obvious.

Her mother had helped Voggo for many years, but she mainly had seen the crazy old man who loved to tinker with stuff and prepare poultices. Firestorms and region-spanning conflicts were very much beyond their day-to-day.

It felt lonely to have drifted apart so much without even realizing it.

Her parents would always be a safe haven from the world, but her life was now on a different track.

I love them so much. I'll have to do my best to protect this. I won't allow anything to threaten it.

Resolve burning inside her, Dorea decided to redouble her efforts to train herself into an absolute powerhouse. Only then could she be sure that the world's dark realities wouldn't touch her family.

Voggo's house was as messy as always, but the atmosphere differed from what she was used to.

Ed the hunter and Mark the scout were both already present and acknowledged her with a nod. They sat with the old man at the table they held their last talk at, though this time, the table was covered by a parchment map.

From what she could see, it depicted the surrounding lands all the way down to the end of the grasslands. Beyond it, a gray area was left open to mark the Ergasters' territories, which they apparently didn't know much about.

"Welcome, Dorea, sit down," greeted the shaman.

She took her usual seat and picked up a cup of red tea from the nearby tray. The ability to enchant things went up several notches in her mind as she was once again reminded of the possibility of keeping things warm for long periods of time.

"Mark already told us about what happened during the mission, but I wanted to hear your impressions. I've found that having a fresh perspective weigh in can be illuminating." Voggo smiled.

Dorea nodded, taking a deep breath. "If you already know, I should focus more on my personal thoughts." She looked at the three for confirmation.

Once they agreed, she continued, "I was honestly surprised at the lack of enhanced beasts that we found during our travels, but I'm guessing that since we kept to the more well-beaten routes, it was to be expected."

She rolled her neck, trying to get more comfortable. "The therium was something of a surprise, in both sheer size, as it was the first time I ever saw one alive and moving, and in the ease the scouts had in bringing it down."

Mark smiled in satisfaction. "Being given time to prepare some actual traps and having the certainty that we would have backup were something to go wrong made it much easier than it normally would be. I wouldn't want to tangle with one that can use some magic, though."

"Yeah, that would be a hard fight. I'm also happy we could bring it back to the village; leaving it there would have bugged me to no end," Dorea replied. The thought of fighting one of the giants with magical abilities was terrifying. While she believed in herself and her growth, she knew she was nowhere near that level of power.

That brought her back to her report. "The grasslands were boring, but I guess I can see how its resources could be useful to a village. The Heidels, on the other hand, were pretty standoffish. Even after the first contact, when things would obviously be more tense, none of them ever relaxed enough for us to talk to."

Voggo chuckled at her words. "Always one to make a friend everywhere, little

Dora. I'd say you'll have better luck trying to chat up one of them away from the old hag; unfortunately, she has them on a tight leash."

"Yeah, that was my thought as well. No matter how relaxed she seemed, I have the impression that she runs a very tight operation."

And now for the actually important bits. I'll be honest, though I don't like admitting how much she rattled me with her show.

"I think that my casting of Lightning Sphere, which is what I'm calling my spell, was timed well, as it allowed negotiations to proceed in a more balanced manner," she continued, getting nods of confirmation from all three.

"I still don't know why she allowed us to think she was rattled, though? I think she engaged in good faith negotiations, but the fact that she waited until things were done to reveal her actual strength makes me think that they went exactly how she wanted them to."

"It wouldn't be wrong to say that both sides already knew how things would go," explained the shaman. "We had mostly the same knowledge of the situation, and since we are relatively friendly, it would only be natural to get guarantees that no hostile actions would be coming from the other. The negotiations were a necessary formality, and things could have gone worse had you not shown the might of our next generation, but at a guess, I'd say Yaomi felt the need to balance the scales."

Dorea bit her lip in thought. *It still feels a bit excessive. It's like play-fighting with a kid and pinning them to the ground with full force just to show them who's the best.*

"Think of it this way," interjected Ed for the first time. His voice was much deeper than the others, but he had a gentle quality to him.

"What we put to the table is our future might. We showed her that our next generation will be great, and even if that was not assured, we believed in you. She had to do something, and considering she didn't bring any new Gifted to show off, she had to do it herself. Both as a show of strength to us and to reassure her people."

That's probably it, huh. If we actually took her by surprise, not so much in the level of power I showed, but in the boldness of me being there at all, she would have felt the need to respond.

"Thanks, that makes much more sense." She bowed lightly.

"As for her level of power, I will explain more in tomorrow's lesson. I wanted to wait more to go into detail about it to avoid giving a warped idea to everyone, but I'm sure that what happened will be the talk of the village very soon if it isn't already," Voggo chuckled.

The conversation wrapped up soon after that. The three men needed to discuss the increased patrols and what to share with the Heidels, and however much they valued her opinion, Dorea was aware that she didn't have much to contribute there.

Walking back home, she felt her insecurities subside and her curiosity about the following day's lesson grow.

Their usual clearing was packed. Word had gone out about the day's subject, and everyone decided to attend.

They had asked Voggo at the beginning of their lessons what level of power a mage could reasonably accomplish in their life and had only gotten vague answers.

Until now, they had to rely on legends of mythical figures, like Jorr the Sea Splitter, who had opened the stormy seas up to protect his village from being destroyed by the waves.

Such feats were theoretically possible, but the sheer amount of mana necessary to even attempt and to maintain it for such a long time—as the story went that he kept up his spell for a night and a day, without ever resting—were astronomically high.

Beth had once told her that even if all of the village's Gifted, Voggo included, gave every drop of mana they had for a whole month, they still couldn't do it.

But then again, those are legends for a reason. If someone could do that, they would deserve to be remembered forever.

"Quiet down!" boomed the shaman, a spark of mana lazily floating around his neck, signifying the active use of his spell to increase the volume of his voice.

"You pests have been bugging me about this for weeks now, and I guess it's time to actually tell you how far you are from the top," he began.

The speed at which everyone shut up was something to behold. For once, there was no doubt that he had gotten their interest.

Voggo smiled in satisfaction. "Good. Now, I suppose I'll start from the bottom, which is where you all are. That is called being a Neophyte. Someone who just started their journey on the long road to learn the deeper mysteries. To advance, you need to be able to cast at least two spells of a different origin. Which means no going from Water Ball to Water Arrow. You have to show mastery over two different aspects of your element."

That makes sense. I had to work very hard to finally cast Lightning Sphere. I can tell that developing a similar spell, even in a different element, would be significantly easier than crafting an entirely new one.

"Once you have done so and have proved to be able to reliably cast both, you'll be considered a Journeyman mage. Generally, nine out of ten mages reach this level within a few years from their Trial." He stopped to see if anyone had questions but was met with silence. Everyone was waiting for him to continue instructing them on their future path.

"Now, most Gifted stop here. There is nothing wrong with that. I myself am a Journeyman and have been for many decades. Advancing beyond that requires both an iron will and a great deal of power," he said without an ounce of shame.

I knew he wasn't particularly powerful in the grand scheme of things, but I bet he has more than one trick up his sleeve. He hasn't lived this long without reason.

"I can see that you are not content with just that, so I'll explain further. I want to make it clear that these ranks are very much not a hard limit. I've met Masters who, for all their power, still fell to the tricks of a Journeyman, but if we are talking just about power, then to become a Master mage you need to explore elemental manipulation to the fullest. Your skill needs to be such that you can craft new spells on the go. Your power has to start weighing upon everyone around you. That is the limit that most Gifted cannot surpass," he finished heavily.

Everyone took their time digesting that. The only mage they had ever met before their Trial had been Voggo and, for the oldest among them, a couple of the last earth mages from Dorea's grandmother's generation. None of them could have claimed the rank of Master.

I bet that Yaomi is a Master. It's the only thing that makes sense.

"Is there anything beyond that?" asked Mark the Blue loudly. It was a question whose answer interested everyone, so they all refocused.

Voggo sighed, fondly exasperated. "There is no real certainty about anything more powerful than a Master, especially because the mages who are not battle-crazed do not go around flaunting their power. But I have speculated, reading our ancient records, that there is at least one rank above Master, that being Archmage. From what I could gather, to become one, you'd have to fuse with your own element, thus shedding at least some of mortality's limitations. I want to make sure you all understand how little there is known about such individuals. I have certainly never seen one in action," he concluded.

Questions kept coming, mostly about how one would speed up their ascent through the ranks, but Voggo fielded them all with a variation of "Hard work and luck."

Soon, the lesson ended, and Dorea made to go back home, head filled with thoughts about her possible future might.

She was soon stopped by a hand grabbing hers. Looking at the offender, she found Beth and Jonah looking very annoyed.

"You didn't think you could leave us in the dark about what happened, did you?"

CHAPTER FOURTEEN

The grip on her wrist was just short of bruising, which told Dorea exactly how annoyed Beth was with her.

To be quite honest, she had forgotten about her promise to share what happened with her friends, which she felt was perfectly understandable given all that she had gone through.

She allowed herself to be led away from the clearing and toward Jonah's house, their usual hangout. Protesting now would just make the whole process longer and more painful.

I guess I have been a bit too absorbed in my training and duties. I shouldn't have neglected my friends like that.

They got to the bench that was their unofficial personal spot, and Beth finally let her go.

"Now, spill!" the brunette ordered.

Faced with faces more worried than angry, Dorea gave up even on the token resistance she had planned. "I suppose I should start from the very beginning. It all started just after the Trial when Voggo came to our home to discuss my three elements . . ."

She tried to keep the story as devoid of worrying details as possible, but she wouldn't lie to her friends.

They listened in silence, though from their expressions, she knew there was much they wanted to say. *At least they know not to interrupt, or we'll never end.*

By the time she got to the last meeting at Voggo's, lunchtime had passed, and the sun was beginning its descent.

They agreed to stop for a quick break to eat something. Luckily, the bakery was always full of seasoned rolls, and the influx of fresh meat from the therium meant they could also have some stuffed ones.

The pause allowed Dorea to wet her parched throat and prepare for the influx of questions that was about to come.

As soon as they ate the last bits of bread, Beth spoke again, "First of all, I just want you to know that I am proud of you. I know how hard you've worked, and getting recognition for it is something you deserve."

Flummoxed, Dorea stared dumbly at her friend for a moment. Both Beth and Jonah burst out laughing at her expression.

"Didn't expect that, huh? I guess if you were that worried about a grilling, it means that you started thinking about what you did wrong, which is good."

Dorea scratched her neck in embarrassment. *I guess I was expecting them to just go off on me. It's nice that she's proud of me.*

The warm glow of accomplishment would stay with her for a while.

"Now, what exactly do you think Voggo meant when he said there are much worse possibilities after the Trial?" her friend asked.

"He implied that some Trials fail differently than just death. Some people come back warped. It's honestly very disturbing to think about."

Beth hummed in thought, apparently not shocked by the revelation. "I think there are some legends like that. I remember once my grandfather telling me about doppelgängers: demons that take the place of someone who goes missing for a while and attack their loved ones. It could be related."

It fits, though it would mean they can also originate from a wild Wrath. The thought of finding a wellspring of mana in the wild, undergoing a trial you are not prepared for, and ending up losing yourself and attacking your family is a terrifying one.

"We don't know if it is exactly the same occurrence. It could be two completely separate things," commented Jonah. He seemed disturbed by her words and looked around to make sure no shadowy demon was about to attack them.

The talk went on for quite a while, with Jonah interjecting once in a while to add something when they talked about the mission or to congratulate Dorea once more on being chosen as the representative for the Gifted in the unofficial village council.

By the time they were done, it was almost evening. Though there was more to clarify, and Dorea felt like she could keep chatting with her friends to no end, dinner was waiting.

Armed with a few more stuffed rolls, courtesy of Jonah's father, she said her goodbyes to Beth and Jonah and trekked back home, her heart lighter from sharing her burden.

The following day, having no lesson planned or mission to prepare for, Dorea returned to helping around the ranch.

Though the worst damage had been patched up, there was always some work to do. The anoas and moas needed to be let out to wander, their enclosures cleaned, and the perimeter checked to make sure nothing had gotten in.

She happily spent some time ensuring their enhanced anoa, Bebe, wasn't making any trouble. The little buffalo was a cuddly thing and got along splendidly with the rest of the herd.

Mimi, the alpha, also seemed to like him well enough and didn't show signs of having any pressing needs.

I need to tell Dad that Bebe has his power fully under control by now. He isn't particularly strong, being weaker than even the lowest of the Gifted, but since he has no power, he should still be careful. We're lucky he's so calm.

The moas, flightless prideful things, were more of a problem. According to Dodro, the death of the crazed enhanced ones after the Wrath passed had set off a bit of a leadership struggle. The old alpha still held on to his place, but the younger ones had been trying him more and more.

It was getting to the point where she started to wonder whether they needed to cull a few of the more feisty ones to prevent an all-out brawl.

Having to put down an animal is always sad, but letting them do their thing would mean a much more significant loss.

After having checked the enclosures, finding them clean enough, and letting out the herds, Dorea began to track around the fence to ensure it was still standing.

Though they had managed to put it back up after salvaging most of it, the wood was weakened and, in some places, had started to rot. It would take many months before Whitecliff's woodworkers would have enough pieces to spare to replace everything, so they made do.

We have been lucky so far, with no attack from wild animals, but I know it cannot last. The pecking order should be established by now, and those who have lost will be looking for easy prey.

As she passed by the rockier side of the ranch, where the anoas liked to perch and climb, her senses alerted her to something that didn't belong.

Though she wasn't as precise or long ranged as Jonah, who had been making it his specialty, Dorea could still identify large animals at a distance of almost five hundred feet, if she concentrated fully in a specific direction.

It was too blurry to precisely determine what it was, but its gait and shape told her it likely was a smilodon. A younger one, if she was correct about its size.

It probably lost a fight. But from what I can tell, it's definitely enhanced. The air shouldn't be that dense around its face otherwise. And it's keeping any noise from escaping. That's genius!

Shaking herself from studying its air manipulation, Dorea quickly looked around while keeping her senses trained on the approaching feline.

The anoas were frolicking without a care. Mimi was alert as always, but it seemed he hadn't noticed the coming danger. Bebe, the electric bovine, was close to her, having just enjoyed a nice belly rub.

Luckily no animal had strayed too far, so she could move to put the entire herd behind herself. This way, the smilodon would have to pass through her to get to one.

She remembered her father's instructions from when she first started helping him with the herds.

"If it's a singular predator and not injured, do not attempt to save its prey. Your life is worth much more than theirs. Make some noise and let Mimi deal with it. If you can, shoot it with an arrow but don't approach it."

Well, I don't have my bow. I haven't been bringing it along since I became a mage. Not like it would make any difference, considering that my opponent could simply move it with an air current.

A world where she ran away from a single enhanced beast and let it feast on their animals was one she didn't want to live in. No matter how many problems had come her way since the Wrath passed, she was still grateful to the Mother for her powers.

With this, I can protect my home.

The smilodon was still approaching, slowly and silently going up the rocky hills. The time to tend an ambush was long gone, but there still was something she could do to inconvenience it.

Air was out, as it would feel her gathering it. There were better choices than lightning manipulation because of its loud crackling and the time needed to do anything worthwhile.

Her first instinct was to simply blast it with Lightning Sphere and be done, but she had no idea how keen its senses were, and if it somehow managed to dodge, she would be left with very little mana.

Water was the way to go, it seemed. Luckily, the sky was overcast, and the air was dense with humidity. This would help reduce the cost of pulling water from her surroundings.

Now, I can't just lob water balls at it and hope to do any damage. Condensing it too much is also out, as it would require more mana than I'm comfortable with using in my first real fight. I'll need to be sneaky about this.

Dorea felt surprisingly calm. She had thought nerves would prevent her from doing any planning, but they simply never materialized.

Oh, she was still scared, of failure and for her and the herd's safety.

After being praised so much for her achievement in casting a spell so soon, she had felt the pressure mount to keep ahead of everyone, and her lack of raw power was making itself heard.

If I had as much mana as Mark the Blue, I would simply cast Lightning Sphere on repeat until the whole area around it melted into glass.

Unfortunately, that wasn't an option, so she started pulling on the moisture around herself. She first gathered just a small amount, keeping her senses trained on the smilodon.

By now, it was less than three hundred feet away, and as soon as it crested the next hill, she should be able to see it. It didn't react to her preparations, maintaining its smooth but slow gait.

Heartened, Dorea carefully increased her pull. She created several different puddles around herself and along the path it should take to get to her.

Finally, she saw some movement with her eyes. The beast was a grayish color, almost indistinguishable from its surroundings. She was able to see it just because she could feel where it was precisely by now.

Her initial impression was correct, as its size was that of a juvenile specimen. A barely healed gash around its neck told a story of losing a territorial fight and being chased out.

As soon as she saw it, it saw her. Their eyes met momentarily, and it decided not to bother with stealth anymore.

It sprang toward her, closing the ground much faster than she expected. Surprisingly, she didn't manage to use the first three puddles she had prepared but pulled herself together and enacted her plan as it was halfway to her.

Water surged from the ground, coalescing around its snout in an attempt to suffocate it.

The beast was startled by the sudden movement but managed to create a cushion of air to prevent its untimely death.

This was part of her plan, thankfully. She had noticed its ability to quickly manipulate air currents and therefore devised her plan with it in mind.

The smilodon had stopped in its tracks, busy keeping the water from pushing into its orifices. Dorea didn't let the opportunity go to waste.

She pulled on the water from the puddles it had passed by in its earlier sprint, working to her limits to simultaneously manipulate so many different sources.

To ease her burden, she started pushing the water that engulfed the beast's head uniformly, not bothering to find a weak point as its usefulness was more in keeping it contained than harming it.

At the same time, she condensed the three puddles into rock-hard balls, not having the ability to shape them into something more useful like an arrow.

She launched them at top speed, the bullets concentrated on the smilodon's hind legs. All three hit, though one splashed into its rump, causing more pain than damage.

The other two smashed into its calves with bruising force, sweeping its legs from under it. The animal fell into an ungainly heap, and Dorea redoubled her efforts to drown it, taking advantage of its surprise and pain.

Already high on her plan's success, she didn't notice the blast of wind until she was sent flying.

She landed roughly, rolling to a stop against a bigger stone, bruised and bleeding from minor cuts all over.

Her lapse in concentration had been enough for the smilodon to finally push all the water away, and it started limping in her direction.

Another blast of wind came at her, but she was prepared for it this time and met it with a wall of air. It didn't hold it back completely but weakened it enough that it just sent her hair flying.

A bit dazed from the blow, Dorea stopped worrying so much about conserving mana and recalled all the water she had created into a single stream, whipping at the beast like a lasso.

It jumped over it, aided by his air manipulation, but the fall was more than a little painful, going by its howl.

Grinning madly, Dorea brought the whip down, stomping the animal into the ground again.

Not willing to let it take any more shots at her, she kept pummeling with the compressed water. Subconsciously, she had molded it into a hammer, with the rocky ground being the anvil.

The metaphorical sword being hammered didn't last long. In fact, it stopped using the air to protect itself after the second hit, and by the fifth, Dorea was more than sure it was dead.

As she finally dropped the construct, now dyed red with the smilodon's blood, a small bolt of lightning struck the creature's carcass.

A happy moo told her of its origin. The enhanced anoa, Bebe, stood proudly next to Mimi. Tiny sparks traveled between his horns.

He trotted forward, coming close to her and rubbing his head on her thigh.

Dorea huffed out a laugh, patting him in thanks. "That was definitely useful, little guy. Thank you so much."

Satisfied that the smilodon was actually dead, as it didn't move beyond the usual twitching that came from muscles being hit by lightning, Dorea checked her reserves to see how much the fight had cost her.

She was startled to find them fuller than she had expected. It wasn't by much, but she swore they felt deeper.

What in the hell is going on? I should be almost at the bottom, but I'm over one-third. I'm certain I put much more than that in my last attacks.

The water hammer had been expensive, but she felt safe using it because it ended the fight. Had there been a second enhanced beast lying in wait, she would have been deep in trouble, but she gambled that the smilodon was alone, and luckily it seemed she had won the bet.

Still flummoxed by her fuller reserves, Dorea took the time to dive into herself after doing a quick sweep with her senses.

Satisfied that nothing was trying to sneak up on her, she sat down. In her mind's eye, the currents of mana inside her twisted in incomprehensible ways, there but not.

However, she could figure out the reason for her increased reserves. A decent quantity of air-aspected energy was present, which she could tell did not come from her.

It was slowly being absorbed into her native mana and becoming part of herself, but it had an obviously different source.

From its . . . taste, let's go with that, I can tell it is the smilodon's mana. How it came to be here, I have no idea. It's so difficult to adequately put into words the things you can only feel through a metaphysical sense . . .

While she couldn't possibly begin to understand the why, the how was quite simple. Whatever she had done to herself, which Voggo had noticed but told her not to worry about, had allowed her to absorb a portion of her opponent's strength.

She had both refilled her own reserves and expanded them slightly. Definitely much quicker than training herself to exhaustion, though.

This . . . this could be it. My trump card. If it's not just a fluke, and I'm not horribly mistaken, I have found a way to bridge the gap in power between me and everyone else.

First, she had to clean herself, wear new clothes, and try not to appear suspiciously happy. Her mother would be able to patch her up quickly, but she might send her straight to Voggo if she thought something weird had happened to her.

She would tell him, of course, but in due time. After understanding the phenomenon herself.

Tomorrow, she would hunt.

CHAPTER FIFTEEN

Dorea woke up determined to achieve greatness.

Well, to step on the path of it, at the very least. She was still giddy at the thought of finally having found her edge.

She had to live with the fact that she was one of the weakest mages in her village for weeks, even though her talent was obviously among the best. And now she might just have found a way to bridge the gap.

Dreams of becoming so powerful to make Yaomi, the old fire mage, green with envy aside, Dorea decided to approach the situation carefully.

I'm sure I'll still get an earful once I tell Voggo. He's gonna tell Mom, and she's gonna tan my hide, magic or not.

Considering how worried her mother had gotten the previous afternoon when she had come back home battered and bruised, with the carcass of a smilodon held in midair by a water construct, she was right to fear her reaction.

She had been scolded, fussed over, healed up, and fed so much soup that she was close to bursting.

Dorea was aware that it was her mother's way of helping and regaining a bit of control, which she felt she had lost ever since the Wrath changed everything, but it was still overbearing.

If I added on top of that, telling her I'm some weird mutant thingy that came out wrong during the Trial, she would just keel over and die from the shock.

Her father had been more reserved in his worry, though he still held her tight for a few minutes. He had also been proud of her, and that warmed her more than any amount of soup ever could.

Little Lia's starstruck eyes had been the last push she needed to commit to her decision.

A single smilodon, weakened from territorial battles and caught by surprise, had been enough to give her a hard fight.

Considering what she knew about the movements of the surrounding tribes and the likelihood of increased beast attacks in the future, she needed to get stronger.

Her family required her protection, even if they never would want her to place herself in danger for them. Her village needed her protection, especially since they had given her a preeminent role in the leadership.

The expectations on her were heavy, and she might just have found a way to deal with them.

First of all, I need to see if what happened yesterday is a repeatable feat. After all, I killed the lightning snake in the grasslands and didn't feel anything weird afterward. Though it was quite a bit weaker than the smilodon, and I was preoccupied with everything else that happened after . . .

The uncertainty had been eating at her since she first remembered that the feline had not been her first kill.

Having the opportunity of growing stronger—much quicker than she had thought possible—dangled in front of her and snatched away seemed cruel.

Mother Nature, please, please let me have this.

Though she wasn't one to pray much, the previous evening and that morning she had taken the time to make a small offering to the Goddess in the hopes of receiving her favor.

She had contemplated the option that something unique about the smilodon had allowed her to absorb some of its strength. Still, considering what she could remember from her Trial, where she had grasped and brought into herself the surrounding energy, it felt wrong.

No, whatever she had done to herself to survive her terrifying encounter had allowed her to take a small part of her defeated opponent's strength into herself.

Now she just needed to prove that it was repeatable, and if possible, do it enough to climb the ranks, and then she'd tell Voggo about it.

She tamped down on the little voice that told her how reckless she was being. Nothing terrible had happened after she unknowingly did it with the smilodon, so it should be safe, right?

After breakfast, Dorea set out to continue her examination of the fence's stability. Her father had asked whether she wanted to do easier work for the next couple of days, but her cuts and bruises had already almost fully healed, thanks to her mother's poultices, and so he said nothing when she refused.

No lesson was scheduled for the next few days, so she decided she would go farther into the forest than usual, look for enhanced beasts to beat up, and get stronger without anyone bothering her.

Despite her eagerness to start her hunt, she still dutifully let the animals out, cleaned the enclosures, and checked another part of the fence.

After she was done, she ensured no one was looking for her and set off toward the forest. Jumping over the wall was trivially easy with the help of a water platform.

This side of it was much more familiar to her than the southern reach, as she had been exploring it since childhood.

Her father had taken her inside to forage for mushrooms and berries, showed her the safe paths where animals usually didn't wander, and told her never to cross the stream almost a mile from their land.

That morning, she did exactly what she had been told not to do.

In my defense, he said it to seven-year-old me. Now I have magic on my side and am almost an adult.

Despite the knowledge that she was much stronger than even a village hunter, Dorea still felt like she was doing something she shouldn't.

As she hopped on the other side of the stream, she forced herself to focus more. Her senses opened up and swept around herself in every direction, looking for prey.

Finding nothing worth her time, she kept heading deeper into the woods, walking through the undergrowth.

Green ferns and barberries accompanied her on her path. She trailed her hands between dogwood and holly trees, breathing in the forest.

Light came through more scarcely as she walked farther, giving everything a magical feeling.

There was nothing special about this patch of the woods to her mystical senses, but to her mundane ones, it was an almost religious experience.

Mother Nature didn't require much in the way of worship, and the rites were more about celebrating important occasions or the passing of time rather than stuffy ceremonies that the southern tribes held. Still, these kinds of moments, where you could almost feel her presence with you, were treasured.

Dorea let her hands hang low, brushing the vegetation with her fingertips as she walked. She kept an eye on her sensing but allowed herself to unwind momentarily.

She bent down to pick a few blueberries, delighting in the tart taste. It was still too cold for them to ripen, but they were her favorite.

Lips red from the snack, she followed an imaginary path, passing by mushrooms hidden in moldy-looking trunks that had fallen with the Wrath's passage.

The forest as a whole was less damaged than it should have been by such a powerful storm, which explained why people believed them to be the work of the gods.

No other explanation held up, as she had gone through much less violent squalls that devastated the environment.

Finally, she sensed something at the far end of her range. Although she couldn't say what it was exactly, a decently sized mass was sitting in the waters of another stream, which were moving in unnatural ways.

From what she could sense, there wasn't too much energy in it, but that it was using its power outside of a fight, be it for training or playing, told her that it had a modicum of intelligence.

The world was vast, and Voggo had taught all Whitecliff's children that not all animals were simpleminded. Supposedly, there were entire villages built by beasts enlightened during a Trial by the Mother's benevolence.

Just because most of them were simple, it didn't mean that all of them were, especially the enhanced ones.

I'll approach and study it for a bit. If it shows signs of intelligence, I'll retreat and alert Voggo. Observing it will serve me well in a possible fight even if it is just an animal.

Aware that most magical creatures developed at least a rudimentary sense of their element, Dorea condensed a small ball of water and held it just above the ground, ten feet in front of herself.

If the beast reacted in any way to it, she'd know the range of its ability.

Of course, there was the chance it had known about her long before she found it, but she was already done for if she was playing with such a mighty foe.

Just like humans, some beasts that developed intelligence liked violence and deceit. There were horror stories about young boys and girls being lured in by something that feigned sickness or injury and used its animal likeness to lower its would-be savior's defenses.

They usually ended very badly.

Dorea paid particular attention to her prey's movements as she walked on. Although her senses weren't precise at such a distance, she could make out when it shifted around if she concentrated.

Every once in a while, she stopped after making sure it hadn't noticed her, and swept her surroundings like Voggo had taught her in class, to prevent any-thing from sneaking up on her.

When she was only one hundred feet away, she started to worry that it either had noticed her long ago or was an entirely mundane animal surrounded by weird water currents.

Finally, it twitched. Its head turned toward her direction unerringly.

She dropped the water ball, it having fulfilled its purpose. She found that fighting against someone or something with their own element only worked if you were much better than them. Otherwise, it would be a tug-fest as both tried to take control of the other's construct.

Of course, if one could use spells, things would be very different, but she was still the only one to have successfully cast one in her class.

At that distance, she could tell that the thing she had been stalking was a glyptodon. It had a hard, almost rock-like armor covering its back, all the way down to its stomach and head. Its tail was also covered in the bony shield but tapered into a menacing club.

Oh, and it's damn huge. Not as big as the therium, but quite a bit larger than the smilodon. It can't be too old, or it wouldn't have survived receiving its powers, so it must be an enormous specimen.

Dorea gulped, suddenly anxious at tackling such a large foe in the middle of its habitat.

While she was busy studying it, it had sat back down in the water, though it had stopped playing. It was obviously wary after sensing her water ball but was confused at the same time.

Since it didn't appear to be readying anything, Dorea took the time to strategize a bit. After all, it was what had won her the last fight she was in.

The main problem is that it's in the middle of a stream and has access to as much water as it wants. I could try to lure it out, but I doubt it would follow me away from its main advantage.

Depending on its capabilities, it could try to snipe her from its safe position without ever needing to move. While its range was much smaller than hers, it didn't mean that it was necessarily weaker.

Lightning Sphere is probably my best bet, but even with the bit of power I gained from the smilodon, using it once is almost enough to put me out of the fight. I'm not worried about it dodging, but if it survives the hit, I'll be in trouble.

Even though Dorea had consciously decided to undertake such a dangerous endeavor, she still wanted to be as careful as possible.

The hope that if she didn't get hurt, the scolding she would receive would be lesser was an alluring one.

I could try to shock it from afar, but nothing I could throw at it from this distance would affect it. I need to get closer to hurt it; no two ways about it.

Unfortunately, she didn't have the punch necessary to do anything more than annoy it.

"The vaster the distance you need your construct to travel, the more mana it will require to maintain its shape and strength" had been Voggo's words, which now echoed in her mind.

Lightning was still her best bet, given its ability to travel through natural water. It would have been a different matter if it sat in a pool of conjured water, but she could work with that.

Gathering her courage, Dorea broke into a sprint. Tiny arcs of electricity condensed around her hands, ready to zap her prey.

As soon as she crossed the virtual line she had determined to be the glyptodon's range, it rose back up with a bellow.

Water streamed off its armor, heavy tail swishing back and forth in the churning waters.

By the time she was fifty feet away, she had brought her hands up and let out the charge she had been building in her run.

Immediately after, she dropped to the ground in a roll that saved her life as a lance of condensed water speared through the holly tree behind her, obliterating it.

Her attack hit it simultaneously, making the glyptodon groan in pain. Its muscles twitched, and it fell gracelessly back into the waters.

Taking advantage of the moment of weakness, Dorea sent as many bolts as she could without exhausting herself. After all, in their studies of the local fauna, the armored beasts were always described as unyielding tanks.

Her senses alerted her to a rapidly approaching mass of water, which she tried her best to dodge, but it still clipped her shoulder, sending a white-hot lance of pain through her.

She spun in the air, crashing back down into a bush and scratching herself even further.

My poor dress, was the almost hysterical thought. Her mother had purchased it back when she passed her Trial, but she hadn't worn it. In hindsight, it hadn't been the best idea to put it on when she knew she would have to fight.

The linen was definitely dirtied and scrunched up, but she'd make sure it wouldn't end up ruined further. It was a weird thing to focus on, but it helped her regain her mental faculties.

She abruptly decided that she had held back too much, her mind concentrating on the fractal that made up the matrix for her only spell.

It sucked mana like a starved leech, leaving her at one-fifth of her overall reserves, but seeing the ball of lightning hit the glyptodon felt like sweet vindication.

The water it had been accumulating for a finishing strike fell back into the stream with a great crash, compounded by the screeching of the beast.

The rugged exterior held up well under the assault, but with it being submersed in mineral-rich liquid, it had nowhere to escape. The great creature cooked inside its armor, skin splitting and blood boiling.

Once it was over, Dorea limped to it to make sure it was done fighting. She had learned that the twitching didn't necessarily mean anything, as residual electricity ran through the nerves.

It's a horrible way to go, but I'd much rather it cooking than me being smashed into a paste.

She approached it with a spark ready to transform into a bolt on her fingers. Now that she was closer, she could tell it was still breathing.

"What an absolute monster," she said to herself.

It was obviously out for the count, and had it been any other occasion, she would simply leave it to die on its own terms, but the whole point of coming all the way there had been to see if she could replicate the previous day's feat.

She carefully stepped onto a dry rock, wary of electrocuting herself.

Assured it wouldn't react, she placed her hand below its neck, the least protected part she could reach, and sent a continuous stream of lightning into its system until she felt its brain shut down.

Dorea staggered out of the waters, dropping down the grassy bank to rest.

The fight had been quick, lasting only a minute or two, but it felt like hours. Her reserves were almost entirely depleted by the time it died, but she felt them recover much quicker than they usually would.

With a massive grin, she let herself lie fully down, laughing with joy at her success.

Adrenaline still pumping in her veins, she let out an almost crazed laugh, genuinely happy to have survived the encounter.

She kept an eye on her mana pool, feeling it stretch in impossible-to-describe ways. She was both stuffed and hungry at the same time.

I got much more out of that than yesterday's fight. Almost double, I'd say. It's crazy that I can get stronger just going around killing things . . . Well, maybe when I put it like that, it sounds bad.

She was now comfortably half-full, though most of the mana still didn't entirely feel hers.

She quickly decided that bringing the carcass with her would be impossible. While she could theoretically lift it on a water platform and levitate it as she stumbled through the forest, it would exhaust her completely and leave her defenseless.

Maybe I'll come back to see if it's still here tomorrow . . . If I manage to avoid everyone's attention.

Keeping a wary eye on her surroundings, with her senses fully open to any movement, she hobbled back toward the ranch.

Crossing the forbidden stream was a problem, but she helped herself with some water manipulation. She kicked herself for not thinking about it earlier, but with the compact liquid seat's help, she floated over the wall and back to her family's lands.

That was when her good luck ended, as her father spotted her from a hill and immediately ran to her side in worry.

As soon as he was sure she wasn't fatally wounded and had a look at her guilty expression, he sighed in defeat.

"You have a lot of explaining to do, young lady."

CHAPTER SIXTEEN

The walk back home was done in shameful silence.

Dorea wasn't even going to try to justify herself. Her parents knew her too well, and she had never managed to successfully lie to them.

After making sure she wasn't in need of urgent care, her father had picked her up as if she weighed nothing and brought her back home like he would a troublesome anoa who had gone missing.

She felt a mix of satisfaction at having succeeded and shame at having been found out. Technically, she hadn't broken any rule beyond the "don't cross the stream" one, but that was easily explainable since she now was a Gifted.

Nonetheless, Dorea knew very well that she was about to receive the scolding of her life. She could try to lie and say that she had been attacked by the glyptodon, but her mother could always tell when she wasn't being truthful, and doing so could make the whole thing even more painful.

She wasn't afraid of corporal punishment. Her parents had never subscribed to the theory that slapping your child could make them behave like Jonah's father always said, but their disappointment could be heavier than their fists.

Once inside and after Dorea had been carefully lowered on her cushioned chair, her mother rushed to her side, stripping her of the dirtied dress with quick motions to check all her injuries.

Dorea avoided her gaze, feeling she would spill everything and start crying if she met her worried eyes.

The woman clicked her tongue at the bruising that was starting to spread all over her chest and left shoulder from being clipped by the devastating water attack.

She pulled an ointment from her bag and started applying it, shushing her when she startled at its coldness.

At a gesture from Lilian, her father used his right hand to lift her face, seeking her eyes. When Dorea met them, she felt a pull and a white-hot spike of pain going through her system as her mother realigned her shoulder.

She yelled in pain but was only met with a snort of contempt. "This is what you get when you go looking for trouble. Don't think I don't know what you did."

She has to be a mage; how can she read my mind otherwise?

"I'm not reading your mind; you are just as clear as spring water."

Her father's laugh startled from her spiraling contemplations. He stopped abruptly when his wife turned her glare to him, and he gulped in fear.

He cleared his throat before addressing her with a forced frown. "Yes, Dorea, how could you enter the forest after you barely survived yesterday's fight?"

"But that's exactly why!" she burst out. "I need to get stronger, and what I've been doing is too slow. I need real experience if I want to live up to the expectations that were placed on me!"

Lilian sighed. "I told Voggo not to push you this much. It was obvious that you would start being increasingly reckless to prove yourself."

With tears of frustration stinging her eyes, Dorea rebutted, "But it works! I'm getting stronger! I won against a glyptodon so strong it could go through everyone else here without trouble!"

Her tirade was stopped by her father's warm hand on hers. "We have all the trust in the world in you, little Dory; your mother and I are just worried that too much has been put on your shoulders. Maybe if you could take a few steps back—"

"NO!" she yelled. "You don't get it; I've finally found a way to get stronger much quicker! I don't need to step back!"

As it came out of her, she knew it was the wrong thing to say. She had admitted to doing something that no one else knew of and was sounding like a petulant child. Still, the thought of her parents asking the shaman to let her off her duties was too humiliating to contemplate.

"What way to get stronger are you talking about? If there were a quick and easy method, everyone would be doing it," asked Lilian in a warning tone. She had worked with Voggo for many years and knew very well that there were no shortcuts to power.

Well, good job, Dorea; you basically told them everything already.

"It's just something I noticed yesterday; I grow much quicker if I fight something than with traditional training. I was a bit reckless, but I'm not doing anything wrong!"

Evidently, her parents weren't entirely on board but didn't know enough about magic to refute her words.

"Tomorrow, after you have recovered, you'll accompany me to work and explain exactly what you are doing to Voggo in front of me. If he even hints that you are doing something dangerous, you'll really get it."

Dorea bit her lip. She couldn't get out of this without admitting to her experiment, it seemed. "It's not a conventional way of doing things, and I think I'm the only one who could actually do it like this. I was gonna talk to Voggo about it after I ensured it wasn't just my imagination or a onetime thing . . ."

From the frowns on her parents' faces, that wasn't enough to convince them, but lying at this point would only make things worse.

"So you've known that something weird was going on since yesterday, and rather than telling us immediately or asking for the shaman's expertise, you went and tried to make it happen again? Am I wrong?" summarized her father, now looking worried.

"Voggo already knows something is a bit different about me; it's why he came by the first night after the Trial. I just wanted to know what it was before I went to him with it," she justified.

Lilian sighed. "We are not trying to interrogate you, Dorea. We just want to make sure you are as safe as possible. All of this is still new to us. We can't help you beyond patching you up. We are just scared for you," she finished quietly.

Dodro gathered them both in his arms, holding tightly. "We don't want to lose you, little Dory."

Tears finally came out, and she didn't attempt to stop them. She let out everything, releasing the fear and uncertainty that she had held on to.

The sound of small steps alerted them to Lia's presence, who joined the group hug without needing anything to be explained.

Dorea basked in her family's embrace, reaffirming once again her decision to get stronger to protect them.

If Voggo tells me that I'm not turning into an abomination, I don't care how dangerous what I'm doing is; I'll keep at it until nothing can threaten us.

After the heart-to-heart was done, Dorea was brought to her bed by her father with strict orders to rest for the day and to not even attempt to do anything magical until Voggo could take a look at her.

So there she lay, staring at the ceiling in boredom.

Even just two months ago, the thought of being involved in this kind of mess would have been unthinkable.

Dorea had never been one for staying still too long. She was an energetic young woman, always looking for the next adventure, and gaining magic had only made her more willing to throw herself into the fray.

Still, this didn't make her opposed to reflecting back on her mistakes. While quiet contemplation wasn't her favorite pastime, she wasn't a stranger to it, having had to spend many tedious hours watching the animals graze.

I guess I was a bit too reckless, especially when I decided to attack a beast whose power I didn't know much about, beyond it being stronger than the one I barely won against . . .

She had gotten a bit too into the belief that she needed to gain power quickly, which made her rash, but she still didn't feel like she had made a particularly dangerous mistake.

She felt nothing wrong within her mana, even after observing it for quite a while in detail. Instead, she had fully absorbed the glyptodon's power and increased her reserves.

To her estimate, she was now one-third stronger than before the smilodon's fight. She couldn't hide the satisfaction at the results she had gotten, even if she would have liked to have come about them without worrying her parents so much.

It is inevitable for me to fight with an enhanced beast sooner or later. It would have come up even if I were more careful.

She fiddled with her grandmother's amulet, which she wore wherever she went. Although it hadn't done anything of note and didn't seem to protect her from being noticed by the glyptodon, she still felt much safer with it on.

It felt like a cold lump of metal to her senses, but for all she knew it was doing its job perfectly well, considering its primary purpose was to hide her from anything too strong.

There are still many things that remain a mystery along the path of magic. I'll just have to live a long enough life to learn about them, then.

Voggo could probably shed some light on whatever was going on with her, but Dorea doubted he could fully explain it.

Mainly because he already tried to examine me and was stopped by the pendant. I doubt he'll get a different result this time.

Though the amulet was likely still not fully recovered from protecting her during the Trial, its defenses would prevent anyone from looking too deeply at her.

Dorea felt conflicted about it. On the one hand, it felt good, knowing that she could count on it; on the other, knowing what exactly was happening to her would be quite relieving.

We'll just have to make do. We could still call it a success if he has some examples of a similar condition in the village's records.

She didn't even contemplate stopping her rush to gain more power. She was one of the front-runners of the village's Gifted and, considering what they knew about their neighbors' movements, would likely be required soon to help in Whitecliff's protection.

Whatever she had done to herself during the Trial was the likely culprit for her ability to absorb some of her defeated foes' strength, and Dorea consciously chose to think of it as a blessing.

Being deemed the weakest of the bunch from the beginning had grated on her something fierce, and the fact that a solution appeared so soon just had to be the Mother's intervention.

Being woken up at dawn was never a pleasant experience, but Dorea didn't put up a fight, knowing that it would be useless.

Thanks to the poultices her mother brought back from the shaman's, she had recovered enough to be let out of the house. Not to say that her shoulder was okay, as it would take at least a week more of being slathered in smelly creams before she could use it without pain.

Voggo's element-free mana manipulation might be weaker in a fight, but damn if it isn't useful.

The old man had single-handedly reduced untimely death and crippling injury in the tribe to almost nothing. Even in the case of the scouts and hunters, who dealt with dangerous wildlife and rarely with skirmishes against other tribes, his potions and salves saved many lives.

He couldn't do much about the loss of limbs and deteriorating illnesses but had dedicated his life to healing and had arguably been successful.

According to him, the only weak point was the need for him to be present at least at some point during the production process to infuse his creations with mana.

Of course, Lilian was perfectly able to make them herself, but the full effect wouldn't be achieved without the mystical power only he could provide.

That was the reason he had been so obsessed with enhanced beast parts or magical plants. If he could substitute his power with the ingredients', his potions would be able to work even long after he had died.

Once they arrived, Voggo just had to look at her mother's stormy face and her bruised form to know that she had done something stupid.

He sighed and gestured for them to follow inside. Dorea felt grateful that at least he would grant them some privacy rather than airing out her dirty laundry for anyone to hear.

They settled in his less official living room, as this was a matter of family rather than village welfare.

"What did you do?" he asked with a long-suffering look.

Dorea pursed her lips, annoyed that he would assume she had done something wrong, but being aware of her situation, she wisely avoided complaining. "Two days ago, I fought an air-aspected smilodon that was trying to eat our livestock and found my reserves larger than expected after the fight. To ensure it wasn't a fluke, I went into the forest and found a water glyptodon yesterday. I was right, and I have become stronger after."

She had decided during the night not to try and hide anything, but that she would keep her report concise. There was no need to let them into her worries and expectations, as they would only make her look immature.

"She went looking for a fight after barely surviving the previous one. And she's trying something weird to become stronger . . . Can you check to make sure she's not doing anything bad to herself?" Lilian asked worriedly.

Voggo's lips had been pursed ever since she admitted to the increase in power. He had distinctly told her to go to him with anything weird but evidently decided that berating her would be counterproductive.

"Give me your hand. I want to try something to avoid the necklace's protection. I'll send a stream of mana into your system and not do anything. It'll just circulate for a while before I lose control over it. This should allow me to observe you better."

"What defenses are you talking about?" her mother interjected.

"Doressa's last present can protect her from any inspection but the most cursory ones. It's generally a good thing, but it makes it hard to see if anything is wrong with her," he distractedly explained.

It was evident that her mother was feeling a bit out of place. Though she was used to Voggo's experiments and much closer to magic than any other villager, she still had no control over it. Still, she chose to trust in her mentor and settled down.

"Dorea, please take it off and put it in this box." He gestured to a metal chest. It felt mostly like a void to her senses, which told her its purpose was to try and limit the pendant's influence. She complied, taking her grandmother's gift off for the first time in a while.

The shaman's eyes glowed, and his brow furrowed in concentration. Dorea felt a stream of mana enter her system and actively stopped herself from pushing it out.

His touch was very light, but it still felt like an intrusion. He kept feeding a small amount to maintain his connection, but otherwise, he let it be. It began to follow her natural flow, moving through her body in ways that weren't entirely physical.

After a few minutes of silence, he dropped her hand and stopped his effort. He was handed a cloth by Lilian to wipe the sweat that had accumulated during his exertion.

Immediately after he was done, Dorea flushed her system thoroughly. She overwhelmed the remaining mana with her own and broke it down.

Paying close attention, she noticed that a small fraction of it was absorbed into her network and turned into her own.

"I was partially successful. The pendant still managed to obfuscate most things, but I got a general idea," he announced.

"The damn thing still works, even in the sealing box I made, and it interfered enough that I could only get glimpses. Whatever happened to you during the Trial seems to have made you much more receptive to outside energy. It's like your system has been primed to receive something; in its absence, it's trying to absorb everything it comes into contact with."

His explanation made sense, especially considering what flashes she could remember of the Trial. It also sounded like there wasn't anything too bad, giving her hope.

"I had to feed it much more mana than it should have needed to maintain the connection, which tells me killing an enemy isn't a necessary component for your growth. That would have been quite bad, as it would have come close to the darker arts. Instead, you likely have some benign form of a mutation. Possibly more than one."

Lilian had taken hold of her hand, listening worriedly to her mentor's explanation. Although she wasn't an expert in magical problems by any means, she still understood enough. "Does that mean she could further mutate if she keeps this up?"

Voggo shook his head in denial. "No, I don't believe that to be the case. I want to do this examination again every month to keep an eye on it, but for now, I feel confident saying that there shouldn't be any problems. It's a peculiar condition, but it's not worrying."

Dorea felt her shoulders drop in relief. *I knew I wasn't doing anything wrong!*

Still, she had one last question "But if it doesn't require me to kill anything, why am I getting all this power after doing so?"

The old man smiled at her, happy to be able to explain anything. "When anything with a mana system dies, unless it completely expended its reserves, the remaining power disperses into the surroundings. Generally, this isn't a great enough phenomenon to be noticed, especially in battle, but it seems your . . . ability allows you to drink some of that scattered power in. More efficiently than what you did with mine just now, as there is no will to contest your hold over it."

He handed her the pendant back and asked, "Now that the difficult bit is over, tell me about these fights."

The conversation was lighter from there. Though she got some more scolding, her biggest worry was gone.

I'm a bit weird, but not a monster. That's good enough for me.

INTERLUDE 1

Voggo

He was getting too old to do this much longer, but unfortunately, Voggo simply didn't see a way to pass on the torch yet.

There were many promising youngsters in the new crop of Gifted, but none were ready for the responsibilities that being chief of Whitecliff in all but name brought with it.

Looking at Dorea's retreating back as she left his house, he only felt affection for the girl. He had been worried they were too protective of her, that they risked stifling her growth, but she was a resilient one.

He hadn't expected her to go look for trouble this soon, but considering how boisterous she had been even as a little tyke, he really should have.

Voggo sat down heavily on his favorite leather chair, the one that was stuffed with moa feathers and allowed some respite for his poor back.

"Is she really going to be okay?"

He turned to face his daughter in all but name. Lilian might have been getting older, as all mortals did, but to him, she would forever be a beautiful little girl, more interested in poultices and brews than dresses and dolls.

"She'll be fine, as far as I can tell. Doressa's little gift makes things harder to understand, but she has none of the characteristics of an upyri if that's what you are worried about," he reassured her.

The woman dropped down to sit next to him heavily. She sighed, running a hand over her face. "I didn't even want to think about it. I couldn't have lived with myself if we had to put her down."

And hadn't that been the crux of the matter? Upyri often didn't know what they were the first few months of their lives and simply mimicked the previous behavior of the body that they now inhabited.

There were signs, like constant hunger for something that wasn't food, or a preference to wake in the night, but Dorea hadn't shown any of those, and after the first general checkup he had done on her when she told him about her control of three elements, he had put his fear to rest.

The news that she could gain strength from the fallen enemies' mana was terrifying.

It would have been a disaster. Explaining why she had to be put down to everyone in the village after they had seen her acting normally for days would have been impossible, and even their trust in me can only go so far.

That wasn't to think about what killing his granddaughter in all but name would have done to him.

Voggo had lived through very harsh times, both in war and famine; he had seen his friends and many families killed and torn apart by man and beast alike, but he wasn't sure he would have been able to look into Dorea's eyes and snuff their light.

"It doesn't bear thinking about. She's clean, and Doressa's pendant is likely what saved her from becoming one. As long as she keeps it on, we should have nothing to fear."

His words had the expected effect of calming Lilian down. She had the terrible habit of trusting him too much, and Voggo could only hope he was genuinely correct here.

"All right. Well, I need to start on those pastes if we want to be able to up production." She got up, already in work mode and tackling the next task in the way he had always admired.

"Ahh, what would I do without you, my dear. There is only so much these old bones can handle, and all that bashing and mixing is getting too much," he chuckled.

Lilian just shook her head with an indulgent smile, knowing that he liked exaggerating his condition to exorcise bad thoughts.

He took a final sip of his tea, grateful as ever for the ability to keep its temperature at the perfect spot, and got up himself.

Dorea's little adventure, if stripped of its scarier implications that they had hopefully put to rest, had been very impressive.

For a girl whose most significant conflict so far was beating back amorous anoas from females in heat or struggling with a fish too big to catch, she had taken to fighting like a duck to water.

Not only had it been incredible to witness her first spell—and he could tell that it had really been her first time casting it, as she had looked as surprised that it had worked as he had felt—but that she hadn't been discouraged by her meager reserves and instead kept working on them day and night proved that as long as there was a strong will and grit, magical talent meant little.

He himself hadn't been impressive in any way when he first acquired his powers, but dedication and necessity had made him into a respectable mage.

He was well aware that he couldn't compare to the Witch of Immolation in the south or Samos the Bright Shield in the east, at least in terms of raw power. Still, his skills were much more suited to healing and growing a community than destroying it, and he had long since made peace with it.

Voggo walked back to his lab, patting a seemingly empty spot over a chair, which produced a hoot like an owl.

Shimmering into the visible spectrum, his oldest companion tilted its head questioningly.

"It's as you thought it was. No sight of corruption in her. I can't even begin to fathom just how much power Doressa put into the damn thing to protect her from such a fate."

The little brown owl ruffled his feathers happily, somehow conveying a feeling of smugness.

"Yes, yes, I should have listened to you, but this is something I couldn't really gamble on. Upyri are a calamity that has to be eradicated as soon as possible, you know that."

Another hoot, this time of acceptance, ended the conversation, and the avian tucked his head under his wing, apparently going back to sleep.

Voggo shook his head at his familiar's antics but knew that he, too, was getting on with the years. Their bond might have lengthened his life dramatically, but they were getting close to the end nonetheless.

Still, a few things left to do. I can't leave it all to the next generation yet, not until I know they'll be able to handle it.

He picked up the glass shard from the small table next to the left wall that he had been given days before by one of the scouts and admired its ability to reflect the light.

There were several possible culprits for its creation, even just considering the older generation of beasts still residing in the forest.

They generally kept to their territories and rarely bothered to exit them, having achieved some sort of balance many years before. Still, once in a while, a new upstart came knocking on their door, and they needed to make a show out of dealing with them to ensure everyone knew they were still capable of holding their own.

We're all getting old, even those damn animals, but that doesn't mean we will go silently.

Old Titan certainly wasn't involved, since the bear's territory was much farther northeast, and even then, it simply wasn't in his capabilities. He was a scary bastard, but making glass was not one of his skills.

No, this likely was the work of either a particularly powerful new lightning-enhanced beast he didn't know of, or one of the salamanders that came a couple of decades ago.

Their control of fire would allow them to reach the necessary temperatures to create the glass. Though they were generally passive and content lazing around, they could be terrible foes if angered.

There had been seventeen of them when they first came and had risked setting the entire forest on fire, but with time and effort, their numbers had been reduced to only five. Those remaining ones, though, were the strongest and brightest of the bunch and had entrenched themselves so that trying to take them out would risk far too much collateral damage.

If a new beast, drunk on their acquired power, had tried to square off with one of them, well, that would explain the destruction the scouts had found.

"It seems like your little project can still go on then, huh?" asked a deep voice from behind.

Voggo had sensed the man long before he entered the house, and allowed himself a smile of amusement at how he still tried to spook everyone when he had the chance.

"You'd think you would grow out of this, Edward. You are almost old enough to be called elder by now."

The hunter snorted in amusement. "Everyone has to have their little ways of having fun. You like tinkering; I like keeping people on their toes."

The man settled into his usual chair, pouring himself some tea. They waited a few minutes, knowing they'd need to repeat it all if they started so soon.

"Sorry, sorry, I just wanted to check on the gates one last time," muttered Mark as he got in, throwing his pack over the table that had housed the glass shard a few minutes before.

"So, how did the test go? By the fact that you don't look distraught, I'm guessing little Dorea is free from any taint?" he asked.

"Indeed she is. My message might have spooked you, but it would have been a terrible blow. You needed to be ready in case I had to act," the old shaman explained.

The two younger men exchanged a look that said a thousand words but evidently decided not to press the issue further. Though they might have been spooked by the sudden letter explaining how there was a possibility that Dodro's daughter was an upyri and needed to be dealt with immediately, they trusted their leader to know what to do. If he believed there was no danger, they would behave accordingly.

"Now, what is the word from the north? I'm expecting those damn barbarians to start moving soon."

CHAPTER SEVENTEEN

Her parents had been somewhat heartened by the news that she wasn't horribly sick, nor had she injured herself beyond repair, but they were understandably wary of a condition that seemed too good to be true.

Only Voggo's assurance that he would continue monitoring her periodically and alert them to any important changes had been enough for them to lay off her.

Dorea had endured their fretting with stoic countenance, more than happy to have avoided any further scolding, and been proven right.

Her method worked, and that was all she really cared about. She now had a viable way of getting stronger much faster than average.

I can fulfill my potential. Just the thought of being left behind by everyone else once they manage to start casting spells is enough to give me the shivers. No, I'll keep my weird mutations, thank you very much.

Although she had been given the go-ahead for any further fight in relation to her condition, she was very much still recovering from being tossed around by the glyptodon.

While no expense had been spared in making her better, as she was considered quite important to the village's defense, there was only so much that could be done without taking Voggo away from his duties to attend to her constantly, and that was simply not an option.

Therefore, unable to go out for a patrol or help around the ranch, Dorea had been booted out of the house and told in no uncertain terms to spend some time relaxing with her friends.

She had wanted to object that surely the time was near for their enemies, animal or human, to start testing them. However, that had been accounted for by the shaman, who had set up rotations to allow everyone to have some downtime between their duties.

It had, apparently, been a harsh lesson to learn during the great war with the Ergasters. Pushing people to the breaking point actually broke them. And putting them back together was a much more complex endeavor than just preventing the problem in the first place.

Dorea was quite curious about that time in the village's history, but no one was willing to tell her more beyond vague generalities.

It felt a bit unfair since there was obviously much to be learned from such campaigns. Still, because only seven people in Whitecliff were old enough to have lived through those times while fully conscious, and they were respected elders whom she couldn't easily pester, she hadn't yet been able to find out more.

Of course, Voggo had also been present, but he was so busy with everything and had already dedicated his time to the collective lessons that she didn't want to annoy him too much.

Ultimately, I trust the old man to tell us about anything important. I'm just so curious though . . .

The fact that she could find out more about Yaomi only made it more alluring, but she could wait. She knew how to be patient.

Shaking her head to clear her slightly obsessive thoughts, Dorea made her way toward Jonah's place.

The bakery was finally fully operational once again and had started producing crackers as rations for the frequent patrols beyond its regular bread and the occasional sweet.

In his spare time, the poor boy had been enlisted by his father to help him keep the production going. The village leadership wanted to enlarge their food reserves, and whole grains could generally keep well by themselves; already such products were given to those tasked with going out into the wilds.

He can never say no to his father, but I'm sure he'll take the chance to get out if I pose it as something I was told to do by Voggo. Which is even true. So I'm just following orders, really.

It took a bit of convincing, but the thickly built baker finally released his son. He gave them some stuffed bread for lunch, as was his usual way of expressing affection.

Dorea didn't even try to pay for them, knowing that he would take it as an insult. Under the grumpy and rough exterior, Joe was a man who cared deeply and had always treated her and Beth like his own.

After saying her goodbyes, she hurried to join Jonah, who had been walking so fast it was almost a sprint. "If you move a tiny bit faster, you'll be running."

"I just need to get away from there for a while. He has been using any excuse he can think of to keep me busy. I get that he's worried for me, but it's a bit much," he huffed back.

Once they were a good distance away from the bakery, he finally slowed down and looked her over. "I can't believe the amount of trouble you manage to regularly get yourself in."

Dorea smiled sheepishly, scratching at the bandages that still covered her shoulder. "I won the fight, though. That's what counts, right?"

Jonah shook his head in amusement, knowing her too well to simply take her at her word.

"Well, once we get Beth, you can fill us in. Afterward, I wanted to show you something I've been working on. I think I'm close to finally getting it," he said, referring to his attempts at casting a spell.

Dorea grinned sunnily at him, more than happy to help him along. "If you manage to be the second, and we get Beth to third place, our little group will be the strongest. It doesn't really matter how much water you can summon if it takes you long enough that you've been sent to sleep by a spell, after all."

He smiled back, blushing at her faith in him. His golden hair covered his eyes as he tugged on a lock, embarrassed but happy at the same time.

Finally, they arrived at Beth's house, a reddish building much larger than the average home. Her extended family all used it as their residence, forming something of a clan within the village.

It had apparently been a bit of an issue long ago, as they had produced several earth mages who had started acting in unison and imbalanced the village's politics.

But that was long ago. These days all they have is just a bigger house. Beth is their only mage, and she'd never try anything like that.

One of their friend's aunts spotted them, waved at them cheerfully, and gestured toward the back.

They found her busy hanging the laundry, evidently having been co-opted into helping with the monumental task. The downside of living with so many people was that this kind of chore could require hours.

The moment she saw them, she dropped everything and ran to them, yelling distractedly about having forgotten some duties.

She gripped their hands and marched them away without giving anyone time to protest. "C'mon, move! If we let them think about it, they'll find another excuse to keep me there."

Dorea and Jonah shared a chuckle, amused at her plight.

"Are they still going on about becoming the perfect wife?" the blond girl asked.

"Yes," Beth huffed. "Apparently, the fact that I'm a mage has no bearing over my future. At least Papa isn't rushing things. I have some time to convince him . . ."

While talk of marriage wasn't exactly foreign to any of them, as they knew they would have to do it sometime in the future, it still felt too nebulous a subject to pay any serious attention to.

Especially considering all that happened recently. I know my parents would never force me to marry someone I disliked, but some people would try. And attempting to force a mage to do something they don't want to never ends well.

"Well, whatever. I'll deal with it when the time comes. What are we actually doing?" Beth asked, shaking herself from her musings.

"Jonah wanted to show us something he has been working on," Dorea interjected immediately.

The boy blushed at their attention but nodded. "I've been thinking a bit about how to go about casting a spell. I don't think my previous approach was correct. Dorea's success made me think I should try something closer to my specialty."

"I believe in you!" reassured Beth.

As they talked, they took the path toward the beach. It was still too cold for anyone to be swimming, and going too far from the village was not a good idea, especially when experimenting with possibly dangerous magic.

More spots could be used for practice, like the clearing they used for lessons, but that was usually quite crowded, or the cliffs, which were most often devoid of anyone, but ever since the Trial, no one had felt like using them for something so unimportant.

Our friends died there. It would feel disrespectful.

The beach was close to the cliffs but still far enough not to feel weird about it. It was also secluded, which meant having some privacy.

They weren't doing anything worth hiding, but who liked being seen repeatedly failing as they tried out something new?

Once they finally got there, they were happy to find it empty. The sandy beach wasn't particularly long, but one side had the pier from which the fishermen sailed into the sea and was off-limits.

The southern side was more open to the elements but still sheltered enough that unless the wind really picked up, it wouldn't be a problem. Considering the brightly shining sun and the absence of dark clouds, they felt safe enough.

"So, what is it that you've been working on?" asked Dorea, too curious to keep her silence anymore.

Jonah sat on the grayish sand, picking some up and letting it trickle down from his hand. "It's nothing special. I've just been thinking I should try to cast a spell that suits me before I start on battle magic."

Beth patted his shoulder encouragingly, sitting close to him. "That seems like a good idea—I should try that too. I was so focused on replicating Dorea's success that I didn't think about my specialty at all."

By then, the blond girl was almost vibrating with excitement, with all her attention turned toward her friend. "Show us! Show us!" she chanted.

Laughing to shake off the embarrassment, Jonah closed his eyes and, curiously, placed one of his hands over his mouth.

"Is it working?"

With a shriek, both girls jumped in surprise at the voice that sounded like it came from just beside their ears.

"What in the hell?"

Jonah rolled in the sand, holding his stomach as he laughed at their reaction.

"How did you do it?" Dorea asked.

Once the red-faced boy had finally recovered from his bout and had shaken the majority of the sand from his clothes, he answered, "It's not that hard. We all figured out how to keep sound from escaping as we move, right? So I just used that as a basis to encapsulate and release it at a different spot."

Their mouths hung open in surprise. It wasn't such a complex operation, but the ingenuity behind it was startling.

Beth scooped him up in her arms, rocking him like a doll in her enthusiasm. "That was great. You are great!"

The boy let himself be manhandled for a bit before putting an end to it. He looked at Dorea shyly, seeking her thoughts.

"I think you were very smart about it. Considering your sensing range, which is the greatest in all of Whitecliff, this kind of thing is right up your alley." She smiled with pride.

He scratched the back of his head. "Yeah, that was my thought too. I'm still not there with the fractals, but I think I'll have it down not too long from now. It just lacks something to be complete."

Looking back at her experiences, Dorea tried to help. "I know what you mean. Until the last bit clicked, it was very frustrating. I don't know if it will be the same for you, but what helped me was concentrating on the sensation of lightning alone. The buzzing within a person, so to speak."

Jonah twisted his lips in thought. "That's actually what I started from. The feeling of the air moving and sound propagating through it . . . What was the first concept you used to craft the spell?"

Instantly getting what he meant, Dorea recalled the very frustrating days she spent trying to successfully cast Lightning Sphere. "Mmm . . . I remember starting from simple manipulation, making sure that I had the shape done right; after that, the main thing was using the element, in its condensed form, to attack. So I focused on its purpose."

Beth, who had been silent for a while, finally interjected, "So it's important to think of the elemental shaping, the reason behind the spell, and the origin of the element, and to find the proper fractal pattern . . . It's a lot of work, but it kinda makes sense."

"Yeah, it's a lot to keep in mind. But once you get it, casting a spell is easier.

It becomes like second nature. The pattern is always there, at the back of your brain."

"Why do you think Voggo hasn't explained it to us in these terms? It's much easier than all the long-winded speeches about matrices . . ." the only brunette complained.

Dorea scratched her elbow as she considered it. The old man wasn't one to overcomplicate simple things. Not that even their formula was straightforward . . .

"It's probably because he has to go through a different method than us all. He uses unaspected mana, don't forget. He likely has to rely on records and what he remembers from the previous generation's struggles. But considering how basically everyone gets it after a while, it's unlikely to be something they talked about often or considered important," Jonah shared.

The boy's words felt right. Since everyone managed to cast a spell within a year, there wouldn't be much in the records about it. And Voggo couldn't even use his own personal experience.

"Well, you are probably correct. Still, even if it's not a great discovery, if our method makes it easier to cast a spell, it could be useful." Beth gestured for Jonah to try again, with all they talked about in mind. "I still have to do some thinking, but since you are so close, why don't you test our theory?"

What followed was a few hours of attempts. He first attempted the spell as it was, just keeping everything in mind, but they tried more things when that didn't immediately work.

The distance seemed to make it more complex and expensive, and after three hundred feet, it just became prohibitively costly. The golden point was two hundred feet, as it wasn't so expensive to drain him, but it was far away enough that it would allow them to be in different positions in the forest.

Now that I think about it, trees will probably be an obstacle. That would reduce the range. Damn.

In the end, they didn't get it that morning, but everyone felt satisfied with their work.

Jonah took out of his leather bag the stuffed buns his father had given them for lunch and distributed them around.

"It's a pity that we don't have a fire mage in the village. Just think how useful it would be to reheat stuff without it being such an ordeal," Beth complained.

"I know what you mean," joined in Dorea. "My lightning is enough to start a fire if I build a log base, but it's nothing close to the immediate result you'd get from fire manipulation. I tried to reheat stuff with electricity and mostly just burned them."

They all shared a laugh at that. Even cold, the stuffed rolls were lovely. The grumpy baker might have a terrible personality, but he was fully dedicated to his craft.

He woke up very early every morning to start making bread and ground grains into the finest powder possible, thanks to the stone mill he was left by his father, an earth mage, which kept the prices very affordable.

"There is no need for me to be richer if it means my people are poorer," he was wont to say.

Money was used to buy things in the village, but people could also barter. Everyone did something valuable to the tribe and had something to give even if they didn't have enough coins.

And in the rare case that one's trade stopped being profitable, the whole village pitched in to help them until they found something else.

It wasn't a perfect system, but it worked as long as no significant disruption happened.

In the distance, they felt a pulse of mana be released in the signal every Gifted was taught, which meant that they needed to assemble.

The three friends immediately stopped their banter and started packing their things. They ran for the village, their direction the clearing where the lessons were held.

Something big had just happened.

CHAPTER EIGHTEEN

They ran back to the village silently, their breaths and the crunching of their feet the only sounds that broke the silence that had settled after the emergency signal.

Although normal animals and people couldn't directly feel mana, they all had a primal instinct that alerted them to its presence, and it seemed like everyone got the message that something was wrong.

With her sense fully extended, Dorea could tell that all animal life, from the seagulls to the crickets, had felt something. They had either retreated in their burrows, flown away as far as they could, or kept perfectly still, primordial instinct telling them not to attract attention to themselves.

I really hope we are not going to war. We just aren't ready yet.

"They are all in the class clearing. No one seems to be gearing up for battle yet," announced Jonah as soon as they were in sight of the village. His air sensing was much greater than anyone else's, so it made sense that he was the first to know.

"Then why in the hell did Voggo send out the emergency signal?!" complained Beth, wiping her forehead with a hand, though she didn't stop running. Her breath was short, and sweat dripped down her brow, but she kept pace with them.

Speculating too much was useless, considering how they would find out in just a few minutes, but Dorea's mind couldn't help but reach for the worst possible conclusions.

It could be an enhanced beasts' stampede. Maybe the Heidels betrayed us. Or they were overrun by the southern tribes. The Ergasters could have taken over all of the grasslands, and we'll be next. The northern clans are finally attacking us . . .

She cursed her vivid imagination. However helpful it might be for casting magic, she really hated it now.

Finally, they reached the clearing, where almost every mage, hunter, and scout had assembled. Voggo was whispering with Ed the hunter on the side, but upon seeing them arrive, he moved toward the podium he usually gave lectures from.

"Now that we are all here, at least those that aren't out on a mission, I can share what we know," he began.

Everyone quieted down immediately, an undercurrent of seriousness keeping them from acting out.

"Approximately four hours ago, a scout unit patrolling the forest's northern side came into contact with a large group of people. Since they didn't seem armed for conflict, they were approached after being deemed unlikely to be a threat, and contact was established."

What? From the north? Then are they survivors of a clan raid?

"They claimed to have come from a valley to the northeast, where their village was destroyed by a mudslide after the Wrath. They tried to resettle but were harassed by other clans. Those who managed to survive the raids packed up their things and left the mountains." He coughed to clear his raspy voice and took a swig from his flask. It was evident that he had been talking for quite a long time, even before this speech.

"They chose to approach us because we've had dealings with them in the past. According to them, and to the best of my knowledge, they are right; they were once part of a village neighboring ours when we still resided in the mountains before the earthquake, two generations ago. I was able to verify this because their shaman still remembers some of our old warriors, whom no one else possibly could."

The news was both very welcome, as it meant that there wasn't about to be an all-out war just yet, and problematic, as refugees would strain their larders and could possibly bring disorder in the village.

There is also the fact that their presence means that things are moving quickly in the mountains. Sooner or later, we will have to fight.

"So they want to mooch off us?!" yelled an annoyingly familiar voice from behind.

Dorea turned to see Mark, the farmer's son who had hit on her some time ago. Luckily her demonstration of power had been enough to cow him, but it seemed like his attitude was still the same.

"They offer quite a bit in exchange for our hospitality," replied Voggo, unruffled by the questioning. "Not only do they still have a lot of food that they brought with them, but they have at least ten Gifted in their ranks that could bolster Whitecliff's protection."

The news that they wouldn't entirely depend on them for sustenance was well received, but the fact that foreign mages wanted access to their village was much more of a mixed bag.

On the one hand, they really needed the help. Having more people that could defend their lands could only be a positive thing, especially as they already fought with others in the mountains and could share their tactics.

On the other, it was scary to think of so many strangers, whom they knew next to nothing about, living in the village.

What if it's all a ruse? It could be true that they were once our allies and that they now want to hurt us. I don't like this, but can we really just send them away?

It was a dilemma that everyone was feeling at the moment, except for a specific few.

"Why should we care? They are barbarians from the north anyways; you can't trust them!" Mark yelled again. The fact that he wasn't reprimanded meant that Voggo was taking all points of view seriously, despite his preference.

The old man smoothed out his beard as he replied, "It is true that there is a degree of risk involved, but there are ways of ensuring they are not deceitful. I've sent a message asking them for a few volunteers to answer my questions, and I assure you I have my ways of guaranteeing I'm not being lied to."

His image was no longer that of the slightly ditzy shaman or their grumpy but patient teacher. No, Voggo was a leader, and his stern expression told them he wasn't playing around.

"If they refuse, we need to be ready to deal with them." A dark cloud seemed to pass over his face, his eyes like ice and his tone uncompromising. His words chilled Dorea to her core, but no matter how much she disliked the idea of attacking an already battered group of people, she would do her duty.

The moment passed, his expression smoothed out, and she felt her shoulders unclench from their unconscious tensing. "But if they comply, and I have all the indications that they will, I see no reason to condemn them to a life of vagrancy."

That seemed to be enough for most people. Trust in the refugees wouldn't come quickly, but everyone had relied on Voggo for so long that if he thought it was okay, it was also okay for them.

I wonder if he has a spell to differentiate truth from lie. That would be very useful . . .

Some holdouts grumbled further, but their main complaints had been addressed. The old shaman would ensure there was no foul play in the refugees' request for aid and shelter, and that was enough.

"Now, for the good part. Not only will they bolster our numbers, with both hunters and Gifted, and share what they know of the happenings in the northern ranges, but they bring with them some very interesting things. Their village sat on an iron mine, and they brought quite a bit of the ore with them. With that, we'll be able to make much better weaponry and shields."

These refugees are surprisingly well equipped.

Evidently, she wasn't the only one to think so. "Why come here if they already have all that stuff? Couldn't they just settle on an empty spot in the forest?" was asked from behind.

"That's a good question. The answer is that they tried, but their population isn't enough to sustain a village by themselves, and they have no idea how to live in the forest since they are mountain people."

That's a good point. No matter how many mages we have, I don't think we'd be able to easily transfer to the rocky mountains and thrive there without someone to explain things. It must be hard leading a village. We are very lucky to have Voggo here.

With the questions taken care of, Ed the hunter and Mark the scout started calling people's names to divide them into three groups.

Two groups would remain in the village, strategically placed north and south to avoid subterfuge. The remaining group, the biggest one, would set off toward the temporary refugee camp.

Jonah and Dorea were part of the latter, while Beth was in the team entrusted with the southern defense. They said their goodbyes, though none were particularly worried about foul play, given Voggo's reassurances.

The blond boy would be tasked with scouting from afar for any sign of preparation for a conflict while Dorea stood with Mark the Blue and a few others to make up their heavy assault.

I'm probably more lethal than any of them at first, but even with my increased reserves, I can only cast Lightning Sphere twice at most before I'm wiped.

It felt like everything was moving quite fast, but considering the situation, there wasn't much they could do about it. If the refugees were planning something nefarious, they needed to deal with them immediately, whilst if they were just seeking help, they needed to escort them to safety inside the village's walls.

The groups moved out quickly. Though they weren't exactly running, they marched out at a sustained pace, with Jonah and Mark the head scout leading the charge.

This side of the forest wasn't as familiar to Dorea as the northern reach close to the ranch, but she had walked through it enough times to be able to orient herself.

It felt surreal to be there with the possibility of having to do battle still pretty high, when she had wandered through the same trees with her friends just last year, looking for berries and mushrooms.

My life changed radically the moment the storm came. I need to stop being surprised by it.

Only the hope of not needing to fight calmed her down. No matter how many beasts she slew, the thought of having to face another human and possibly having to kill them was still enough to form a pit in her stomach.

She'd do it, she knew, but that didn't mean she had to like it.

Some kids in the village, primarily young men, were socialized with the idea of violence in mind. They were taught how to kill animals from a young age and instructed on their future duties to protect the tribe.

Dorea wasn't one of them. Although her father had desensitized her to death early on, having taught her about the need to slaughter their animals, she had never expected to end up here as the first line of defense.

It doesn't matter what it once was. I wouldn't have wanted to marry and settle down soon anyway, so I don't get why I'm getting worked up about it. I have more freedom than ever before! Stupid, why are you so scared?!

Her spiraling thoughts were interrupted by a call from the front of the group. The group of hunters and scouts that left to observe the refugees' movements had finally been sensed.

Soon, two men she recognized as hunters emerged from the trees and made a beeline for Voggo and Ed. Their relaxed demeanor was enough to calm her and everyone else. After all, they wouldn't be strolling so placidly if they needed to prepare for battle.

"The refugees have accepted our terms!" called out Voggo in an enhanced voice, being met by relieved cheers.

"This doesn't mean you can lower your guard, but it is a good sign."

That's right. If they really wanted to ambush us, they would do it the moment we thought we were safe.

Getting to the temporary camp took them another two hours of marching, but spirits were higher, and the mood was lifted from the darkened one that had settled.

Finally seeing what her senses had been telling her for a couple of minutes, Dorea counted at least a hundred people, from squalling babes and surly teens to white-haired elders and all in-between.

It obviously wasn't the whole village, but a good part had managed to escape and make it all the way there.

There probably would have been less than a third of these people without mages. Just having access to fresh water and not having to fear the typical fauna is more than enough to save many lives.

Dorea's eyes were drawn to the hobbling figure led by two teens toward them. The shaman of the tribe with whom they had been negotiating was a middle-aged woman whose left leg was missing. She determinately walked forward using wooden crutches, but from the hovering figures surrounding her, she likely wasn't too stable with them.

Voggo walked forward to meet her, flanked by Ed and Mark, and Dorea snapped her attention back to the surroundings.

She probably could have muscled her way into the meeting. Still, considering her abilities, she had been asked to make sure nothing interfered with the talks, and after the stress of the last diplomatic mission, she had gladly accepted.

Unlike the Heidels, the people here were part of the same branch of humanity as her tribe: the Sapiens. More specifically, the Northern Sapiens.

Considering how they had apparently once been neighbors and allies, it was likely that there were some blood ties between them, though it was so far into the past that no one would know for sure.

To her senses, there were three lightning mages, four water, and two wind ones. They made no effort to hide themselves, either too tired to do so, or rightly knowing that they needed to show all their cards to be welcomed.

It was still a bit surprising, considering that the first element was supposed to be the rarest, but she didn't know what they had gone through and how many people they had lost.

The original group that had survived the Trial might have been more balanced, but the following tragedies had whittled them down into what they were now.

Their shaman was likely an unaspected mage like Voggo was. According to him, it wasn't necessary for one to manipulate free mana to become a shaman, especially if the tribe worshipped a minor elemental god, but it was much more likely.

Mana Geysers and similar events were quite rare and often occurred in the wilderness with no one around, but they still happened with much more frequency than the Wraths, which ensured that most villages of a decent size had at least one mage.

The refugees' faces weren't as dirty as she had imagined, possibly thanks to having fresh water at their disposal, but from the way they moved sluggishly and their tired eyes, it was apparent that they had gone through quite a lot.

In the end, several people were brought forth for Voggo to test. His eyes glowed as he asked them questions while holding their hands palm up, but he must have found no falsity or deception, because after the fifth person, he stopped the spell and declared, "I have confirmed their truthfulness. These people are our brothers from the distant past, and though time might have weakened our bonds, they have not broken! Today is not the day we turn our back on our family! Today is the day we welcome them back into the flock, and as we shelter them, they shall strengthen us!"

Smiles and cheers broke out from both sides of the clearing, and the tired refugees hugged each other in relief, some crying at the end of their struggle.

It took a while to pack everything up, as they had managed to bring a surprising amount of things, but once they were done, they started the trek back to the village.

A group of fast scouts had been sent ahead to alert everyone of the news, while the rest split around the refugees to lead them on and cover their rear.

Dorea found herself walking close to a red-haired air mage who was supporting two large chests filled with iron with an air construct, holding them just above the shrubbery.

"Do you need any help with that?" she asked, sure that if anything were to get close, Jonah could alert them well before she noticed.

The boy looked at her from beneath his bangs with tired eyes but shook his head. "No thanks. I've gotten so used to them that I almost don't feel it . . ."

"It's an interesting shape you are using. I can feel how tight it's compressed, but I still wouldn't think to use such a thin layer to move heavy chests," she commented, curious at how these people went about their magic usage.

The boy sighed but answered nonetheless, "It's mostly the only thing I'm good at. I can compress air into pretty sturdy walls, which saved me from the mudslide, but anything beyond that is still too difficult for me."

There was a moment of awkward silence as Dorea was reminded of just how much the refugees had gone through to make them leave their lands.

"Sorry to hear that. I'll leave you to it, then. I'm Dorea, by the way; it was nice to meet you."

He gave her a small smile in response. "Yeah, we'll probably get to know each other better in the future. I'm Leo."

The rest of the march was mostly done in silence. Everyone was curious about the new people, but they had the good sense to realize how tired they must have been. There would be time for socializing and integration later.

As Dorea walked through the verdant forest, breathing in the fresh air, she could only hope the poor people would have time to recover before the next problem.

CHAPTER NINETEEN

Word had spread through the village very quickly, and they were welcomed by a sea of curious faces.

It seemed everyone had dropped what they were doing and came out to watch the tired refugees march in.

The atmosphere seemed to settle between bemused and relieved, so Dorea guessed that the scouts Voggo had sent to explain the situation had done a good job. No one appeared to be particularly worried, even though she was sure that problems would crop up in time.

The fact that they're bringing with them food and resources has probably done a lot to smooth things over. Also, they don't look too different from us.

No matter how simple a thing it was, allowing strangers into one's land was much easier when there was a shared culture.

The stone gates of the village had stood strong and proud ever since her grandmother's time and had never been breached in a direct confrontation. Just passing through them gave everyone a sense of safety that was priceless.

They led the refugees into the practice clearing behind Voggo's house, where they helped them set up temporary tents. In time, they would build new homes for them all, but considering the distinct lack of earth mages, it would take some time.

Someone should dedicate some time to creating utility spells to help with the construction. Water is probably the best element at our disposal . . . Well, when they crack casting.

While she probably could do it herself, Dorea felt it would be a waste of her talents, especially now that she had found a way to catch up with the others.

I really need to go hunt some more enhanced beasts. Knowing they were around in the forest but having to stay in formation was torture. And more meat is never a bad thing, especially now that we have so many mouths to feed.

No matter how many sacks and barrels of grains and preserved meats the refugees had brought with them, the reality was that in the medium to long term, they would weigh heavily on their resources.

There was already talk of putting them to work around the fields since it was still planting season, and having more hands on it could mean utilizing plots that had been left fallow for many years.

The village's population had once been almost double what it was now, but the previous generations had had to deal with wars, raids, and pestilence. It was only thanks to Voggo's efforts with healing, which had saved many mothers at childbirth, that they had managed to repopulate a bit.

Following the latest Wrath, there were no more empty houses, as those built and reinforced by the earth mages had survived much better than the newer ones, but that didn't mean there was a shortage of land.

The walls of the village encompassed a large area, stretching from the southern coast, where the forest met the sea, all the way to the rocky hills where her family's ranch was.

Apparently, the protection offered by the natural barrier was enough that they didn't need to build the wall to be as tall there, but considering the chaos in the north, Dorea sorely felt its lack.

We'll just have to deal with it. Nothing to do about it now.

As she ensured everyone had a decent spot to sleep, she heard her name be called. Turning around, she saw her father in the middle of the village's men, who waved at her to come closer.

"I heard that they were our cousins or something, and suffered a lot to get here, but how sure are we that they are safe?"

Dorea thought back to all the precautions Voggo had taken and what she herself had observed. "I'm certain they won't try anything. I don't know exactly how close our tribes might have once been, but these people just want a safe place to live, nothing more."

She noticed his shoulders dropping in relief at her words, followed by everyone in earshot. It was a bit funny how all the dads had their little congregation, but she stifled her laughter.

"How's everyone?" she asked, just to distract herself.

"Good, good, Lia really wanted to come but your mother managed to distract her by teaching her how to make poultices. She had been increasingly interested in it, so she might just follow Lilian in her line. You'll just have to bag a good lad who doesn't mind working with animals!" He laughed heartily.

Dorea rolled her eyes with a smile, knowing he wouldn't mind if neither of his daughters took up the profession. He'd already spoken about getting an apprentice, so she wasn't too worried.

The afternoon passed quickly as everyone pitched in to build the temporary camp. The mages used constructs to levitate heavy things while the more experienced men directed them on where to place them.

Large pots were brought out where stews were set to boil in quantities large enough to feed everyone twice over. The leftovers would serve as breakfast the following morning since they would need all the energy they could spare to begin building new housing and, for those with a trade, start helping in those.

For now, as they had made sure that the situation was truly safe, everyone had come out, children and elderly included.

The kids ran around the bubbling pots, shrieking with laughter and easily making friends with the newcomers. Heavy topics had been shelved for the moment, and everyone seemed to enjoy themselves.

At Voggo's order, alcohol had been restricted, as they didn't want anyone to make a scene, but the tense situation had been turned into a sort of festival, and the mood was high.

Dorea sat beside the old shaman, handing him a big bowl of hearty therium stew—the meat belonging to the beast she had seen be taken down days before—and a piece of day-old bread.

"Things have been going even better than I expected," he commented lightly.

"Yeah, there seems to be no sign of discord for now. And the refugees look happy enough with the reception."

He hummed, tasting the meat and dipping some bread into the brown sauce. "The real job will be in the coming weeks. Once we have done all the easy things, we'll have to carefully pick what to give them and how to integrate them. Letting them do it themselves is an option, of course, but we can't risk their craftsmen coming into conflict with ours or their farmers trying to use weird methods on our lands."

"Wow, that's a lot more than I thought they would need . . ." she said quietly while tucking into her portion.

The long cook had broken down the tough meat and made it into a succulent meal. Truly, the grannies who took care of the meals had perfected their art.

Voggo patted her head with a chuckle. "Don't worry too much about it; while in the future you might have to deal with stuff like this, for now, your role is to just learn. If you really want to help, tomorrow you can test their Gifted to see their level so that we can use them better."

Dorea brightened up, nodding vigorously to confirm her willingness. That was something she felt perfectly suited to do, and it would save the shaman precious time.

Soon after, they were joined by a woman she had seen only in the distance until now. The refugees' chief, who had led them through the treacherous mountains and the dense forest to safety, wasn't an imposing woman. Still, Dorea had learned her lesson after underestimating Yaomi.

"I hope you don't mind me joining you," she said. Her voice was deeper than she had expected, and now that she was closer, she could see thin scars crossing her face in an elaborate pattern, looking like the aftermath of a lightning strike.

As Dorea made to get up to let the two leaders speak, she was stopped by Voggo's hand. He gestured for her to sit back down. "You didn't disturb us at all. This is Dorea, a wonderful mage and extremely intelligent young woman."

She was gifted with a small smile and an inquisitive look. "Pleasure to meet you. I saw you in our escorts but didn't have the chance to say hello. Thanks for welcoming us to your village, Dorea. I'm Noele."

"Please, it was the right thing to do." She smiled back.

On these occasions, it's better to say less and not put your foot in your mouth.

They all sat quietly for a moment, enjoying the last bits of the stew and wiping the bowls clean with the remaining bread.

"I don't want to bother you, Shaman Voggo, but I wanted to give you an assessment of my people to better allow you to direct us," Noele began. She kept her tone light, but it was obvious that her words were carefully chosen.

She gave all authority to Voggo while highlighting the importance of her role as a bridge between the tribes. She gave him the go-ahead for integration while implying that it would be a more complex task without her.

Mother Nature, I'm so glad it's not me that has to deal with all of this. I just want to blast stupid monsters.

The old man didn't even twitch. "I'm sure you'll be able to shed some light on the problem. Your knowledge will be most useful when we get to assigning positions."

The following conversation felt more like a high-stakes hunt than a sedate discussion about job opportunities. The two shamans never said anything impolite, and Noele maintained an air of submission all throughout, but to Dorea, it felt like two predators testing one another.

The fact that they chose to have it the same night of the refugees' arrival and out in the open possibly had multiple meanings, but she decided not to twist her mind in too many knots and try to read more into it.

In the end, they reached a tentative agreement about the nonmagicals and deferred the decision about the Gifted until after her assessment. That put quite a lot of pressure on her, but having gone through weeks of tests and lessons, she felt reasonably confident.

All in all, if one forgot the underlying tension, it was a positive meeting, and the festive dinner had managed to dispel the last vestiges of reluctance in the villagers.

* * *

The next morning found Dorea and a few more of her friends waiting for the newly arrived mages to gather. Their usual practice spot was obviously being used to house the refugees, so they needed to pick them up and move somewhere their examination wouldn't disturb anyone.

Soon enough, the nine new Gifted came out of the camp and filed out. She recognized Leo, the air mage she had made conversation with during their march back to the village, and smiled at him.

He nodded back, rubbing the sleep from his eyes. His long red hair was a bit frazzled and messy, but he looked better than he had the day before. There was a lightness in his eyes that had been absent.

The poor guy probably has gotten the first decent night of sleep in weeks.

"All right, everyone, we'll move toward the beach where we won't have to worry about making a mess or accidentally hurting anyone. Don't get too nervous; this is just to get an idea of what you can do. The results are not permanent," Dorea explained as she started to walk.

They followed her in silence like ducklings, and she saw both eagerness and fear in their expressions.

They probably want to show us how useful they can be. I'd bet a honey cake that Noele had a talk with them to explain how important it is to make a good impression.

As they trundled upon the path she had taken just the day before, she explained a bit about the village and the surrounding landscape. "That is the bakery. Jonah's father owns it and is fantastic at it but is a bit grumpy. Don't get scared by his gruff exterior; the bread is really worth it."

She tried to keep her tone light to drain some nervousness away, and she thought she was doing a pretty good job. "On the left, you can see the fields where Brock, his family, and others farm the land. The Wrath came just as they were done planting, but by now, they have managed to get it back to normal, and there shouldn't be too much delay in the harvest."

That was always a sore sight, as she was used to searching for Rupert's figure as he helped his father in the tilling. He'd smile at her and make a joke, and she'd go about her day a little bit lighter.

Her life had gotten much more exciting than it used to be, but his absence was still keenly felt.

Shaking the sad thoughts away, Dorea refocused on her task. She needed to ensure everyone gave their best and to observe all they did to report it back.

Finally, they arrived at the beach. The pier at the northern end was still empty, as the fishermen would return only in the afternoon, but she still took care to bring everyone to the opposite side to avoid any potential damage.

"All right, everyone! I already know your specialties, so separate into three groups depending on your elements. We'll start with wind, then water, and finish with lightning. I want you to show me everything you can do beyond basic manipulation. If you can cast a spell, do so. If you can't but are working toward it, show me."

The nine mages silently separated. Seeing how no one was starting, she gestured toward Leo, the only person she had had a conversation with.

He sighed but stepped forward. Holding his hands out, he condensed the air in front of him into a thin shield that started rotating around him.

To her senses, it felt very dense. She'd probably need to use Lightning Sphere to have any hope of breaking it.

"It's not a spell yet, but I think I'm close. I can make it in several different shapes, but the oval seems to give the best result. The goal is to have it be reactive to attacks, but I think that is far into the future," he explained.

It seemed like these types of constructs were his primary focus, but he could use them very well and even demonstrated how he could step on them and float.

It wasn't true flight, mainly because he could only maintain one such platform and was very vulnerable to outside interference, which would send him plummeting into the ground. However, it was an interesting application.

I need to keep it in mind.

The next air mage, a dark-haired girl who looked to be eighteen but had a scar over her throat, was apparently able to use the wind to enhance her voice to an excruciating and debilitating level.

Her normal tone was almost inaudible, likely due to whatever injury gave her the scar, but she had adapted very well.

The water mages were a more mixed bag. The first two were brothers, who had focused more on the utility side of things and could conjure large quantities of water and control its flow in an exact fashion. Together, they could create a suction of all moisture around, but the range was quite short, and it took far too long to do any damage.

Still, it was interesting seeing how they could seamlessly piggyback on one another's manipulation.

The following two were more martial in their focus, though while one used jets of compressed water to damage rocks, the other preferred sending large waves around him to bludgeon anything that got too close.

The three lightning mages were all girls and were evidently the main protectors during their flight from the mountains.

They hadn't yet managed to cast an actual spell, but all three were quite powerful and could switch seamlessly between long-range bolts and short-range usage of their iron weapons to channel electricity and give a nasty shock to any unwary enemy.

Lara, the leader of the three, was a stocky nineteen-year-old with a friendly predisposition. She was the one to talk to in case they needed to assign missions, as everyone else looked at her when they needed to make a choice.

I don't know precisely how much fighting they went through before arriving here, but they are obviously well practiced.

Deciding that since it was her role to know these things—it wouldn't be rude to ask—she turned to Lara. "I can see that you know your stuff, and you don't waste power in flashy displays, but how much actual experience do you have in a real fight? I'm just asking this to know what I'm working with."

Luckily the girl didn't take offense. "Last week, we only fought a few times against beasts that thought we were a snack, but before that, we had to face several raids from different clans. Most people who didn't die in the mudslide were either killed or taken. I personally killed three men."

Her words were enough to put an end to the light mood that had persisted throughout the day. The fact that they, too, would likely face such things soon enough was a somber reminder that the time they had to prepare was a luxury they couldn't waste.

Determined to put some time into her own personal training, Dorea soon called an end to the examination and led the new mages back to their camp.

"I want to thank you all for your cooperation. I think we will be able to find a good place for everyone. I know you have gone through a lot, which is why I appreciate your willingness to contribute to your new village even more."

She said her goodbyes and left them to help their tribesmen in their tasks, but she already felt better about having the refugees with them.

"I'd say that went well enough," commented Beth from her side. She had kept silent for most of the day, merely being there to accompany her and not leave her alone.

"It did, and they seem like nice people. A lot of bad things happened to them, but I'm hopeful for the future," agreed Jonah. He had managed to get the morning off from his scouting duties thanks to having to serve as a sensor for the whole time the day before, and had decided to spend it helping her, which she really appreciated.

Though she knew there would be tough times ahead, Dorea was sure she would face them standing together with her friends.

CHAPTER TWENTY

The previous day's demonstration had not been particularly shocking, no pun intended, but it had shown Dorea that there were different ways to go about things.

Not everyone who was incapable of blasting a beast into a smoking mess was useless to the village's defense. On the contrary, they could become a great asset if one could better mesh the different specializations.

They hadn't really delved into collaborative casting, but it was something she would have to suggest. Even people like Beth, who wasn't particularly powerful or interested in fighting, could be essential during an assault if they had trained in specific strategies that used their strengths to complement others'.

That morning she had woken up bright and early to give Voggo her report on the new mages and her considerations about their possible uses. He seemed receptive enough and told her they would have another, more in-depth meeting once the housing situation was solved.

Once she was done there, Dorea walked to the eastern gates, where she would meet her team for the day's patrol.

Though she didn't particularly like having to wander through the forest, having to pay attention to anything that moved without being able to pick a fight with interesting beasts unless they seemed hostile, she didn't complain.

It was, unfortunately, a duty that anyone with a smidgeon of propensity for combat had to undertake. At the very least, she wasn't as swamped as Jonah was. The poor guy was by far the best sensor in the village and had been the center of many fights between teams, as everyone wanted him on theirs.

She might not have his range or accuracy, but Dorea felt like she made up for it in the sheer security she provided. She was nowhere near the level of power she needed to feel comfortable, but she was still the only one who could cast spells in the village, which meant something.

At the gates, she met with her team. The familiar faces of Tom and Eddie reassured her that, at the very least, it wouldn't be too boring.

"Look who it is. Has the princess decided to join us?" asked a high-pitched voice.

Dorea turned to see Mel, an air mage and the newest conquest of Mark, the farmer's son.

"Oh, hello, Mel. I didn't see you there." She smiled blankly. When dealing with this kind of person, her mother had taught her it was better not to give them anything. Indifference was a powerful weapon.

"That tells me all I needed to know about your senses then . . ." the short brunette replied.

Oh, it's gonna be like this, huh?

The girl's specialty had been her ability to go unnoticed for quite a while. She managed to dampen her sound, smell, and even presence in the air. The fact that Dorea hadn't immediately noticed her, especially when she wasn't paying particular attention, shouldn't be a great surprise.

"All right, girls, enough chatting," intervened Eddie, Beth's cousin and, by the looks of it, the leader of this mission.

Although she was the strongest person present, Dorea was well aware of her inexperience regarding patrols and such missions. She'd defer to the appositely trained people until she was confident in her ability.

This sentiment wasn't exactly shared by everyone, as evidenced by Mel's snort of contempt, but Voggo had been very clear that no one was to make problems during these troubled times, and it seemed that his words still held power.

I doubt it's gonna last much longer. I have seen how some of the Gifted are starting to think of themselves as above everyone else. At least it's a minority . . .

She said hello to the other three scouts that would go along with them on the patrol, whom she recognized from seeing around the village, even though she had never personally spoken with them, and they set off.

Passing through the stone gates was always a weird sensation, but it was happening more and more these days, and she was getting used to leaving her village behind.

Who would have thought that this would be my new routine?

"That girl is gonna be trouble, I'll tell you that," Tom commented from her side. The water mage had come along as he was getting especially good at quality-of-life magic and was in the process of developing a tracking spell.

If he managed to do so, it would be quite a boon to the village, and Voggo thought that getting some experience tracking things in real life would help him break through.

"I know that, Mother, do I know that. Why she would get entangled with Mark is still a mystery, but if she keeps this up, we're gonna have a problem."

He looked at her in the eyes, unsure of how serious she was being. She gave a small smile to show she was joking, but he didn't seem too convinced. Luckily, they had a job to do, so she didn't need to explain herself further.

Patrols generally split in teams of two or three, depending on whether they had a mage, roaming in specific patterns, never too far away from each other but distant enough to cover a lot of ground.

They took most of the day, as they needed to pass through the same spots several times at different moments to ensure nothing was trying to sneak in like the smilodon had managed to.

Her specific one that day twisted northeast to cover the short wall where her family's ranch was, the stretch of the forest she fought the glyptodon in, and farther east into the woods, to the border with the Forest tribe.

Dorea knew that a diplomatic mission was being prepared to try and reach the same agreement they had with the Heidels, but since they were very reclusive people, contact still hadn't been made. They didn't want to force them out by entering their territory as it could be taken as a sign of hostility.

Walking deeper into the forest, they divided into groups and began their range.

She was coupled with Matt, one of the scouts. He was a bit older than Eddie, but his passive nature had seen him passed over for the mission's leadership.

Luckily, he didn't seem to mind the situation much, as he silently nodded at her in acknowledgment. The man was known to be silent, and for all that she might have preferred going with Eddie or Tom, she was glad not to have been assigned Mel as a companion.

I don't think we'd all walk out of the forest if that had been the case.

That seemed to have been Eddie's thought as well, as he picked Tom, the least powerful mage, leaving the girl with the remaining two scouts.

It was a standard procedure, and no one complained, but she could see the will to live being snuffed out in their eyes. Or maybe she was projecting a bit; who could possibly tell.

With her senses fully extended, Dorea could appreciate just how much life was in the forest at any time.

Squirrels jumped from tree to tree in their never-ending search for nuts; birds perched high in the foliage and looked for tasty treats to swoop down to, and insects built kingdoms just as intricate as Whitecliff, if not more.

A couple of red squirrels helped their hunt by launching from the highest branches and floating down, aided by air manipulation, but they didn't seem to be interested in doing anything more than just building a mountain of nuts.

If they haven't gone murderously insane, they are among the lucky few to manage control over the mana in their bodies. To think that such small and simple creatures can do it. Mother Nature is undoubtedly amazing.

As time passed and they went through all the proper calls to ensure the others of their continued presence and hadn't found anything interesting, Dorea had to force her mind not to wander too much.

While she could keep an eye on her senses without having to scan actively all the time, getting too distracted while in the field could be a death sentence, especially since Matt was relying on her to alert him of anything out of place.

It was a bit weird how their profession had been so quickly subsumed by the arrival of magic, but she had no idea how to reproduce the sounds he made to communicate with the others, nor could she tell a type of marking on trees from another.

They swerved around Old Titan's territory, a gigantic bear who could use earth mana to impale anything he set his sights on but who was luckily very passive and, as long as no one bothered him, would never leave his patch of the forest.

He had resided in the same spot for decades and had to have been by far the oldest specimen they knew of, but since they found fresh scratches to mark his lands at every patrol, no one dared go in to see in what condition the bear was in.

According to Voggo, the beast was quite intelligent and perfectly aware that he'd face harsh retaliation if he pushed too much toward the village. Still, since he had no intention of doing so and actually served as a bulwark against any newly enhanced animal who thought of itself as the strongest around, it was much better to leave him be.

It took them a few hours, but they finally got out of the forest and into the rocky hills that followed the coast all the way up to the mountains. The open space made traveling more manageable, but the uneven terrain hid many things they needed to check before considering the area safe.

Indeed, shortly after they had gotten there, her senses alerted her to some movement.

She immediately signaled to Matt, who gave out a soft call. After a few seconds, they received a confirmation.

Crouching down to not be noticed but aware that if what she was feeling was right, there was not much of a point, Dorea crawled through the rocks to get closer, immediately followed by the more experienced scout.

There were at least ten presences, though two of them felt hazy in a way that told her they were doing something to camouflage. She relayed this to her companion, who gave out another call imitating the indigenous birds.

The protocol they had been taught told them they needed to encircle and gather further information, to see if whoever it was had hostile intentions.

However, to do so without being noticed by any dedicated sensor they might have was a foolish endeavor.

Finally, they received another bird call, which Matt whispered to her meant that Mel's team had gotten in position and could confirm the presence of ten men.

Dorea actively focused on the group, trying her best to learn as much as possible before a confrontation.

The two hazy presences were obviously air mages, given how they controlled the winds around them. There was also at least one water mage playing with the contents of his flask.

The rest were just milling about, checking their bags, or, in one case, oiling a blade. Although she couldn't be sure, she seriously doubted they were refugees. They felt too organized, and the fact that there were only men was also a red flag.

Another exchange of birdsong later, they had confirmation that they were hostiles. Mel had sensed severed heads in some of the sacks that Dorea had also felt but was too far to distinguish the contents of.

No one who wanted to receive help or exchange goods went around with that kind of grim package.

Now that they were sure there would be a fight, they needed to stack the odds in their favor. Having to battle three Gifted, with the possibility of there being more, was not a simple thing, especially since they had only three of their own, along with the nonmagical scouts.

It went against her instincts, attacking before even an exchange of words to ensure they were making no mistakes. Still, everything they had learned so far implied that this was a raiding band, and considering their position, the first target would be her house.

There is absolutely no way I'm letting them through. Just the thought of them falling upon Dad, Mom, and Lia is too much.

Unfortunately, she didn't have a large-scale spell at her disposal, but she would have to make do. Taking out the mages first was essential, and Dorea was quite sure that Lightning Sphere would be enough to do the job.

The problem, of course, was ensuring she had a clear shot without alerting her enemies to her presence.

They had been lucky that no one with Jonah's range seemed to be amongst them, but there was a clear limit to how close they could get before being noticed.

Then, she had an idea.

It was something she had been thinking about ever since the new mages had shown their ability to work together to get greater results.

Training with someone else to manage the timing and power perfectly was not an easy feat, but what if she could do all of it by herself?

If there is an advantage to having more than one element at my disposal, beyond the sheer range of options, it is the ability to use them together.

Now, this would require a lot of work and concentration, so she quickly relayed her plan to Matt, who gave his approval after a short moment of thought. He then sang to explain it to the others, but she had already focused on her task.

In her study to get her spell down, she had to test the hows and whys of all the elements. One thing that she noticed was that natural lightning formed quite quickly when there was a change in the atmospheric charge.

It was a concept that Voggo had introduced to them in one of his lessons. He didn't have much research on their elements, but a few scrolls detailed the attempts of allied mages, during the war with the Ergasters, at exploring weather-related magic, and she thought she might be able to use it.

Strictly speaking, this was less direct magic and more manipulation of the environment, but if it accomplished the task, she'd go for it.

There were two preconditions to her plan coming to fruition: first, there needed to be suitable weather, and luckily the gray clouds that hung above them would suffice; second, and this was the hardest one, she had to manipulate the winds to rub the droplets in the sky hard enough to create friction.

Once that was done, she could call down lightning pretty easily, but the problem was doing all of this without being noticed.

There are no two ways about it; I just need to hope that what I'm doing is far enough that it's beyond their senses.

Technically, she could create such winds already in the clouds, but the distance was enough that doing so would sap her of all her mana. And she did not believe that her plan would be enough to end the fight.

But if I can take out at least the two air mages, our lives will be much easier.

Dorea worked silently, softly increasing the winds above them to move the water and ice around. She did so for several minutes before she noticed that enough charge had built up.

Opening her eyes, she found Matt looking at her in concern. She nodded to show her readiness, and he let out one last call.

They received one back, which he translated as a go-ahead, and she returned to her task.

Using lightning manipulation, she increased further the buildup of negative charge around the enemy camp and did her best to limit the area that would be struck.

As soon as she felt one of the air mages start looking around, she let all hell loose.

With a blinding flash of light, a dozen lightning bolts arced from the sky and hit the ground. The roar of thunder that followed was extremely disorienting even from where they sat, but it couldn't cover the manic laughter that spilled from within her.

Since their cover was blown, she poured more power in, attracting more bolts.

It was as if an angry god had decided that a specific patch of land needed to stop existing.

Dorea felt power enter her system and knew that she had gotten them. The rush was intense this time, much more noticeable than what it had been in her previous fights.

Using her increased reserves, she decided to make sure that they could never threaten her family again.

Her arms had raised themselves unprompted as if in prayer. With wild mana coursing in her system, she let out a roar drowned out by the rumble of thunder.

She kept going until there was almost nothing left in her. Her arms dropped, and she lay down, trying to regain her breath.

The thumping of her heart was enough to deafen her, and her eyes stung from being subjected to the repeated flashes.

The smile that had painted itself on her face finally dropped as she realized what she had done. Although it hadn't been confirmed, and she was too exhausted to tell if what she could sense were charred corpses or miraculously alive survivors, the fact that she had gained power at all told her that she had killed some men.

I killed them. It was me. I did it, knowing that they would die.

It was the right thing to do, but it still feels wrong. It feels wrong. It feels wrong.

She tried to get up but only managed to raise and turn her head enough not to choke as she threw up.

The acidic bile burned in her mouth, and Dorea was very grateful when a flask filled with water was proffered to her.

Matt helped her up and cleaned her using his cloak. Silently, he checked that she was okay before calling out again like a bird.

The response made his shoulders drop in relief, and he turned to her. "You got them all."

CHAPTER TWENTY-ONE

Dorea blearily stared at the clouds, too physically and emotionally tired to move. They rumbled with thunder and, now that she wasn't tethering the charge in one spot, flashed with distant lightning.

That she had merely redirected nature's power rather than using her own didn't lessen her accomplishment.

She had unleashed the fury of the elements upon her enemies and kept doing it repeatedly until she was sure that no one had survived.

Numbly, she drank some more water, trying to get rid of the awful taste in her mouth. The worst of her vomit had been cleaned by Matt, but she was still queasy enough that just the aftertaste risked being too much.

Around her, she could feel her companions start to approach. Mel's group was first, but they headed immediately toward the enemy camp after asking her if it was safe. To which she just nodded her head.

Eddie and Tom were next, and they stopped to check on her. By then, she had recovered enough of her faculties to answer with words.

"How do you feel?" The water mage sat beside her. His eyes were gentle, and his demeanor was as if speaking to a lost animal.

"Like I've been kicked in the head," she rasped.

"It was the right thing, what you did," commented Eddie softly.

Her lips twisted in distaste, but she nodded and acknowledged his words.

"I know. It still feels horrible. It doesn't help that I'm the emptiest I've ever been, mana-wise."

A small huff of laughter came from Tom. "Yeah, that would do it," he said, sounding a touch unbelieving.

"I thought you weren't particularly well known for your power . . ." trailed off Eddie.

She explained her actions, keeping in mind that he wouldn't have any of the frames of reference she used. It probably came out too dumbed-down, but she was too tired to think further.

"I just used what was already there. The stored energy in the clouds was ripe for pickings, and I simply directed it where I wanted it to go."

Though she tried to downplay her efforts, by the awed look on his face, she hadn't been particularly successful. She turned to the other mage for help, but he just raised his hands in defeat.

"Don't look at me like that. There is absolutely no way I'd be able to do anything similar. The fact that it was all manipulation and not an actual spell might be even more impressive, to be honest."

Giving it up as a bad job, she turned her attention elsewhere. "They are coming back."

Indeed, in just a couple more minutes, Mel's group had returned, looking very pale and holding with them one sack. "This is all we could salvage. Everything else is too charred to be worth bringing along."

Tom gestured vaguely in the direction they came from. "What about the heads?"

The three grimaced, but one of the scouts responded, "They weren't as burned as everything else. Three children, as far as we could make out. We buried them there."

No one tried to protest at that. Had they been people they knew, a decent funeral would have been organized, but this was the best they could do for strangers, even if they were kids.

Dorea sent Mother Nature a quick, silent prayer to welcome their souls in her embrace and deliberately put it out of her mind. If she thought about it too hard, she might puke again.

"As for the rest of them, well . . . there wasn't much left to go on. We think there might have been two water mages because two people had signs of shielding themselves. They were less burned than anyone else and had water residue around their bodies."

So it would have been four mages against us three, with six nonmagicals to fight our four. The odds were not in our favor, especially if they were ruthless enough to kill children and bring along their heads . . .

"As far as we could tell, these men were Sapiens from the mountain clans. Beyond that, it's impossible to know. Three of them had melted metal around their ears, indicating the typical earrings, which is what clued us in. Their features were not recognizable," he ended in a quiet voice.

Despite how sick it made her, one part of her wanted to go look at what her handiwork had resulted in. She wanted to look at the remains of the people she killed and whose power she had taken for herself.

Luckily, no one else wanted to go near the site, and the pressing need to go back to the village to alert them to the presence of such a group prevented her from fulfilling the sick fantasy.

As soon as everyone felt stable enough to resume their path, they marched directly toward the wall. From their position, passing through her family's ranch was the most efficient path, so she took the lead even as they separated into groups once again to ensure nothing else was trying to sneak up on them.

Nothing stirred, even the mundane animals were too scared to come out of their burrows after such a display, but the protocol was there for a reason. If they missed another such group just because they were all walking together, they'd never forgive themselves.

At least I scared Mel enough that she's unlikely to bother me much in the future . . .

Soon enough, they arrived at the border. Dorea easily jumped above the wall, helping herself by using it as a stabilizing factor.

It had once been unnaturally smooth, according to Voggo, but the weather had turned it into a much more gritty surface, which helped one's grip.

In the distance, she sensed the anoa herd and made sure to relay to everyone that she should be the only one to approach them to avoid angering Mimi or Bebe. Her father appeared next, apparently busy trying to shoo them back into their enclosure.

She called out to him, and he just needed to look at her face once she got close enough to know that something horrible had happened.

"What's going on?" He rushed to her side.

"You need to gather Lia and Mom and come with us. We met a raiding band from the north just a few miles from here. It might not be safe in the village either, but the walls there should hold much more than the ones here, and the shelter will protect you."

His pursed lips told her that he very much wanted to know more and protest at her putting herself in danger, but there wasn't anything he could do about it.

He nodded and took off toward the house. She used some of the power she had recovered to float the animals back into their enclosure and shut its door before resuming her march toward the village, with Matt a silent companion at her side.

They found the two other groups as they came toward the gates of the property and didn't need to wait much for her parents to come out with her sister.

Eddie turned to regard them. "We'll move more quickly ahead and alert everyone of the danger. You gather them all and lead them toward the shelter."

Although she wanted to protest, as she was the most useful one in case of an ongoing attack on the village, she hadn't still recovered fully after the previous expenditure of mana, and beyond that, her system felt strained from overuse.

Seeing no problems, he nodded one last time and started running toward the village's center with the others.

She smiled at her sister comfortingly but couldn't offer her more than that. Seeing her worried little face broke her heart, but saying anything to calm her would have felt too much like lying.

Instead, she began marching out of the ranch. Soon they passed by the closest properties, where people came out hurriedly and joined her group.

It became almost a procession, and Dorea seriously worried about her ability to keep everyone safe in case an enemy mage managed to get in.

She'd be a sitting duck, trying to shield everyone while they attacked from afar.

But then again. If they penetrated the walls so far, we would be done for anyway. Leaving them at home would have just meant them being picked apart one after the other.

Her expression must have been bleak because no one tried to question her further. The previous groups had explained the basics, and everything else could wait until they were safe.

Finally, they arrived at Voggo's house, whose owner was waiting for them outside. As he spoke, the old man gestured for the villagers to get inside the shelter. "There were three different attacks on the village today. We have repelled them all, but please stay in the shelter until we are sure it's safe."

That was new information even to her, but even as she stretched her senses to their maximum, she couldn't feel anything to indicate a successful raid.

There were multiple presences already underground, but no one was lying down, nor did they feel particularly weak.

She joined Voggo, standing at his side, and received a small, proud smile in return.

"You did well. I dare say you were our most successful protector today."

The sensation of wrongness that had accompanied her so far finally receded a bit at his words. Something in his approval told her she had done the right thing in ways that no one else, not even herself, had managed to convince her of.

The villagers quickly filed into the shelter, less afraid now that they knew the attacks had been repelled but still worried.

As soon as the last one was in, Voggo spun away, and she followed, hot on his heels. The refugee camp was empty, as thankfully there was enough space for them to take refuge beneath the shaman's house, since it had been built in times when the village's population was much larger.

Soon, they reached the gates, where a few dozen people were standing, agitatedly speaking with each other.

The old man broke up whatever discussion had been going on and set about making some order.

"Has anything more happened?"

Jonah, who was standing close to the gates, replied: "No one has gotten close that wasn't part of the patrols. The signals have worked so far, and there is no sign of other enemies."

The blond had evidently been tasked with sensing any suspicious movement since his range was, by this point, around a mile in radius. It was a ridiculously large area to cover and an amount of information that would have befuddled anyone else, but he had a real talent for it.

"The patrols have also reported that the enemies who managed to run away have fully retreated from our territory."

Voggo turned to regard the speaker, a young woman named Nila, who was the only female scout as far as Dorea knew.

"Which direction did they go in?" he asked.

"Two men made the mistake of crossing into Old Titan's lands. They didn't make it out. The rest retreated toward the mountains, but that doesn't mean they are giving up."

Voggo hummed in thought as he stroked his beard. "How many people were in the group you took care of?" he asked Dorea.

"Ten men, four of whom were mages," Dorea replied.

"They are all dead?" questioned Nila, who obviously hadn't heard directly about what had happened yet.

"Definitely."

She might have been too curt in her answer, but Dorea didn't feel like spending more time thinking about what she had done.

There was a moment of silence before it was broken by the question many had internally debated before they got there.

"Should we not go after them now that they are weak? Next time they'll come back with many more men, and they'll know what we are capable of."

It made sense to her, beating the iron while it was hot, but the risk of leaving the village unprotected was too much. The thought was evidently shared by Voggo.

"To send a strike group strong enough not to fear ambushes would mean depleting the village's defenses. It's possible that this was simply a probing strike, and while we may have repelled it with more force than they had expected, it doesn't mean that we should underestimate them," was his reply, and no one tried to gainsay him.

"I know it might seem appealing, the thought of hunting down those that would dare hurt our tribe, but I've seen too many people fall into that trap to allow it."

He has been through a war. I'd forgotten.

"Now, that doesn't mean that we should just be sitting ducks and wait for the moment the enemy will come. We have learned quite a lot from these skirmishes; first of all that, while they are ruthless, their training doesn't hold up to ours."

That seemed to calm the spirits better. They had all taken for granted that other tribes would be afforded the same level of attention by their older mages, but not all had one in the first place, and those that did, did not necessarily want to spend their time like that.

They had been put through a condensed course meant to get everyone to the level where they could defend themselves and contribute to the village's protection.

"We have to tread the fine line of not underestimating our enemies, without thinking of them as incredibly powerful absent a reason to do so."

His speech done, Voggo went to speak more with Nila, who was coordinating the patrols.

Dorea approached her friend, whose brow was scrunched up in concentration as he scanned as far as he could.

"I don't think they are returning so soon," she told Jonah.

"I agree that they'll need to think it through much better if they want to attack us again, but that doesn't mean we should let our guards down," he replied distractedly.

"I know what happened north, but how did the attacks here go?"

Jonah turned to look at her, catching something in her forcedly light tone. "You'll need to tell me everything once we are out of the emergency."

She smiled tightly, not looking forward to it but wishing for the comfort of her friends at the same time.

"There were two different attacks, one that came from the northeast and was met by a patrol, and the other from the south. There they made it to the gates before being discovered."

"From the south? Are we sure they were northern clansmen then?" she interrupted.

"Yeah, they were all dressed the same and ran away in the same direction, up north. I wasn't there when it happened, but apparently Ed, the lead hunter, recognized one of them."

She hummed in acknowledgment and gestured for him to keep going.

"The group down south was taken by surprise, apparently because they had a mage who could hide his group's presence until they were very close. According to Ed, they weren't particularly interested in raiding anything but wanted to test our defenses."

"Which explains why everyone is so sure that they are going to attack again soon," she finished for him.

He nodded at that. "They managed to take down two men, mostly thanks to Mark the Blue, who fried them with lightning, but the rest ran away and they lost track of them soon after."

Dorea kept her face impassive, though hearing how their strongest mage had dealt with their enemies wasn't pleasant, nor were the similarities with what she had done.

"Some people were injured, mostly by arrows, but Voggo's poultices that we keep at every gate allowed them to be saved. Up here, on the other hand, was more chaotic."

As he spoke, he kept his concentration on his task, monitoring the length of the wall from top to bottom and making sure no one got close.

His ability to sense things at such a distance was a great boon to the village, but it also meant that people started relying on him for it all the time.

From the bags under his eyes, Dorea could tell it was taking a toll on him. The fact that the moment he took a break this happened had probably only reinforced his sense of duty.

Not that she could speak on the subject, seeing how she had taken upon herself the task of dealing with a group of enemies by herself.

And I'd do it again. Knowing that maybe they'll think twice about attacking us, no matter how sick I feel to my stomach, makes it all worth it.

"The eastern patrol intercepted them about a couple of miles away from the walls. From what I could understand, the enemy had set up an ambush by aggravating an enhanced glyptodon into a rage and attacking as our group dealt with it. Luckily, they had been sensed ahead of time, even though they also had someone who could hide their presence at a distance, and Mark, the lead scout, led the group as they counterambushed them."

Dorea tilted her head, trying to imagine everything he told her happening simultaneously. "That sounds like a right mess."

"It was, which is what helped us win. They managed to turn the glyptodon against the Northmen and picked them apart one by one. A couple even ended up in Old Titan's territory, which meant certain death. From what I heard, at least three men managed to run away, but they should have put the fear of the Wrath into them."

It was very comforting to know that the village was perfectly capable of defending itself even without her.

Times would come where that sentiment was tested, she was sure of it, but for now, she welcomed it warmly.

CHAPTER TWENTY-TWO

The day passed in anxious vigilance as everyone was too keyed up to lower their guard.

Some villagers had wanted to return to their homes for the night, but Voggo had decided that doing so would be too dangerous, so they had to make do with sleeping on hay.

Some elders had gotten the best spots, but there weren't any complaints. Their bones would already creak in normal conditions, and no one wanted to hear them moan through the night.

A rotation of patrols was set so that people could still get some sleep, and with the increased protection, Dorea finally felt safe enough to share what had happened with her friends.

Jonah was the most sought-after Gifted, as his sensing was by far the best, but Voggo had put his foot down and only allowed him to do as much as everyone else.

Beth, who had been sent to the southern wall, had finally returned and was full of additional details about what had happened there.

"And then Ed said, 'Is that you, Kannis the Wolf? Is this what you have lowered yourself to?' and it was him! And he actually looked ashamed of himself but still attacked. I heard him say that he was following his people's will."

She was animatedly recounting everything but conspicuously avoided saying anything about her own actions. Since her best attacks were more blunt jets of water than anything threatening, and Dorea knew from the grapevine that her best friend had taken down one man, drowning was the only possibility. That or she had bludgeoned him to death, which sounded even more traumatizing.

She gripped her friend's hand tightly in a show of tacit support. In moments of great stress, such as this, Beth often talked about anything and everything, desperately trying to keep her mind off whatever disturbed her.

Knowing this, Dorea decided to hit two birds with one stone. She'd tell them what she had done and definitely distract her friend.

"Our side went a bit differently," she began.

All in all, it had been a relatively quick operation. According to Matt, whom she trusted much more than herself to have kept a cool head, from the moment they had first sensed the enemies to the end of her attack, less than a quarter of an hour had passed, though it might have been a bit more since the clouds had covered the sun.

Jonah had evidently heard something about it, since he wasn't particularly surprised when she told them how she decided to simply fry them all at a distance.

They were both suitably awed at her manipulation of charges and winds to create the lightning, especially since to do so alone was impossible to all but her.

Of course, other lightning mages could have achieved a similar result by simply dumping aspected mana into the clouds and forcing it down. However, that would have been quite a bit more noticeable and required a lot more power than she had available.

"I got the idea from watching the new mages' demonstration. Their coordination was much better than ours, and since I can use more than one element, I decided to give it a try."

Her casual tone alerted her friends to her state of mind. Although she had decided to open up so quickly to distract Beth, Dorea was still not over what she had done, and she doubted she would be for a while.

Thus, focusing on the more technical aspects of her magic made it easier to talk about what had happened.

In the end, her friends were surprised by the sheer power she had been able to unleash but also proud of her, which helped immensely.

The night passed quickly in a mixture of dozing off and sleepy vigilance, as she was afraid of what she'd see if she dared to slip into a deeper slumber. In the early morning, she was woken up for a patrol, thankfully in the opposite direction to the previous day's.

It was uneventful, beyond a couple of river shrews that could use water magic and made a nuisance of themselves when they passed through what was evidently their territory.

She could have zapped them easily and gained a little boost to her reserves, but she wasn't really feeling up for any unnecessary fighting, so she let the others take care of them.

The patrol was done mostly in silence, though she could tell that everyone already knew what had happened to the northern group of enemies, given the looks they gave her.

Luckily, no further interruption happened, and she was able to go back home alongside her family.

Indeed, it had been decided that while the enhanced vigilance would continue, the villagers could return to their houses since the wait wouldn't be short.

"We can't let them dictate how we live our lives," Voggo had said, and that seemed to be the shared sentiment, even if everyone had been told to prepare a bug-out bag in case the alarm needed to be sounded.

The arrival of the refugees had been, in a sense, a godsend, as the influx of mages and fight-capable people made their lives much easier.

Of course, they weren't left to themselves, nor could they form their own teams, as both Voggo and Noele saw this as an opportunity for them to prove their worth to the villagers.

Some had raised the question of whether they would eventually leave, given that they had traveled all the way to Whitecliff to get to a safe place, but that line of reasoning had been shot down quickly as Noele leaned on her people.

She had been unequivocal that, given what the Wrath had done to the region, there would never be a completely safe place, and their new village was the closest thing to home they could ever find.

War was coming for everyone; all they could do was find a secure place and pour everything they could into its protection.

There is also the fact that no one else would take that many strangers in. It's very likely that they tried it with neighboring neutral tribes first and were rejected. The cousin people story is nice and all, but I sincerely doubt they would have come all the way here if they had any other choice.

The following couple of days passed in tense vigilance but nothing seemed to happen, and people did what people could, which was adapting to the new circumstances.

Every mage, scout, or hunter now had less free time than before, just like the people who started producing more food under the expectation that they could come under siege or that the surrounding lands could become more dangerous to forage in.

No one liked it, but it was the current situation, and they dealt with it as they could.

It's not like we didn't know that we were under threat of attack from the north; it's the entire reason behind the mission to the Heidels, but knowing something because you have been told it's likely and having it happen are two entirely different things.

Dorea had taken, in her free time, to experiment further with her spell creation in the hopes of a further breakthrough.

Although she might have managed to take out a large group of enemies, the conditions for such a thing weren't likely to repeat themselves.

Having the targets close enough between themselves to be all taken out together, in favorable weather conditions, without a sensor strong enough to detect her and having the time necessary to set the stage without any interruptions was something a mage could usually only dream of.

No, she couldn't hope to be given such a golden opportunity again. Dorea felt the need to be strong enough not to care about such a thing rearing its head again and was determined to reach her goal as quickly as possible.

The increase in power she had gotten by killing the four mages had been enough to double her reserves, which admittedly wasn't as large a boost as it might have seemed since she had so much less than others, but now she was squarely in the middle of the pack.

Even just a few weeks before, she had been completely exhausted after a single casting of Lightning Sphere, her only spell, but now she was able to use it five times and still have something left.

If she could just develop one more spell to give her some more versatility, she'd be much more confident.

Following her earlier success, she decided to keep doing what she was good at and apply the idea behind Lightning Sphere to a water spell.

She had considered air, but she felt better using the element as support for now, since she didn't want to sink so much mana into creating a construct robust enough to do damage.

Embarrassedly, she realized that her original spell might have been a bit too strong to have any practical use, especially considering how weak she had been when she first cast it.

Thus, she tried to recreate it in a miniature form, using a different element but from the same principles.

Immediately, she ran into the problem of water not working in the same way lightning did. She couldn't confine herself to just the latter, though, as that would mean essentially abandoning her main advantage.

Thus, she kept trying different combinations. Going about it the way the glyptodon did wasn't really feasible for her. Not only was she still only a middling Neophyte mage, not even capable of casting two different spells, but she simply didn't have the reserves to do much damage with blunt force yet.

The river shrews she had met the day before had propelled themselves using compressed water, which sounded like a pretty decent mobility spell. The problem with that was the need to stop.

They could shoot themselves into the water without much trouble, considering how little energy was required to move their bodies, but if she applied the same logic, she'd splatter herself on a tree the first time she tried it.

Beyond the fact that she was about to lose her position as the only spellcaster in the village, not considering Voggo, as the other Gifted got better and better, she felt the need to prove to herself that her achievements so far were not just flukes.

I need to be able to fight without worrying about every minute change in the environment, if I want to be actually useful.

To be recognized as a Journeyman, you needed to be able to cast two entirely different spells, which meant you couldn't piggyback on the previous one's framework, and you had to be able to cast them both repeatedly.

What she was working on wouldn't give her such a distinction yet, but it certainly would bring her closer to it.

The idea of a spherical cage of churning waters didn't seem too bad, but was apparently unsuited to being used as a projectile.

Something to keep in mind. I'll definitely revisit it in the future.

That, however, didn't mean that she couldn't use anything from Lightning Sphere to make her newest spell. The intensity of the electrical currents transposed itself very well, and the idea of condensing it to have it explode on impact was definitely something to explore further.

Mobility magic might have seemed like a better idea, but they were still too far from anything she had ever done and would probably end up taking her weeks, if not months, before she had a working spell.

Also, considering how she had never seen anyone use one, if you discounted Leo's display with his air platforms, it was likely to be a challenging endeavor.

Not one to be discouraged, Dorea tried out several versions of her prototype, splashing compressed water balls against one of the broken trunks left from the Wrath.

At first, the strength was enough to damage the tree, but it took way too long to be usable, and she needed to maintain its cohesion the whole way.

The second was even worse, and she found out after being splashed that the speed of the internal rotation, if not stopped by an external force, would cause the construct to explode early.

Soaked but not defeated, Dorea continued her experiments. Luckily her recent increase in reserves allowed her to go on much longer than she had been capable of during the first spell's trials.

It took her many tries, but she noticed a pattern where the tighter the balls of water were made, the less power they would require to shoot toward the target.

It wasn't a massive breakthrough, but it gave her something to work with. Of course, condensing the liquid further meant expending more power initially, so she set about finding the point of equilibrium.

She ended up with marbles the size of an acorn, much smaller than she had initially anticipated. However, when they hit, the resulting explosion was still capable of leaving an impression on the bark of a sturdy oak.

Considering the increase in power and efficiency that came with finding the proper mana pattern to turn a simple manual manipulation into a spell, she felt it was an excellent first step.

It would take some time to work out all the finicky bits and even more to be familiar enough with it to be able to actually cast it, but Dorea was very satisfied with her efforts for the day.

Lunch was a simple affair, consisting of some of the remaining meat from the moa they had to put down, alongside stewed herbs her mother and sister had picked early that morning.

Little Lia had been suffering from nightmares after all the agitation of the previous day, and Lilian had decided to distract her with something useful. It had worked well enough, as the girl proudly explained how she had found a fantastic spot for garlic mustard, which could be eaten stem and all.

It felt surreal to Dorea, going from a massacre, to high alert for a whole day, to sitting at the table with her family as if nothing had happened.

I know that Voggo said that we can't allow them to rule our lives, but this is just jarring.

Still, she did her best not to show her feelings and instead tried to pay more attention to her sister's chatter. She had been told repeatedly that these moments should be treasured, and she'd try her best to do so.

A strange sort of quiet had settled over the village. Everyone went about their day normally, but they all knew that they could come under attack at any moment.

People greeted each other with a bit more feeling, as if it could be the last time they saw each other. They showed more respect for their protectors, aware they were the only thing keeping their families safe.

Not to say that they had been rude or dismissive before, but there was a difference in how you treat the little girl you saw grow up, who used to steal cherries from your backyard, and how you treated a mage who had killed ten men to keep you safe.

Dorea wasn't sure she liked the change but decided it was likely a temporary effect of the scare they all had.

One good effect on Whitecliff was that the refugees were now much more integrated with the population. Not to say there weren't differences, and problems would surely arise in time, but people now felt much more compassion toward them.

Intellectually, they all had known what the poor people had gone through, but having it happen to you, even if in a tiny percentage, had done wonders to make the villagers more understanding.

The increased patrols hadn't picked up on any strange movement, and, according to Voggo, the Heidels hadn't either.

They had been informed of the attack and the subsequent response as part of their pact and had been reportedly very happy with the black eye they gave the Northmen.

Dorea could just imagine the old hag, Yaomi, cackling at the brutal end they met. In a way, it was calming to know that she was on their side. She still gave her the shivers, though.

The other big news that day in the village was that two more people finally managed to cast an actual spell.

To her and Beth's pride, Jonah was one of them. His Whispering Wind might not have seemed like a great deal, but he was able to communicate with anyone within half a mile. That was huge.

Also, the fact that he had been able to find the time to reach such a goal, considering all the work he had had to do, was amazing.

Or maybe it's precisely because of it. Working on his air sense so much might have been the thing he needed for it to finally click.

The other person was, unsurprisingly, Mark the Blue, whom everyone had thought would be the first to cast a spell.

Still, his Lightning Bolt was impressive enough, even if a bit too banal for her tastes. No one could comment on its effectiveness, as having an entire thunderbolt thrown at you would definitely put you out of commission.

The fact that he could do by himself what she had done to the enemy group she dealt with, without the need to set the conditions right at will and using only a portion of his mana, felt very unfair, but Dorea had long since made peace with her situation.

It would take some time, especially since everyone else kept growing too, but she'd surpass them all one day.

CHAPTER TWENTY-THREE

The following day, something that shouldn't have been so surprising happened.

A merchant caravan, belonging to the nomadic people of the southeastern grasslands, approached the village.

It came as a shock since they had been so busy worrying about a possible attack that they had almost become hostile when they first noticed the group approach, but luckily, beyond a few short minutes of tension, the situation was resolved quickly.

They usually came twice a year, once in the spring, like the one that had just arrived, and once toward the end of the summer, when they sold supplies for the winter months.

This season's was quite a bit smaller than usual, but they opened the gates and welcomed the nomadic people with great cheer.

The caravan was composed of four carts pulled by two shaggy-haired horses each and a set of ten guards armed to the teeth with bows, spears, and knives.

Their stony expressions had always frightened Dorea in her childhood, and their reputation as unrelenting warriors had only compounded it. Even the northern clans were reluctant to attack them, as the losses were always more significant than the gains.

These people served another crucial role, beyond supplying them with iron and food and buying their surplus. They were the ones that made information move along the region of Loisos.

While Dorea considered Whitecliff to be relatively advanced, she was aware that when compared with some of the eastern settlements, it might have seemed like the boonies.

Which meant that almost no one passed through their lands without a very specific reason to do so.

That was good because their isolation guaranteed their security, but bad in that important news took a long while to arrive. And one of the only ways information traveled was thanks to these few caravans that braved the journey through the forest.

Voggo stood before the village gates, arms open wide to welcome the merchants.

One person was helped out of the first cart, which was more of a carriage now that she looked closely, and went to hug him back.

It was another elderly man, whose long beard was tied in a braid that went down his waist. He wore the typical dress of the nomadic tribes, flowy and decorated with stitched shapes of birds of prey.

"Voggo! My dear friend, it has been too long!" the man shouted.

"Mos, you old dog, I thought you were gonna sit this year out."

They released the embrace, and the merchant scoffed, "Bah! It's going to take much more than a few upstarts and a couple of bumbling Neophytes to make me stop my business."

Considering the more limited size of the caravan and the fact that she could sense at least two mages within the guards, Dorea wasn't sure he was really that unconcerned, but she could appreciate his courage.

"The usual spot is being used by a group of refugees for now, but we can set you up just a bit farther south . . ."

Their conversation got harder to hear as Voggo led the other man toward his house, but Dorea's attention had already been shifted away.

I need to get back home to gather my coin. I'm sure they'll have some interesting stuff. And maybe an artifact! I can't lose it to anyone else; I need to hurry.

She ran down the road much quicker than she usually would have. It would take some time for the caravan to set up shop, and they would generally stay the night and depart the following afternoon, but the best things always got bought in the first couple of hours, and Dorea had no intention of having them be snatched away.

Especially because this year I have money! You can't do much with it in the village normally, but it's the best on this occasion. I don't want to spend hours bartering just to get what I want.

She rushed down the path, entering the house like a woman possessed.

"The caravan is here!" she yelled to alert her family.

Considering the noise that followed her proclamation, the news was well received.

In the time that it took her to find her satchel filled with coins she had been accumulating ever since the last caravan passed by, everyone had gathered at the entrance, all holding a bag of their own.

These kinds of visits always came unannounced, but were definitely very welcome.

Lia was vibrating with suppressed energy, and the moment she saw Dorea come down the stairs, she ran to grab her hand and physically force her to go faster.

The elder blonde didn't resist, too amused at her little sister's enthusiasm.

Her parents followed only slightly more sedately behind. They met several people along the road, this time luckily for a much happier occasion.

I'm so happy I don't have to patrol until tomorrow. I would have died if I had to roam around the forest looking for Northmen while the caravan was here.

Dorea also decided to take the day easy and finally enjoy some time in her sister's company. They had been very close before the Trial and still were, of course, but the time they managed to spend together had gotten much shorter, and it was something that she wanted to remedy.

I'll train in the afternoon. It's unlikely they'll attack now anyway, since we'd be supported by the caravan's guards. And they don't mess around.

It had taken about an hour since she left the gates and returned, but the merchants were almost done setting up.

People were crowding the stalls, even though they weren't technically open yet, and Dorea allowed herself to be tugged toward one where they displayed dolls and stuffed animals of all types.

The vendors looked to be rubbing their hands in glee at seeing their fat pouches ready to be emptied. It was, after all, the main perk of coming all the way to their village. Since no one else did, this was almost the only moment money could be spent.

Lia had gotten her eye on an exceptionally well-made stuffed smilodon. Its size resembled a barn cat, but it looked highly realistic.

The merchant noticed her longing gaze and immediately started hyping his product up. "I see that you have a very discerning eye, young lady. This is a piece from an Ergaster artisan who uses real animal pelts. Truly exquisite."

Yeah, this is gonna be expensive.

Her sister's longing gaze only increased in strength at that, well aware that what little she had gotten from her parents to spend wouldn't be nearly enough.

Dorea was lucky that she had accumulated more coins than she knew what to do with, so she conceded to her unspoken request.

"And how much does this 'piece of art' go for?"

"Why I couldn't possibly bear to depart from it for less than ten iron coins, and that's only because you seem like lovely ladies!"

Dorea sputtered at the ridiculous price. That was enough to buy a dagger.

"I see; thank you for your time then," she replied in a final manner, acting as if she was about to leave.

"Now, now, there is no need to be hasty. Nine iron coins and five coppers, that's all I can do," he said quickly.

So we can negotiate. This is still going to be way too much money for a stuffed animal, but it's not really about the price in the end.

Lia had been quiet as they haggled, knowing that her sister was simply trying to get a better price. Dorea had been taught by their mother when she was younger and would now slowly teach her sister.

"That's a proper robbery. It can't possibly be worth more than six iron coins. That's enough to buy a decent shield!"

"Well, yes, but it would be wooden and rot on you in just a couple of years. This wonderful piece will last decades, I tell you! Nine iron coins, and it's yours."

The following negotiation was a fierce one. It wasn't enough to just say a lower price, after all. You needed to justify your request in a manner that wasn't easily dismissible.

Ultimately, they got to the final price of eight iron coins, which was still much more than an average plushy would cost, but not as egregious an expense as it would have been.

The delighted look on Lia's face as she held the smilodon to her chest was more than enough to soothe Dorea's phantom pain at spending so much money on the first item of the day.

The market was, by then, in full swing. Wares were being hawked, and stalls were filled to the brim with all kinds of stuff.

Dorea saw beautiful bolts of cloth, which she knew the elders would fall upon with glee, hunting tools, sacks of grains of all kinds, and even a stall with fresh fruit.

How they could have lasted so long was a mystery, and so she got closer to try to resolve it.

Surprisingly, the air was quite a bit chillier in front of it than it should have been, which gave her a hint as to what might have been the cause of the fruits' mysterious lasting power.

"Are you using an artifact to conserve your wares better?" she asked the woman manning the stall.

She was definitely not a classical beauty, but had an intense look that gave her a weird charm.

"Indeed. My grandfather bought it from the northern tribes many decades ago, and to this day, it's one of the best things that have happened to our people."

Her voice was surprisingly deep for a woman, but Dorea found herself particularly interested in the long-lasting efficacy of the artifact.

"How have you managed to keep it working for so long?"

The woman smiled at her curiosity. "It was made by a Master mage. This kind of powerful, intricate magic can last for a very long time. I know for sure that sometimes ruins are found where there are still-working artifacts."

It was a somewhat disappointing response, but she couldn't really blame the woman for not knowing the intricacies of the rituals used to create it.

The bit about ruins was interesting, but she already knew they existed. Indeed, one of her father's brothers had left long ago to explore the world in search of such things.

They hadn't heard from him in many years, though according to Dodro, he was more likely jumping from one shiny new thing to the next than just dead.

"Can I see the artifact?" she asked. Usually, she knew that it would be guarded very thoroughly, but considering how the woman used it to preserve fruits, it wasn't likely to be that big of a deal.

It also helped that she could feel two guards paying close attention to what was happening at the stall, apparently having been tasked with its protection.

"Tell you what, you buy something, and I'll show you," was the reply.

She had already intended to do so, having noticed a few particularly interesting-looking fruits that she had never seen before, and, more than that, she could feel some kind of fluctuation coming from a yellow and green dried prune of some sort.

She pointed to those she wanted and was told to eat them before the next couple of days, as once outside the artifact's protection, they'd start to go bad like regular fruits.

The price was, as was apparently the norm now, higher than she expected, but she didn't fight too much for it. She was already getting to examine an interesting piece of magic, and considering how the woman had sold her the weird prune without batting an eye, she was also bagging something that only she could tell the worth of.

She was then brought to the back, where a sturdy iron chest lay. Two different keys were necessary to open it, but a weird sight was revealed when the stall owner did.

What looked to be a perfectly cut piece of ice in the shape of a cube sat there, softly glowing with an inner light.

Even now that she was looking directly at it, she could barely feel it with her senses. There definitely was power, and it was at least tangentially related to water, but it was so tightly contained and so efficient in whatever it was doing that she was left feeling like she was grasping smoke.

There was a tenuous sensation that told her it was affecting specific objects in an area and that it would continue to do so without much trouble for many, many years.

Lia let out a sound of awe, this being her first time in an artifact's presence. The little girl looked at the cube with wide eyes, mesmerized by its shine.

It wasn't anything like Dorea's pendant, whose entire job was to mask its and her signatures from scrutiny above a certain threshold, and might simply have been too advanced for her to learn anything from for now. Still, it wasn't like Voggo's artifact, whose function was quite simple to discern even at a glance.

This was made by a Master mage with the express purpose of maintaining the freshness of produce. Why anyone of that level would waste time making this and then just give it away was beyond her, but since she couldn't even tell how old the thing was, maybe it had simply been passed down after the original owner had died.

After all, ice magic was not part of the package of the last two regional Wraths, so it had either been a localized awakening event or had to have been from the time before her grandmother's. At least a century before, if not more.

She could have stayed there for quite a long time, just trying to grasp at its inner workings, but the stall owner was getting a bit antsy and evidently wanted to return to her place but didn't feel up to leaving her alone with her heirloom.

Unsatisfied but still grateful, Dorea thanked her again and said her goodbyes.

Just as she was leaving, her senses alerted her to something incorporeal, quickly moving in her direction with unerring precision.

She only had half a second before it splashed against her hastily constructed air shield, which thankfully held without trouble.

She then heard Jonah's voice, as if coming from a considerable distance, telling her to go to Voggo's house.

With a startled laugh, she realized she had felt Jonah's spell, Whispering Wind, approach and had mistaken it for an attack.

I'm going to need to get used to it soon. Otherwise, it will be useless.

She hadn't yet found the miraculously unnoticed artifact she dreamed of, but she supposed that her duties were more important than a futile search. And if it wasn't something too serious, she might have some time left to browse the stalls before all the good things were bought.

Extending her senses, she quickly located her mother, who was haggling at a stall that sold jugs of all sizes. She then dropped her sister with her, briefly explaining that she had been called by Voggo, and left.

She could feel several of the village's most influential people moving toward the shaman's house, which told her that whatever was going on required immediate deliberation.

I just hope we aren't about to be attacked . . .

Once she finally got there, she nodded in greeting to the two leads of the hunters and scouts, who had just arrived as well and were ushered in.

Sitting at his usual table was Voggo. Beside him were Jonah, who was thanked for his efforts and shooed away, and the old man who was the caravan's chief.

Dorea exchanged a look with her friend as he left, telling her he was worried about whatever was going on but that it wasn't immediately urgent.

"Come in, sit," they were told by the shaman.

"I'm sure you all know my friend here, Mos. He's the leader of the nomadic caravan that is draining us of all our hard-earned money." He laughed.

The other man huffed at his words, a smile pulling at his lips. "Well, you can't expect us not to do anything about it, what with you having fat purses of coin and not having anywhere to spend it. We're doing you a favor, I say, relieving you of the weight."

Once they sat, Voggo presented them to the other man, who didn't bat an eye at her being there.

"I called you here, interrupting your day of relaxation, because he just informed me of something very important. The reason for all the chaos up north, and very likely the culprit of the attacks on our village, is one and the same. The youngest son of an old chief, known as White Wolf, became a Gifted after the Wrath, a mighty one, and immediately usurped his father, starting a war of conquest. He apparently has the stated goal of uniting all the Sapiens tribes of the region of Loisos under one banner. His own."

There was a minute of silence as they digested the information. It had been relatively obvious that someone was stirring up trouble in the mountains, and the fact that they had been attacked in an organized fashion meant a mind was behind it. But an actual war of conquest was beyond that.

"I wanted to hear your opinions, but at the moment, I'm inclined to increase our relationship with the Heidels into a fully-fledged alliance. The game is quite a bit more complex than we expected, and we need to adapt as soon as possible."

CHAPTER TWENTY-FOUR

Unfortunately, the rest of the day had been spent away from the hustle and bustle of the market. While it might have sounded simple enough, requesting the Heidels' help without seeming too weak was a delicate issue.

Soon enough, Voggo had thanked old Mos for his information, and the merchant left them to their strategizing. Though he was an ally, and an important one at that, they couldn't really reveal all their cards to him.

In the end, they found a proposal they all could agree on. Joint patrols would be the final objective, and if the northerners attacked one such mixed group, they could count on the grasslands people to want revenge.

It was a bit of a dirty tactic, forcing them into a conflict that, by all rights, wasn't theirs, but Voggo had explained that it was likely that Yaomi would have tried to do the same had the Ergasters moved aggressively. And she still would try to do so if there ever was a need.

Their main point of strength was that they had already repelled the first attack without taking any casualties. Theoretically, that meant they could stand up to the enemy by themselves.

Ed the hunter had argued precisely that point, not wanting to rely on outsiders for the village's defense.

"We have managed to break their attack without losing a single person. Whatever their skills might be, no matter the brutality they used against Noele's people, we have shown ourselves to be perfectly capable of dealing with them without having to bow our heads to the old witch of the south."

He passionately appealed to their strength and even used Dorea as an example, but it wasn't enough to move anyone.

"Dorea has taken out an entire squad by herself, for the Mother's sake. Our Gifted are growing stronger every day, and we are developing better tactics to work alongside them. Our people are more than enough."

The old shaman, though, wasn't one to be blinded by pride. "I do not doubt our strength. I do not fear our enemies. I am simply aware of what a protracted conflict is like," he lightly chastised.

"If we were to fight the coming battles by ourselves, we'd probably manage to hold on to our lands for a while. But the price we'd pay for it in lives is simply unacceptable. Especially when we have a relatively easy solution at hand."

It had taken a while longer to field all the points Ed had raised, but no one begrudged him that. The entire reason for this kind of informal council was to develop and refine their strategies. And to have the best possible ones, they needed to be able to stand up to scrutiny.

And considering that we expect the situation to keep getting more chaotic region-wide, for quite some time at that, we need allies.

Luckily for her, Dorea hadn't been chosen to take part in the delegation to the Heidels to discuss their proposal. Still, she had been volunteered as the leader of the first joint patrol in case the cantankerous chief agreed without trying to extort too much.

It's not really volunteering if I don't have a choice in it, is it?

Mark, the scout leader, had once again been chosen to command the mission and had left to gather the necessary people.

They further discussed the patrols' scheduling, now that some people would be out of the village for a few days, and moved things around to avoid any holes in the defenses.

By the time they were done, it was almost dinnertime, and Dorea left Voggo's house, both more worried for the future, given what they had learned from Mos, and hopeful that the alliance with the Heidels would help them brave the coming storm.

The negotiations had gone suspiciously smoothly, which told them that Chief Yaomi thought she would need their help sooner rather than later, and a group of Heidel warriors and mages was sent to participate in the new joint patrols.

Of course, a separate group of their people had gone down south to do the same. Nothing was ever free, after all.

It might have seemed foolish since the available number of fighters was still the same, and they had taken in people who were simply not as committed to the village's defense as their own men, but Dorea knew that that hadn't been the point of this exchange.

No, Voggo had ensured that the Heidels would have a bone in the fight between them and the northern clans trying to conquer everything.

After all, they could have sat in the grasslands, well aware of how difficult it was to assail from the north, and simply monitored their borders closely.

If they had done so, however, they would have lost a valuable ally in case they were attacked either by the tribes farther south or, in a much more threatening case, by a force of Ergasters from the southeast.

It was a complex calculation, but the balance had been tipped in their favor.

Still, this means that not only do I have to go on more patrols, but I have to make sure no one causes problems for the Heidels. Somehow, all the work ends up on me.

Commiseration aside, Dorea was relieved that the diplomatic efforts had gone well. It was an additional layer of security in case things truly heated up.

The first such patrol was relatively unremarkable. She met their allies bright and early the morning after they arrived.

The gates were opened just enough for them to pass through, and she waved in greeting to the poor people tasked with the dawn shift.

Their usual team of seven to eight people had been expanded to at least ten after the recent attacks, and in this instance, it was made up of six from Whitecliff and four Heidels.

She was in overall command, though she had Matt—whom she could rely upon if she needed counsel—Luke, and a veteran hunter, and had chosen to bring Beth and Leo as their mages.

Unfortunately, Jonah was unavailable, as he had just returned from his mission.

On the other hand, the Heidel side consisted of Melu, a tan young woman whose entire body felt like a watery construct; San and Nas, twin warriors; and Eol, an air mage with a permanent smile affixed on his face.

Dorea was quite confused the first time she sensed Melu, as it appeared as if the girl were no more than an elaborate piece of magic, but it was soon explained that it was her spell, Armor of the Rivers.

No one had many details about it, but all agreed that it was a form of passive protection that couldn't cost too much to keep on at all times.

Still, it was the first example of a semipermanent spell she had ever seen, and she had stealthily paid careful attention to it.

The fact that their allies had several people capable of casting spells by now was notable but something they had expected, given their own successes.

They divided themselves into the usual team of two, and Dorea took one of the two warrior brothers with her. Their communication was even better than it used to be, thanks to the abundance of mages on duty these days.

Everyone pulled their weight, even though no one had made them do it. Beth wasn't a very aggressive person, and she didn't enjoy the thought of hurting wildlife or other humans. Still, she had volunteered for more patrols, just like everyone else, because they knew they were the one thing defending the village from ending up like Leo's people.

Their integration wasn't a done deal yet, and given the recent tensions, it wouldn't have been out of the ordinary for some to want to leave, but it seemed that Noele's efforts were bearing fruit. Their new home was under attack, and they would help.

The first few patrols were mainly done to show the Heidels the land and teach them what to avoid, like Old Titan's territory.

On the second day, they encountered a particularly ornery pair of smilodons in the rocky hills up north, both enhanced. They appeared to have been fighting amongst themselves, likely in a territorial scuffle, but had set aside their animosity for each other immediately upon noticing them.

It didn't take long to deal with them, given the sheer amount of mages they had on hand. Dorea herself could have taken them without any help and, indeed, would have done so had she not needed to show herself to be a good leader to the Heidels.

At first, I couldn't attend the market; now I can't even take a few animals out by myself. Truly, life is suffering.

Her complaining aside, Dorea felt satisfied with the way things had been going so far. The boosts she got were smaller in scope and came less frequently, since the surrounding territory was so well beaten, but the increase in safety made up for it.

Also, the Heidels' presence here, and the fact that we are getting along decently well, means that our fledgling alliance could actually bear fruits.

She still hadn't forgotten what she had seen during her first mission. Yaomi's display of power was engraved in her mind and would likely be for quite some time.

Now that she was getting stronger herself, she could appreciate her feat even better. She had noticed no buildup, and the power had been so overwhelming and controlled that comparing it to her efforts with natural lightning was a joke.

No, she still had a long way to go, and she was very glad that the old monster was on her side.

It was on the fourth day since the Heidels arrived that something changed.

They gathered at the village's gates for their usual morning patrol with the team that was starting to become familiar.

Dorea exchanged greetings with Melu, with whom she had begun forming a tentative friendship. The other girl was witty and always smiling, making it easy to want to spend time with her, even outside their duties.

I should bring her with us to the beach next time. We should have some free time coming up this week . . .

She breathed in the fresh morning air, taking in the dew still hanging on to the grassy underbrush. It was her favorite smell.

They stepped out of the gates into the forest and split into their usual teams. Marching through the trees always relaxed her, and even though she had had so many violent encounters, she couldn't bring herself to associate these woods with anything negative.

Her teammate, San, wasn't one to chat endlessly, but he had evidently been tasked with gathering more information about her and had spent the last few days trying and failing to be subtle about his inquiries.

He was so bad at it that Dorea had initially thought that it was a ruse to make her guard lower, but had been forced to reconsider when faced with questions such as "I have always been fascinated by spells. Are you working on any?"

Truly, a mastermind at work.

He had been trying to devise new avenues of inquiry when she raised her hand to stop him abruptly.

Something was buzzing at the end of her senses, and her instinct told her it wasn't an animal.

Quickly, she signaled to the other teams via short pulses of mana, trying to keep them away from whatever she sensed.

Even as she sensed her allies respond and start to gather at her position, she felt surer that it wasn't a simple beast testing her range. No, this felt too deliberate.

It reminded Dorea of her efforts in hunting down the glyptodon, where she used an unremarkable water ball to discover its sensory range.

We are being hunted.

She took stock of the situation with a grim set on her face. They had ten people, five of whom were mages. It was a better starting point than her last encounter with the enemy, but back then she had the advantage of surprise, while now it was on the other side.

She considered their position relative to the village, but they were too far away to receive any help, and something told her it was a deliberate choice.

They have been observing us while we patrolled. But for how long? How have we not noticed them?

Deciding to leave such questions for later, Dorea kept a wary eye on the movements she could barely feel at the end of her range as she went through their realistic possibilities.

They were in the northeastern quadrant of the forest, relatively close to Old Titan's territory but not close enough to bait the enemy there unless they tried to chase them. Going farther northwest, into the hills, was possible only if the ambush hadn't already been set, which she seriously doubted.

No, they would need to stand their ground.

Finally, the others arrived, grimly aware that their fate was about to be decided.

"I only sensed three or so different people, but that doesn't mean anything. So far, they have been operating as teams of ten men, but it's also possible they were originally a squad of thirty and split up to accomplish their goals. We should think of them as outnumbering us three to one."

Beth made a sound of shock at her words but accepted them resignedly. No one wanted to fight thirty people stalking them for who knew how long, but it was happening whether or not they wanted it.

"We should try to find a more favorable position, but since we all changed pattern abruptly, I guess we won't have long before they spring their trap," Melu commented in a light tone that clashed with the hard look in her eyes.

Unfortunately, they didn't have the time to reposition. Dorea felt a large number of people quickly move in their direction, some with magic already formed in their hands.

"They are coming! Nonmagicals, disperse and harass; mages, break them!"

However much she might have wanted to start blasting people with her Lightning Sphere, with this many opponents, she couldn't waste mana at the beginning of the fight.

This is the entire reason why I've practiced so much with my water bullets.

It wasn't a spell yet, but she had the manipulation down to pat. She could create the exploding balls with little effort, and they drained a tenth of what her lightning magic did.

Leo cast several air barriers around everyone, apparently focusing entirely on defense. Considering how little he could contribute to the offense, it was a good idea. Dorea was glad that the redhead was showing initiative.

Finally, the first enemy came into range, and she saw them. It was a band of mostly men, unwashed and dirty. From the bone necklaces and armbands, they were obviously part of the same mountain clan.

The front line, if she could call it that given the haphazard way they were running between trees, was made up of ten nonmagicals, all holding sharp spears ready to tear into their flesh.

Behind them, at a slightly more dignified pace, ran the mages. One of the only two women caught her attention.

She was tall, with a wicked scar that cut her face from ear to ear. She was smiling madly, lightning crackling at her fingertips. There was no mercy in those eyes, no one to reason with.

These people were battle maniacs, one and all. They could only be made to stop against their will.

Arrows of lightning splashed against the shields, but Dorea didn't let them break her concentration. She could feel their strength and knew they would hold under the assault for quite a while.

She let go of every distraction and focused on compressing water. Dozens of acorn-sized balls floated in front of her shield, as she had the foresight of creating them outside their protection.

Having readied the first volley, Dorea pushed.

She felt a blade of water emerge from Melu's hands, ready to cut their enemies to pieces. She felt Beth preparing liquid whips to harass their enemies and allow their stronger members to finish them.

She felt the arrows being nocked by their nonmagicals, the tension in Matt's arms as he waited for a perfect shot.

Time rushed back in, and with a staccato of loud bangs, her bullets exploded against the front line.

Not all of them hit their intended targets, but that was part of the plan. Those that did, however, left behind mangled bodies.

The explosion wasn't enough to completely destroy a human, but it certainly was enough to send arms and legs flying.

The screams of pain and the sight of people crawling desperately toward their limbs should have sent her reeling, but all that Dorea felt was cold vindication.

The time for reflection would come; now, she needed to defend her village.

It was challenging to maintain her attention on everything happening, even if it was within her range. Her brain simply couldn't keep up with so many things.

Therefore, she didn't notice the massive bolt of lightning headed her way until she was thrown back by the force of it slamming against the wind barrier.

Dorea was sent rolling, stopping roughly against a tree. She scrambled up, knowing that to stay still in such a situation was tantamount to giving up.

Her senses alerted her to another bolt being formed, and she responded with her own. Though Lightning Sphere was a costly spell, it was still the fastest in her limited arsenal. She simply didn't have the time required to manipulate an element.

The crackling ball shot toward where she felt the concentration of power and exploded in its usual light show.

Immediately, she knew that she hadn't hit her target. The damn woman had used one of her injured allies as a shield.

Still, it had been enough to distract her from her attack, giving Dorea time to recreate the water bullets and send another hail.

This time, the enemy mages were hit directly without the human shield in front of them.

Her allies took advantage of the lull in attacks and sent whatever they could, be they physical arrows or elemental bolts.

She felt an influx of power coursing through her and knew she had killed at least one mage. It bubbled within her, restoring strength to her spent limbs.

Dorea straightened her spine, assessed the situation, and decided it was tenable.

On their side, Beth had been clipped by something and was hiding behind a large oak, occasionally sending one of her whips to harass the enemy.

The brothers San and Nes drew and shot arrows almost inhumanly fast. Both were banged up, but it seemed nothing serious. Leo was still reinforcing his shields, recreating them when necessary. Melu danced with watery blades at her side, scattering enemy mages like a smilodon through an anoa herd.

Her senses told her that the others were down for the count, Matt included. She could feel him breathe, though, which would have to be enough.

The enemy was in worse condition. Luckily it hadn't been the entire thirty people she had feared, but it wasn't the ten she had hoped for either.

Twenty-one people had attacked them, two-thirds of which were nonmagical warriors. Not skilled ones at that, luckily for them.

The mages still standing were only three, two of which were busy with the dancing Heidel. The remaining one was the burly woman who had sent her flying earlier, who was now picking herself up from the ground.

There was a choice to make here. They could attempt annihilating the enemy for good, focusing everything they had on the attack. But doing so would leave the injured to their fates, likely resulting in several deaths.

Or they could try to send them fleeing, gather their people and some prisoners, and return to the village, still victorious.

No matter how much she wanted a clean win, Dorea knew what she had to do.

She started battering the enemy with more water balls, though only some were compressed enough to do any damage.

Still, the sheer amount of projectiles sent their way made them reconsider their chances.

She didn't let up and noticed how Beth and Melu started following her lead, apparently on board with her strategy.

Considering the weakness of their attack, it wouldn't have worked typically, but for an already bruised and halved force, it was simply too much to deal with.

With a scowl that promised revenge, the burly woman roared out, "Retreat!"

Her people, to their credit, immediately followed the order. They gathered as many of their men as they could and started running north as fast as possible, being covered by a rain of weak arcs of electricity.

The woman waited from behind the cover of a large mossy stone until everyone that could move had left and then legged it herself.

There was no last shot, no parting words. But that was okay with Dorea. She needed to hurry back home if she wanted to save her people.

CHAPTER TWENTY-FIVE

Speeding through the woods while holding injured men aloft in an elemental construct was not easy, but no one complained.

Leo had to be almost entirely drained, after protecting everyone from the worst of the enemy barrage. However, he still projected his air platforms to transport their prisoners while Dorea, Melu, and the twins took care of those who couldn't move by themselves.

Beth was by Dorea's side; an arm was obviously broken and in a lot of pain, but she held the forced march without emitting a sound. There was an almost wild look in her eyes as she stared straight ahead, but the fact that she could move under her own power would have to be enough for the moment.

The time for talking about what they went through would come once they were sure they would all survive.

Dorea held Matt's still form in a watery hold, worried that if she put him in a too rigid environment, she'd risk hurting him further.

They had applied the medical salves as soon as they left the battlefield, hoping to gain more time, but the scout looked paler and paler with each passing minute.

He would have died if I had gone on the offense and left him behind. He might still die now. But it would have been a certainty.

The enemy leader, the large woman who wielded lightning like a javelin, had been more powerful than she had expected, given what they had fought during the last attack. Luckily her men weren't disciplined, nor did they fight with a notion of what going against a prepared mage meant.

That, and only that, had allowed them to come out on top of the stacked odds.

Also, I'd bet my pendant that we sprang their trap before they had prepared completely. I shudder to think of what would have happened if we had kept going through our patrol without noticing them.

Finally, the village walls came into sight. Still too far away to be heard, Dorea sent a pulse with as much power behind it as she could to alert the guards of the incoming medical emergency.

She wasn't in range to sense them receive it, but she'd bet that gave them quite the scare. Unless Jonah was on duty, which would have meant they already knew they were coming.

The second turned out to be true; soon enough, they were met by an armed group from the village.

"Are you being chased?" she heard being shouted.

"No, we scattered them, but we need medical help immediately!" she responded at the top of her lungs.

They were escorted back to the village, as another group peeled off the walls and started moving toward the battlefield they had just left, to ensure the enemy was truly gone.

As soon as they passed through the gates, they were met by Voggo, who directed them to the medical tent he had the foresight to have prepared after the first attack.

Dorea gently lowered Matt into a cot and quickly shared what she could remember of his injuries.

"He was hit by a part of the explosion after the enemy managed to break Leo's barriers. I lost track of him after that, but I know he got hit by at least another concussive attack."

The shaman's look was grave, but he thanked her and gestured for her to find a place to sit. He then proceeded to open his patient's eyes, taking his pulse and using a spell that made his hand glow a radiant blue.

As he worked, the tent opened again as Noele, the refugee's leader and a shaman herself, entered and immediately set about caring for the others.

Soon after, Dorea's mother came in, holding a chest containing several jars and bottles, given the clinking that could be heard.

Lilian looked her over worriedly, stopping on her side when her touch made her jump in pain. The adrenaline of the fight was wearing off, and Dorea started feeling all the aches she had suppressed in her mad dash.

Her mother pursed her lips and carefully tugged her shirt up, revealing an ugly, bloody abrasion. Her whole side, from hip to armpit, was red and sticky with blood.

Dorea looked at it in shock, not having realized the extent of her own injuries.

It must have happened when I was hit with the explosion . . .

She was quickly tended to by her mother, who slathered a pungent-smelling paste on and carefully bandaged it. She was then proffered a vial of murky liquid.

"Drink. You need to give your body the energy to heal. It's still too soon to know if you broke anything, and I doubt Voggo will be able to see you for a while, but it doesn't seem like anything too dangerous. Do not sleep, even if you are tired."

Her voice was controlled and methodical, but the way the woman held on to the bandages with a deadly grip told her she was extremely worried.

"Thanks, Mom. I'll try not to," she replied, unsure what else to say.

She received a tight nod before Lilian bustled up to check on Beth, who was holding her arm in pain while sitting on her own cot.

The triage continued for a long time, though Dorea couldn't tell if it was an hour or three, given the afternoon light from outside.

I don't even know how long we fought for. It couldn't have been too long, but it felt like an eternity.

Finally, she was visited by Voggo, who looked over the bandages and nodded to himself. He then repeated his diagnostic spell. "Remember to let me in, little Dory. Otherwise, I won't see anything."

His voice was soft and relaxing, reminding her of simpler times. She allowed his mana to flow through her channels, fighting the urge to reject the foreign power.

Luckily, it only took him a few seconds before he got what he needed and retreated.

"You definitely bruised your ribs, but they aren't broken, thank the Goddess. Beyond that, your system is acclimating well to the influx of power. You have gotten a lot stronger, little Dory."

She replied with a slight hum of contentment. Now that the medicines were doing their job, her pain had dulled, and she was quite sleepy.

"You have no concussion, luckily, so go ahead and rest."

Dorea only barely acknowledged his words, already halfway to sleep.

Waking up was a violence upon the sanctity of the human soul, Dorea decided.

She was forced away from the warm embrace of her cot by a building pressure in her bladder that brooked no argument.

She stumbled up, groggily looking for a night vase to relieve herself. It took her a moment to realize that she was still in the triage tent, not her room.

Somewhat more awake and aware of aches and pains all over her body, she navigated in the dark around the cots containing her team's sleeping forms and got out.

There was barely any light out, which told her it was very early in the morning. Her observations were cut short by a more pressing need, and she finally located a small copse of trees by the wall that could serve her purpose.

Once she had finally relieved herself, Dorea felt ready to take on the day. And by that, she meant to get another dose of pain reliever because she was aching everywhere.

The rush one gets during a life-or-death situation is insane. I ran through the forest without feeling anything, and now I'm moving as if I were eighty years old.

"'Lo there!" she called to the guards at the gate. They were startled, having been paying attention to the outside rather than the inside.

"Dorea, is that you?" asked a familiar voice.

"Eddie?"

Beth's cousin waved at her enthusiastically from atop the wall and gestured for her to get closer.

"How's the shift? Did they send another group?"

He shook his head. "Nah, everything's been quiet since you came back. The team we sent to harass them didn't find them, but apparently they took the road back toward the mountains, so we should be fine for a while."

That was good to hear and lifted a weight from her mind. She had been worried that her choice not to pursue the enemy and make sure they were truly defeated would lead to disaster, but she couldn't have lived with herself if she had abandoned her comrades.

"How is everyone that was with me?" It was a question that should have probably come first.

But apparently, I'm much more worried about myself than the others.

Eddie shrugged. "As far as I know, everyone pulled through. We'll probably need to wait a few hours for a better assessment."

That was a fair point. Sometimes, especially when hits to the head were involved, the only thing you could really do was wait.

"All right, thanks."

"No worries, this and more for our village hero!" he smirked.

It took her a second to compute what she had heard. "Hero?!" She strangled out a gasp.

Eddie sniggered together with the others tasked with the night shift. "Well, you defeated the clansmen twice, heroically leading our people to victory and ensuring our allies would survive the attack."

Dorea felt herself pale. She wasn't one to hate recognition, but she'd very much enjoy it better if it came thanks to better reasons.

Being known as a good killer is not really a girl's dream . . .

"I imagine you are very busy with your guarding. I'll leave you to it. Bye!"

It wasn't her best excuse, and given the barely suppressed laughs she could hear in the background, it hadn't worked at all, but she was too achy and annoyed to care.

Dorea returned to the tent to see her mother standing by her cot, obviously having come to check on her and not having found her.

The woman merely gestured for her to lie down immediately with a stern look, and she complied. It wasn't as if she enjoyed hobbling everywhere anyways.

She was then stripped, and her bandages were removed to reveal the thick green paste slathered the day before. Luckily, it seemed to have done its job, and no pus or bleeding was present.

The smell wasn't the most inviting, but considering its effectiveness, Dorea decided not to complain.

"How are you feeling?" asked Lilian quietly, trying not to wake the others.

She took a moment to look her over, finding the woman somewhat haggard and evidently not well rested.

"I'm okay, Mom; I'm sorry to have worried you."

Lilian sighed, patting her cheek in affection. "You foolish girl. I'm always worried for you, especially when you go out in the wild. But I'm also so very proud."

Dorea felt tears sting in her eyes. In the dark of the breaking dawn, hidden from any observer, she let go of her fears.

She was cradled in the arms of her mother, who caressed her back as she cried her heart out. She cried because expecting her to lead and defend was too much. She cried because she wasn't enough, never strong enough, always having to compromise.

Lilian gave her the warm, silent support that she needed. She kissed her brow and combed her hair with her fingers.

"My beautiful little girl. You are so strong and so loved."

They enjoyed the moment of closeness, taking strength in the other's embrace.

"Now, let's get you treated."

Soon after she was done being treated by her mother, Voggo came in to check on the more injured patients. Although her mother was a skilled healer, the old man had access to an entire lifetime of experience, which, coupled with his magic, made him simply superior.

Indeed, he had managed to save two lives thanks to his healing spells. Matt, who had suffered a rather severe blow to the head, had needed much help as fluid had flooded his brain and would have killed him in a few more hours.

Eol, the Heidel air mage, also had necessitated particular attention, as a broken rib had punctured his lung. The boy might have survived on his own, but his chances would have been slim, and their allies were well aware of it.

If I think about it, this whole situation went as well as it could have. Not only did we not lose anyone, but we ran the enemy out and we furthered our alliance with the Heidels. I know the patrols were set up like this to invite such a situation, but it's still crazy. If Voggo weren't on our side, he'd be terrifying.

As for the prisoners whom the groups sent after their enemies brought back, there was one inevitable death, as the man had been brought to the village with a still heart. The other three were alive and should wake up in a few hours, though their mangled limbs weren't easy to fix.

Seeing the effects of her magic like that was much more impacting than a broken tree trunk. She had purposefully attacked them, knowing what would happen, and it felt horrible. It also felt horrible to feel bad for the enemy.

Her emotions were honestly all over the place, which definitely wasn't helped by what happened soon after they were released.

Jonah, who hadn't taken part in the patrol but was by then aware of everything that had happened, came to see them as they finally got out of the tent.

The boy had tried sneaking in, but Lilian's stern gaze was enough to scare him off. No one had ever accused him of being too reckless, after all.

Beth launched herself at him as soon as he was in sight, wrapping her arms around his neck and bringing him down for a passionate kiss.

Dorea was left staring at them, befuddled by the sight.

She hadn't known that Beth had feelings for their friend, nor that they were reciprocated.

It felt like the kiss went on for a long time as she awkwardly tried not to gape.

Finally, the brunette released her grip, and they split apart. By the looks of it, Jonah was confused at what happened, but since he hadn't rejected her, Beth grabbed his hand.

"I've really wanted to do that for a long time." She grinned at him.

He smiled back tentatively, still apparently not fully there.

"I realized I couldn't wait after yesterday. Life is dangerous, and we should live as we want," she explained further, staring into his eyes.

Jonah looked at Dorea, only to find her looking at her shoes in apparent interest, and his expression firmed up.

Another kiss, shorter this time, broke him out of his stillness. He responded with enthusiasm, scooping Beth up in the air.

The brunette laughed with joy, hugging him close. He held her tight for a while before letting her down.

"I was so worried for you when I felt you run back. There was so much blood . . ." He tucked one dark lock of hair behind her ear, making her smile softly.

"It was scary, but Dorea led us to victory!" Finally, it seemed that the two remembered her presence and turned to her.

She shrugged back. "I did what I could. Your water whips were very useful in keeping their attention away from me so I could attack properly."

It felt bizarre to Dorea not to address what had just happened and, given their closeness, what was likely to keep happening for a while, but if they didn't want to act like it was a big deal, she wouldn't make it.

They chatted normally, though it was a bit stilted, given the new couple's closeness and the occasional kiss.

It's not that I'm not happy for them . . . Of course, I am! It's just that I wasn't expecting it.

As they passed the fork in the path that went to her family's ranch or toward Beth's compound, she said her goodbyes to the two, who gave her a hug and went back to holding hands, and headed away.

It's not just me, is it? This is kind of weird. No one said anything, and now they're acting like they have been a couple for months?

Dorea decided that thinking about it further would only confuse her more. She'd talk to them both, possibly individually, once she recovered and wasn't feeling so weak.

She had a long soak to look forward to for the moment that no one could take away from her. And probably thousands of questions from Lia.

Dorea was called for another meeting at Voggo's house the next day. The pulse of mana that served as a signal scared her awake, and for a moment, all she could feel was her madly beating heart.

Thankfully, when Voggo had developed such methods, he had made sure they could all recognize the different meanings, and once her brain could process more than a hamster's, she realized that it wasn't an emergency and that she had simply overslept.

For some reason she couldn't possibly fathom, Dorea hadn't been able to sleep well the night before. The medicinal paste took care of most pains, and being in her own bed should have calmed her further, but her thoughts were murky, and sleep hadn't arrived quickly.

After stumbling down the stairs, she found her family preparing to start the midday meal. They all looked at her with degrees of amusement, which told her that her bed hair was out in full force that day.

She mumbled a greeting and dashed into the bathroom to clean herself up.

Once done, she grabbed a thick piece of bread and some cheese to eat on the way, alongside a couple of boiled eggs, and left for the meeting that disturbed her sleep.

Thankfully, her mobility had mostly returned, and her aching ribs didn't bother her much as she marched down the path to Voggo's house.

Those poultices may smell terrible, but damn if they do not work. By all rights, I should be in bed for a week at the minimum.

Finally coming in sight of her destination, she felt the three presences she had expected to feel alongside two more.

Curious, she jogged the last bit, wincing at the jostling. Once there, she went inside the house and toward the usual room to the back. Outside sat the two unexpected guests, Noele and Melu.

"Go ahead; we are waiting for our turn," shared the one-legged woman.

Now even more interested, the blonde quickly entered the meeting room.

"Come sit, Dorea. We have lots to discuss," Voggo greeted her.

She took her usual seat, murmuring a greeting to everyone, and looked at the shaman curiously.

He smiled kindly before finally explaining, "We have several points to discuss, among which the response we are expecting from the Heidels. But first, the reason I called the meeting: we have finally received word from the forest tribe. They want to meet in three days to discuss a possible alliance."

CHAPTER TWENTY-SIX

We have finally received a response from the Forest tribe. They want to meet in three days to discuss a possible alliance."

Voggo's words sent a pulse of shock down Dorea's spine. It had been so long since they had first tried to make contact with the reclusive people that she had almost forgotten about it.

Her first thought was that something had to have changed, and the most likely thing to have happened was that they, too, had been attacked.

The sentiment was evidently shared by Ed, who spoke up, "Knowing what we do about them, they are probably in dire need of help. They wouldn't break their isolation otherwise."

Mark hummed in agreement. "They are a reserved tribe, almost skittish, I'd say. If they are finally coming out of the forest, something has to have happened."

"That was my thinking as well," replied Voggo, pulling out a piece of parchment. "This message was found by a patrol during the eastern route. It simply says they want to establish friendly contact and will wait for a delegation at Tumbling Lake in three days."

"I'm sorry to appear so ignorant, but what do we know about these people? Are we sure they'll be friendly? Or that it's even them and not another northern trick?" she queried.

The three men considered her words before the shaman shook his head. "No, they used a specific type of parchment made only through the skin of a particular species of sheep they breed. And it's a monthslong process, which means that either their village has been sacked completely, but we have no indication of such, or it's them."

Mark let out a startled laugh at that. "Man, it's good to have you with us, old man! You are the only one in the world to know so many apparently useless but actually useful things."

Voggo scratched his beard in embarrassment, cheeks reddening. He took a long sip of acidic red tea and changed the subject. "Well, I think we are all in agreement that we need to go. We'd be much safer if we could expand our newborn alliance to include them."

Seeing that there were no objections, he moved on. "Speaking of our alliance, I have called young Melu here to share her thoughts about what happened and how it could impact our relationship with the Heidels."

There was a knowing smile on everyone's face that they made sure to wipe the moment the girl came in after being called.

"Hello, my dear; I hope you didn't wait too much," he greeted.

Melu shrugged uncaringly. "It doesn't matter; not like I can do much until I'm fully recovered," she said, gesturing to her bandaged arm.

Dorea recalled her being hurt, but the haze of combat made it much more challenging to place the exact moment.

Voggo gestured for her to take one of the empty seats, and Dorea, who was the closest, served her some tea as was the traditional hospitality.

"Then, if you don't mind indulging us, how do you think the news of your battle is going to be received back home? We sent a messenger as soon as possible, but they won't return until tomorrow evening."

The old man's tone was innocuous, like a grandfather chatting with his favorite granddaughter. It was kind of scary to see him manipulating the girl in real time.

Melu's shoulders dropped in relief, probably having been worried that she had done something wrong and was going to be reprimanded.

Leaving her outside to wait was likely done on purpose; he could have asked her before the meeting and let us know, but this way, she had the time to work herself up. Scary.

"Eh, if I know our chief well, she's gonna be on the warpath against those damn northerners. It's good that no one died, or she'd go up the mountains and burn them all to a crisp. She's probably going to send someone to talk with you about organizing a counterattack, to be honest."

That was in line with their thinking; even though many still wanted to keep being passive, they couldn't live their lives waiting for the next attack.

Of course, that meant committing most of their forces, though, and it made gathering more allies much more important.

Melu relaxed as she drank the tea, ate some honey cakes when offered, and was a perfect guest. Unfortunately for the poor girl, she was in a den of vipers, and they made sure to pose several innocent questions that let them have a much better idea of the Heidels' forces.

Once they were done squeezing her for all she was worth, they sent her out with a smile and called the other shaman in.

"Are you done sucking her dry?" Noele asked bitingly.

"Now, now, we just had a cup of tea with the poor girl; no need to be so rude," Voggo replied.

Oh Goddess, here they go again. These two really enjoy insulting each other in their faces without being explicit.

Preparations for the diplomatic missions had been underway as soon as they decided to go, and Dorea had unfortunately been chosen to go.

She might not have enjoyed the politicking and power struggles that ensued in such situations, but she was never one to say no to duty, especially if it got her away from the village for a while.

Though she was happy for them, Beth and Jonah made for a sickeningly sweet couple. They were always all over each other, even in public, and seemed not to have boundaries, especially when alone with her.

I'm glad they suddenly fell in love, but there is such a thing as too much. If I hear a suppressed moan again, I'll start blasting.

Thus, she hadn't even put up a token complaint at having to go on a mission that she would have usually done her best to avoid. The fact that she would be able to go much deeper into the forest than she ever had before was also an alluring benefit.

Though exploration had taken a backseat since the attacks started, at heart, Dorea was still yearning for adventure. If she could ignore the more tedious parts, which thankfully wouldn't fall on her, she might even enjoy it.

Since she was going along primarily as muscle, she spent her days recovering physically and working toward finishing her spell.

It felt unfair that after using it so much in a real fight, she still hadn't managed to properly cast her Exploding Water Bullet, but magic didn't really work like that.

It was more about fully understanding all the minutiae that went into making something work; evidently, she was still missing something.

More people had finally managed to develop a spell of their own, and by now, almost half of the village's Gifted could be counted amongst that number.

According to Voggo, it was significant progress. He had expected to be at this point in a couple more months, which gave them the advantage over other tribes.

I wonder what it is that is making us advance faster than the others. The only different variable in our experience, when compared to what Masi told me, is Voggo's potion. Could it really have that much of an effect?

The question would likely be forever unanswered, as the Wraths came so rarely that it was impossible to fully understand how they worked.

Still, Dorea felt like she had made good progress. The fractal was almost fully formed in her mind, and once again, she just needed to push through the last bottleneck to achieve a proper spell.

She didn't know what it would take, but she could feel how close she was and hoped she might get inspired by going on the mission.

They'd need to wade deeper into the forest until they found Tumbling Lake, a decently large basin of water formed by several streams uniting into small waterfalls, thus giving it its name.

Mark, the scout leader, had been there several times and would be their guide and foremost diplomat. Tom, the water mage, would also come along as their support. Eddie, Nila, and Luke would also be part of the team, which reassured her that she'd have people to talk with.

Unfortunately, her usual teammate, Matt, hadn't woken up yet, which was starting to worry her. According to Voggo, they had done what they could and healed what had broken. The rest was up to him.

With a deep breath, Dorea exited her home, taking care not to make too much noise. They needed to leave at first light since the trek would take hours, and they hadn't been given an exact time to be there at.

If all went well, they'd return the following day with a new alliance and more information about the northern tribes' movements.

By the time she got to the village's gates, dawn was starting to break. She greeted all her companions and went to the triage tent to receive the two potions that were part of everyone's kits nowadays.

Her mother was there, having taken up the night shifts to ensure Voggo could get some sleep, and proffered the brews with a warm smile.

"Good luck, darling."

"Thanks, we'll try to make this one quick. If everything goes well, I'll be back for dinner tomorrow."

Lilian patted her cheek before moving on to the others, giving everyone their own jar.

Soon enough, they were done with the preparations and left the village at a quick pace.

"We can't go to the lake directly, as the path would take us through Old Titan's territory, but if we move along its border, we shouldn't lose more than an hour," Mark called out from the front.

Dorea hummed in agreement, taking in the wonderful smells of the still-waking forest. She could feel birds start to wake up, chirping and fluttering about, and squirrels still in their dens, sleeping surrounded by nuts of all types.

This close to the village, there were no predators of any kind, and many smaller animals took refuge in that calm.

She stepped over the verdant grass, maneuvering around roots and stones with the grace of someone who had lived all their life there. Not only had she always been an adventurous girl, but her senses allowed much better balance than ever.

Indeed, even without knowing who was a mage and who wasn't, one could infer such by looking at them move. The scouts and hunters were obviously very practiced, but their smoothness came from observing their surroundings carefully. The mages never stumbled, even though their attention was focused elsewhere.

It was one of the many little privileges that came with passing the Trial.

The hours passed by quickly and undisturbed. The more dangerous animals had long since learned that picking a fight with such a large group was a foolish endeavor, and the ones strong enough to threaten them were too old to come out of their territories, which they avoided thanks to Mark's expertise.

Dorea felt several enhanced beasts along the path, but none got close enough to justify stopping the group to fight them.

It's unfortunate that I can't seem to fight anything other than humans these days. I really should do another trip in the woods by myself. Maybe that would help push me over with my newest spell.

Finally, after a short break for lunch, they arrived at Tumbling Lake. She felt it long before she saw it, with all the water rushing in its direction.

Four different streams converged into a dozen small waterfalls, creating a beautiful sight. The roar of the water wasn't too loud, and the lake itself was crystal clear.

She could sense hundreds of fish in it, ranging from schools of small red ones to giant catfish that scoured the depths for nutrients.

Her exploration of the lake's depths was cut short when the people they were there to see finally came into range.

"They're here," she called out.

Soon enough, a dozen leather-cloaked figures emerged from the woods. If she hadn't been able to feel them coming, Dorea would have been very surprised.

Indeed, they made no sound, nor did they disturb the plants, appearing as if they had always been there.

Very dramatic, nice.

"Welcome, neighbors, to the deeper forest," a tall man greeted, arms raised as if to hug them all.

He was wearing a peculiar headdress of deer antlers and colorful feathers, which told them he was likely a shaman.

Mark stepped up before their group and reciprocated. "Thank you, neighbor. In these difficult times, we should all help one another. After all, that is the Mother's creed, isn't it?"

He received a warm smile in exchange. Those had been the right words, as the atmosphere relaxed even further.

Now that they were coming closer, Dorea could make out the forest people's features better, and if one could get over the leather straps and cloaks, they looked just like normal Sapiens.

A bit paler, perhaps, but they wouldn't have looked out of place in their village.

It's so strange that we live relatively close to each other, and I've heard less about them than the Heidels, who are at least thrice as far.

Voggo had instructed them about their possible new allies and how they were gentle people who preferred to keep to themselves. However, it seemed like their self-imposed isolation was finally ending.

As the two men in the center talked and tested each other, Dorea focused her observations on the three figures that stayed in the back.

They were mages; that was a certainty given the weirdly dense air she felt surrounding them. It took her a few minutes to realize it was a variation of Melu's water armor, though more pliable.

It might have been in a passive mode since it didn't feel like it would protect them from much as it was, but the fact that all three could use it was a testament to their efforts.

The shaman was obviously a mage, though she couldn't tell if he was unaspected like Voggo or had a more esoteric element.

That's something to keep an eye on. He's shielding himself well, which tells me he's an old hand. Why would he do so if he never left this village so deep in the forest?

Putting her suspicions aside for the moment, Dorea refocused on the situation at hand.

"I'm sure you are all tired from the long trek through the woods; why don't you join us for a meal so that we can show you our goodwill?" The shaman gestured toward a set of logs that could serve as benches, and his people started to bring out baskets full of food.

The other thing Voggo had explained was that this tribe was known for its adherence to the Mother's teachings, and an offer of a meal was basically the equivalent of them assuring beyond doubt that there would be no backstabbing for the day.

After all, if you shared a meal with someone, they were your brother or sister for that day.

Or something like that. I can't really remember exactly, but it's a very good sign.

Mark discreetly signaled to go with it, and everyone moved to the logs even though they had eaten just a couple hours prior. It would have been terribly rude to refuse and might have caused the talks to break down.

Not that anyone complained. They had been marching through the forest since dawn, and one single meal wasn't enough to satiate any of them.

Dorea sat beside Eddie, who welcomed her with a smile and passed along a bowl of some kind of herby porridge. It had speckles of dried meat and smelled like a mixture of one of Voggo's potions and an actual meal.

Trying not to show her thoughts, Dorea dug in and was surprised at the taste. It was actually delicious, both in texture and flavor.

I wouldn't say it's up there with therium stew or Mom's best, but it's quite decent. If you could add some cheese to it, I bet it'd be even better.

Unfortunately, meddling with the meal she had been given as an offer of peace was a big no-no. She had a small packet of aged anoa cheese in her rucksack, which would have gone perfectly with the meal, but Dorea restrained herself.

Eddie had already finished his portion to her left and was attacking a second with gusto. She turned to regard him for a moment. "So, did you see Beth and Jonah?"

She kept her tone casual as if making light conversation.

He made a disgusted face. "Ugh, not when I'm eating, please. Those two are like limpets. Honestly, I think their faces might get stuck if they keep kissing that much."

That startled a laugh out of her. The image of her two best friends frantically trying to unstick their lips was just too funny.

"Maybe I'll have to prank them with that." She dried a tear of laughter that had escaped her eye.

Shaking her head at the silliness and now in a better mood, she took a moment to observe how the mission was going.

Mark sat next to the shaman, both speaking softly. It seemed that things were going quite well there for the time being.

The other forest people had mainly kept to themselves, but Dorea could see they were relaxed now that they all had a meal together.

She decided it would be a pity to just sit there chatting with Eddie when she could easily do so at home.

Picking one of the mages, who she could see had sat apart from the rest, Dorea walked over to make some connections.

CHAPTER TWENTY-SEVEN

The boy was quite a bit shorter than his companions, and sitting by himself, huddled in his ample cloak, he looked even smaller.

Dorea plopped down beside him, taking care to announce herself by making noise, crunching leaves and sticks beneath her feet.

"How are you doing? My name is Dorea; nice to meet you!"

He recoiled back, apparently too distracted to notice her approach.

"Wh-what? Huh?"

She waited patiently for him to recover, smiling sunnily in what she had been told was a disarming manner.

His cheeks pinkened once he focused on her, and he cleared his throat awkwardly. "Hello, I'm Jasper. What are you doing here?" he finished in a confused tone.

"Well, I was getting bored of waiting for those two"—she gestured toward the still busy leaders—"to finish speaking, and you seemed interesting enough."

The boy pushed his hood off, revealing messy brown hair that fell to his shoulders. He scratched his neck, not meeting her eyes. "What's interesting about me?" he muttered moodily.

Dorea was undaunted by his resistance. "Well, first of all, whatever you are doing to the air around you looks pretty neat."

That seemed to do the trick as some pride entered his eyes. "It's cool, isn't it? I'm the youngest to have managed a complete Zephyr Armor."

Dorea crinkled her eyes encouragingly. "That sounds hard; you must be pretty good, huh?"

He turned to face her better, the topic evidently being a favorite of his. "Man, was it hard to do. I can't give you the details. Obviously, it's a super secret spell from our ancestors. But I worked really, really hard to get it down, and I did it! And no one can take that away from me!"

He had gotten more heated as he spoke, but since that risked attracting attention from his companions, Dorea adopted a more soothing tone. "My village's shaman always says that magic and free will are the only two things no one can take from you. If you can cast a spell, it's yours forever."

Jasper nodded furiously in agreement, sending his messy hair flying all over. "That's right! I'm even working toward the Gale Arrows, and I bet I'll become a Journeyman before everyone else too."

It didn't take a genius to figure out that the boy was starving for positive attention. It made her feel a bit dirty, using such a weakness to extract information from him, but the current situation didn't allow for them to willfully blind themselves.

It's not like he's sharing anything we wouldn't discover with time, but it's better to know about their capabilities, so we can plan around them now, rather than later.

She kept chatting with Jasper, keeping an eye on the other tribesmen to see if any of them decided to intervene, but it seemed like they didn't think much of it.

Possibly, it was that the boy simply didn't know anything significant or that they believed her to be just an innocent girl making conversation.

Whatever it was, Dorea appreciated it. The juiciest find was that his tribe had had both air and water mages within the last three generations, and had recorded training methods and spells for posterity.

According to Jasper, most of the stuff wasn't useful since it detailed advanced spells that required much more power than any of them could produce, or exact manipulation, which was equally out of the question.

Still, the basics they could utilize allowed them to have a series of standardized spells they could work on.

It would be a great boon to Whitecliff if they could get their hands on that. It might even have been worth reconsidering their alliance if they hadn't had the Northmen breathing down their necks.

Satisfied with her results, Dorea moved the discussion away from possibly incriminating subjects and toward the boy's daily life.

"We don't really train together, but since the first attack, we have started sharing a duty to guard the borders. We don't want to lose more people to the damn clansmen," he growled.

The fact that they had been subject to an attack confirmed their original thoughts about the nature of the alliance. Had they been able to, the forest people would have much preferred maintaining their isolation, but the choice had been taken from them.

Suddenly much more interested in his words, Dorea was about to ask him to explain further when Mark's voice cut through the chatter. "All right, people, I want three of you for a little excursion with our new friends here. Dorea, Eddie, and Nila come over here!"

She stood up and smiled apologetically to her unwitting victim before joining the other two as they walked to their leader.

"I was talking with Chief Samos here, and he told me about a fascinating cave about an hour northeast from here. It apparently has drawings from the ancestors, which could be interesting to Voggo, so go there and try to imprint everything you see in your memory," Mark explained.

The tall shaman next to him inclined his head in greeting. "There is nothing dangerous on the way or even inside, but if you haven't walked through these parts, it's better to take a guide. Jasper, Leila, come here and guide our new friends to the Cave of the Ancestors!"

The boy she had been talking to scrambled to his feet and joined them hurriedly, while a tall woman with a dark ponytail peeled off her group more sedately.

"There isn't anything spectacular in there, but Mark was telling me that your shaman is a student of history, and that place definitely has a lot of it. It's just an hour's walk from here. Think of it as a token of our new friendship," he finished, smiling widely.

Mark nodded seriously. "Indeed, and by the time you are back, we should be done with the more practical talks regarding our alliance."

That was more than fine with Dorea. Sticking around for the talks as they first met the neighboring tribe and were unsure of the reception was one thing. Staying for the boring minutiae when it was understood that the alliance was all but formed was another.

If it meant that she could have an adventure and learn something interesting, well, she was all for it.

Jasper bounced up to her with a much friendlier disposition than he had had when she first approached him. On the other hand, his companion merely inclined her head in greeting, much more aloof.

They set off without fanfare, sedately following the two tribespeople further into the woods.

In only a few minutes, the waterfalls' sounds were gone entirely, the chirping of birds and rustling of the leaves their only companions.

Though Dorea and her two companions were used to moving through the forest, it was apparent to them that they were not on the same level as the ones who had spent their entire lives in it. Jasper and Leila glided between roots and rocks as if the impediments weren't there.

It wasn't the smooth walk of a mage who knew where an object was. This was closer to the old hunters' and scouts' experience but extended even further.

"The cave is something every tribesman has to go through by themselves when they reach adulthood, to see what life was like long before our time. I have already done so, of course," chattered Jasper.

That the boy had been allowed through a rite of passage early didn't particularly surprise Dorea. He was evidently precocious and likely one of their most talented mages.

If going through a cave was a cultural requirement to be considered an adult and thus be able to participate in the village's defense, then waiting for years until he reached a proper age made no sense.

"It's not really anything scary like they used to tell me; it's just a bunch of cave paintings and broken ruins, but it's pretty enough, I guess."

Leila's suppressed smile of mirth told her that the boy hadn't understood all the implications of this mysterious cave, or maybe she just found how he talked funny.

I need to stop getting ahead of myself. I'll know what's inside in a few minutes; there is no need to build my expectations up like this.

The forest was now much denser than she had ever seen, with creeper vines running from tree to tree. The light came in more sparsely, barely shining through the dark canopy.

The path had become less secure, almost overrun by moss and shrubbery in places, but never entirely gone.

This road was not often traveled but kept with just enough care not to allow it to be overrun.

Even Jasper's chatter had quieted, as if in respect of the sanctity of a place he didn't know the meaning of.

The atmosphere had become solemn without them noticing it. Even the birds fell silent as they arrived at the gaping mouth of a mossy cave.

Without prompt, Dorea held up a hand and gathered a spark of electricity, twisting it into a softly shining sphere.

Although an air mage's senses were enough to navigate the cavern even in the dark, only she and Jasper had that ability. Going by his embarrassed expression, he had forgotten about that little detail.

Dorea extended her range into the dark and was surprised to find it much more extensive than expected. The cave ran deep into the ground, and though the incline wasn't particularly steep, they would be under several hundred feet of dirt by the time they got to the end.

Stepping inside, they found the walls covered in soft moss and lichens, with the occasional bug skittering around. On the other hand, the floor was unnaturally smooth, confirming her suspicion that the cave wasn't entirely natural.

It was impossible to know if it had already been present and a mage had changed it to their preference or if it had been made wholesale.

"Wow, is this natural?" Or she could always just ask like Eddie had just done.

"It's not. As far as we know, the original cave was only a couple hundred feet long. You'll be able to see the change once we get farther in, but it runs at least a mile more, and it's definitely artificial," replied Leila.

The woman had been quiet so far, but evidently she was chosen to guide them for a reason.

"Our ancestors built it many generations ago; some say as much as twenty, while others think only five or six. It is an ongoing debate, but the fact is that it is old," she explained further.

Indeed, after a few minutes of walking, they passed through what had to be the original end of the cave, and all the walls took that unnaturally smooth appearance that the floor had.

"Were they earth mages, then?" Dorea asked Jasper, who was walking next to her.

The boy rushed to answer her, more than happy to prove himself helpful, "They had to have at least a few earth mages, but more than that, they had to be Master-level ones. Working in concert, all of them must have been incredibly powerful."

Considering how her village had, as far as she was aware, only produced one such Gifted in the last generation, her grandmother, it sounded a bit improbable to have multiple Masters at the same time. Still, she didn't bother voicing her skepticism.

"We think this was originally meant to be a temple to Mother Nature, but it evolved into a place of learning and was used extensively for many years," Leila continued.

"Of course, we don't have any earth mages anymore, so if there are any secrets hidden there, we'll never find them. It's a bit of a pity that this Trial didn't awaken any as well, but at least it gave us a decent spread of elements."

Finally, they entered the large room she had been feeling for a while, and Dorea had to increase the luminescence of her magic to fully appreciate its size.

The cavern opened up enormously, the ceiling being a good two hundred feet high, and was at least half a mile deep. Inside, carved into the stone, was a temple. It was taller than her village's walls and looked just as sturdy.

Two columns held up the facade, though Dorea didn't doubt it could have stayed up by itself if it was genuinely made by a Master.

As they got closer, she could make out intricate designs all over the stone pillars, depicting fractal shapes that felt both alien and familiar at the same time.

"This is definitely not just cave paintings, that's for sure," she commented, startling a laugh from her companions.

She stopped for a moment to take it all in. This was by far the most beautiful building she had ever seen. The houses her grandmother's generation had built were austere and functional. Although they had their charm, this was in an entirely different league.

Here, a Master had taken the time, possibly a long time, to carve intricate fractals and nature scenes with vegetation and all kinds of animals.

Her air sense gave her a more in-depth knowledge of the reliefs, telling her how it was all at the same specific depth without any error.

This is beyond the realm of what an average human can do. Only by wielding the power gifted to us by the Mother can we reach such heights.

Even though she wasn't one to lose herself in religious fervor, Dorea felt something like it swelling in her chest.

Finally, they entered the temple. Inside was a ten-foot-tall statue of the Goddess, easily recognizable by the flora that served as her clothing and a cowl made of stitched holly leaves.

She held her palms in front of her, cradling a pine cone. There was an indescribable emotion etched on her face, seeming to shift from sorrow to a welcoming smile depending on where Dorea looked at it from.

"Whoever made this, they were a genius. Not only a powerful mage but an actual artistic genius," Nila murmured.

Dorea shared the sentiment. When she looked at the statue, it felt like it was about to come alive. It was only thanks to her senses that insisted it was a cold stone that she felt sure it wasn't about to move.

Behind it was a complex tapestry of paintings on the wall, each describing different moments of the tribesmen's life, from their birth to their death.

Hunting scenes were present several times, and a few figures that could recognizably use magic were there too.

No explanation was offered, but none was needed. This was a temple of Nature, of the cycle of life and death. All things had a beginning and an end, glorious or miserable; all were birthed from the Mother, and all would return to her to nourish the future generations.

On the opposite wall, above the entrance, was a different painting.

Colorful spheres orbited around a brilliant, much larger one. Small, ungainly rocks traveled through the empty spaces between the spheres, filling the scene with reflected light.

"What does this mean?" Dorea asked curiously.

She didn't expect a dramatic slumping of her guides' shoulders. "No one really knows. Some think it might be the elements moving around the Goddess, but not many agree. It's a mystery, and we have found no explanation."

Not knowing seemed to grate on Jasper as he glared at the painting. "Everyone understands the cycle of life, but here they could have added a tagline!"

Dorea snorted in amusement. Though it was a fascinating piece of art, she doubted they would ever know its true meaning if even its makers' descendants didn't know. Still, she would report to Voggo. He'd be interested, she knew.

They spent at least another hour exploring the temple and its surroundings, fascinated by all the carvings they kept finding in the dark cavern.

A suspicion formed in her mind, fomented by her failure to find any critter or animal residing in the cavern.

There is something at work here, keeping the wildlife away. The entrance was perfectly normal, with insects everywhere, but here there is nothing.

It was even stranger when one considered who this temple was in honor of. The Goddess certainly wouldn't mind being surrounded by her bounty.

The more she stayed in the cave, the more Dorea was weirded out by its sterility.

It's certainly a peculiar way of worshipping the Mother . . .

The fractals, or at least some of them, had to be the anchor for a ward of some kind, though it was far too advanced for her to sense.

Considering it likely was earth-magic-based, she was simply out of her depths. Still, she impressed in her mind as many patterns as possible and subtly gestured for her two companions to do the same.

Soon enough, it was time to head back. The talks were likely in the final stretch if they hadn't already ended, and a feast would likely follow.

Dorea doubted they'd get invited to their ally's village, but more people were surely coming, and she'd be interested in studying them further.

The trek back was done mostly in silence, everyone busy digesting what they had witnessed in the cave.

No matter its weird absence of life, the temple was still majestic and would forever be etched in their minds.

Soon enough, the waterfalls' sounds started filtering in, and they stepped out of the dense woods and onto the lake's shores, where their people had made camp.

The atmosphere was relaxed, and people had finally started chatting among tribes.

They were noticed by Mark, who waved them closer. Dorea turned to her two guides and thanked them sincerely. "This was a wonderful experience. I'll forever treasure it. Thank you, from the bottom of my heart."

Her sentiment was echoed by her two companions. Always the aloof woman, Leila waved them off while Jasper blushed deeply and muttered a quiet "Don't worry about it."

CHAPTER TWENTY-EIGHT

The evening feast had been more or less what Dorea had expected. About a dozen more forest people had joined them, bringing food and mead.

The atmosphere had been merry, though never completely relaxed. It wasn't that they didn't trust each other so much as that it wasn't good practice to let your guard down so far from home.

Also, they had finally learned the reason behind the entire diplomatic effort. Their new allies had been suffering from smaller but more common raids against their foraging parties.

Several people had been taken away, likely never to be seen again. More than that, their ability to gather food was severely hampered by the constant harassment.

They had obviously beefed up the parties with mages and hunters, but considering the frequency with which they had to exit the village's safety, they were leaving themselves open to trouble at home.

It wasn't a tenable situation, which meant either going on the offensive—a daunting prospect—or gathering more allies.

The second being much easier to accomplish than the first, especially considering the already existing relationship between the two possible neighbors, Whitecliff and the Heidels, the choice was easier than expected.

Of course, that didn't mean they could expect to simply join in after having rebuffed any kind of contact for decades, but with a bit of generosity, they could expect to grease the wheels.

This had all been revealed to Dorea by Mark, the expedition leader who tried to keep her appraised of the most important happenings.

While she had no official role, Dorea was still invited to the council meetings and was considered Voggo's favorite in the new generation.

That, by itself, brought her a lot of power and influence.

Still contemplative from the almost mystical experience in the cave, Dorea hadn't paid as much attention to the man as she probably should have, but luckily nothing that required her touch had come up.

The party ended relatively soon, as they would need to leave early in the morning if they wanted to be back before the afternoon, and so with less pomp than one might expect in such an occasion, they all said their goodbyes to their new allies and went to sleep.

Guard rotation had been set up the previous day, and it continued without any modification apart from substituting one hunter who got too tipsy to stay awake reliably.

The man, Jon, would be severely scolded once they had returned to the village, but for the moment, no one wanted to end the day on a sour note.

The night went by without trouble, and morning arrived soon enough.

Still sleepily rubbing her eyes, Dorea broke up her camp. The rollable sleeping mat went back into her rucksack, and she made sure to erase the traces of her presence with some magic.

Though not strictly necessary in this case, they had been taught to always do so, and she had developed a habit.

Samos, the forest shaman, and a few others saw them off. A separate group would shadow them until they reached their territory, as they began participating in the joint patrols.

It made less sense for the forest tribe to send people to live with them since they were much closer than the Heidels, but they had set up overlapping patrols in the northern quadrant of the forest with dedicated meeting spots where they could share info or call for help.

It wasn't yet the full alliance they had with their southern neighbors, but it would help them fend off further incursion much more easily.

Soon they left the lake behind and began marching back home. The air was much more relaxed now that they had been successful in their mission.

The eastern border had been secured against possible attacks, and they had expanded their burgeoning alliance against the northern clans.

Whoever the new bellicose chief was, he'd find a much more difficult enemy in the south than he would expect.

They honestly didn't seem like mighty warriors, but having them on our side is much better than not. This was still useful, since we can count on them to alert us should anyone try to flank us from the east.

Shortly after, they left the forest tribe's territory, saying goodbye to their escorts, and entered much more familiar woods.

Minutes later, a cry cut through her pondering, returning her back to the present. Extending her senses in its direction as far as she could, Dorea found what seemed to her like the wreckage of a cart and at least two people surrounding it, though it was too far to tell.

Everyone switched immediately to high alert, and she reported what she had found.

They split into three groups, each approaching from a different side to avoid getting caught in an ambush.

After quickly running to where they could still hear the desperate voice, they found a worrying scene.

Three carts had been abandoned on the side of the path, each sporting significant damage, while two were still intact enough.

Several people were trying desperately to lift one of the good ones out of a muddy patch while a young woman cried her heart out over the cooling corpse of an elderly man.

They were immediately noticed, and given their fearful, desperate expressions, these people thought they would only increase their suffering.

"We aren't here with any ill intent. You are passing through our tribe's territory, and we noticed you as we patrolled. Can you tell us what happened while we help your wounded?" Immediately Mark tried to defuse the situation.

Dorea could feel only two Gifted amongst them, the crying girl and another one lying in one of the carts and holding his own blood inside his body with magic.

His words were met with skepticism and a desperate hope for their troubles to finally end.

Once the two other groups emerged from the woods, signaling that no one was lying in wait, nor did there seem to be anybody in pursuit, they slumped in defeat.

"Do what you will; we can't stop you either way," a middle-aged man holding a wounded arm close to his chest called out.

"Have you been attacked by the northern clans?" Dorea asked.

The man spat on the ground in disgust. "People with whom we have traded for centuries turned on us when we refused to submit to them. And when we packed up to leave, they harassed us, kidnapped our women and children, and did their absolute best to drive us to ruin!"

That lined up well enough with what they could see. These people might be trying to deceive them, but the whole charade, with the dying and wounded who did not appear to be under duress to keep their mouths shut, seemed too much.

Dorea walked to the poor water mage she could feel desperately trying to avoid bleeding to death and quickly applied some of her mother's poultices on his wounds, removing clean bandages from her bag, and after receiving a desperate go-ahead, she used them to shut the blood flow.

Once she was sure he wouldn't bleed out, she gave him a potion to drink to replenish his strength after losing so much blood.

Now that I look at him closer, he can't be much older than me. He's just very dirty and very pale. He looks like a ghost.

Now out of immediate risk of dying, the boy did his best to make himself presentable, weakly forming a sphere of water and using it to clean up.

"Thank you. I'm not sure I could have lasted much longer," he said with heartfelt gratitude.

He had deep green eyes and a rather pretty freckled face, but he still looked weak and sickly, taking away from his charm.

"Don't worry about it. We know very well how brutal those barbarians can be, and helping you didn't cost us much. I'm Dorea; what's your name?"

He gave out a startled laugh, only then realizing that they hadn't even greeted each other or said their names in the haste to save his life.

"I'm sorry, I'm Nettle."

She gave a warm smile, trying to set him at ease. Around them, similar scenes played out. The wounded were cared for thanks to their potions, and the dead were cleaned up and appropriately buried.

The crying girl who had alerted them had tired herself out and was now resting on the one free cart guarded by a haggard but severe old woman.

Done with her rescue and seeing that her companions had it all well in hand, Dorea extracted the water from the mud keeping the cart trapped and used it to slowly push it out of the ground.

It was heavier than she had expected, but thanks to the boost in power she had experienced, she could lift it without much trouble.

Done with that, she approached the dark-haired man who had answered her earlier question and decided to learn more about what had happened.

"Do you mind if I sit here?" she asked, smiling kindly at him.

He looked tiredly at her but gestured toward the open space beside him.

"Do you need medical attention?"

"No, kid, I'm fine. The others need help more than me," he huffed back.

Undeterred, Dorea channeled her mother at her strictest. "Sir, I can see the blood caked on your arm. My companions are caring for your people; please let me help you."

He grumbled some more but finally consented to be helped, seeing how she remained undeterred.

"My name is Dorea, and my mother is a healer; you can be sure I know what I'm doing."

After a moment of silence, he looked into her eyes and nodded in greeting. "Mav."

Luckily, his wounds were more painful than dangerous. He had several long cuts on his right arm, which looked to have been made purposefully to inflict as much pain as possible.

She pursed her lips at the sight but didn't comment, simply getting to work.

The man hissed in pain several times as she applied the salve but stayed remarkably still.

Once she was done with her task, she decided to ask some of the questions that had been burning at her.

"Can you tell me what exactly happened? Beyond your earlier summary, this seems too cruel, even for those barbarians."

He regarded her silently for a moment before sighing. "It's because we defied them. We have always been somewhat under their yoke, depending on them to hunt meat and paying for their protection for decades."

He cleared his throat and swung out of his almost empty flask. Dorea refilled it silently, to his shock, but after a moment, he inclined his head in thanks.

"Our village sits in the next valley to the Mondeans—"

"Sorry, Mondeans?"

"Yeah, it's what they call themselves. It comes from the peak they sit at the base of, Mount Mondeo. You can't see it from here, but it's the highest peak in the range."

"Sorry, go on. I didn't mean to interrupt you," she apologized.

"Don't worry. Now, the Mondeans are warlike, but their old chief had always managed to strike a balance between their more dangerous impulses and suppressing them too much. Sometimes, they would hunt in our lands, and there wasn't much we could do about it. At other times, they'd demand a tithe outside the agreed upon ones, but we couldn't do anything about it either."

He was getting more heated as he spoke, evidently bearing a deep grudge for how his people were treated.

"But there was a limit to what they would do to us. Our women were out of bounds. Our food stores weren't to be touched. They harassed many other tribes, but we were left alone as long as we paid our dues."

The thought of being subjected to another tribe's whims for so long left a bitter taste on her tongue, but Dorea could recognize that if the balance of power was too tilted in one direction, there wasn't much they could do.

"That changed after the Wrath passed. The chieftain's son gained terrible, terrible powers and used them to usurp control of the tribe. A few of his father's lieutenants attempted to stop him, but his strength was too great. Many of the younger warriors flocked to his banner, and with the mages' loyalty, there wasn't anything the rest could do." His eyes took a faraway look as he spoke.

"He killed his own father during a hunt. No one knows for sure, but it's almost certain. He didn't seem too broken up about his old man's death. After that, he immediately took control of the tribe and started attacking those that had long refused to pay their tithes."

That lines up with what we were told by the caravan's leader. A young and ambitious but powerful chief alongside a bloodthirsty tribe of warriors is a terrible mix, especially when you add magic.

"It obviously didn't stop there," Dorea commented, getting a huff of laughter from the man.

"No, it did not. He enslaved and subjugated all their old enemies in just a few weeks. Then, they turned to us. First, by increasing their demands. Then, when we couldn't match them anymore, by simply taking people away to make up the difference." He had a sorrowful look as he explained the depredations his people had suffered.

"And then it was too much for you to bear any longer," she finished for him, seeing how hard it was to go on.

"Yes, we couldn't stay. We packed what we could and left in the night." He shook his head ruefully. "In hindsight, we should have known they wouldn't let us go. They didn't care enough to send a proper fighting force, but enough of them came after us to be able to kill several people as a parting gift."

The scene they came to was explanation enough for the rest. If the Mondeans truly had dreams of conquering the whole region, behaving cruelly and making enemies everywhere would only make the resistance fiercer.

Of course, they might not care about it if they are that powerful.

"How many mages do they have?" was the pressing question that kept her awake at night.

If the enemy had only slightly larger numbers than their own, they had already demonstrated superior quality. Especially after they allied with the Heidels and the forest tribe, it wouldn't be such a worrying prospect.

On the other hand, if they had many more mages and warriors, the situation could already be lost.

"I don't know exactly, especially because they conscript more and more with every passing week as they go through the villages, but at this point, I'd expect at least two hundred, if not more."

Damnit! This is bad, really bad. Even being optimistic and counting everyone who can use magic, we only have seventy or so if we put the three villages together. This is not a gap we can fill with simple preparation.

The forest people might have a bit more in reserve than they had disclosed during their talks, but they weren't warlike people, and even though they had their ancestors' lessons, they hadn't seemed keen on aggressively applying them.

"And you say that they keep adding more to their numbers? How can they do so without the new mages mutinying?"

The man shrugged. "I don't know. Their chief is terrifying, which I think is more than enough, but who knows if they can use some weird magic to force people. I wouldn't put it past them."

Evidently, she had reached the end of his knowledge. He'd be questioned further once they were back home since they needed to know what kind of threat they were dealing with, and verifying his words was now a priority.

Still, he had been very useful, and Dorea counted it as a net gain, even considering the potions they had to use to save the wounded.

"Of course, they can't really bring all their people to one place since they made so many enemies. If they left their valley unprotected, many would attempt to take it," he added as an afterthought.

Dorea jumped on it, suddenly revitalized. "Who are these other enemies?"

He smiled slyly, obviously having expected her to want to know. "Can you guarantee aid and shelter for me and my people?"

Oh, you son of a . . . All right, if you want to negotiate, we'll negotiate.

"We have come to your aid without anything to gain, didn't we? Your people will be treated well, whether they want to leave after you have recovered or you want to remain in our village's safety. Of course, the more you contribute, the better we will be disposed toward you."

This kind of bartering with human lives left a bitter taste on her tongue, but if it was what it took to receive precious information, she'd do it. Voggo would uphold her words' worth.

"Can you really promise such things?"

His skepticism was warranted but still hurt. After her tending to him, being treated like that was a low blow.

"I can; I assure you of that."

Mav opened his mouth to retort but was interrupted by a slap on the back of his head by the old woman she had previously seen by the crying girl. "Leave the lass alone, you old coot! She has saved Nettle from certain death and even helped you! Treat her better, or we'll see if I can't still tan your hide."

She left immediately after, leaving them flabbergasted. The man shook his head ruefully before bowing in apology. "That blasted crone is right; you've been nothing but good to us. I'll tell you everything I know."

CHAPTER TWENTY-NINE

Their talk ended up being put on hold, as all the wounded had been stabilized enough to move, and the dead had been buried to become one with Mother Nature.

No one seemed to be pursuing the poor people, but Mark had decided not to wait too long and tempt fate.

Having to fight the Mondeans while protecting their new charges was a nightmare they wanted to avoid if possible; therefore, they quickly packed everyone up in the two usable carts and decided to abandon the damaged ones for the time being.

If no further attack came, they'd send a squad to pick them up, but for the moment, no one wanted to risk their lives for junk.

They marched back with all due haste, maintaining two separate groups that served as an early warning in case anyone or, just as likely, anything got too close.

Dorea led the northern flank, having by then the most experience in combat of any mage.

It's crazy to think that so many people are depending on me. That I have a duty to kill anyone who approaches with bad intentions. And that I'm already used to it.

Every once in a while, such thoughts shook her up, but she had long learned not to allow them to run free. The time for contemplation was once they returned to the village and she reported to Voggo all that she had learned.

So much has happened in just a day. Sometimes weeks go by with nothing interesting happening, and at other times everything happens simultaneously.

Luckily, they were able to reach the village gates undisturbed. A team had met them shortly before they came in sight of the walls, thanks to their system of mana signals.

While the meanings they could send across were limited, it was still much better than just showing up, bringing wounded that needed urgent care to unprepared people.

The triage tent had been in the process of being expanded and would likely need to become a permanent building if things kept going the way Dorea suspected they would.

"Anything that needs my immediate attention?" swiftly asked Voggo, who came out of the tent to start processing the wounded.

"Nothing urgent, but we got a lot of interesting information about our enemies. I'll be hanging around once you are done to give a proper report," she replied, even as he started to walk off.

Dorea didn't take it to heart. The old man had made it a mission in life to save as many as possible, and while this conflict would likely bring death and destruction to their village, she knew he'd try his very best to prevent as much of it as possible, in the best way he could.

It was unfortunate that he was both too old to take part in the patrols and that his specialization didn't allow for much effectiveness in direct combat, because his mind was sharper than any blade, and she knew he'd be a right terror.

Dorea was looked over by her mother, who had come bustling out of the tent to help with the wounded, and received a quick kiss on the forehead once Lilian had ensured she was whole.

Knowing it would take a while before she could give her report, the girl jumped on top of the wall, aided by solid air platforms she had been working on in her spare time, and decided to help guard the village.

To pass the time, she tried out her Exploding Water Bullet against much smaller targets than usual, attempting to improve her accuracy and clear the last hurdle before it became a proper spell.

Extending her senses to their fullest potential, Dorea attempted to snipe any dangerous insects and wildlife that dared get close.

After a full hour, she had tallied up seven cockroaches, four spiders, and one rabid skunk.

Not all her shots got close to their target, but she had become slightly better after the practice. By the second hour, hitting her chosen victims only took four attempts.

It was, she found, also a very good anti-stress method, because her anxiety about the coming confrontation with the Mondeans had softened after her inflicting so much destruction on the forests' ugliest inhabitants.

Of course, that kind of exercise wasn't very useful in an actual battle since the chaos of it required an almost all-out approach, and the targets were much larger there. Still, Dorea felt that she shouldn't develop her magic with the sole objective of being more efficient at killing humans.

No matter how much she needed to hurt and kill other people to ensure Whitecliff's safety, she wouldn't let it swallow her.

Magic was a gift from the Goddess, and using it only for war felt like heresy. It'd be like saying that Mother Nature only presided over death and not life.

Finally, she was alerted by a runner that Voggo had finished doing what he could and was ready to see her. She gave one last parting shot to a particularly lucky arachnid and hopped down the wall, aiding herself with another air platform.

These things are handy. I need to get better at making them stable, because the slightest shift in the winds risks making me fly, but if I manage, I'll be much more mobile.

The old man waited for her at the tent's entrance, and as soon as he saw her arrive, he started walking toward his own abode, gesturing for her to follow.

He was evidently tired from the days of hard work, but his eyes were clear, and his back was straight.

As soon as they got in the house, he started putting together a meal for them both, not even questioning whether she had taken the time to eat.

Admittedly, she hadn't. She had been too engrossed with tormenting the forest's critters to think about eating, especially since she had still been too keyed up to stomach anything.

A plate full of warm bread, eggs, and cheese was placed in front of her, and Dorea decided she was hungry. The pungent cheese wasn't her favorite, but Voggo loved it, and she supposed its creamy texture was good enough.

They ate in silence, both desperately needing the energy. Once they were done, the old man sat back in his chair with a sigh, patting his belly.

"What a mess, huh? And it's only going to get worse as more and more people flee from their depredations."

She took that as a cue to give her report. Although Mark had surely filled him in on all the essential bits, she still had things to add, especially because she was the one to visit the temple and speak with Mav personally.

Thus, she explained what she had found, going in-depth about her worries over the Mondeans' overly aggressive behavior and her experience in the cave.

Voggo hummed in thought as he listened, smoothing his beard. He let her speak without interrupting, though she could see he had questions.

"As far as what this Mav told you goes, we can only trust it once we have verified it. It might explain some things, but I'm wary of any story where a clearly evil group behaves irrationally. Though we may never know it, there is likely an actual explanation behind the Mondeans' behavior," he finally commented.

That both made sense to her and didn't, because the man had felt a genuine rage when speaking about the abuse they went through, and she had seen the damage with her own eyes, but she supposed his perspective might have been colored by his personal experience.

"That's not to say that people cannot behave evilly. The Goddess knows I have seen too much of it in my life, but large groups generally have motivations or, at the very least, justifications they tell themselves. No one is the bad guy in their own mind, after all."

That struck a chord within her. No matter how badly one's behavior reflected on them, people generally didn't consider themselves evil.

"As far as the cave goes, I had heard that they had a temple of some kind, possibly even more than one, since their people have been in the forest for centuries, but it's certainly not what I was expecting."

I don't think anyone could expect that, honestly. If I hadn't seen it with my own eyes, I would be hard-pressed to believe such a thing exists in the middle of the forest.

"If we have the time, I'd like to see it myself. For the moment, I'll look through our records to see if anything references it," he said.

Soon after that, she left. She was too strung up to sleep and honestly didn't feel like being subjected to Beth and Jonah's mushy sweet behavior.

Not that I have anything against it. It would be nice to spend some time like we used to, though. I hope it's just a phase . . .

The only thing that remained was to see if her father needed any help at the ranch, although she doubted it.

He had found two men from the first refugee group with experience in animal husbandry and hired them to help.

That it would ensure the ranch always had someone present to sound the alarm were anything to get in from the northern wall was just an additional benefit.

Of course, patrols at the northern border had been increased the most, especially after the alliance with the forest people had secured their eastern one. Still, no one wanted to take chances after the scare they had during the first attack.

As she had expected, Dorea found her father directing one of his new hires, Monty, as they finished the repairs to the barn.

It had taken quite a bit longer than they had expected, because the influx of people needing housing had taken precedence for the village's skilled construction workers. So they ended up doing it mostly by themselves.

Dorea had helped when she had the time, especially by using her magic to lift heavy things or keep stuff affixed to a spot as Dodro hammered it.

Finally, two months after the Wrath had passed, they had rebuilt the ranch completely.

Without magic of any kind, which meant no speeding up the logging and processing of wood or helping in the construction, it would have taken them much longer, but it still felt like a lot for such a simple thing.

Unfortunately, my magic is not very good at building things. If you want to destroy something, though, I'm your gal.

She was waved off by her father, who told her not to worry about the animals as the other laborer was caring for them.

Thus, Dorea found herself with some free time to dedicate to training. Not the slow and steady kind she had been doing before her talk with Voggo, where she experimented with various mana patterns in the hopes of finding a stable one or where she perfected a specific skill.

No, the kind of training she had in mind involved much more explosive growth.

Out of habit, she swept the ranch with her senses and found nothing out of place, beyond her sister's attempt at getting to the honey jar that had been strategically placed too high for her to reach.

With a chuckle, she set off toward the forest she had gotten out of in such a hurry just a few hours before.

Dorea considered her options and decided to head toward the northeastern sector, where fewer patrols went through, in the hopes of finding some enhanced beast that wanted to try its luck.

That she might be able to wash herself in a stream was also a good incentive. She had taken care of the bloodstains and dirt with a simple usage of water manipulation, but nothing could really beat dunking yourself in a clean river.

Thanks to the increasingly helpful air platforms, she hopped over the wall and set off into the woods.

With her senses fully extended, finding a possible target didn't take long.

A large brown boar snuffled at the base of a fallen tree looking for tasty treats, its tusks occasionally sparking with leftover lightning.

Dorea observed it from a safe distance and carefully examined the broken trunk beside it, trying to divine exactly how it had been felled.

The base was obviously broken by a powerful impact, its smoldering center telling her everything she needed to know.

A lightning beast that fought at close range wasn't something she had personally fought before, but she would gladly take it instead of a long-range slugfest.

Her most powerful attack was out, as while Lightning Sphere should be more than strong enough to deal with it had it been of any other element, she didn't want to lose the surprise effect with an ineffective move.

It wasn't that beings that used a specific element were immune to it, so much as they could shield themselves more efficiently against it and, if the difference in power and skill was enough, even take control of it.

She wasn't worried about the boar usurping her spell, but it felt like a waste to bombard it with it several times, when using a different element would do the job much more quickly.

Therefore, she decided to use her work-in-progress water spell, albeit in a slightly different manner.

Her previous practice had given her an idea of how it could be made into a fully functioning one. She had started with her Lightning Sphere as its basis, knowing that working on an entirely new matrix would require much more time, but had soon veered off its course by splitting it into several bullets.

That had likely been her mistake. She had tried to do too much all at once.

In front of her, a singular watery ball formed before shrinking in size as she applied more and more pressure. It churned and twisted dangerously in her ethereal grip, but she didn't let it worry her.

Instead, she carefully examined the boar's signature and aligned the shot.

Once the sphere was twisting so fast to almost seem still, something finally clicked in her mind, and she let it go with a whoop of joy.

The bullet shot forth with incredible strength, burrowing through a tree trunk and not slowing in the slightest.

It hit the boar before it even knew of its danger, exploding on impact with such force to pulp its head entirely.

The rush of power she felt was an almost unnecessary confirmation of what she had seen with her own eyes. Her new spell, Exploding Water Bullet, had done its job perfectly well.

She approached the carcass and decided that, if she had the time, she'd bring it back home to process it since most of its meat looked to still be edible.

She levitated it thanks to an air platform and left it high in the canopy, where unless a bird of prey swooped from the skies, it would be left alone.

I wasted a lot of time hoping it would solve itself while making it more difficult for it to happen.

Though she blamed herself, Dorea was riding high on her success. She now had two spells in her repertoire, and though she couldn't call herself a Journeyman mage yet, as they were simply too similar to demonstrate the needed competence, she felt much closer to that goal than she had been.

This was, she felt, a lesson she would treasure going forward. She wasn't a genius who could understand the weavings of mana at a glance, nor was she blessed with incredible power from the get-go, but she had tenacity in spades and a possibly eldritch constitution.

All my future spells that branch from an existing one will need to maintain their original purpose. Otherwise, I might as well just start a new one from scratch.

The cost of her Bullet had decreased significantly thanks to it being completed, and the damage was increased by an order of magnitude.

Just a few days prior, she had used it in its unfinished state against the

Mondean team they had battled with, and though she had done great damage, the most she had gotten was broken bones and a couple of severed limbs.

Now, she could kill a man with a shot as surely as the sun rising.

Dorea looked up at the sun to find it still high in the afternoon sky and decided to keep hunting until dinnertime.

She set off to find a new target with her reserves refilled by the successful kill.

That day, the cries of dying beasts were heard all over the northeastern forest. So much so that she had to explain to a passing patrol that she wasn't just hunting for sport or to relieve stress but as a training exercise to test her spells.

They looked at her weirdly, but Dorea didn't care to explain herself further.

She had Voggo's blessing, which was enough for everyone to overlook any eccentric behavior.

CHAPTER THIRTY

Deep within the Loisosian Forest, a power struggle had been going on for more than two months.

Every morning, beasts of all shapes and sizes woke up knowing that that day could be their last, just like it could be their most triumphant.

Nature's Wrath had brought significant change to the ecosystem, though it would be hard to know if one simply observed from a distance.

Small creatures that hadn't dared raise their heads for fear of predators now strutted around as if they owned the place, confident in their newfound powers.

Great packs had been reduced to few separate survivors in the wake of leadership struggles, their territories much reduced.

Only a few places remained unchanged, where old monsters of an age past slumbered, content in their absolute superiority.

A few contenders had tried their luck, drunk on the power they had received, but none had posed a challenge.

This relative calm within the storm wasn't likely to last forever, as the meat grinder the forest had become forged stronger and stronger creatures, but for the moment, it held.

Outside of that oasis, the battle raged on.

In the last week, a new challenger had appeared, emerging from the human settlement that had, for the moment, simply been observing the ongoing change.

She was deceptively innocuous looking, a blond waif not even at the cusp of adulthood.

Many beasts had underestimated her and therefore paid the ultimate price. Even those with a modicum of intelligence had been surprised at the sheer level of violence she could unleash on command.

The girl had gone through several upcoming contenders to the territory close to the village and had slowly started to move deeper into the forest, looking for more opponents to throw herself against.

While aggressive behavior wasn't outside the norm in the forest, this kind of single-minded efficiency in the slaughter was not.

Hunters and at times scouts took out the more dangerous beasts that got close to the walls, or went out looking for some to replenish the food stocks, while animals killed mostly to eat.

The magical powers they had gained after the storm had made it much more common to attack one another to prove themselves or to expand one's territory, but she had deliberately looked for powerful opponents just to kill them.

That she took back most of the carcasses after she was done with her slaughter was the only thing that prevented her from being sacrilegious.

Still, the girl had been smart enough to avoid those places where creatures far beyond her resided, having been warned by the signs left on trees and the ground.

Her path of destruction had taken her much farther than patrols usually went and left her without easy-to-reach backup.

This would have customarily spelled her doom, as she faced more dangerous opponents while tired and far from home, but the girl had, somehow, never run out of strength.

Indeed, she seemed to be getting more and more powerful as the days passed.

The level she needed to be at to dare threaten the old monsters was still very far, but the rate at which she grew was unnatural.

That day, Dorea faced an unorthodox alliance of solitary smilodons, who had evidently decided to put their internal struggles on hold for the time being and deal with her.

She had been chipping at them for a while, always facing the beasts when they isolated themselves.

It seems like they have something beyond their usual low cunning. This level of coordination is definitely different from their normal behavior.

Although she had walked into some sort of trap, as she had been stalking a water-wielding female only to feel four more beasts close in on her position, Dorea didn't feel particularly panicked.

These animals were all relatively young, they had to be to have received their powers, and none looked to be the leader who had planned the confrontation.

No, it was more likely to have been an older, wiser smilodon who was either too weak to face her or too powerful to bother.

The likelier of the two was the second since she had never heard of an animal gaining that sort of intelligence without a great deal of magical power.

The fact that it wasn't there to crush her itself meant that this was likely a test for the young beasts there with her. To see if they were capable enough to join its pack or something like that.

Well, divining its intentions isn't particularly important at the moment. I need to figure out how to get out of this sticky situation first, then I'll have all the time necessary to understand the feline mind.

The idea of using her air platforms to simply leave, hopping in the sky, had popped up in her mind but she dismissed it as the first and only time she attempted such a thing, she had been sniped by a particularly ornery beaver whose water manipulation far exceeded hers.

She had been lucky it remained in the river and had managed to fry it as she fell. Otherwise, it could have been dangerous.

The next option was to punch through the encirclement, as she was pretty sure of her individual superiority to any one of her enemies.

It was a decent plan that would ensure her survival, so she shelved it for if the situation got desperate enough.

The last one, and her favorite, was to turn this little game of theirs on its head.

Although she generally used her hunts as occasions to test new ideas, that didn't mean she couldn't reuse old ones.

Indeed, some had simply been too successful for her tastes, and she had stopped using them since they would prevent her from getting any experience beyond the increase in reserves.

They were quite helpful in such moments, though, so Dorea started preparing her own little gift.

She kept a wary eye on the approaching smilodons, but it seemed like they were in no hurry, which was just fine with her.

The beasts took a sadistic enjoyment in their pace, as they slowly prowled through the forest toward her position without any attempt at hiding, even though she could obviously feel them coming.

Unfortunately, she couldn't repeat her victory over the first group of Mondeans who had attempted to attack the village, since the weather was too nice to create that much natural lightning.

On the other hand, she was quite a bit more powerful than she had been then, and she needed much less help from the environment.

Were she in an open space like the northern hills, her options would have been much more limited, but in the forest and at such distances, where the only way to tell something's position was to trust your senses, she could do much more.

Her main advantage in an otherwise dangerous situation was that enhanced beasts, especially juvenile ones, were more limited than humans in their magical repertoire.

Now, she couldn't tailor an attack for each of the five smilodons that were part of the ambush, but she knew what to expect much better than they did.

First, she had to finish preparing her surprise since she expected things to move quickly once she started her counterattack.

Dorea did her best not to be too obvious about it, but there was only so much she could conceal.

The air vibrated slightly all around her as she raised her hands as if in prayer.

It's not anywhere near an actual spell yet, but when I get this down, and I know I will, it'll be enough to make me a Journeyman mage.

Recently, she had been reflecting on the overlapping properties of the elements, specifically lightning and air.

She had been inspired by Jonah's Whispering Wind and had looked into the matter, only to find that surprisingly little had been written by the ancestors, likely because there was no record of anyone using more than one element at the same time.

Discouraged, she had decided to focus on something more easily achievable, like the Exploding Water Bullet she had completed the previous week.

After she was done with it and had developed a few different offensive strategies, she dedicated herself to a defensive spell. However, experimenting with a mixed-element one wasn't particularly appealing to her, as it turned out more complicated than she liked.

Still, while a complete mixed-mana spell was far in the future, she had managed to get something interesting to work.

Though air and electric mana didn't go together naturally, that changed radically when you gave them a similar purpose. Equal levels of the energies brought a surprising instability to the manipulation, but when she used just enough of one element to flavor her working, she succeeded.

Finding the right state of mind required some time, but luckily for her, it seemed her enemies were keen on letting her have it.

Mixing the two elements while keeping a specific purpose in mind, she gave form to a less visually flashy but still devastating attack.

The female she had been stalking had turned around and was keeping a wary eye on her position, obviously in on the plan but not feeling entirely secure.

On the other hand, the four males had only started to come into range for her to attack. Thus, she decided to keep waiting for as long as possible.

If, in their arrogance, they allowed her to deal with all of them simultaneously, she'd gladly do so.

Finally, the smilodons came into sight. They prowled toward her, licking their chops, taking in her seemingly defenseless form with what would have been glee, had they been smart enough for it.

The female had also gotten closer, feeling more secure with the presence of her companions, but was still warier than them.

It was what saved her in the end.

As soon as she felt them come within twenty feet, Dorea unleashed what she had held for several minutes.

A deafening roar of thunder echoed through the forest, sending birds flying for miles.

Around Dorea, it looked as if a giant had pummeled the earth. Save for a small circle where she stood, the land had been carved by a large explosion as the sound traveled through the air, bringing with it a kinetic weight.

If that had been all, she would have gained the upper hand thanks to a clever bit of magic and probably lightly injured her enemies, but the truly dangerous part of her working was in the sheer loudness.

The four closest smilodons had been thrown back like ragdolls, and they weren't getting up.

Their eardrums had ruptured immediately, saving them from further pain, but the shock wave itself was not simply air moving. The sheer energy it brought was enough to bruise skin and break bones.

The four felines were rendered a heap of broken flesh, though luckily for them, they weren't awake to feel the agony that would surely rack their bodies.

The smartest one, who had kept a greater distance, had still been sent flying by the sheer displacement of air and suffered severe injuries, but had she been left alone, she would have likely survived.

That option wasn't given to her, as Dorea catalyzed a Lightning Sphere and ended her struggles.

She did the same to all the beasts in quick succession, ensuring that none of them would ever attempt such a thing.

Unfortunately, their meat and pelt were too damaged to be worth taking back.

Dorea dispassionately looked at her handiwork and considered what other choices she could have taken.

Trying to face them one at a time would have left me open to sneak attacks as I concentrated on one of them. I could have engaged them at long range with the Bullets, but their precision falters the farther they travel. It's a pity that I won't be able to hunt in this area for a while, but the next time, whatever sent these five against me will be much more prepared.

Dorea didn't bother burying the carcasses since the sheer level of noise she had produced would have alerted anyone to her presence, and left immediately.

Although she doubted anything would try their luck after what she had done, there was the remote possibility that she had disturbed one of the slumbering old monsters that resided in the forest.

Therefore, she decided to cut her hunting short, especially since she had already met her goal for the day of hunting at least four different beasts.

Her power had spiked once again, though the increases were much less dramatic these days.

The first time it had happened, she had felt her reserves grow so much that it felt incredible, and though rationally she knew that they were still getting bigger, she couldn't help but feel like it was becoming a slower process.

It wasn't, she knew, but the growth she achieved by killing beasts such as the smilodons she had just dealt with was a linear addition, and every time it meant a smaller percentage increase.

If she wanted to feel the same explosive increment, she'd need to hunt more powerful animals or human mages.

She was not ready yet to challenge the greater beasts that resided in the forest, and as far as the second option went, she was pretty sure they'd come looking for her before too long.

The last week had been relatively quiet as the new alliance went into practice. Information was being exchanged at a rate unseen since the previous war against the Ergasters, and their border security was at an all-time high.

Nevertheless, no one made the mistake of thinking they were safe from further incursions.

The Mondeans had many possible targets to choose from in their depredations, and while they might have shown them that they weren't an easy one, it was likely that they'd see a punitive expedition soon enough.

Dorea returned to the village and bypassed her house, walking directly to Voggo's.

They likely heard my Thunderclap from here, though it shouldn't have been more than a loud noise at these distances. It's still better to make sure they know it was me and that the enhanced beasts are showing a degree of coordination.

Indeed, the shaman proved to be very interested in her story. He complimented her ingenuity in mixing the two elements and seemed particularly interested in the ramifications of such a skill, but he didn't appear worried about a possible mastermind behind the ambush.

"It is very likely that one of the older enhanced smilodons coordinated such a thing, but they are very aware of how much they can push things. The forest has a delicate balance, and doing too much can have terrible results," he explained.

Next to him, listening intently as she made her report, sat Noele, the first refugee group's leader.

She appeared very fascinated by her ability to use air and lightning mana at the same time, though she didn't ask questions about it.

Dorea had hesitated momentarily when she had seen her, unsure how much to share with the woman present, but Voggo had discreetly signaled to be open about everything that wasn't her secret ability.

"Powerful creatures have long resided in these lands, but they aren't thirsty for greater territory. Whenever a new generation undergoes a Trial, they weed out the weak and the dumb with these kinds of games," the woman added, taking on a faraway look as she remembered something.

"In the mountains, hidden valleys have been off-limits to humans for centuries. Inside live creatures that are just as cunning as the greatest of us, but they generally have the wisdom not to take too much.

"Beings of ages long past, older than our memories, kings of their little kingdoms. Humanity has no foothold there, no recourse to speak of. Keep out of those lands if you want to live long."

Her words had the quality of something long repeated like a nursery rhyme told for generations.

To her side, Voggo nodded in agreement.

"Then can I go back there to hunt more?"

"I wouldn't push it. No matter how little the beast that sent those five against you cares, it still has a reputation to uphold. Taunting it with your continued presence may not be a wise idea."

His expression then took a graver tint as he gestured to the map on his table. "And I don't think you'll have to wait too long before your next battle, my dear. Things have been too quiet."

That tracked with her own impressions. Whoever the new Mondean chief was, he didn't seem like the type of person to leave them alone after they bloodied his nose.

It was unfortunate, but she would have to put her hunting expeditions on hold for a while to avoid being too far from the village in case something happened.

Still, I'm quite satisfied with what I got. I wouldn't say I'm the most powerful mage in the village yet, but I have definitely caught up with the top group.

CHAPTER THIRTY-ONE

As Dorea was returning from an uneventful patrol, a signal came to go back to the village with all due haste.

It wasn't meant for an active attack, but it was the second highest priority, so Dorea accelerated her pace, aided by the winds.

It had been something she had seen Eol, the Heidel air mage who went on patrols with her, do when he was getting tired.

The guy reduced the air drag in front of him and used the leftover currents to propel himself forward.

It wasn't a massive increase in speed, especially since that would have the risk of hitting something at the slightest mistake, but it made walking as fast as jogging.

Dorea didn't know if the guy had invented it himself or if he had seen someone or something else do it first, but she was grateful nonetheless.

Once she had the trick down correctly, she'd make sure every air mage in the village could use it, especially those not focused on battle magic like Jonah.

No matter how annoyed she was with him and Beth for spending most of their free time being annoyingly vapid, she still loved them and would make sure they'd have the best chances to survive future confrontations.

It might even become a spell once I can dedicate time to it.

Indeed, her biggest roadblock had been, for quite some time, the absence of time.

She had dealt with her lack of mana more or less, though there could never be enough.

On the other hand, the skills she needed to master and the spells she wanted to develop kept increasing. She was playing catch-up and was not getting any closer to her goals.

Her world would open to more abilities and applications whenever she got something down, and it would keep going like that forever, according to Voggo.

A boring life, this is not.

Finally coming into sight of the village walls, she pulsed her mana to signal her coming and her status as friendly, though the sensors present should have felt her arriving a while ago.

They had managed to find several people amongst the Gifted not particularly interested in fighting but who wanted to contribute to Whitecliff's safety and had the talent for it. Immediately, they were put to work at expanding the sensory net around the village.

In time, they might even develop a ritual to work together and have a real-time feed of the surroundings like the previous generation of mages had, but that was still quite far away.

According to Voggo, they'd all need to be Journeymen before they could attempt such a thing.

Receiving a return pulse that let her know she'd been acknowledged, Dorea created several air platforms in front of her and used them to bypass the wall entirely.

She cheekily waved at the guards manning it, catching a glimpse of their exasperated looks, before she sped toward the shaman's house.

The village looked quite different these days, as more and more houses had been built or, in many cases, restructured to allow the refugees to properly settle.

The tent camp still housed some, especially with the latest arrivals still deciding whether they wanted to stay or head elsewhere to try their luck outside the walls.

The triage tent was being expanded into a real pavilion, and talks were underway to decide its future.

Their earth mages hadn't seen the need to craft such communal buildings, simply because their battles had all been fought down south, far from the village.

The remnants of their camps were still in use by several tribes as outposts to this day, but were simply too far for them to have any use.

The space behind Voggo's house had been mostly freed up, and there she found the old man alongside Mark the lead scout, Ed the lead hunter, and a team of scouts who looked to have just returned from an extended mission.

She finally let go of the air around her and almost stumbled as her speed dropped dramatically, but caught herself with another bit of manipulation.

Voggo gave her a smirk, evidently having caught her mistake, but didn't address it, instead turning to the tired team. "Thank you all for your hard work. Go rest for now and remember what I've told you."

Dismissed, the men tiredly bowed in their direction and left. They trudged away tiredly, but the prospect of having some time off seemed to give them some energy back.

"So what is going on?" Dorea questioned once they were gone.

"Let's go inside; we have much to speak of," was the shaman's response.

They all sat at their usual table, where, as was tradition, Voggo served them a new tea, this time made with lavender and ginger.

It was a bit too strong for Dorea's tastes, since the spices overpowered the palate rather than being enjoyably present, but she didn't make a fuss about it. Old people liked old people flavors, after all.

"We have received a rather troubling report from our scouts, unfortunately. They have observed a buildup of forces a day away from the northern wall, of what we suspect are Mondeans. The presence of Kannis the Wolf, a skilled hunter who led one of the first attacks, makes it a certainty," he began, setting his cup down.

"So they have decided to deal with us. How many are there?"

"As far as they could tell, more than fifty people were present at the camp, and given the quality of some of the tents and the behavior of some people, we expect at least ten mages to be present, though it's possible for that number to increase."

That wasn't as bad as she expected since ten mages wouldn't be anywhere near enough to take the village, especially if they were at the level of those she had fought with the last few times.

Only the imposing woman who had slung lightning like a toy was somewhat intimidating, but she had been an outlier so far.

"Is that all? If so, we can attack them now and prevent damage to the village."

Ed the hunter, chuckled at her words, shaking his head in amusement. "Well, no one can say that the next generation doesn't want to get their hands dirty."

Mark smiled at her before explaining further, "We doubt they are the only ones who'll participate in the attack. Indeed, we expect that number to at least double before they launch the offensive."

Mmm . . . that would be much worse, yes. Especially if they manage to take us by surprise, get the jump over a patrol, and prevent them from sending the alarm.

Dorea tilted her head in thought as she went through the possibilities. "And I imagine they are still far enough that by the time we got there with a decently sized group, they'd have swelled in size."

Voggo nodded silently, showing that he had already considered and discarded the hypothesis.

"That means that we have to prepare either for a siege, which I doubt we'll be able to maintain for long given our lack of defensive options, or we need to somehow get enough warriors and mages to be able to face them," she finished, looking at the old man for confirmation.

"That is along my thoughts, yes. Although preparing for a decisive confrontation doesn't mean the more subtle tactics are out." He smiled foxily.

I keep forgetting that he has been through a war. He probably has many ideas about how to harass such a group.

"I have prepared a missive to send to the Heidels and the forest tribe to ask them for their support. Considering the timings and the distances involved, I believe you would be the best option to go down south and come back with enough time to spare."

That was less welcome, since it would mean having to deal with that old monster Yaomi by herself. Still, given the severity of the situation, she avoided voicing any complaint about it.

"I get the forest people, they are close enough, but do we have the time to wait for the Heidels to arrive?"

This time, Mark answered her query, "I have seen how fast you can go if you want to. If you can keep it up for a while, and Voggo has assured me you can, you'll be able to be there within a single day. They'd need a couple more to get here, so if our estimates are correct, that'd leave us with a whole day to prepare."

It felt good knowing that her efforts had been noticed, but the growing responsibilities attached weren't exactly welcome. Especially since they would send her out of the village when she wanted to be present in case of an early attack.

"But how do you know it's going to take them that long? And how do you know they will only bring that many people? As far as we know, they could send all their mages and flatten us. No amount of allies is going to do much, then," she questioned, worried about what Mav had told her.

Two hundred mages is simply too much. They wouldn't even need to come into sight of the village. They could simply call upon the elements to batter us until nothing remains.

Voggo took a fortifying sip of tea and sighed into it. "There is the possibility that they'll crush us from a distance, that is true," he admitted.

"But that is unlikely for several reasons. First of all, our scouts have observed behavior in their warriors more akin to those preparing to take prisoners, which would necessitate leaving some of us alive," he explained, getting a nod of confirmation from Mark.

"Secondly, we are not their only open front at this time. Resistance is still fierce in the mountains, and they won't win easily. They simply do not have the capacity to send that many people down south, so far away from their main campaign. And going by their slow speed, I assumed a very tight timeline. If they took their time, they could be here in as much as a week, though I wouldn't count on it," he finished, patting her hand in reassurance.

It seemed to her that the three had thought of everything and had planned out the best course possible with what they had.

Some fear remained in her heart, as it had since she had learned just by how much they were outnumbered, but having a path forward made it much easier to bear.

"And so I need to leave as soon as possible and convince Chief Yaomi to send us more people in the hopes that they don't have a similar situation down there."

Ed shook his head this time, answering her unspoken question for further information. "You won't have much trouble there, luckily. Our people that we sent down south for the inter-village cooperation have reported the absence of any active conflict. You'll have to haggle on how many she'll send, but they don't have a pressing need, and getting more experience in a relatively low-stakes environment would be useful."

It was the most she had ever heard him talk, especially since his low baritone didn't seem suited to long speeches, but his words set her at ease.

If, indeed, there had been no trouble with the southern tribes, then she wouldn't have to face such an uphill battle.

"Yaomi is the type to get as many advantages as possible even in difficult situations, but she's never unreasonable. I'll give you a satchel with a few of my ointments, and you can promise her regular shipments of those if she does send help." Voggo got up and started rummaging through his shelves, picking small jars and putting them all in one spot on the table.

"I'll give you some cotton to wrap around them to prevent any breakage during your travel. This should be enough to entice her; the opportunity to see our worth in a fight should do the rest."

Much could be said about the Heidel chief, but once she gave her word, she'd respect it. They were already in an alliance and had been working toward further integration to some success, and this was simply the next step.

Melu had been quite popular in the village, what with her tanned skin, loose clothes, and sunny smiles, which had helped transform the collective consciousness toward a more accepting mindset.

The constant stress and influx of refugees had, surprisingly, only brought people together more. It may have been out of necessity, but Dorea liked to think that it said something about their strength of character that even in such a situation, her people could be so welcoming toward strangers.

"Of course, all of this will come with a price to be paid at a later date. When the time comes, and unfortunately it is likely to happen, we'll be called to help the Heidels just like they are going to help us now. And we'll have to answer."

Voggo's words resonated heavily with everyone present, though there wasn't much they could do about it.

Trying to take the Mondeans on without the Heidels would be foolish at best and would mean many more casualties, even in the best of futures.

Still, his warning had been heard, and they would all have to keep it in mind.

No matter how much helping each other made sense at that time, there would still be a cost attached.

I'll gladly pay if it means our people can live free from pain and strife.

In the end, Dorea was dismissed to rest for a few hours and told to return as soon as she felt ready to start her journey.

Although she wanted to get it over with, leaving immediately was not a wise choice, as she had just come back from a long patrol.

No, getting a good few hours of sleep would allow her to depart before dawn the following morning, fully charged to sprint to the Heidels' village.

When she got home, she allowed herself to be assaulted from behind the door, though she had felt Lia's presence as soon as the house had come into sight.

She dramatically fell to the ground, taking the little girl down with her to her loud giggles.

They rolled on the floor for a minute, the youngest trying and failing to escape the oldest.

With an amused smile, their father broke up the brawl, picking them up by the scruff of their clothes like errant kittens.

"You two both need to go wash your hands because dinner is almost ready. If you don't want all the steak and liver pies to disappear down my stomach, you'll even need to hurry," he threatened.

The two sisters shared a look of understanding and immediately wriggled free of his grip. They ran to the bathroom and cleaned up as quickly as they could, without making a mess that would see them walked back there by their ears, and reached the table just as Lilian was placing the still steaming pies on it.

"Wait until they have cooled a bit. Otherwise, all the filling will dribble out," she warned them.

The girls sat opposite their father, matching grins on their faces as they banged on the table to signal their hunger.

Lilian rolled her eyes, taking a tray of roasted root vegetables from the wood-fired oven.

They didn't use it often, as it required much more fuel and its temperature was too high for most cooking, but when they did light it on, delicious treats were sure to come.

Indeed, Dorea spied another two pans close to the coals, where sweet pies were baking.

Her mother was not a professional like Jonah's father, but when she dedicated herself to something, she was very good at it, and somehow the woman found the cooking process soothing.

Her pies were famous in the village, and Joe the baker had even once said that she was the only competition he was truly afraid of.

It was moments like this that made it all worth it. Her family laughing together as they impatiently waited for the pies to cool, the warmth of the fire.

That the Mondeans wanted to take this away from them simply to sate a single person's lust for power was incomprehensible.

The Nature's Wrath had brought significant change to the region of Loisos, but it was the humans who actively chose to use the power they gained to bring about so much suffering.

No one was forcing them to use their magic to expand so aggressively, yet they still decided to do so.

This time, it was the Mondeans that were doing so, but Dorea didn't doubt that others would try their luck before too long. And she would be ready for them too.

Whatever it is that I've done to myself during the Trial, no matter what changes it brought to my soul, it's giving me the power to protect this, and that's all that matters.

Her increasingly darker thoughts were interrupted by a thick slice of pie being placed in front of her.

Her father smiled softly, not saying anything but gesturing to her plate as if to tell her to concentrate on that, rather than what had been bothering her.

I should bow to the wisdom of my elders. I'll have all the time I want to brood tomorrow as I travel south; now, it's time for pie.

CHAPTER THIRTY-TWO

A foggy bank was rolling from the sea as Dorea exited her home.

It was an unusual scene, since the high cliffs usually protected them from the worst, but some spring mornings had just the right mix of humidity and temperature to allow the vapor to rise high enough to engulf the village.

Though it usually was a natural phenomenon, Dorea still made sure to check it with her senses for any magical presence.

Of course, if it were me making it, I'd simply help out the fog's natural formation rather than brute-forcing it into existence and leaving my mana everywhere.

Therefore, she slightly deviated to the northern wall to check with the patrol there.

They reassured her that the fog had been forming for a while and had no unnatural origin.

She had expected it since it was still too early for an attack, but it would have made for a perfect cover for an army's approach.

Of course, if they were noticed as they came closer, it would likely spell their doom since they weren't as familiar with the terrain.

Things like that were very much a double-edged sword, but it was good to be reminded that the enemy could also be clever.

She had had it easy so far and feared she had been getting complacent, since the Mondeans seemed to prefer attacking head-on. That, however, didn't mean they would always do so.

She stepped away from the northern wall, and thanks to her new speed-boosting air manipulation, she soon got to the southern gate.

It actually took her longer than she had expected, simply because the high humidity in the air changed the formula required to move at such speeds.

Still, she adjusted soon enough and quickly found herself at the exit, where the current shift had been told to expect her.

She found Nila there, the woman tiredly rubbing sleep from her eyes as she finally got ready to go back home. Before leaving, she handed Dorea a satchel she recognized from the day before.

"The shaman asked me to give this to you. Says you know what it is and to try not to jostle it too much."

She accepted it with a nod of thanks and put it in her rucksack, placing it between her clean underclothes to cushion it further.

Nila patted her on the shoulder and turned to leave. "I'll be off, then; good luck on your mission. Apparently, it's really important."

Yeah, no pressure, though, huh. It's not like the future of our village hangs on me getting the reinforcements.

With a wave backward, Dorea left through the open gate. As soon she felt it close behind her, she took a deep breath and activated her newest experiment.

The wind rushed around her, creating an empty spot in front and propelling her forward from the back.

It wasn't a spell yet and likely wouldn't become one for quite a while since it had so many moving parts, as evidenced by her earlier difficulties with the fog, but for the moment it allowed her to move faster than she ever had, without tiring.

The forest rushed around her, and although she couldn't go at full speed in such a restricting place, her senses allowed her to avoid colliding with anything.

Flora and fauna passed by quickly, and Dorea relaxed in the monotony of the travel.

The southern reach of the forest was more sparse than the rest of it, as it slowly tapered off into the grasslands, which meant that unless she was unfortunate enough to find an enraged territorial animal like the therium her group met during her first mission, she should be safe from any harassment.

Well, unless I veer too far to the east and end up in salamander territory.

She left the forest behind after only five hours and had to stop to take care of an annoyingly persistent sparrow-hawk who used its air manipulation to go even faster than her.

At first, it had seemed innocuous enough, as it raced her playfully, but after a while she understood that the little predator was taking her measure.

She had to halt her race and swat it away with a burst of lightning to convince it not to try its luck.

The damn thing was only as big as my head. How could it hope to eat me? These beasts are getting quite bold; I should hunt down here more, once this situation ends.

She finally broke into the grasslands with a sigh of relief, and after orientating herself with the map she had been given, she took off toward where the Heidels' village should be.

Her speed, unencumbered by trees and shrubbery, was much greater than in the forest, and she made good time.

As she passed by the monotonous landscape, Dorea felt very grateful to have developed the ability to move so quickly; otherwise, having to suffer through such a tedious experience again might have killed her.

Once in a while, a copse of trees sprang up from the otherwise uniform background, and small streams broke it up further, but it was still sorely lacking in excitement.

She stopped for lunch once the sun was up high in the sky and took out a wrapped slice of pie that her mother had reserved from the previous dinner.

Sitting on a white rock by a brook, Dorea watched tiny fish swim in the clear waters as she enjoyed her meal with gusto.

She took the time to refill her flask, as drinking too much conjured water seemed to have slightly adverse effects on people's health.

Voggo explained it in much more detail, but the gist was that while it's okay to have it out in the wilds and for emergencies, drinking too much pure water can take away good stuff from your body.

That tracked with what she had observed in her earlier efforts at combining the elements. She had immediately discovered that, unlike natural water, conjured water was not a good way to transmit lightning while trying out combination attacks.

Soon after, Dorea rose from her crouch, and once she had packed everything and made sure that Voggo's package was still intact, she started moving again toward her target.

It took her only five more hours before she felt a human signature in the distance and immediately slowed down.

Although it was convenient for quick traveling, seeing a strange mage rushing at high speeds toward your village would be enough to put off anyone. Since she really needed their cooperation, she tried to prevent such a situation.

She pulsed out her mana in the pattern that had been established between their two villages for urgent but not immediate requests and, after a few seconds of silence, received an acknowledgment.

Soon after, a group of what she presumed to be Heidel warriors and mages came out from behind a hill while riding horses. At the helm was a tall and tan young man, who felt like a very controlled lightning storm waiting to be released.

She waved with a hand. "Hey! I'm from Whitecliff."

The older teenager at the front reached her shortly after, stopping his horse in front of her. "I could tell. You people are so pale it's like you never leave the house."

Her mouth hung open for a second before she noticed the smirk at the edge of his mouth. She shook her head in mock offense and waved a fist at him. "Why you! I oughta put you in your place, you overcooked chicken!"

The boy burst out laughing, revealing pearly white teeth. He hung from his horse with just his leg strength, holding his stomach with his hands.

"Oh, you have a sense of humor! Considering how dour the people you sent here were, I was starting to doubt it was possible."

Dorea lifted her nose up in the sky. "Well, if I had to live in such a dull place, I wouldn't have much to laugh about either."

He opened his mouth to reply when he got interrupted by an older man with dark shaggy hair and beard. "Masi! You can flirt with the Sapiens girl later; she's here for a reason!"

Both stumbled over their words in denial, but the man merely snorted and turned his horse to leave.

The newly identified Masi then offered to give her a ride, but she declined, too embarrassed to share such tight spaces.

Instead, she reactivated her Air Boost, though not at full speed, and caught up with the man.

Though the Heidels were surprised at her speed, they didn't put up a fuss about it and simply guided her toward the village.

It took them another hour before it finally came into sight, lit by the waning light of the sun.

The village sat on a higher hill than the ones it was surrounded by, spanning from its top and extending for a while as it tapered off into a low wall.

Even at a cursory glance, it was nowhere near as sturdy as Whitecliff's was, which was perfectly reasonable since the Heidels hadn't had earth mages at their disposal.

Its southern border was delineated by a larger river, still shallow enough to wade across with a horse but wide enough to slow down anyone trying to assault it.

A wooden bridge was built on top of it, and though it was evidently well maintained, Dorea didn't doubt that there weren't ways to take it out of the equation if needed.

They finally got to the gates, where two guards stood at the ready with sharp spears. After a brief explanation from the shaggy man, they were let in, and she found herself herded toward the center of the settlement.

The architecture was a weird mix of brick houses and solid-looking tents. The buildings looked commonly used, such as a granary or a town hall, while the tents appeared to be for housing.

Dorea had never seen such well-crafted ones, though she couldn't imagine living in one her whole life.

I wonder how they fared during the Wrath. It definitely hit here as well since they have received its powers, but those really don't look capable of withstanding it . . .

Her musings were cut short as she was brought to the largest tent she had ever seen.

Its green and gold colorings meshed well with the surrounding grasslands, and it looked to be made up of several different ones put together to make up a small palace.

Inside, light came in only through strategically open flaps that functioned as windows but could be closed in case of need with strange golden clips shaped like butterflies.

The man guiding her quickly navigated the rooms to stop before a closed flap.

He stomped his feet and announced out loud, "Yavo is here with an emissary from Whitecliff. We have confirmed her truthfulness."

That gave her a pause. She wondered if someone present during the first talks had remembered her and confirmed her affiliation, since that was the only moment she had ever come into contact with the Heidels.

That has to be it. The other possibility is that they have information on all of us and cross-referenced it, but it seems a bit farfetched, even for one such as Yaomi.

It was the old crone herself who opened the flap, sending the man away with a careless gesture. "Well done, now leave us."

She then turned around and strode back in, seating herself on a low cushion that also served as a recline.

Unsure but unwilling to be intimidated, Dorea let herself in, taking up the spot in front of the chief.

"I can already imagine what you want. The problem now is what you are willing to give," Yaomi said tonelessly, breaking all the images Dorea had built up of an endless discussion where they verbally sparred until she, victorious, managed to trick the woman into assisting them.

What Dorea got instead was a toothy, knowing grin. "Not what you expected? There is a time and place for word games, girl, and now it is not. The only possible reasons for you to be here is that either our people's contingent in your village got killed, but you would be much more contrite were that the case, or you need more men for a possible attack."

This is why I didn't want to come. This old witch is way too wily for me to deal with.

Nevertheless, she had been tasked with getting at least thirty warriors, amongst whom there had to be ten mages. It was vital to the village's defense, and so she avoided showing any distaste.

"You are correct in that we have knowledge of a future attack from the northern barbarians. They should get to Whitecliff in three more days, and I'm here to formally request your assistance in the form of manpower."

She kept her tone steady so as not to give the woman anything, but luckily it seemed she wasn't interested in dancing around the subject too much.

"Are those we sent not enough? Did they not suffer grievous injuries while defending your land?"

Dorea pursed her lips, not amused at what the woman was implying. "I was there with them when they got hurt. We covered each other's backs like comrades do. I am the one who sent the enemy commander packing. What we are asking you to do is simply a continuation of that."

Yaomi leaned forward, scrutinizing her face as if in search of falsities. "You speak of great struggles for such a young girl."

Again, Dorea restrained her first instinct of rejecting her words. The Heidel chief was prodding at her weaknesses for whatever reason, but she wouldn't give her the satisfaction of thinking she had gotten through her.

Then, the woman leaned back with a satisfied look. "But you have some restraint. That's good; you are going to need it in the future," she shared cryptically.

"As for the men, I can offer you a dozen more for the promise of two when we call upon you."

And there she is. I knew she was going to haggle me like a sleazy merchant. She's even trying to treat this like a loan . . .

From that moment, the talks descended into little more than fighting over wares.

Dorea offered a supply of potions for forty men and was laughed at and, in turn, rejected out of hand the chief's proposal.

They both affected offense and even surprise at how they were being treated, but it was all a performance.

It had long been a tradition in the Loisos region to be as theatrical as possible while bargaining for a better price, be it over a sack of grain at a market or during high-stakes negotiations, especially when the two sides didn't really know each other that well.

It was a way of creating a farcical superstructure that gave both parties a sense of control. If neither was being truthful, as was expected, there was no need to wonder if you were being fooled.

It was something that was taught to every little kid during their first market day, and accompanied them all their lives.

Inside the village it was less common, simply because everyone knew what the worth of a product was, but it allowed for much easier exchange with the outside.

Of course, the situation being what it was, Dorea didn't really appreciate having to haggle so much over human lives, but she'd do it if it meant having more protection for her family.

The old witch was a skilled negotiator and could have pushed for more concessions, but had seemingly decided to refrain from pushing the envelope too hard.

It's not in her interest to let us get overrun after all, since she already invested so much in us. It's scary to think that Voggo predicted this moment months ago.

Indeed, had they not already been in the process of becoming close allies, their discussion would have been very different.

Dorea would have likely had to promise precious materials as payment, and the Heidels would have taken on a mercenary contract to fight for them.

That would have meant less motivated troops and an unreliable ally.

What they had done, by slowly integrating with each other, was create the framework needed to reach accords such as the one they were hammering out, without having to promise an arm and a leg.

Of course, they had bound themselves to help the Heidels out when the time came, but they likely would have had to do so anyways, since any fighting force that could seriously threaten them wouldn't stop at the forest's edge.

In the end, the negotiations ended with a semisatisfactory outcome for both.

Dorea would get her twenty warriors and ten mages, while Yaomi got a steady supply of potions, which they had lacked beyond the most basic preparations, and the promise of help when the time came.

She didn't stick around to see whether they actually went through with it, as while the old woman was annoyingly shrewd, her word was as good as gold.

No, I need to go back home as quickly as possible to help with the defenses in case the attack comes early. They can make it there by themselves.

The Sapiens contingent residing in the Heidel village would also come back with the promised troops and act as guides through the forest.

All in all, she had achieved what she had come to do and could return quickly enough to be present should anything happen before they were ready.

As she started her Air Boost up again, Dorea looked at the tent village one last time, lit by the moon and stars, before beginning the journey back.

CHAPTER THIRTY-THREE

She arrived back to Whitecliff as morning was turning into afternoon without any hiccup, having managed to avoid confrontations with any beasts and after stopping at a grove during the darkest hours of the night.

Her continued use of Air Boost had allowed her to refine it into a more polished form, and she had tweaked the matrix to make it less expensive.

Turning it into a proper spellform would take time she simply didn't have at the moment, but being able to move at such speeds with barely the need to stop once in a while for a breather gave her enough freedom of movement to be exhilarating.

Without a looming invasion, I'd be zipping around the forest looking for decent fights or more hidden temples.

The village's atmosphere was relatively subdued, as people went about their duties with the awareness that it might just be one of their last days of freedom.

Oh, no one liked to think they'd lose. Indeed, the prevailing sentiment between villagers was that they'd send the barbarians running with their tails tucked between their legs. Still, the possibility of losing dear friends and family, even in victory, was very real.

They had been lucky so far, not losing anyone during the earlier skirmishes, but already a toll had been taken.

Matt, the silent but friendly scout who had accompanied Dorea on many patrols, had still not woken up from his coma.

Voggo had done what he could to heal his body, but the mind was a much more difficult prospect, and they could only hope he'd wake in time.

Others had been severely injured, but thanks to the potions the shaman and

Lilian—now with Noele's help—constantly kept brewing, they had avoided any tragedy.

That was not guaranteed to keep happening. Sure enough, Voggo had made sure that everyone who would participate in the village's defense was aware of the genuine chance of dying or seeing someone they knew dying.

While that might have sounded counterproductive to the defenders' morale, it was important that no one broke rank.

Battles, such as the one that would come in a few days, differed significantly from the messy fights Dorea had participated in until that moment.

The shaman had used his previous experience in fighting a war to draw up defense plans while she had been out of the village, and had apparently given everyone a specific role.

There would be long-range bombardiers made up of archers and those mages who couldn't cast if distracted by a physical assault.

There were the frontline warriors, where hunters, scouts, and some villagers had decided to stake their lives.

There were the flanking troops meant to crush their enemies in a deadly trap should they ever overextend.

Some, those who were less likely to be able to hold better under pressure, had been given the role of protecting the other gates to alert the main fighting force of any sneak attack from the rear.

Dorea herself, she found, had been given the role of leading their allies' troops, as she was the most well-known and respected mage.

She accepted the role with a grimace but didn't complain beyond a perfunctory attempt at pushing the position on someone more experienced.

Unfortunately for her, no one besides Voggo had any real-life knowledge of warfare, and though some older men had been in light skirmishes before, they simply didn't command the same respect that she did with their allies.

It was a weird situation to be in, as an almost-fifteen-year-old girl who had been busy flirting with a farmer boy and caring for her family's herds just a few months before.

The Wrath had done more than given her powers. It had radically changed her path in life, for better or worse.

Arguably, had it not arrived, the northerners wouldn't have descended upon their neighbors in their mania for conquest, and she would have been able to spend all her life in peace, but Dorea was aware that such was just a story she told herself.

Magic didn't change who people were. It simply gave them the means to assert themselves.

The old Mondean chief would have died sooner or later, and his ambitious son would have likely managed to take control of his people.

Then, their conquest would have started anyways. It would have been slower and clumsier, but possibly even bloodier.

No, there is no need to fool myself. This confrontation was coming sooner or later. And now I have the power to do something about it.

The news of her successful negotiations had been very well received, and she had been congratulated many times for it, though Dorea didn't feel deserving of it.

The groundwork had been laid out long before she reached the Heidels' village, and she had simply been the most expedient way of making it happen.

Still, she didn't protest the praise too much, aware that people were doing it more to convince themselves that the village's leadership had things well in hand, rather than out of genuine sentiment.

She reported back to Voggo what she had seen and talked about during her mission and was told that a similar, albeit slightly less successful, one had been conducted with the hopes of bringing the Forest tribe into the fold.

They hadn't been rejected since Samos, their chief, was well aware that they'd likely be the next target were Whitecliff to fall, but the men they'd receive were less than what they would have liked.

"They are reclusive people, and we simply haven't had the time to truly make them understand the severity of the situation. I can only hope that the upcoming confrontation will awaken them to it," the old man had said.

It seemed foolish to her, keeping most of their forces when they were aware of no other power in the near distance that could threaten them, but from what she had seen in their brief encounter, those people were stubborn.

They had been brought out of isolation only because they risked extinction, and they likely needed several reminders of it before they fully got the lesson.

Well, wasn't that snippy? I shouldn't blame them too much; they have suffered too, and simply don't want to overcommit.

It was a reasonable fear, unfortunately. It would likely spell doom for all three allies if they were to lose badly. Such a loss in manpower and morale would allow the Mondeans to take control of the forest without much resistance.

That was the exact reason why losing couldn't be even contemplated. Too much was at stake, and the consequences were unacceptable.

The day of the battle was an uncharacteristically hot one. The sun had been shining at full strength since the early morning, and had it been any other situation, Dorea would have taken the time to go to the beach and swim for a while.

Instead, she was sitting upon the northern wall, waiting for their scouts to bring word of their enemy movement.

Behind her stood the Heidel and Forest tribe contingents who, when put together, formed a decently sized force.

She recognized Masi, the boy who had spoken to her as she had been led to their village. He was cheerfully chatting with Melu, the girl who had become quite popular since she came back from the skirmish, and, looking at them together, she suspected they might even be related.

The Heidels all had a long spear and a bone bow as equipment, and they looked the most professional.

To their left were the Forest mages, a small group of five who had assured her they could all use the same spells and should be allowed to work together.

They were less organized, as had been expected, but all still had either slings or, again, bows.

The battle would be fought primarily at long range—Voggo had explained—since the presence of mages on both sides made it foolish to attempt a charge until the ranks were thinned enough.

That meant that almost every warrior had brought all kinds of bows, whether hunting ones, old war bows made during the last conflict, or even practicing ones.

Acquiescing to the Forest tribe's request, she didn't split them up, though she suspected their wish to fight together had more to do with distrust for anyone else, rather than a need to be more effective.

Ahead of them, Jonah was scouring the land with his senses, being far superior to anyone else in the skill.

Still, he shook his head.

"Nothing yet. I'm certain I felt them prepare yesterday, but the guys posted northeast are still reporting no attempted flanking maneuver," he called out.

It was a nerve-racking experience, knowing that the enemy was coming and that battle was about to be had, but being forced to wait for them.

The possibility of attacking themselves had been raised several times. But since the wall and high ground provided an unmatched defensive position in the area, as Ed had explained several times, they would make their stand there.

We just need to wait. They'll come. I can feel it in my bones.

It was also possible that they had sensed not movements indicating an immediate attack, but preparations for one in the following days. Still, no one wanted to be taken by surprise if they got it wrong.

It would be an interesting psychological warfare method, making the enemy think that you would repeatedly attack, only to truly do so when they lowered their guard. However, the possibility that it was what the Mondeans were doing seemed quite remote.

Dorea surveyed the area again, pushing her senses into the ground and the sky to ensure nothing could sneak up on them.

Of course, the latter was more easily done than the former since she lacked any earth magic capability.

However, there was a significant water content in the earth, especially so close to the coast, and if anything tried to tunnel through, she'd be able to feel it coming, unless it was the work of a Master mage.

But if that were the case, we'd have lost in principle.

Unfortunately, there wasn't much they could do against such a powerhouse, especially an earth attribute one, which would mean an old and experienced fighter.

Their intelligence didn't suggest the presence of anything of the sort, but Dorea's thoughts had been filled with such scenarios since she had heard of the upcoming attack.

It was counterproductive, she knew, since imagining desperate possibilities didn't do anything but sap her energy, but her mind had been running against her will for some time.

Finally, something shifted.

Jonah rose up from his crouch, closing his eyes in concentration as he did when extending his range to its fullest extent.

"They are moving. The scouts just gave the signal!"

There was a rush of movement as everyone scrambled to their positions, standing straight and looking as menacing as possible.

Unfortunately for them, their wait wasn't over yet.

Jonah's sensing extended for several miles if focused on one specific direction, and the scouts were placed at the very end of it.

That meant that they would need to stand there, ready for battle, while their enemy marched in the distance.

It would take them at least an hour to come into sight, but the knowledge that there was a battle to be had had sent a charge of adrenaline through everyone.

Dorea reviewed her role and options again, ensuring she had everything down correctly.

First of all, start sending volleys of Bullets as soon as I can feel them. The time for speaking has long since passed, and we aren't here to make any friends.

Try to target the mages if possible; they are more likely to be at the back. Do not concentrate on shielding; there are other people whose job that is.

Once they are finally close enough, blast them with Lightning Sphere. Hit the front line if possible; if not, aim again for the mages.

If we can make them run and break their morale, we'll all be better off.

She had also considered going in and using her Thunderclap, but doing so required stillness and concentration, which was scarce during a melee.

It was possible that in the future, once she had become capable of casting it as a spell, she'd be able to employ it that way, but for the moment she had to shelve it.

Her other destructive ability was out as well. She might have been able to use the natural charge that had built up into the clouds to crush the enemy camp weeks before, but the environment would not allow such a thing again.

I wonder if they are attacking today because it's cloud-free. But again, how could they have known that was how their men were killed?

She decided to leave such conspiratorial thinking aside for the moment.

Dorea realized her nerves were getting to her, but there wasn't much she could do besides start preparing the mana for the Exploding Water Bullets.

Around her, the Heidel contingent was standing at the ready, their long spears gleaming with polish and leather armors clean.

The fact that they were so well equipped made her think that they either had a hidden production capability they were somehow hiding or, much more likely, the old witch had predicted long before the Wrath arrived that there would come a time when such things would be needed.

They were also a more warriorlike people than the residents of Whitecliff, and their skirmishes with the southern tribes tended to be somewhat bloody, from what she had managed to infer.

Getting them on their side had been a great move.

The Forest people looked a bit shabbier in their older leather armor, but not everything was as it seemed.

Their mages were each capable of conjuring elemental armors that could hold up better than any mundane material could, and they specialized in collective casting.

That meant that they had been tasked with shielding the squad from arrows and all kinds of magical attacks that were sure to rain upon them.

"I think it's about three hundred people!"

Jonah's ability to sense so far was pivotal to their strategy.

He'd quickly relay what he felt, and they'd reconfigure as needed to accommodate for the enemy's strategy.

Luckily, they had opted for a more classical approach.

"Mages at the back, archers in the middle, and warriors as front-liners. There is a large concentration of mages at the center!"

For the first time, Voggo raised his voice to speak to everyone. "They might be trying to break through our middle and separate us. Remember to hold steady and switch with someone else before you take refuge behind the wall. This might end in just an hour or two days, but Whitecliff's survival depends on you!"

The old man had been asked several times by the two other leaders to stay behind and run the field hospital, but had refused to do so.

In the last few days, he had produced as many potions and poultices as humanly possible, and ensured enough people knew how to apply them properly under Lilian's guidance.

Staying behind, he'd said, would be an act of cowardice.

He couldn't seem to fathom asking the village's youth to fight for its survival without doing so himself.

Of course he knew that he wasn't well suited to frontline combat, because of his advanced age and his elementless mana didn't lend itself to fighting.

Still, he chose to direct the battle from close behind and, when necessary, supply them with additional shielding, which was sure to be needed were it to go on for long.

Finally, the enemy came into her range.

Feeling that many hostile people approach her home was daunting, but it also ignited a rage in her.

How dare they?! How can they think our land is theirs to take? That our people are theirs to kill?

She used that boiling emotion to fuel her magic, feeling it sing in her veins.

In front of her materialized several Bullets, prepared to wreak havoc.

A flash of light and a boom told her that the battle had started, as a solid rectangle of air intercepted a lightning bolt directed toward Voggo's position.

Dorea recognized Leo's handiwork and immediately felt more relieved that the old man had such protection.

Then, she turned toward the enemy and started doing her part.

The Bullets were buzzing with suppressed energy, and she released them with a vicious sort of glee.

Though they were still too far behind a hill for her to see, she sensed several people being hit by them.

Shields of all kinds covered the enemy's approach, but they weren't positioned well enough to cover everything, and some attacks, especially the smallest ones like hers, still managed to slip through.

They, on the other hand, had the advantage of having several mages who had trained for collaborative efforts dedicated to their defense.

Noele's people had also focused their training on elemental shielding, thanks to a request from Voggo, which proved itself almost prophetic.

To her side, she felt arrows being nocked and loosed as they sang through the air, only to be knocked aside like errant children from a tremendous gale.

Undeterred, several volleys were sent as the villagers attempted to knock as many mages as possible out of the fighting.

The battle still had a sort of organization, Dorea felt. She had been told that chaos descended almost immediately many times, but the addition of so many different shields allowed both sides to keep their forms.

Still, she did her job. Another series of Bullets was launched from her extended hands, aimed at the gaps she felt in the enemy defenses.

A scream pierced her fugue, and she turned to see that a boulder had managed to punch through a shield and had hit someone.

Without even looking, she could tell there would be no saving them.

Death had finally arrived at Whitecliff.

CHAPTER THIRTY-FOUR

The defenders quickly filled the gap created by the boulder, but they were evidently rattled.

They had all known that death was inevitable in such a confrontation but had still held out hope for a miracle.

Unfortunately, it seemed like they would have to take things into their own hands.

The barriers were reinforced by a shimmering blue-white one made of pure mana, signifying Voggo's entrance into the fray.

That the old man had decided to intervene so soon meant that he saw a pressing need to keep their lines tight. Breaking now would spell doom for everyone, and he knew it.

His presence reinvigorated everyone, and they returned to their roles after the moment of stillness. The body was then dragged away by those supporters who had volunteered to help them out, even if they couldn't fight directly.

Dorea pushed her sorrow at such a brutal death to the side, deciding not to be distracted by her emotions.

She had a role to fulfill, and she would do it properly.

Although she wasn't the most powerful mage in Whitecliff, since that distinction belonged to Mark the Blue, she was definitely the most capable if you didn't consider Voggo himself.

That meant that whenever the enemy commander finally appeared, she'd need to engage them in a personal battle to try and limit the damage they could do.

That, of course, required that they show themselves, but considering how recklessly the Mondeans had operated until that moment, it was very likely they would do so.

Whoever it is, whether it's that huge woman from last time or someone else, I need to take the heat off our people as much as possible.

The fact that in the splash zone for their possible duel were only Heidels and Forest people was deliberate. They would need some finessing were that to be called into question at a later date, but the thought of saving more of her tribesmen's lives spurred her on.

The battle raged on like that for a while, with the two formations hiding behind either the wall or the hill and exchanging volleys of arrows and spellfire.

To Dorea, it seemed like her side was doing a better job at defending than the enemy at attacking, and were the situation to go on much longer, cracks would start to show in the opponents' lines.

That thought appeared to be a shared one, as the Mondeans suddenly decided to change the game.

They split into two large groups, and both went around the hill. They were bombarded mercilessly throughout the maneuver, but to their credit, they maintained their structure.

Once they had finally surpassed the hill that had served as a hiding spot, they found themselves directly below the wall, though at a disadvantageous place.

The specific place they had arranged themselves on had been chosen by the village's leadership because, from a distance, it appeared relatively assailable, which would mean that the enemy wouldn't attempt a breach on another spot, but it was actually quite unfavorable.

They found themselves right in a cul-de-sac, squeezed between hills and entirely below the wall.

At that point, they had no other choice but to attempt a frontal assault.

They would have been whittled away if they had kept up the long-range battle. Retreating might have been an option, but it would leave them open to bombardment for quite a while, and, more than that, it would have been a humiliation they simply couldn't stomach.

No, the Mondeans had crossed the mountains and the rocky hills for a specific reason: to put the upstart village in the south in its place, raze it to the ground, and enslave its people once and for all.

To run away after engaging for not even an hour would have been seen by everyone in the region as a humiliating defeat.

Therefore, just like they had hoped, the enemy had decided to press themselves against the wall to overwhelm them.

Considering that it was only about as tall as an average adult male, scaling it wouldn't require special equipment.

Or they could try to break it open like they were doing at the moment.

Unfortunately for them, the walls were built by Master mages. Unless they keep throwing themselves at them for the whole day, they won't be able to break through.

And so, with a hill behind them keeping them from retreating without heinous losses and a solid wall that held against all their tricks, the Mondeans had only one option: kill as many defenders as possible to scale the wall.

It was risky, leaving them no option but to fight, as a trapped animal was much more dangerous than a free one, but they didn't have much choice beyond stacking as many advantages as possible.

Already, they were outnumbered two to one and had much less experience fighting against other humans than the Mondeans did.

No, we need to crush them. We have to send a message to ensure this will never happen again.

A massive bolt of lightning crashed with immense force against Voggo's shield, shattering it and creating an opening for more attacks to fly through.

Several smaller shields flashed into existence, plugging the gap as best as they could, but already more people had been injured.

That was the signal that Dorea had been waiting for.

She left behind the fear for her mentor's life and concentrated on attracting the caster to herself.

Unsurprisingly it turned out to be the large woman she had fought with, and when she managed to turn the man to her left into a pile of mush with a well-placed Bullet, she turned to meet her eyes.

The woman roared in a fury, pushing a crackling stream of electricity toward her, but Dorea calmly redirected it with an arc of water.

It was a trick she had seen a shrew employ. It had used the river it lived in to catalyze an electric attack and push it away harmlessly.

Of course, this was only possible when water with enough mineral content was present, but given the sheer amount of liquid that had been thrown around on the battlefield, she had no problem on that front.

The woman looked surprised at that for only a second before she redoubled her efforts to eradicate Dorea from the world of the living.

The girl didn't let the Mondean be on the offensive for too long, pushing out a rapid staccato of Bullets to break her concentration.

The Forest people close by raised an air shield right ahead of her, protecting them all from the wrathful barrage that came their way.

Dorea and the woman exchanged several volleys that way, some breaking against each other in strangely beautiful explosions.

Then, her senses screamed that *something* was about to happen, and she threw herself back, bowling over two others.

Given the brutally powerful bolt of electricity that fell from the heavens and turned the ground where she had been standing into charred glass, that instinct had saved her life.

Immediately, Dorea grasped what had happened. The woman had taken advantage of the chaos of battle to create a charge high above the shields and dropped it on her head when it looked like she wasn't paying attention.

I'm never fully checked out, you stupid cow.

The woman took advantage of the momentary lull in their duel to blast several archers out of the wall, dropping them like flies with bolts that always seemed to overpower the defenses.

How in the hell is she putting out that much mana and still has enough to fight me?! I've been getting refilled as I kill them, and I still am not that full!

Unheeding her own complaints, Dorea immediately started her assault again.

Even though she couldn't seem to pin the strangely agile giant, the people around her were not at the same level, and she got more than a few hits thanks to the range of her spells.

Lightning Sphere was the least effective against her opponent, likely because she could feel it coming even if it was very fast, but its area of effect was large enough to create too much damage if she danced around it.

Therefore, the woman found herself forced to block hits that would have otherwise been perfectly avoidable to prevent the collapse of her line.

Dorea wasn't naive enough to think that she was doing it to save her comrades, having seen the callousness with which she stepped over their bodies, but the woman's pragmatism won over her pride, and thus, she was forced on the back foot.

She pushed her advantage as much as she could, shooting the more draining Sphere several times to allow her enemy to track the attack and have to put herself in a disadvantageous position to prevent critically important mages from dying.

This game of cat and mouse went on for quite a while, as Dorea gleefully forced the woman into uncomfortable positions and chipped away at her strength as she regained more and more as she hit the surrounding enemies.

Suddenly, it seemed that the giant had had enough, and with a roar of frustration, she crafted a massive lance of electricity in her hand and threw it forward with as much strength as she could.

Dorea immediately stopped her harassment and put all she had into a barrier of solid water as thick as an oak tree.

The spear hit the barrier and went through it without stopping, with barely a deviation in its course.

Before she had time to process her failure, Dorea felt it pass by her, leaving a burning trail of charred flesh on her hip.

It hit the Forest mage behind her, ignoring his air armor as if it wasn't there and killing him instantly.

The following explosion threw everyone around, sending the line into chaos.

Luckily, the Heidel warriors were ready for it and, with their long spears, managed to prevent a breach.

A miniature lightning storm was launched from Masi's hands, covering the gaps and sending back the attackers, who yelped as they held their burned limbs.

The boy stepped up, continuing his assault and preventing any enemy mage from getting ideas. With Melu's help, they managed to plug the gap that had formed, repelling the assault.

He slung around electricity like he was born with it, punishing anyone who came too close and even helping repel another assault farther west.

As soon as Dorea's head stopped ringing and her limbs ceased their spasming, she was dragged away from the fight.

She regained consciousness as she was sitting behind a boulder, where Noele the shaman was administering some kind of ointment over her hip.

She looked down at it only to immediately look back up.

The entire flank was charred, darkened flesh. She turned her head just in time to avoid splattering her rescuer with her vomit.

The taste of bile was foul on her tongue, but it made her focus again.

She then created a small amount of water in her mouth and swished to clean it.

"You need to get to the tent as soon as you can. I've done what I could, but this requires much more time than I can afford you," Noele shouted over the roar of battle.

As soon as she was done placing a bandage over the ointment, she rose up and, helped by another woman, hobbled off to help someone else.

I can't leave now. I don't care what it's gonna look like; if I'm not there to battle that ogre, people are gonna die.

Uncaring of her state, Dorea hoisted herself up and joined back into the fray. Her feet felt heavy, her eyes couldn't focus, and her mind was hazy, but deep within, a fire burned and it would not be quenched so easily.

She looked for her enemy, only to find her facing the lightning trio from Noele's group.

Surprisingly, they were holding their own as far as power thrown around went, though given how much the woman had already used in their duel, maybe it wasn't so strange.

They were, however, much less capable of navigating the battlefield and were being herded around in disadvantageous positions by the more skilled woman.

That lasted until a properly placed Bullet exploded right in front of her, throwing her on the ground.

Dorea took advantage of the moment to relieve pressure from the front lines, shooting wave after wave of her most versatile spell.

Through this, she kept a wary eye on her enemy. Though she had been injured, she still wasn't out for the count, and underestimating her would be a terrible mistake.

As if to confirm her fears, she felt another javelin of electricity being formed, even as the Mondean commander appeared to be too hurt to stand.

That's not going to fool me. You are gonna have to try better than that.

She interrupted her efforts immediately to focus on the woman, keeping her pinned down.

A transparent shield sprang around the enemy, signifying another mage's intervention, but Dorea didn't let it stay up for long.

Although her reserves weren't immense, she had been getting a steady refill as she sniped careless Gifted who left themselves open through the gaps in their barriers, which meant she had much more mana on hand than could be expected, especially after so long.

Most Gifted usually focused more on getting in the occasional hit and protecting their formation rather than sending wave after wave of destructive attacks like they had done in the beginning.

The melee fighters had advanced thanks to this change in the situation, and while they were kept at bay for the time being, thanks to their unfavorable position, that wouldn't last forever.

As soon as the mages got too tired to be functional, the battlefield would be theirs, and the sheer amount of humans the Mondeans had brought would make itself known.

Of course, that was only the case if everyone got tired at the same rate.

On the western side, Mark the Blue and his men had been doing a fantastic job at slowly chipping away at the edges of the enemy formation, bunching them up, and making it easier for those attacks that went through to find purchase.

His powerful Lightning Bolts reverberated through the defenses, shattering some on contact and allowing his allies to get more hits.

In the center, Voggo's shields still held firm, though the old man looked tired and haggard.

There, the greatest concentration of nonmagical fighters made themselves known by sending barrage after barrage of arrows, which slipped into the gaps.

Back on the eastern front, Dorea had broken several shields and prevented the formation of another javelin.

Luckily, it seemed to be a very complex spell, requiring concentration and a great deal of power, and being forced to dodge all the time hadn't allowed her opponent the time to form it.

The tall woman had abandoned her attempts at seeming defeated and was now giving as good as she got, though the difference in shielding capabilities was making itself heard.

Although Dorea wasn't in the best condition, with her entire left side feeling numb, she kept up her attacks with an almost psychotic focus.

I know that if I can take that stupid cow down, I'll be able to mop up the rest. She's literally the only good fighter they have; everyone else is below average. They are just too many. Like cockroaches. Need to stomp.

While her frustration was great, she had long since learned that emotions were helpful only as much as the situation allowed it.

And the one she was in then did not. Battles of such scale, she was coming to find, were peculiarly organized things.

The masses of people obeyed strange laws, moving like the ocean's waves. One couldn't simply push back and expect the opponent not to try to advance again; something, be it an elaborate strategy or a desperate last-ditch effort, needed to be implemented to stop them from coming.

And so, she had been building up to something specific.

Although the weather didn't allow for much that day, since the sun was still the only presence in the sky, a lot of magic had been thrown around, leaving useful material behind.

Through her assault, she had slowly been slipping more and more of her mana into the great mass of water that had been building up below the wall.

Her idea wasn't anything too complicated. She wouldn't be able to divert that much attention to it anyways without stopping her harassment, and so far, it was the only thing keeping her opponent from smashing through their defenses.

On the other hand, sometimes simple things were the way to go.

Once she had finally reached every drop of water, she stopped attacking only long enough to get it under her control, and, with a herculean effort, she lifted it.

All attacks stopped as the great mass of liquid blotted out the sun.

People on both sides looked at it with unease, not knowing who was keeping it under control.

Dorea, on the other hand, was operating under a tight limit. Though she had more mana than she should have at this time, her effort was draining her reserves rapidly.

Furthermore, she could feel several people trying to usurp control of it.

Luckily, she didn't want to do anything complex. She simply couldn't manipulate such a vast amount of water beyond just moving it around.

And that was precisely what she did.

Dorea sent the mass careening toward the enemy lines with a spiritual heave of effort.

It slipped from her control as it hit the ground, but by then, there wasn't anything they could do to stop it.

A great wave crashed against the Mondeans, obscuring them from sight.

After a few seconds where everyone held their breaths, a scene of destruction was revealed. The vast majority of the foot soldiers had been washed away, breaking limbs against the hard rocks that made up the hills.

Some mages had managed to shield themselves, the water-aspected ones doing better than the others, but the majority hadn't managed to avoid taking some damage.

Extending her senses, Dorea located the person she had been battling with, who had barely managed to not be drowned by the wave but had still been rattled enough to lose her orientation, given the woman's confused fumbling, and, without much fanfare, blew her head up with a Lightning Sphere.

INTERLUDE 2

Masi

Convincing the chief that he could be trusted to lead the contingent that would go to Whitecliff turned out to be simpler than Masi had expected.

"It'll be a good experience. I don't expect things to go too bad, and learning more about what both sides can do will be helpful to you" had been her words.

Thus, he had been put in charge of both the warriors he would have to bring north and their tribesmen who were already there as part of their alliance.

Melu's not gonna like this. I just know she'll complain to no end that I'm being shown favoritism again.

He rolled his eyes at what he knew was about to come. His sister was a bright and fun girl, but if someone dared not give her preferential treatment or, worse, gave it to someone else, she would go insane.

The fact that their chief had been showing a preference for him for a while had driven her up the walls. It was why she had volunteered to be sent to Whitecliff in the first place.

It was an entirely new place where people didn't know her; she was like a wolf in a sheep flock.

More important than that, they didn't have much time, so Masi made sure to emphasize to the warriors he would bring along—a group he was used to sparring with thanks to their closeness with his older brother—that they would need to be ready within the next couple of hours.

The possibility of the Mondeans attacking earlier wasn't to be discounted. Still, he would not commit his men to a fight if they didn't have the time to rest, so even if they hurried along as quickly as possible, they'd still need to hope for at least a day of waiting.

Given what the girl had said, they were likely to get it.

And what a girl she was. Her skin was pale in the way of the Northern Sapiens, her hair a golden blond that was impossible to find within his tribe.

The Heidels and the Sapiens might not have been the most different of humanity's branches, but they couldn't be mistaken for the same, even at a cursory glance.

The fact that that a slip of a girl had been given a mission of such importance likely meant that she was held in favor with the old shaman who led her tribe.

The chief had explained clearly that Voggo, the unofficial leader of Whitecliff, was not a person to dismiss, even if he hadn't achieved the level of personal power that Yaomi had.

The old man had managed to stay in power for very long, which meant something. Luckily, he wasn't a direct threat to the Heidels, as he was too wise to alienate one of his only allies.

Masi was well aware that the group he would lead and the contingent coming from the forest wouldn't be all that decisive, especially since they were told under no uncertain terms to all come back alive. Still, these kinds of gestures would go a long way to pave the path for smoother cooperation.

And we want that. If the Ergasters smell weakness in the grasslands, they won't hesitate to restart their conquest, and this time they might just win it.

The battle was somehow both messy and well organized at the same time.

Spells flew around without a specific target, splashing on the surprisingly sturdy walls or against magical barriers. Arrows whizzed past him like great birds of prey hunting for weakness.

The enemy had been forced into an unfavorable position, locked between the wall and the rocky hills, but they gave as good as they got thanks to their greater numbers and sheer aggressiveness.

What stood out the most to him, rather than the great shows of power flashing by, was the difference in how the two armies behaved.

The defenders were divided into three main groups, who all had their own dedicated barrier mages, attackers, and nonmagicals, the latter of whom served as both support and archery. It was evident even to him that there had been some thought behind their formation and that whoever called the shots had some actual experience.

The Mondeans, on the other hand, were much messier. Their entire line was made up of mages casting spells seemingly without any thought for strategy, nonmagicals who either rushed the wall in the hopes of creating a breach—but who had been entirely unsuccessful so far—and the smarter ones who stayed at the back and served as long-range archers.

Still, for all the compactness and preparation that Whitecliff's people had, their warriors were of lesser quality, evidently much more used to hunting beasts than fighting as soldiers.

That wouldn't have been enough to spell their doom by itself, but the presence of a few, better mages in the attacking ranks, made it a much more even fight.

It still wasn't enough for him to start calling for a retreat, especially since he'd never be able to live with himself if he had to run during the first real battle he commanded.

This isn't like one of our skirmishes with the southern tribes. No veterans can pull me out of a deadly situation if I get over my head.

On the other hand, he was now a mage. Lightning crackled at his fingertips, and he unleashed a powerful current, targeting a mage he had seen purposefully directing his attack toward his people.

Power coursed through his veins, and he again thanked the Spirits for choosing him.

Not only had the Wrath brought significant change to their tribe, but he himself had risen in prominence from lowly warrior apprentice to being noticed by the chief.

If he acquitted himself well—and he was well aware that everything happening here would get reported to Yaomi when they got back, especially his behavior—he could expect to continue his rise.

Masi's hair stood up as he felt a powerful lightning spell being worked. He just had the time to turn toward its origin before it was unleashed.

Luckily for him, it hurtled to his left, where it exploded into a mess of crackling arcs.

He numbly watched Dorea, the girl who had come to alert them to the upcoming attack and asked for their help, be hit. She was thrown to the back by the explosive force, skipping across the ground like a doll during a child's tantrum.

He barely had the time to extend his senses toward her, surprised to find her still alive, before he was forced to reenter the fray as one of their best mages was taken out, and her absence meant more spells passing through the layered barriers.

He couldn't help but feel slightly disconnected, his mind still stuck on the scene he had just witnessed.

The spell that had been sent was powerful, yes, but beyond that, it had been aimed purposefully at her, its caster having decided to take her out.

To think that a young girl could be the object of such a decision felt insane to him, even as he shot more and more bolts toward the enemy, ending the lives of people who had wives, sisters and brothers, enemies and friends.

This is what it's like being at war. There is no time for mercy, no place for considering the enemy's situation. I'm sure many of them don't want to be here, dying in a broken field as half their bodies lie charred beyond recognition, but yet, we are all still here.

The battle raged on, uncaring of his realizations.

He was saved from a particularly well-aimed arrow in the eye by a glob of water materializing out of nowhere, and he only had the time to shout his thanks to his sister for the save before he refocused on the fighting.

His reserves had always been considered particularly large amongst the tribesmen, but even they were starting to dwindle. He had been sparing with his spells, not wanting to exhaust himself in a fight he had to force himself to remember wasn't of existential importance to him, but even just that much ended up taxing him more than expected.

Even if Whitecliff fell, his people would be free. It would take the Mondeans much more than such a ragtag army to face the Witch of Immolation, and they likely knew it.

Still, this village served a strategic purpose, being a buffer between them and any possible northern incursion, and so had to be protected if possible.

The battle was still ongoing, and Dorea, looking worse for wear, somehow rejoined it, relieving some of the pressure he had been feeling.

Lightning magic wasn't well suited for defense, at least at the level available to him currently, and having to aim for specific spells he noticed coming their way to knock them off course was becoming tiring.

Suddenly, he heard his sister gasp in surprise. He himself felt a great concentration of power being worked and looked at the battlefield, seeking its location.

Its source ended up being much closer than expected, as all the water collected at the bottom of the wall rose at once.

The great mass of liquid trembled in the air, and Masi couldn't help but send a prayer to the Spirits that it was one of theirs controlling it.

It blotted out the sun, becoming, for just a moment, all that was visible.

His breath rushed back out, and time started running again as he saw it crashing upon the enemy lines.

The battle was over.

CHAPTER THIRTY-FIVE

The following events could best be described as a mop-up.

In any situation, losing one's leader and primary offensive attacker would be devastating. However, this loss occurred when the rest of the line was already scattered, leaving the Mondeans with no option but to flee.

The people of Whitecliff had prepared for such an occasion, and a contingent of the fresher people was sent after the fleeing fighters to ensure they couldn't regroup and take them by surprise later.

As for the rest of the men, who were either too injured or too dead to leave, they were rounded up shortly after.

There were a couple of holdouts, mages who bunched up together and tried to take down as many people as possible with them, but with them being a stationary target for the Whitecliff mages' rage, they didn't last long.

The wave had surprisingly not netted her as much of an energy boon as Dorea had expected, seemingly not having been lethal enough for the Mondean Gifted. Still, it had refilled her sufficiently to participate in the cleanup, and she did so with viciousness.

Generally, she would have been reticent at the idea of killing men who had no more fight in them, but a quick glance at the long line of her tribesmen's bodies being dragged away from the wall immediately cured her of any hesitation.

She battered down whatever flimsy shield her enemies tried to put up and ended them quickly if they didn't immediately surrender.

There was a surprising amount of the latter. She had thought that since the Mondeans were a warrior tribe with a very high level of pride in themselves, more people would be willing to fight to the death, but given what was happening, she might have to reconsider.

It was possible, of course, that they were simply scared of dying. Seeing their army break after being on the offensive for so long would have shocked anyone, and the method she employed to turn the tables was probably more than a little at fault, but she suspected that something else was going on.

Given the relief on some people's faces when they should have rightly been terrified or mulishly reticent, there had to be.

Indeed, it only took half an hour before the first report came that several new prisoners claimed to have been coerced into fighting for the Mondeans after they had conquered their villages, much like they tried to do with Whitecliff.

That would explain quite a bit. Both their weird behavior and how exactly those northern barbarians are capable of fielding such large groups without collapsing when they get defeated.

Of course, they would need to interrogate them about the other prisoners, and then cross-examine their testimonies to ensure no one was trying to slip in alongside the conscripts.

Since Mother Nature forbid the execution of a defeated foe after they surrendered and posed no more threat to one's people, they would need to divide the prisoners between those who had actually been coerced and could regain their freedom after working off their debt, and those who had willingly attacked them, whose lives were forfeit.

Once she was sure the battlefield was under control, Dorea left to check on Voggo.

She had seen him limp away toward the triage tent earlier and had been too relieved to find him still alive to question him about further injuries, but now that things had calmed down, she wanted to ensure that the stubborn old man was fine.

Maybe I'll get someone to check on my injuries, too, while I'm there. I seem to remember someone saying something about me needing to get looked at.

Now that the adrenaline was starting to come down, the buzzing in her skin of fresh new power was the only thing propelling her forward.

Even that had its limits though, and Dorea found herself feeling more tired than she had been expecting to be.

In the time it took her to reach the tent, she received three offers of help getting there, which told her that she might not be looking particularly good.

Finally, she reached it and went in, aiding herself by using the air surrounding her as a crutch.

Inside, there was chaos.

The tent was bigger than the one erected at the main gate to the east, since the villagers had had enough time to spare as they waited for the Mondeans to attack.

Several women and a few men were quickly going through the cots—made of a hay mattress covered in a linen cloth—as they tried to deal with the worst injuries.

Men cried as they held their broken limbs; people of all ages rested as they tried to contain the pain they were surely feeling.

Dorea would have preferred not to bother the harried healers in such a moment, but her mother had made sure she understood her limits very well, especially after she got hurt the last time, and even had she wanted to, the girl wasn't sure she would be able to go far.

There was still some mana in her, but her system felt overworked and stretched to its limits.

I have never used this much power in a single day. Being refilled so often after I killed their mages allowed me to go on much longer than I should have.

She ached in parts she couldn't possibly point to, as it was more a metaphysical kind of pain, but some instinct told her that using what she had left wouldn't be a good idea.

Her side was throbbing, as apparently whatever paste Noele had used on her stopped working, or maybe it had never numbed her completely, and she had simply been too agitated to notice.

That wasn't a good sign, as Lilian always said. "If you can feel pain, it means you are alive. If your eyes said you should, but you don't, run to the nearest healer."

Her shuffling form was quickly noticed by her harried mother, who took a look at her and immediately directed her to a cot.

"Stay there, and do not move!"

The following events were only a blur in Dorea's mind, but she thought there might have been a lot of swearing, some cursing, and even a bit of ranting.

The grass was still wet with dew as they gathered. The sky was tinted by the colors of the dawn, giving an otherwise grim setting a somewhat poetic atmosphere.

It was three days after the battle, and things had finally settled down enough to start dealing with the aftermath.

The groups sent in pursuit of the enemy had returned victorious, having caught up with most of them.

A lucky few had managed to run away by taking separate paths, but that hadn't necessarily been seen as a negative. Indeed, Voggo had commented that they needed someone to bring back word of what would happen to anyone who dared threaten them.

Their success, however, meant that there was an increasingly large amount of prisoners, and, however much they might have wanted to take things slow to ensure there was no mistake in their investigations, they couldn't justify feeding and healing them all.

It was a brutally pragmatic decision, but it was one that no one contested.

Their resources were limited, and would be much better used for those few coerced into joining the Mondean army.

Thus, once he had recovered enough and had ensured that his presence wasn't immediately required at the triage tent, the shaman had started interrogating the prisoners.

He used magic, potions, and his wiles to get confessions out of them, thus speeding up the process significantly.

That meant that thirty-three executions were about to happen that morning.

As was tradition, all the prisoners had been offered a deadly brew that would painlessly send them to the Mother's embrace.

The majority of them accepted and were therefore allowed to record their last words.

Though it all was codified in ancient customs, this was the very first time Dorea had taken part in such a ceremony, and while she appreciated the cleanliness of it all, it still rubbed her the wrong way to simply kill that many men.

Of course, she was well aware that releasing them was not an option. To do so would mean having them regroup with their tribe and come back again, this time better armed.

No, there was no other recourse, but that didn't mean she had to enjoy it.

As for the few who refused their mercy, they were not granted a peaceful ending.

They were the entire reason why so many people had gathered at the crack of dawn.

Of the thirty-three slated to die, twenty-seven had already drank the brew that would end their lives, though not without a great deal of hesitation.

The remaining six were the rowdiest of the bunch and, if allowed, would have tried to break out.

Unluckily for them, Dorea and several other Gifted had taken the time to ensure that such a thing was not possible.

The executioner's axe had been brought out of storage, since it hadn't seen any use for many years, and had been sharpened until there was no doubt it would cut through necks like a hot knife through butter.

Ed, the hunter, had taken up the post as he waited for the tree stump to be positioned in place, so he could begin.

His face was even graver than usual, seemingly etched into stone.

Though he was never a particularly cheerful man, he had become even more dour since the battle. The loss of his nephew, whom he had been grooming to take his role in the future, had struck deep within him, and a glacial resolve had taken root.

Dorea and others had offered to do the deed by themselves, using magic to ensure it would be as efficient as possible, but the man wouldn't budge.

Tradition dictated that they be executed with a weapon made from the bones of the earth, and since none of them were Master-level earth mages capable of wielding iron as if it was dirt, such a thing had to be done by means of the old axe.

The prisoners didn't go quietly, thrashing and screaming through the cloth that covered their mouths, but there wasn't anything they could do.

Dorea kept her gaze steady, not wanting to give the impression that she didn't agree or was too weak to stomach such things.

The *thump* of the axe hitting the wood and the eerie quiet that followed were not enjoyable experiences for her, but were cathartic for many of those present.

No matter their eventual victory, the battle had been bloody, and they had lost many. Too many, even if it could have been much worse.

Catching their army in the cul-de-sac signified having a better position to rain death and destruction upon them, without allowing them to remove themselves from it easily. Still, it also meant that the Mondeans fought much more desperately.

With their greater numbers—no matter how valuable the reinforcements Dorea's tribe got from their allies might have been—the Mondeans had been able to turn a disastrous situation into something of a stalemate.

Their commander, by herself, had been more than enough to equalize the situation.

Her spells had packed a terrifying amount of power, being capable of breaking through even Voggo's shields, and whenever she was allowed to attack freely, the people of Whitecliff fell.

The fact that Dorea had killed her after keeping the woman occupied for the better part of the engagement had skyrocketed her fame. Luckily, she had managed to avoid the worst of it thanks to either being too sick to receive well-wishers or too busy ensuring no prisoner escaped.

The only part of her new fame she appreciated was that no one would dare voice complaints about her being included during the council meetings anymore.

Voggo hadn't technically announced her as his successor, but it had been unofficially understood to be the case.

The fact that she had been quite a bit weaker than the other mages in the beginning had been causing skepticism, but her recent feats had quieted those voices down, and her latest victory had definitely put them to rest.

Dorea hadn't had the chance yet to take some time and figure out exactly how much stronger she had become thanks to the infusion of power from the battle, but she could tell that she had finally reached the top of their village's power rankings.

Mark the Blue might still edge her out, but her versatility more than made up for it.

One last *thump* interrupted her thoughts. It signified the last of the executions and meant they would need to proceed with the burial.

Noele the shaman hobbled up to check on those who had decided to drink the poison and declared that they were all genuinely dead.

Dorea could have told her that none of them were breathing anymore, but she supposed that making sure hurt no one.

Finally, they started levitating the bodies away from the cliff, where they had held the ceremony and, in something of an improvised procession, brought them all the way to the southern gate, gathering more and more followers as they went.

A deep grave had been prepared for them at the forest's edge, so that their corpses could nourish it.

Some had proposed leaving them out in the open, where animals and the weather could deal with them, but it had been shot down by Voggo.

Beyond the sacrilegious idea of ignoring the proper burial rituals, doing so would be asking for illnesses to start festering.

They deposited the bodies in the prepared ditch and went to work filling it up.

The earth was soft under her efforts as she manipulated a water shovel. Others used what they could or simply threw handfuls of dirt down.

It took them a while, but finally after almost a whole hour, the grave had been filled and they could leave.

There were no last words, no family members to lead a eulogy. These people had tried to take their homes away and had been afforded all the respect they deserved. Nothing more would be given to them.

The meeting room was in its usual configuration; the many maps that had started adorning it as they tried to follow the Mondean contingent's movements had been deemed no longer useful and had been put away.

On the table, a sweeter brew of tea than Voggo usually preferred had been prepared, and for that, Dorea was grateful.

The floral aftertaste was much appreciated and went wonderfully with the ground almond sweets.

The more relaxed atmosphere than their last meetings' meant that Dorea didn't feel too guilty about indulging.

Her mother had informed her unambiguously that she needed to eat more to aid her recovery and that, while the various poultices and potions she had used had done most of the work, her body desperately needed the proper nutrients to finish the job.

Not one to be told twice or willing to face the woman's wrath, she took every moment she could to fill her stomach.

That it helped distract her from the metaphysical ache she could sometimes feel when she used her magic meant that she was only more enthusiastic about it.

"We shouldn't lower our guard too much. We gave them a black eye, and they will likely think twice before attacking us again, but when they do, it'll be with overwhelming force," Ed said, bringing down the mood.

His words were tiredly acknowledged by the elderly shaman. "That is likely, yes. It's also possible they'll try to whittle away at our allies to face us alone, so we must be ready to send help to the east if they need it."

She hadn't thought of that before, but it made a lot of sense.

While the Mondean chief might have the reputation of a bloodthirsty maniac, the fact that he had been able to accrue so many victories and gather such a host meant that he had some tactical acumen.

Dealing with the three allies individually was likely much more appealing than facing them together again, especially if he still couldn't bring his best to bear in the south.

"We should send a mission to the north. Not knowing the situation there will make us paranoid as we wait for them to gather their forces," Mark suggested wisely.

"I don't think establishing an outpost too far is a good idea, but I'm all for a periodic scouting mission. We have several people who once lived there with us by now, so we should make use of their knowledge," she added, gaining a nod of approval from Voggo.

They further discussed the specifics of the mission, arguing for or against some people, but the basic idea was one they all shared.

While they had won a significant victory and could likely expect a bit of slack for the coming period, not knowing anything about their enemies was simply unacceptable.

Regular patrols had already started back up, and their allies' contingents were preparing to leave with their spoils, having taken some of the Mondeans' equipment beyond the promised resources.

Life wouldn't be the same ever again. Since they had lost more than two dozen people, it simply couldn't, but it would go on as it always did.

They would get used to the absences, even if they would never be truly forgotten.

People she had known all her life were gone forever, just like others she had met only weeks before, after helping them find peace in Whitecliff.

War was tragic, but their victory would allow them the time needed to grow even stronger so that the next time such a loss of life could be avoided.

CHAPTER THIRTY-SIX

Dorea walked toward the beach, idly kicking a rock along the path.

The excitement of the previous days had been followed by forced monotony, as she was deemed too important to Whitecliff's safety to go on the scouting mission to the north and still not fully recovered enough to do any strenuous work in the village.

Indeed, it seemed like Whitecliff's people had decided communally not to allow her to exert herself in any way.

Elderly grandmothers who would usually welcome any help suddenly only wanted company for tea, and farmers who had never been as short in manpower somehow did not need a capable mage.

It's obviously a conspiracy. Either Mom or Voggo have put the fear of the Goddess into them. No other explanation.

Thus, she had found herself more bored than she could remember ever being.

More frustratingly, she knew her friends and peers were active in various essential tasks. Jonah was tapped as a sensor for the dangerous northern scouting mission. Beth had been working overtime to clear the mess left on the battlefield, and everyone else, weak or strong, had been given something to do.

Everyone apart from her. Her contributions to the village's protection had been deemed more than enough, and she was refused at every point.

Power churned within her, greatly increased by the spoils of the battle, and she had nothing to use it on.

I'm not even that injured anymore! My mana has fully recovered, and my wounds have almost closed. I get not seeking combat, but there must be something I can do.

Thus, she hatched a plot.

Dorea knew perfectly well that if anyone saw her do any strenuous task, she'd get an earful from her mother within minutes. Therefore, she decided she'd just need to help others do their jobs in ways that wouldn't tire her.

And if, somehow, I annoy them enough to start wanting me to go away and do something on my own, well, that's on them.

Her target had been chosen carefully. A gathering of the least able Gifted in Whitecliff had been meeting at the beach every afternoon after the battle in an attempt to practice their magical skills.

Apparently, having been relegated to the back lines for almost all the fighting had lit a fire under them, and they decided to do something to make themselves useful.

Dorea wholeheartedly approved their efforts and was sure they wouldn't turn away her help.

Though she didn't like bragging about it, she was the only Journeyman mage present in the village from the current generation, and everyone knew it.

Her prodigious growth, alongside her many successes, had lent her an air of competence that she'd usually feel was misplaced but would gladly use on this specific occasion.

Finally coming into sight of the group, she noticed that they were operating similarly to how Voggo's lessons went. They'd take turns showing what they had been working on and receive either praise or critique depending on their achievements.

That, however, was a very inefficient way to go about it.

While the shaman had both a wealth of knowledge and hard-won experience to analyze their efforts and steer them in the right direction, alongside a whole hour of lecturing on specific topics, they didn't have anything close to that and were simply either showing off or repeating the same mistakes.

That she immediately noticed such a thing told her that, for all their enthusiasm, the mages hadn't put much thought into it.

Either that or they just want to do something to not feel useless. Which I can understand, honestly.

Soon enough, she was noticed by Tom, the friendly water mage with whom she had gone on a few missions.

"Are we to be your latest victims, my lady?" His tone was joking, but his expression showed he dreaded a severe response.

"I just thought I might be able to offer some advice, good sir."

She knew that no one would refuse her help in this field. She had been a leading combatant in the Battle of the Rocky Hills, as it was being called.

Turning her down was tantamount to ignoring her accomplishments.

The boy scratched his cheek in thought. "We are delighted that you took the time to come help us, but as you can see, we are doing perfectly fine ourselves. No need to spend your precious time on us."

Several others had noticed her by then, and they all seemed torn between being grateful for her presence and terrified to go against the directive of letting her rest.

"Honestly, I'll just observe and give some pointers, nothing more. There won't be any magic on my part; I'll promise you that," she countered sweetly.

That did the trick. They couldn't possibly reject her without coming off as rude, and if she truly kept to giving simple advice, well, no one could gainsay them, right?

Tom's shoulders dropped as he knew that he had lost the argument then and there.

"I'll keep close to ensure you don't overexert yourself," he added as a last point, looking directly at the poorly hidden bandages beneath her dress.

She huffed a laugh and pulled at it to cover herself better. Then, she sat down on the hot sand, looking expectantly at Nora, an air mage who usually acted as a lookout on the wall and who had been about to show off her progress.

The girl shook herself and gained a determined gleam, apparently wanting to make a good impression.

She raised her hands and sang under her breath as the air in front of her started twisting oddly.

What followed was an excellent example of pushing the basics to their logical limits. As they began their forays in wind magic, they had all been taught that one of the most efficient ways of dealing with an opponent who was unaware or couldn't move was to simply deprive them of air.

To do so, one needed to keep the atmosphere from rushing back in to fill the void at all times while they kept the magic on their possibly moving target, or they'd need to create a shell of compressed air to do that job for them.

Dorea had used something similar—using water as her medium—months before against the smilodon, who had attempted to hunt her family's anoas. It hadn't been enough to win her the fight, but it had certainly done its job in distracting the beast enough for her to finish it.

What Nora was doing was somewhat similar to the second option. Her spell, and it was a spell given its speed and efficiency, allowed for the creation of small orbs devoid of anything.

By themselves, they wouldn't be much more than a nuisance even just to a competent warrior, but as a swarm, Dorea could see how they'd be a dangerous weapon.

The fact that the girl almost collapsed after she was done detracted a bit from their purported usefulness. Still, Dorea supposed that not everyone could have weird magical mutations that allowed them to grow stronger freakishly fast.

Nora turned to her expectantly, ignoring the applause of her companions.

Though she had come intending to create trouble and make a nuisance of herself, Dorea didn't have the heart to deny the girl. She smiled and joined in the applause, to her great joy.

It's a bit weird how she's a year older and still looks up at me as if I were Voggo.

Her contributions to the village's safety had seen her rise from simply being a mage with a lot of potential that the shaman was grooming to one day have a leadership position, to someone worthy of being recognized on her own.

Several more mages went up after Nora in an attempt to receive such praise again, but their efforts were lackluster in comparison.

It was apparent, then, that it wasn't so much a lack of talent that saw the gathered Gifted fall behind the others, so much as them not putting in the necessary effort.

Dorea gestured for the only surprise of the morning to join her, and the brunette quickly did so, looking still exhausted but happy.

"I was surprised at the level you brought such a simple exercise. I can see it being handy in a pinch," she commented.

Nora grinned, dropping beside her. "I'm thinking of calling it Swarming Void. It's definitely not on your level as far as power goes, but Voggo always tells us that every spell has its own specific use."

Not wanting to give the wrong impression, Dorea quickly replied, "No, no, I agree. I'm sure that as you keep growing, you'll be able to turn it into a deadly weapon. But even as it is, I bet it would give whoever was on the receiving end a very nasty shock."

Not everyone is up to killing as quickly as me. I need to remember that.

They continued chatting for a while, casually observing the ongoing demonstrations. Once in a while, Dorea called out a piece of advice or chided someone for their reckless usage of magic.

Indeed, there was more than one case where the mages evidently thought they had stumbled upon a shortcut to power, somewhat similar to what she had done the first night she had her magic.

Attempting to compress an element so much that when released, it exploded violently, was a legitimate tactic when trying to explore one's magic capabilities, but using it as a weapon when you couldn't control it once let go was the height of foolishness.

At least I was just starting out. These people have had months of lessons and experience to realize that it's idiotic.

She knew she was being a bit hypocritical, considering how that kind of experimenting led to her Lightning Sphere and Exploding Water Bullet. Still, she had done so by herself, having taken care to be in a place where no one else could get hurt.

Admittedly, maybe that wasn't the wisest thing to do either since if she did get hurt, it would take time for anyone to find her, but she wasn't feeling particularly charitable lately.

"That kind of harebrained showing off is exactly why you haven't managed to cast a spell yet. Always going after the low-hanging fruit to avoid hard work is never going to pay off, I hope you know."

The boy opened his mouth to rebut something, but she didn't allow him. "You have no significant achievement, have received no particular praise for your skill, and yet you dare think you can reject my words?!"

Her scolding had significantly chilled the atmosphere, and the subsequent demonstrations were done with a much more stilted air.

"Was there really a need to go off on him like that?" asked Tom from her other side.

She turned a frosty glare on him, making him raise his hands in surrender. "If he had been even just a bit more unlucky, that kind of explosion would have reached us before we could put up much of a shield. If he learns his lesson now, we'll prevent future disaster."

He gulped, evidently not having expected her fervor, and visibly gave it up as a bad job.

The glances she received after were enough to tell her that Tom wasn't the only one to think she had gone overboard with her scolding.

Self-reflection had never been her strong suit, and she might never be able to be a particularly calm person, but Dorea didn't think she had been too harsh.

Just thinking about what damage he could have done had he attempted such a thing with nonmagicals around—who couldn't feel the instability of his construct—made her blood boil.

Her emotions had been all over the place since the battle, and being forced to rest without doing anything useful had only heightened her frustration.

I'm getting too angry about this. What's going on?

It was easy to be swept by the frustration she had been feeling for days at her forced rest and lay the blame there, but something told her it had been going on for longer than she was comfortable with.

Undoubtedly, what she had just witnessed had been foolish, and she was perfectly justified in her lecturing, but Dorea wasn't so blind that she couldn't see the uncomfortable looks around her.

There was a profound discrepancy between how she perceived her behavior and how others saw it.

It's possible that they simply don't know what kind of damage this type of thing can do. But again, that sounds way too elitist.

She distractedly gestured for them to keep going, not wanting to stop them for longer than she already had, and tried to dig deeper into her mind.

Some of it is legitimate. It was stupid what he did. Some of it comes from feeling useless for days and enduring praise that I don't think is warranted.

She was well aware that dealing the final blow to the enemy commander had been what broke their assault, but the niggling thought that she had taken too long, leading to more deaths than necessary, was not leaving her.

The praise she received felt like ash on her tongue. The looks of awe and gratitude were like hidden daggers. The power she had gained—which she could feel humming beneath her skin, just begging to be released—now felt stolen, not earned.

Instead of the glory and fame she had been foolishly dreaming about just months before, she would have much rather gone back to being relatively unknown.

Expectations were sure to pile up on her in the future, and when she inevitably failed at one thing, the whole castle of cards would come crashing down.

Dorea felt like a fraud, as if somehow she had convinced her tribesmen that she was something she was not, and that led to at least some of the frustration and anger she was dealing with.

After abruptly standing up, she barely remembered to say goodbye to Tom and Nora, and quickly left the beach.

Although she had come with a plan in mind, the thought of staying there longer than absolutely necessary gave her the hives. She was sure that something else would crop up and she would lash out again, and until she had a handle on her new temper, she'd have to keep away from such situations.

Dorea didn't even realize she had been running until she reached the spot on the cliffs where they had buried those who hadn't survived the Trial.

Unconsciously, she looked for a specific one, stopping before it.

A great white stone had been placed where Rupert had once sat, with his name carved onto it.

There were no epitaphs like those reserved for the warriors, as the boy simply didn't have the time to become one.

He had been too young to gain the achievements necessary to get such an honor, but Voggo had ensured that everyone who didn't make it that day would still be remembered, by granting them a unique grave.

As was tradition, the tribesmen were buried in the dirt and left there for Mother Nature to welcome back in her embrace. They'd serve to nourish the soil, and new life would spring from them.

Only grass and shrubbery grew on the cliff, and the graves had been carefully dug.

Their last breaths had been taken while undergoing a Trial, and as such, they would still be considered heroes to the people of Whitecliff. Everyone had known that there was a possibility they wouldn't make it, and they still drank the potion.

Their bravery would never be forgotten.

Standing in front of his grave for the first time, Dorea felt a tear make its way down her cheek, swiftly followed by more.

"He was such a beautiful soul," she murmured, tracing with a finger his carved name.

Rupert had been a bright young man, always up for a laugh and ready to tease her out of her funk.

That they didn't have the time to explore a relationship felt horrible. In her darkest moments, she wondered if she could have done something to save him during the Trial. Had she taken the right bag and left the pendant with her parents, she might have been taken instead of him.

Would he have been a more powerful mage than me? At least he'd have been able to handle his emotions better than me, that's for sure.

Dorea had made a concerted effort not to think about him ever since that day, knowing that the guilt and despair would be too much to bear, but as she stood there at his grave, the only emotions she could muster was overwhelming sadness at how short his life was cut.

He had had the potential to be a much better leader for Whitecliff's Gifted than she did. He would have managed to help the struggling mages with a smile, and they would have loved him for it.

If only he were still alive, he could have chased her roiling emotions away with a teasing remark, brightening her day. Unfortunately, his cold grave had no answers for her. There was no sudden epiphany, no great moment of realization.

She was alone, with a burden she shouldn't have to bear by herself and the sinking feeling that something was wrong with her.

CHAPTER THIRTY-SEVEN

The following few days exercised Dorea's patience like nothing before.

Her temper, which had been steadily getting worse, kept her on her toes. Every annoyance she met risked becoming a massive blowout, and being aware of it didn't necessarily make containing herself easier.

With a lot of effort, she managed to avoid a repeat of her lashing out at the beach, and people had stopped treating her like she were made of glass, which helped, but the wait for the northern scouting mission to return still kept her anxiety levels high.

She couldn't even take the time to blow off some steam in the forest by fighting powerful beasts, as they simply didn't know whether the Mondeans were about to send another army to attack them.

She had been one of the most successful mages during the Battle of the Rocky Hills, and that came with its responsibilities. Dorea couldn't simply leave as she pleased now.

Mark the Blue had briefly commiserated with her about the need to stay within Whitecliff's borders for as long as they had no intel on the enemy's moves, but the man had no more than that to share.

They were the two most powerful mages in the village alongside Voggo, though, on a grand scale, they had barely started their journey, but they had lived lives that were simply too different to find much in common.

"I respect you," he had said, "but I have my thing, and you have yours. You can sit with Voggo and the others and occasionally come down in the field. I live there."

It hadn't been said with hostility, but as a statement of fact.

That didn't mean that she had taken it well. Dorea had been looking for someone who could understand her burdens, and the blue-haired man had been the most likely candidate, but he had rejected her before she even made an attempt.

Dorea had been severely tempted to make him eat his words about her not belonging to the field, but she remembered that he had been a scout and was used to spending more time outside the village than in it.

Luckily for them—and everyone else—Voggo interrupted what could have been a disastrous fight before it could be started.

They had met outside the shaman's house for a meeting about the village's defenses and had been invited in for a spot of tea afterward.

Mark the Blue was obviously somewhat uncomfortable with the attention, as he had done his best since the Wrath to avoid such situations.

He gratefully took his cup and buried himself in it, using it as a crutch to not speak.

"It's nice sometimes to make yourself a good brew and share it with others," Voggo hummed.

He's either utterly oblivious to what was about to happen or doing this to lower the tension. Knowing how crafty the old man can be, I'll bet on the second.

Dorea could logically recognize how it would be bad for everyone if she and Mark fought, especially in the middle of the village, but seeing his unconcerned face as he metaphorically slapped her hand made her teeth grind.

She held back out of love for the shaman, angrily chewing some almond cookies. They were her favorites, and she was determined to enjoy them fully, even if the company wasn't the best.

The awkwardness was finally broken when a message carried by the winds arrived for Voggo, though Dorea also managed to listen in.

"Mission successful. We have tracked their movements and have determined their goals. No immediate risk for Whitecliff. Coming in fifteen," she recognized Jonah's voice saying.

It had taken them a day longer than initially expected to return, but no one had been particularly worried at their absence.

It was, after all, much more likely for them to have decided to do a more thorough job of it rather than them having been ambushed and killed. No matter how many Mondeans there may be, time and time again, the people of Whitecliff had managed to demonstrate their individual superiority.

Still, it was good news that nothing bad had happened to them. Although she hadn't spent as much time with Jonah and Beth as she used to since the start of their relationship, Dorea still considered them her closest friends, and losing the boy would have been devastating.

The message was followed by a flurry of activity as they prepared to receive the tired scouts. The tea was thrown out, and a new, much larger pot was put on the fire while Dorea busied herself in the kitchen alongside her mother, preparing some food.

It was somewhat nostalgic, sharing a cooking space with Lilian. Once, she used to help with dinner almost every night—since turning ten until the Wrath, to be precise—and though she wouldn't go back to those times if she had to leave behind her magic and independence, she still missed the simplicity.

They operated as a well-oiled machine, frying up some of the meat that Voggo always kept on hand for such occasions and roasting root vegetables over a spit. It wouldn't be a feast, but they were sure the scouts would appreciate it after days of trawling through the mountains.

Half an hour later, they served the dishes. The shaman had cracked a cask of mead to welcome the mission's success, and the small group sat down to eat.

Dorea was called to Voggo's side, and as she joined him, she gave a quick side hug to Jonah, who happily received it and assured her of his well-being.

"Mark was about to relay what they found out, and though it's not one of our little councils, I thought it'd be better if he had to say it only once," the old man explained.

Mark the lead scout, gestured to the empty chair next to him, and she smiled in greeting. On the other side, Ed the hunter and Mark the Blue sat.

"The trip through the rocky hills was actually pretty quick, as we met no resistance, and most of the beasts had been culled by the Mondeans just days before," he began.

"The problems started once the mountains began. I have been there a few times in my life, but I'm only capable of following the easiest paths. It would have been impossible to find anything worth reporting if it weren't for Mal." He gestured to the dark-haired young man sitting next to Jonah. He was one of Noele's tribesmen, if she remembered correctly.

He was stuffing his face as if he had been starving, but no one tried to stop him, instead watching with indulgent looks.

"He insisted on coming with us to serve as a guide in case we got lost, and after seeing us fumble around for a couple of hours, he took over. I thank the Mother he convinced me to come. Otherwise, I don't know how we would have managed."

Voggo hummed in thought as he spooned some more hash on his plate. The shaman had been keeping quiet as he allowed his lieutenant to give his report, but his bright eyes showed he was following everything.

"Mal managed to find a hidden trail soon enough, and after following it for a few hours, we noticed several traces of people going through. And they were fresh, which meant those Mondeans that managed to escape had passed there a day or so before us."

That was one of the many reasons they allowed some of their enemies to escape. Ed had argued that destroying them utterly would send a stronger message, but the resources needed to follow them up the mountains and deal with them before they could reach their people were better spent elsewhere.

Also, Voggo had decided that it would serve as a message. If none returned, it could be argued that they fell against a powerful beast, sickness, or a thousand different things. This way, their defeat would be perfectly clear.

"We followed the traces, being very careful not to be spotted. Jonah was instrumental there, allowing us to move quickly without fearing an ambush," he continued between bites.

The team had brought rations with them—as was the norm for anyone going on a mission longer than a few hours—but wanting to avoid using fire, they had only eaten dried meat and hard bread.

I can see why they would be so famished. Even if it fills your belly, it's still not a good meal.

"It took us almost two days before we started seeing more signs of activity. From there, we followed the paths and were led to a valley where a large host had gathered. About five hundred people, to our count."

Dorea felt herself pale, and from the look of it, many others around them were in the same predicament.

That many warriors, even without much magical support, would mean a terrifying foe. And knowing what they knew about the Mondeans, the absence of mages was unlikely.

"I see it on your faces. I can assure you that having them in front of you is even scarier. It took us a while to decide what to do next, but we couldn't simply run back here with our tails tucked. So I asked for volunteers and went as close as possible." He raised his glass of mead to his men, who all raised theirs in response before taking a large gulp.

"Jonah was instrumental there as well. He can listen to conversations happening hundreds of feet away without being noticed, so we left most of the eavesdropping to him. I tried to get a better picture of their numbers and composition."

Jonah's specialization might mean he's not suited to direct combat, but he's invaluable to Whitecliff. If we lost him, our capabilities would take a huge blow.

That had been Beth's argument against leaving for the mission in the first place, and Dorea sympathized with her. The boy had never been particularly adventurous and wasn't exactly thrilled at the idea of getting so close to their enemies' seat of power. But the level of information he could grasp from a safe distance was unmatched by anyone else.

A nonmagical couldn't get close enough to overhear anything without getting noticed by the mages that, without a doubt, were tasked with securing the perimeter.

On the other hand, Jonah could do so while staying out of everyone's but the absolute best's range.

"What he got from that is mostly good news. The few bastards who escaped us have done their jobs and let everyone know of Whitecliff's might. Also, unlike what you are thinking, the main group wasn't there for us. They were using the valley as a staging point to attack another mountain tribe."

Everyone exhaled the breath they had been holding in. If such a host had marched toward them, they would have been annihilated no matter how much time they had to prepare.

The fact that the Mondeans could produce that kind of army, even after all the losses they had inflicted upon them and months of warring with other villages, was an indicator that their enemy was still very capable of being dangerous.

"Obviously, no one was discussing their plans in an easy-to-understand manner out in the open, but from what Jonah could gather, alongside our observations, they were dealing with a coalition of villages on the eastern ranges, and the army we met was only one part of their strategy to deal with them."

It's so easy to forget we are not the center of the world. Though we have inflicted some losses on them, especially at the Battle of the Rocky Hills, it's likely to be only an annoyance for them. We just aren't that important as they conduct a war against thousands upon thousands of people.

Mark wet his throat with more mead before continuing, "We stayed close enough to study them for a whole day, and the best piece of information arrived just as we were making to leave, happy that they weren't about to try anything."

The tension ratcheted up again, and the scouts who had just returned looked like a mix of resignation and determination.

"It took us a while to identify a command tent, but when we did, we concentrated our efforts there. And they paid off, as we noticed the men who looked the most haggard, and who likely were the survivors from the attack against us, being called in. Jonah did his best to listen in, and from what he could gather, the commander of the force thought that their humiliation couldn't go unanswered, even though he didn't have the means to do anything about it at the moment."

That had been Dorea's biggest fear. It was unlikely that people known for their warlike ways would simply accept having been defeated so harshly by a small village like theirs. Especially not when they were in the midst of a seemingly successful campaign to absorb and unite all the Sapiens tribes in the vicinity.

"Of course," Voggo replied. "It's a matter of pride. Men who win wars and who butcher their enemies are men whose pride takes first place in their lives. They can't possibly stomach our presence. So, tell us, how do they want to deal with us?"

Given the tranquility in his voice, the old man had likely been expecting such a thing.

Mark hesitated in answering for a second before exhaling. "It's not as bad as it might seem. The commander acknowledged that they simply didn't have the men to spare to 'pacify' us," he replied, using his fingers to create air quotes, "but that they'd need to do something, and that something is likely going to be an attack against the Forest tribe. Their reasoning is complicated, and if you want, you can have Jonah explain it to you, but in short it boils down to wanting to split up any possible alliance that is forming here so that when they can spare the time, they'll be able to sweep us."

Everyone breathed a bit better, but the uneasy fallen silence remained.

Knowing they could expect an attack on their ally meant it wouldn't happen to them, at least for a while.

Of course, they'd never abandon them that easily and would send a contingent to help in the defense if necessary, but that Whitecliff would be safe from reprisal was excellent news.

"I'll go and inform them of the situation," Dorea volunteered.

Voggo smiled at her enthusiasm, clearly knowing that the restrictions she had been under lately had been grating. "Are you sure you are feeling up to it? I'm certain we'll be able to find someone else who'd go," he teased.

Dorea didn't dignify him with an answer, already going through the supplies she'd need in her mind. Luckily, the Forest tribe wasn't that far, so she should be able to get there within the day if she left in the morning.

Her Air Boost wasn't yet ready to be called a proper spell, and it certainly wouldn't work as well in the dense forest as it had in the grasslands, but it should still allow her to cut quite a few hours from the trip.

"Did you find out when they expect to be ready for the attack?" she questioned Mark.

He shook his head. "Unfortunately not. We already stayed longer than I was comfortable with at that point, and the Mondeans were preparing to move, so we decided to cut our losses there."

It was understandable. Their findings would allow them to plan for the future in a much more precise fashion.

Asking for more would be too greedy. Even if I wish they'd been able to get a timeline. There could already be a group en route by now, or we could be looking at weeks of waiting.

No matter how much they learned, their thirst for new information was never-ending. This was something that Dorea had been noticing more and more. Their manpower disadvantage meant they'd need to stack all other factors in their favor, and having time to prepare was the biggest one they could get.

If only we could have someone in their high ranks relaying their thoughts . . .

Unfortunately, such a dream would remain in the realm of the fantastic. While there were stories about mages using their powers to subvert others' wills, such things were heavily warned against, as they corrupted the caster's soul.

And beyond that, I wouldn't even know where to begin attempting such a thing. Voggo might be able to, but knowing him, he'd consider it anathema.

There was much one had to give up as they fought to protect their people, but such principles couldn't be put aside. They were the foundation of their civilization; without them, they'd be nothing more than savages.

With the report given, Mark and the rest of the scouts dug in the small feast with gusto and were left to it without any further disturbance. There would be time for a more accurate recounting of events after they had rested, but the salient details had been given, and they could start preparing for the future.

Dorea and her mother soon left the shaman's house, taking some left-over meat for a quick dinner at the ranch. Voggo saw them off with a smile. "Remember to be here in the early morning, little Dory. I'll have more detailed instructions then."

She acknowledged his words with a nod and quickly ran to join her mother, already looking forward to finally doing something important.

CHAPTER THIRTY-EIGHT

At the crack of dawn, Dorea found herself standing at the village's gates, ready to get back into the fray.

"Remember, we don't know when to expect this possible attack, but it should still happen after a couple of days, considering the travel and organizing time. A contingent of Gifted will leave tomorrow and should be there before the shortest timeline," reminded Voggo.

The old man had been worried about her since the Battle of the Rocky Hills but had done his best not to stifle her too much. His edict of enforced rest had not been taken well, and he was obviously restraining himself from mothering her too much.

"I remember. It will be okay, trust me." She smiled back.

He sighed before patting her cheek as goodbye and finally letting her go.

Dorea's mission was to alert the Forest tribe to the upcoming attack and prepare the ground for Whitecliff's contingent, who would join her after two days at the latest.

They had long deliberated what kind of assistance they should offer and had decided to go with only mages since the nonmagical warriors would be much less effective in a siege.

And it's very likely to come to that. We have shown the importance of such a defensive positioning, and since they aren't particularly well versed in combat, they are likely to adopt it as well.

The war her grandmother had fought in had been one of great armies clashing on open plains, where spellfire from powerful mages would turn the environment into a wasteland and torch entire contingents.

Though magic still had a very prominent role in the current conflict, the speed at which it had started meant that no one had managed to develop their Gift to such a degree yet, so individual powerhouses mattered less than military strategies.

That will likely change with the years as mages reach greater highs, and nonmagicals become more superfluous in direct battles.

There was at least one person who could probably face an entire army by herself, but Yaomi was unlikely to leave her village, and no one was yet foolish enough to tempt her wrath.

Rumors abounded about the Mondean chief's strength and capabilities, but it was improbable that he had reached anything beyond Journeyman level since he was from the newest generation.

Still, it would be better to prepare for him to be a true monster, rather than hoping he's not that much of a threat.

Dorea spent the trip thinking up possible scenarios, using her almost complete Air Boost to speed through the forest.

Though not as keen as Jonah's, her senses were still more than enough to avoid collision with the trees. She'd also decided to follow the path she'd taken the last time—the one that went to Tumbling Lake—and get picked up there by the Forest people's scouts.

Their isolation meant that, officially, no one was supposed to know where their village was located.

Unofficially, they had a very good idea thanks to old maps and their scouts' efforts. Not much could escape an earth mage's detection, after all, and the previous generation of Gifted had thoroughly mapped the lands surrounding Whitecliff for posterity.

Dorea stopped briefly to eat lunch, consisting of a baked bun filled with soft cheese and some berries she found in the nearby bushes.

One of the things I appreciate the most about this whole magic business is the quality-of-life upgrades.

Purple and red sticky liquid dripped down her hands and chin in what would have ordinarily been an incredibly annoying mess to clean. However, her water manipulation allowed for a quick and easy solution. The freshly conjured liquid churned around her fingers, scraping every last drop of juice and leaving her completely pristine.

A quick airbrush later, Dorea was once again presentable. She lifted the remaining berries she had picked but didn't feel like eating up a tree, where she could feel a family of polecats napping away.

There was a small one, whose use of magic to ensure clean air in their den hinted at a brighter mind than the norm, so she decided to leave them a little gift she was sure they'd appreciate.

Done with her break, Dorea started up Air Boost again and quickly left behind the clearing.

It took her two more hours to finally reach Tumbling Lake, during which she only had to scare away a curious bear cub that had plopped itself in the middle of her path.

It was adorable, but I could feel its mom looking for it, and magic or not, it's never a good idea to put yourself in between a mama bear and her cub.

Finally, her senses alerted her to the presence of other humans. She pulsed her mana in the pattern the two villages had decided on to signal their friendliness, and after a moment of hesitation, she received one back.

Dorea happily waited as she drank in the beautiful sight. Though she had been there not too long ago, the lake always left her awed with its numerous waterfalls and sheer amount of life.

Shortly thereafter, she was met by a long-nosed man whose dark hair dripped with oil.

He had evidently been in the process of applying it when she disturbed him with her arrival, and given his disgruntled expression and the very noticeable stain on his shirt, he had been startled.

Dorea kept a passive expression, determined not to show the amusement she felt inside. "Good afternoon. My name is Dorea, and I'm coming from Whitecliff with urgent news I have to share with Chief Samos."

The man snorted contemptuously. "That won't be possible. Say what you need to say, and I'll ensure it gets to the proper ears."

This is gonna be a bit more annoying than I thought.

"I must insist. This is crucial information, and I have been instructed to share it with him first," she replied, keeping an even tone in an effort not to escalate.

"And I have been ordered not to let anyone pass through here. So we are at an impasse." His crooked grin told her he was actually enjoying making her life difficult.

Dorea was sorely tempted to show him how little she cared about his orders, and she could feel her temper start to flare up. Luckily for the unpleasant man, another joined them, whose predisposition was much more agreeable.

"Dorea! What are you doing here?"

Her shoulders relaxed from an unnoticed tension when Jasper's presence bloomed from behind a tree.

Though his method of arrival intrigued her, she felt too relieved that someone she knew had arrived.

"I have important news I have to share with your chief. Voggo's orders," she explained quickly before the other man could attempt to poison the well.

The boy bit his lip in thought.

"And we can't let you in, as I've already told you, girl," replied the oily-haired man.

"If you wait here with Ryul, I can alert the chief to your request, and he can decide what to do about it," Jasper finally replied, ignoring what his companion had said.

He was rewarded with a sunny smile that made him blush, and he took it as assent as he scampered away before Ryul could object.

They were left alone at the shore of the lake, the man dumbfounded at how quickly his tribesman had acquiesced at her request.

Dorea allowed herself a smug little smirk. "Jasper is always so useful."

All she got in response was an eye roll, as Ryul evidently decided it wasn't worth the time to argue any further.

"We'll see if the chief is interested in whatever you people have to say. I doubt it's that important. We would be much better off on our own anyway."

Luckily for him, Dorea had been extensively prepared for this kind of resistance. The Forest tribe was an insular community, and many of its members would have much preferred it to remain as such.

It didn't matter that the Mondeans had ripped their way into the forest and slaughtered their people; their new alliance with Whitecliff and the Heidels was bound to suffer some blowback from the more hardline people.

This kind of resistance had been expected and prepared for. Dorea knew the man didn't have anything against her specifically. She was just the closest scapegoat.

That she had run all the way through the forest to alert them to a certain danger made it more than a little annoying, and with her temper flaring up lately, she was extremely grateful that it took less than an hour before Chief Samos appeared from behind another tree, Jasper in tow.

A gesture from him and the ever-annoying Ryul silently left them, returning to his post.

"Welcome, young Dorea. I have been informed that you have urgent information you need to relay to me alone," he greeted.

Apparently, Jasper's presence didn't count—even if he had kept a distance of about twenty feet, his air magic would easily allow him to pick up their voices. Dorea gave him a look but didn't protest further. If the shaman thought it was okay for him to be present, she wouldn't waste energy arguing.

"That is correct. Our scouts have just yesterday returned from a difficult mission in the north and brought grave news," she began. "They have confirmed the preparation of a punitive mission meant to break up our alliance. The Mondeans have apparently realized that the resources they can dedicate to us are too little to meaningfully challenge all of us, and therefore want to deal with us piece by piece."

Her words were met with a grave silence. The tall man rubbed at his shaggy beard as he observed her and gestured for her to continue.

By the stifled gasp she heard, Jasper had indeed been listening in.

"From what our scouts could gather, we have at least another day before they get here, possibly more. We shouldn't expect an army like the one we fought at the Battle of the Rocky Hills, but we still need to prepare for a significant force," she explained.

"And are you meant to be the reinforcement we can expect from Whitecliff?" Samos asked lightly. "Though your exploits have reached even here, I wouldn't want to put all my hopes on a single person, no matter how successful they have been so far. Nothing personal, of course."

No matter how much it rankled to have her abilities be questioned, she knew to expect such. "Of course not. In the spirit of our alliance and as thanks for the support you lent to us when we called upon you, Whitecliff will be sending a mage contingent that should arrive tomorrow or the following day at the latest."

Diplomatic language required one to use flowery words and unnecessary compliments interspersed within the actual meat of the issue, and it definitely wasn't her favorite thing. Still, Dorea had been developing something of a skill with it, simply out of necessity.

The chief observed her for a moment before gracing her with a smile of approval. "Well then, I suppose we should prepare ourselves for their arrival."

And that was that.

The Forest village was much more normal than Dorea had been expecting.

In her mind's eye, she had pictured tree houses joined together by floating bridges and people jumping from the canopy thanks to lianas.

On the other hand, she found stone houses built in a series of clearings encircled by a wall of vegetation. Stout oaks and willow trees surrounded the village, creating the feeling of stepping into another realm. On their trunks were carved runes, and though the meaning escaped her, Dorea could recognize some from Voggo's lessons.

That type of magic required constant upkeep and a dedicated mage to ensure nothing interfered with the schema, on pain of disaster.

It does explain how they have managed to avoid direct attacks. If their wards are more oriented toward misdirection and concealment rather than active defenses, finding them would take a sustained and concerted effort.

The village was smaller but more compact than Whitecliff. Dozens of houses sat clustered together, with a cobbled path running through them. A few of the bigger ones had a backyard with some animals, but space was obviously at a premium.

"Beautiful, isn't it?" asked Jasper, apparently taking her silence as awe.

"It certainly has a unique charm," Dorea replied. The tribesmen were evidently very proud of their home, and sharing her thoughts would only incite trouble.

I like it, and it's picturesque, but I can't imagine living so close to other people. You'd hear them all the time!

The boy grinned at her proudly before scampering up the path to join the chief.

"As you can see"—Samos gestured to the wall of vegetation—"we are quite well protected from possible incursions, but that doesn't mean we don't appreciate your help."

Though Dorea had brought them grave news, the tribesmen didn't seem particularly worried, trusting blindly in their protections.

"Are the wards capable of hiding you from an entire army looking for you?" she questioned curiously.

The amount of power needed for that seemed simply out of the realm of possibility for anyone who wasn't a powerful Master, and however skilled he might be, Samos was not one.

He chuckled at that. "Always doubtful. The defenses make it much harder to find us in several ways, and only some are active. We'll be fine."

I suppose that if the wards work on the forest itself rather than on the enemy's perception, it might be more mana efficient. However, a good enough sensor should still be able to tell if they were being messed with, and from that, it's only a matter of time before they find where the distortion comes from.

Whitecliff had once had wards on the wall, but as the conflict with the Ergasters ended and the need for active defenses became lesser, they weren't maintained as often. With the death of the strongest earth mages, they simply faded away.

Their upkeep was meant to be taxing even for the previous generation. Unless the Forest people had an incredibly efficient method they kept secret, Dorea doubted their protections would last long against the Mondeans.

The tribesmen bustling about gave her weird looks, but no one seemed overly hostile, and the presence of the shaman prevented any who were looking for trouble from approaching her.

The population looked roughly the same as Whitecliff's before the first refugees arrived, but the compact size of the village gave it a denser feeling.

Her mystical senses also alerted her to something particularly interesting. Now that she was inside the circle, she could freely feel everything in the settlement, but the outside world had become blurry and undefined.

Before she was led in, she had barely noticed anything weird about the clustered trees and couldn't have guessed they hid an entire village.

I'm still not a particularly good sensor, though. I bet Jonah could pierce through these wards with much more ease.

Finally, she was led to a larger house, whose stone bricks were covered in ivy. Clothes of different sizes were hung at the back, and from what she could tell, several farm animals were also being held there.

"Welcome to my humble abode," the chief said as he opened the door, letting her in.

She thanked him and ducked inside, taking in the beautifully carved wooden furniture.

A very short woman came out of what she guessed to be the kitchen, wringing her hands dry with a towel. "Well, what do we have here? An outsider, huh?"

Her face was very delicate, but her tone would have been at home on an old sailor. The discordance shook Dorea out of her contemplation, and she replied, "I'm indeed from Whitecliff. My name is Dorea, and I thank you for welcoming me into your home."

By that point, the standard set of greetings had been engraved in her mind almost at the same level as her spells.

"Bah, I didn't welcome you. But if that old lump wants you here, you can stay."

Somewhat mystified at the sheer brass of the tiny woman, Dorea turned to her host, who seemed to be perfectly content watching the byplay.

"You'll have to forgive Thea, my wife. She can be a bit much at first glance, but she has a heart of gold once you get to know her," he finally explained.

The newly identified Thea blushed deeply at his words, swatting at the man's arm ineffectually as it came to rest around her waist.

She grumbled inaudibly for a couple of seconds more, but settled into the embrace.

"Love, would you mind preparing something for young Dorea as well? She'll be staying with us for a couple of days," he asked, giving his wife a peck on the lips when she wordlessly requested one.

Satisfied with her reward, the woman left, not bothering to say goodbye.

A bit lost, Dorea looked to Jasper for some explanation, only to find him with an exasperated look.

Deciding that it simply wasn't worth asking, she sighed.

I just hope the others get here soon.

CHAPTER THIRTY-NINE

Life in Samos and Thea's household was chaotic.

The couple had three natural children of their own and three more kids, including Jasper, that they took care of for several reasons.

The woman warmed up slightly to Dorea over the course of the next day, especially once she offered to help with the cleanup after the messy affair that was dinner.

Having to care for two toddlers, one preteen, and three teenagers was enough to send anyone mad, but the couple shared the burden equally whenever Samos wasn't called upon in his vest of shaman or chief.

The man loved his family deeply, as evidenced by his open affection for them all, and treated his adopted children with as much warmth as his natural ones.

Dorea's presence had been the subject of much of the dinner's conversation, and having to explain what she was doing there without mentioning the impending attack—as she had been asked to do to prevent the spread of panic—proved difficult. Still, she successfully distracted the children by recounting tales of her hunts.

That seemed to increase her worth in everyone's eyes, even the adults, as she proved not to be a "soft outsider." Apparently, it was a common stereotype in the community to consider the villages outside the forest full of ninnies who needed to cultivate their foods, vegetables, or animals, because they couldn't forage it by themselves.

It was a fascinating look into a reclusive society, and Dorea was glad that her temper didn't flare up when they described ranching as a task for sissies.

The image of her burly father and his helpers being told such was funny enough to distract her from any offense she might have felt.

She had spent the whole day waiting for word to arrive of Whitecliff's contingent, but there had been nothing so far, even though Samos assured her they had people waiting for them. She had been told there was a possibility of a day's delay, though, so she tried not to worry too much.

Instead, she spent her time trying to pry the secrets of the wards away from the shaman, who luckily didn't take offense to her curiosity. Since the Forest people considered them to be their greatest defense and were all so certain that they would protect them from the Mondean attack, Dorea speculated that there was something different about them.

Voggo had, during one of his early lessons, explained how warding was a complex and demanding piece of magic that only Master mages could sustain by themselves, thus without placing undue strain on the Gifted population.

That meant that putting them up for Whitecliff was not feasible, especially considering how vast its territory was compared to its population.

The only ones in the village were those defending the shelter beneath Voggo's house, which he carefully maintained.

But those only need the occasional refresh since they are rarely active. These ones have been working for decades, maybe even centuries!

What little she had managed to pry told her that there wasn't even a schedule set up for the village's mages to dump all their mana into them, which was her first idea of how they could maintain them.

Samos also didn't leave her sight for long the whole day, certainly not long enough to power the entire thing, which meant they had found another way to sustain them.

Since there wasn't any particular concentration of mana she could feel in the air, Dorea decided they had to be hiding whatever it was with further wards, which meant an even more potent source.

I shouldn't show that I learned that much. They seem awfully jealous about them, and so far, I've been treated decently, if a bit roughly by some. Being seen snooping around the wall is a good way of demolishing all the goodwill I've built up so far.

The arrival of her comrades would likely give her a much better chance of learning more.

She would observe carefully how they were led in the village, which would at least reveal some of their workings, and then use their presence to look for the possible source.

I can't really share this with anyone yet. It's literally all a conjecture I've built up in my head. No proof to be found anywhere yet.

Thus, she spent the day carefully suppressing her curiosity. If she could learn about and replicate such a feat, her village would be much safer, but doing so at the cost of alienating one of their only two allies would not be worth it.

That evening, she enjoyed another simple but tasty dinner courtesy of Thea, who had laid out a beautiful spread of grilled meats and tubers.

There was no dairy, and the few eggs the village produced were kept for special occasions, but they had an abundance of herbs and spices to flavor their meats with, and Dorea appreciated the craft all the same.

"How many people can we expect to come tomorrow?" asked the chief between bites of deer ribs.

"Should be about a dozen unless something has changed," she replied, enjoying a wonderfully herby tuber salad.

"Do you think something could have changed in the last two days?" worriedly questioned Jasper from her other side.

"Well, I'm sure they didn't send another group up north, but you never know. In the forest, even just a territorial fight between old monsters could be enough to slow them down."

Any further talk was halted as Thea placed the main dish of the evening, a smoked deer rump, in front of them. "You can speak about boring stuff after dinner. Now we eat," was the proclamation, and none dared gainsay her.

The rest of the evening was spent in a cheerful mood, as Dorea and Jasper entertained the younger children by passing around air constructs and making them unravel at unexpected times, to much laughter.

The following day was spent in anxious wait. Although she had affected nonchalance with Samos, Dorea was increasingly worried about the absence of Whitecliff's contingent.

The possibilities were endless, and she knew she'd go mad if she started entertaining all of them seriously.

Her greatest fear was that the attack was meant to target Whitecliff, and the scouts had somehow been fooled. If that happened while she was away, she'd never forgive herself.

Why did I volunteer to come here? Just to get out of the village?! Goddess, please don't let anything happen to them.

Her nervousness grew as the hours passed, and no one was spotted. Even the possibility of learning more about warding didn't seem that appealing anymore.

Others were starting to take notice of her distracted behavior, as she was busy scouring the edge of her senses all the time in hopes of feeling someone she knew.

Jasper, who had been assigned as her chaperone for the duration of her stay, tried his best to interest her with the Forest tribe's traditions, and though she was fascinated by their usage of bone ash in smithing, and their method of desiccation for meat and tubers seemed particularly useful, she simply wasn't in the right frame of mind to appreciate his efforts.

The boy became increasingly gloomy as he realized that nothing he could do would bring her attention back to him, and they must have made for a somewhat comical sight since even the gruffest tribesmen chuckled as they trudged past.

Dorea, however, didn't find the situation to be particularly funny.

By the time evening fell, she was convinced that something terrible must have happened and decided she needed to go look for her comrades.

The problem with that was getting past the wards. Chief Samos likely wouldn't allow her to come and go as she pleased, and since she was technically on a diplomatic mission, leaving abruptly after she had assured him of her help wouldn't go down well.

That meant sneaking out during the night and coming back before she could be missed, if possible.

Of course, there would be several problems with achieving that. First of all, leaving the village without being noticed would be very difficult. Though there weren't guards on the inside of the wall, the outside was different; if even one of them was close enough to sense her, she'd get found out in a very compromising position.

Secondly, getting back in once she had confirmed that nothing terrible had happened might be impossible. Though the wards' efficacy would likely be lesser since she knew where to go, they might still work well enough to prevent her from getting back in unnoticed.

Dorea brooded about her options all through the dinner, barely making an effort not to seem too distracted. From the looks she got, the two adults of the house weren't fooled, but they didn't comment, so she didn't volunteer anything.

In the end, the choice was inevitable. She couldn't go on another day with the constant fear that an invading army might be burning and pillaging her village while she sat safely, so she started preparing.

The consequences of her actions would likely be challenging to deal with, but not doing anything was simply unacceptable.

She hadn't packed much when she departed Whitecliff, not having expected to stay longer than a few days, so her belongings fit into her old rucksack.

Her grandmother's pendant, the only truly valuable thing she had brought, was safely tucked beneath her shirt. The only thing left was waiting for an opportune moment to sneak out.

The nightly routine she had observed in the household the previous times was luckily still respected, and all the kids were put to bed not too long after dinner was done.

The teens had been working hard during the day, helping their father with several tasks, so they didn't protest much beyond a bit of grumbling as Thea herded them up the stairs.

Dorea laid on her bed, fully clothed, waiting for the house to fall silent. Then for an hour more, just to make sure she wouldn't be sensed as she moved about.

Time was a precious resource, but she decided that meeting less resistance as she got out was more important than doing so earlier.

Fortunately for her, the gamble paid off. As silently as she could, using her wind manipulation to prevent any noise from escaping, Dorea snuck out of the house and started moving toward the western tree wall.

Though the Forest people didn't have a main gate the same as Whitecliff did, there was one spot where most people got in and out from, which she had carefully made a note of during the day.

She purposefully avoided heading for that spot, sure that the biggest concentration of guards would be there.

According to her senses, almost no one was still out and about, but those few had to be avoided at all costs.

Thus, she diverted her path several times to prevent an encounter. Even though it added more time, she was committed not to completely muck up the diplomatic mission.

Twenty minutes later, she found herself at the edge of the wards.

From the inside, they didn't actively prevent one from sensing beyond them, but the magical currents running through them did make it more complicated.

Still, with some more time to ensure no one was waiting for her on the other side, Dorea felt confident stepping through.

A weird tingling feeling ran through her as she passed them, signifying the concentration of power the protections held.

Still can't believe they can power these things. I really need to find out how they are doing this.

Unfortunately, there hadn't been time to do so before, and her preoccupation with the fate of her comrades had taken precedence during the last day.

Dorea promised herself that she would uncover their secret after coming back, though she knew she'd be lucky to still be able to find the village.

Finally, out in the forest, she extended her senses to their maximum, seeking to find anyone who might have noticed her. She must have been blessed that night, since she felt no one. Reassured, she quickly reoriented herself with the stars, finding the Goddess's Tear, a bright dot that always led to the west, and set off.

Her Air Boost was a fundamental part of her plan because without it, she'd never be able to make it in time, and the urgency of the situation spurred her to use it in ways she hadn't attempted before.

The corona of air that surrounded her during its use shrank as she concentrated on efficiency. A low buzzing noise became audible—instead of the howling of the winds that her passage previously emitted—as she sped through the vegetation, leaving it rustling.

As she wondered whether it would be too noisy and lead to her discovery, Dorea felt the spell crystalize.

The fractal completed itself in her mind, and finally, she got her third true piece of magic to work.

The actualization process smoothed out some of the kinks, reducing the sound to a barely audible humming. The corona shrank further, becoming almost invisible to the naked eye. Her speed increased enough that she wondered whether she would lose control, but her maneuverability grew with it.

The difference between what was free manipulation—even if she had gotten used to doing it—and a genuine spell was night and day.

With this, I'll be able to be at the village and back before dawn, if nothing stops me.

Dorea didn't know if her prayers to the Goddess had been answered or if she had simply reached an unknown threshold, but she was extremely grateful nonetheless.

Her plan had been desperate, but this new addition might allow for it to work.

As she sped through the forest, she got more and more used to the new and improved version of Air Boost, and ideas about using it in a fight started blooming in her mind.

I've been blasting my enemies from a distance so far, with Thunderclap being my only short-distance attack, but it takes way too long to charge and is not usable in any situation where I'm not fighting alone. This, though, gives me more options.

With her senses fully extended, Dorea could avoid every slumbering animal and even the few night predators on the hunt.

She had just slipped around Old Titan's territory when a flash of light in the distance alerted her to something going on.

Air Boost had become much more sophisticated with its evolution, but it was still not the stealthiest of movement magics, so she let it go, stumbling to a stop.

Quickly condensing an air platform, Dorea rose into the air to get a better look.

Very few people think to look up into the sky. Actually, now that I think about it, I could have probably avoided all the sneaking around in the village I did by just bypassing the wards from above. Or do they reach that high in the air? Ugh, now is not the time.

The flash of light she had noticed in the distance revealed itself as a torch held up by a man she hadn't seen before.

That meant that she had just found a Mondean camp.

Sitting at the edge of the territories of the two villages and Old Titan meant that this group, at the very least, had done some scouting beforehand and was taking advantage of the terrain not to be noticed.

Dorea lowered herself until she was just barely skimming the trees to not be seen in the full moon's glow.

She repeated her usual trick with small elemental balls as she got closer, though she projected them close to the ground and twenty feet ahead.

It might have been simple, but so far it had been the best way to determine a mage's sensory range.

Of course, it only worked because she hadn't met people with a greater range than her, which was a genuine possibility considering that there were at least four such mages in Whitecliff alone.

Still, it's better than nothing.

Carefully getting closer to the torchlight, Dorea learned more about her target. It was a scruffy-looking blond man with a long beard reaching his chest and a scar coming down his left eyebrow all the way down his neck, barely avoiding his eye.

It certainly wasn't a face one would like to see in the middle of the night, but she only felt vindication. Her paranoia had proved itself to be grounded in reality, as the man's presence obviously meant there would be more enemies.

He didn't twitch as the elemental balls got closer, merely peering into the darkness as a lookout was wont to do.

Having gotten close enough to sense more behind him, Dorea found a make-shift camp to have been set up.

Inside, several dozen people were sleeping, surrounded by at least a score of guards.

Tents of various make hosted men and a few women, and to her count, at least fifteen Gifted, given the energy she could feel around them. It was possible that there were more, especially amongst the guards, but she didn't want to get too close and risk being found out.

What captured her attention the most, though, was a wooden pen set up in the middle of the encampment, where she could recognize twelve different signatures she knew very well.

She had finally found Whitecliff's contingent, and they had been taken prisoners.

CHAPTER FORTY

Her first instinct was to go in immediately. Magic thrummed in her veins, just below her skin, ready to be unleashed. It would be messy, and the likelihood of someone dying was simply too high to attempt, but Dorea just knew it would have felt very satisfying.

These men had taken *her people*. The moment she was sure of their safety, there would be hell to pay.

The problem, of course, was removing them from danger. Though she might have preferred direct combat to subterfuge, even she was not foolish enough to believe she could take on the entire encampment.

To her count, there had to be at least sixty people present, which, while nowhere near as many as the army she fought at the Battle of the Rocky Hills, was still a sizable amount.

They'd definitely be able to wreak havoc, if they found a way to locate the Forest village.

Those considerations, however, would have to wait for a later moment. Since a frontal assault was out, Dorea decided that she needed more information to craft a plan.

Thus, she turned her senses to scoping the layout of the camp.

The tents were surprisingly well made, and rather than cloth, like those usually used by Whitecliff's scouts, they were made of leather.

That made her idea of setting them on fire much harder to achieve. Had she been a fire mage like Yaomi, she could have still produced enough heat to burn them down, but her lightning was simply not suited to the task.

If I were Yaomi, I'd simply walk in and turn anyone who dared stop me into ash. Unfortunately, I'm nowhere near that level yet.

The more she grew in power, the more Dorea realized the gap between her and the old witch.

She was sure there would come a time when she'd catch up, but she'd have to work long and hard for it.

Refocusing on her task, she started using one of her favorite pieces of magic: manipulating the air to overhear conversations at a great distance.

She couldn't claim to have been the one to develop such a skill, the merit belonging to Jonah, but she definitely refined it enough to be serviceable.

Every air mage in Whitecliff could use the simple trick, since almost all took part in patrolling their borders, and being able to listen in without getting close enough to be sensed was too great an advantage.

"—and that bloody bastard. I'll tell you now, if he tries to do something like that without permission again, I'll fry him on the spot, consequences be damned," came a feminine, high-pitched voice.

Tuning into its direction, Dorea focused hard not to miss anything.

"I know. Just because he's a wood mage, he's acting like he can do whatever he wants."

A wood mage?! They have a wood mage?! Damnit, this has just gotten a thousand times worse.

"Marcus has allowed him too much leeway. He could be useful down the line, yes, but he's simply not worth the treatment he's been receiving," complained the first voice further.

An affirmative hum was the response, which the high-pitched one took as permission to keep going. "And also, can we talk about his breath? The man stinks worse than a pig! I'm honestly considering arranging for an accident just so I don't have to smell him again."

Laughter followed her words, but Dorea was still stuck on the crucial piece of information she had just heard.

Wood mages weren't just simply Gifted. No Wrath could give an entire population control over the vegetation. Only localized events, similar to Mana Geysers, could, but their rarity was even more extraordinary.

One had to encounter an enhanced tree, recognize it for what it was, eat its fruit, and survive the experience.

The problem with that was that enhanced trees, unlike animals and humans, had their life spans drastically reduced. They put all their energy into producing one single fruit, ripe with power.

Which, when eaten, could grant powers that were the closest to the Mother. One could be said to be an apostle of her will.

Of course, not everyone used the blessing for good purposes, but the sheer level of change a wood mage could enact was simply mind-boggling.

Being capable of controlling crop growth alone would have made anyone the single most important person in a tribe. Producing wooden buildings on demand, ensuring the health of the surrounding lands, and communing with the forest were just the cherry on top.

For a village, a wood mage was the greatest blessing they could possibly hope for. It meant no one would ever die of starvation. It ensured the safety of the tribe, especially if they were located close to a forested area.

To see one in the ranks of an enemy was a terrible blow. That he apparently was a horrible person just made it even worse.

Dorea felt lost. All she had been taught told her that wood mages were the closest to Mother Nature's will and should not be questioned.

That such a person would then take part in kidnapping her friends and prepare to attack an ally, whom she knew had done nothing to provoke it, broke something in her.

It's either us who are in the wrong since he's theoretically the Goddess's apostle, and all we have fought for so far has been a horrible mistake. Or . . .

She knew the real truth. Putting it into words was difficult, even in her own mind, but Dorea was not one to back down.

Or he doesn't actually represent the Mother's will. Or if he does, she's wrong.

That blasphemous thought was not one she could share easily with anyone else, but after she had it, it crystallized into a hard belief. It was the truth; this she knew in her very core.

The idea of abandoning her people and letting the Mondeans have their way simply because a single man happened to have similar powers to the Goddess was absurd.

"The only reason to keep him around is that he's gonna shock the hell out of these idiots. Just the look on the ones we captured earlier was too hilarious. I can't wait to see what happens when we reach this stupid village."

That gave her pause. It made sense that her companions had been taken prisoners without much in the way of injuries, if they had surrendered when faced with a wood mage.

Dorea would have liked to think she would have fought to the end even in such a situation, but she couldn't begrudge them. She had been stunned when first faced with the man's existence, and coupling it with being surrounded by so many enemies would have been terrifying.

The woman's words also explained how exactly they expected to find the Forest tribe's village.

A wood mage would likely be able to navigate through the wards' misdirections much better than anyone else, especially since their power should still work upon the ring of trees surrounding the settlement.

For the tribesmen, being faced with the loss of their vaunted protections and having to battle against one of the Goddess's chosen would be too much.

It would end in a rout. Though the village had hundreds of people in it, they'd lose the will to fight, leaving the Mondeans to mop up the remaining defenders.

It was a brilliantly cunning plan, and Dorea was suddenly extremely glad her paranoia had made her leave the village soon enough to learn of it before it could be put into motion.

Her objective had suddenly changed. Not only did she need to save her comrades, but she'd also have to deal with the wood mage.

Letting him leave the forest alive was simply not an option. He seemingly wasn't particularly appreciated by his companions, but that didn't mean they wouldn't use him against Whitecliff, once the Forest village was under their yoke.

No, the path was charted the moment they decided to send the supposed Mother's chosen to fight against them. There could be no mercy against such an act.

More determined than ever, Dorea resumed her scouting.

"I know," replied the second voice. "It's still almost not worth it. Just seeing him get handsy with the prisoners was bad enough. Can't he just wait until we are done with our jobs before he gives in to his urges? Ugh, he's such a pig."

Dorea's blood froze in her veins.

"The fact that Marcus decided to allow him to have one of them after he's done with his duties is disgusting."

Laughter followed, as apparently, the two women didn't think they should do anything about it.

It was an ancient custom to treat one's defeated enemy with respect, even to their last moments. That the Mondeans would hand over a prisoner to one of their mages, knowing what he would do to them, broke whatever vestiges of doubt Dorea had left.

There is no way this is the Goddess's will. Breaking this tradition is such a taboo that people get exiled from their tribe if they attempt it.

Her unwitting informers finally decided they had taken a long enough rest, and started moving away, shifting their chat to the less exciting topic of who was courting whom.

If it had been any other situation, Dorea would have laughed at how the human experience repeated itself in different flavors in such disparate moments. This time, she could find nothing funny about it.

One of her friends was about to be given to a seemingly perverted wood mage, and she needed to act as soon as possible to prevent it.

She moved away from the women, taking advantage of the momentary cloud cover, and rose up in the air. Her platform wasn't made to move at impressive speeds, but it still beat having to sneak around the encampment with the genuine chance of being found out.

Careful not to dip too low, she floated toward the center, where the prisoners were being held.

As she got closer, she could finally put names to the signatures. Immediately, she recognized Tom's. The water mage was bound in a wooden block that kept both his hands and feet stuck together and, going by the small amounts of moisture she could feel on his clothes and skin, had likely been wounded at some point.

The second person she was able to identify was Mel, the girlfriend of Mark—the farmer's son—and an air mage. The girl was also bound like Tom, but her constant shivering told a story about a very different treatment.

Next to her was her boyfriend, though he was unconscious or sleeping, given his even breath.

It didn't take a genius to realize what had happened to him once she got close enough to sense his broken limbs.

The wood mage had chosen a girl, and it was unlikely that such a thing had not been met with disapproval from the prisoners. His condition was probably a direct result of an act of defiance.

That also meant that the girl who'd receive the unwanted attention of the "chosen" was Mel.

Dorea didn't have the best of relationships with her, given the antagonistic way the girl had always approached her, but even had she been her sworn enemy, she'd still do her absolute best to get her out of the situation she was currently in.

No one deserves such a fate.

The rest were banged up, but not terribly injured, giving credit to her theory that the shock of having to face a wood mage had made them surrender.

It was also confirmation of the fact that the group that had been sent was somewhat battle oriented, but still not the most powerful that Whitecliff could muster.

That had been a point of contention during her talks with Voggo, as she argued that only those they knew could handle themselves should go, while the shaman wanted it to be strictly voluntary.

Well, voluntary for everyone but one. Mark the Blue definitely would have liked to come, but someone needs to ensure the village is safe. It was either me or him, and I was simply the better choice, since some diplomacy was required.

The fact that some of the prisoners weren't exactly on friendly terms with her didn't weigh on her decision. She'd fight to the death for every one of her tribesmen.

Still, there were more imaginative ways to go about it than simply dropping in and attacking everyone.

Around the enclosure, two guards stood alertly, armed with iron spears and leather armor. Every once in a while, they'd walk the perimeter and relocate to a different spot, where they would resume their watch.

The two men were young but had evidently been instructed well on how to conduct their duties. There was simply no way to bypass them and get out with all the prisoners without them noticing immediately and raising the alarm.

That was doubly true because Dorea suspected that if she were to touch the fence that made up the enclosure, the wood mage would be immediately alerted to her presence.

Indeed, her choice to approach the encampment from above rather than sneaking in from the ground might have saved her life, as she avoided contact with any plant life he might have under his control.

There would have been nothing she could have done had she been identified in such a manner. Only luck had saved her.

Or maybe it wasn't luck . . . Thank you, Mother. I know what I must do now.

A plan started forming in her mind. Since sneaking in without being noticed would be impossible as things stood, she'd just have to change the current situation.

I need to take care of the wood mage first. Do it in such a way that it will get everyone's attention away from the enclosure, and only then can I go in.

First of all, she'd need to identify where exactly her target was. Luckily for her, he didn't seem to know the meaning of discretion and therefore had built himself an actual hut on the eastern side of the camp.

She could tell a single person was inside thanks to the air that slipped through the space beneath the door, but the construction looked to be sturdy enough that it might hamper her mana going in, so she'd need to find a way to open it without waking him up.

Why did he even build a door? He could just create a passage when he wants to get out. It's how our earth mages used to do it. Is he stupid?

If he wasn't a particularly bright man, it might explain why he had been sent down south rather than being deployed against the other mountain tribes.

Not all of them worshipped the Mother, as some had different gods they answered to, but the shock value alone would have been enough for any decent commander to want him there.

That meant that either the Mondeans already had one or more wood mages operating in their northern war, or this one was considered too low level for such a conflict.

It might even be both. Or maybe they just don't see the need to have someone who uses an entirely different system when the battles they face are of armies clashing against one another. No matter how peculiar his skills, one man cannot do much in such a situation. At least not until he reaches the Master tier.

Fortunately for her, this specific Gifted was nowhere close to that level, or his comrades would have referred to him with much greater respect.

For a brief moment, Dorea contemplated trying to entice Old Titan, the monstrous earth bear that lived only half an hour away, to come in and deal with the Mondeans for her, but several problems presented themselves.

She wasn't sure she'd be able to survive such an encounter long enough to bring him where she needed to. And even if she somehow managed to do so, the beast would likely kill everyone present, not just her enemies.

Thus, that idea got shelved.

She didn't have all night, though, as the Mondeans were likely in the midst of preparing for an attack on the Forest village, which meant they would wake up earlier than usual. Possibly even before dawn, and she intended to be long gone before that time.

Dorea went through her repertoire mentally, trying to find something she could use in this specific situation.

Finally, she had a thought. It might require some finagling, as she had never done it in such a way and at such a distance, but she believed she might be able to do it.

Furthermore, if it went off as she envisioned, she wouldn't need to do much more than swoop in and lift the prisoners out of the enclosure.

Well, I'll need to cut them out of there, but if everything goes well, it won't be much of a problem. The only thing that worries me is if they set up contingencies to deal with the prisoners in case of an attack, but they likely left that up to the guards.

The Mondeans, at least those sent south to fight them, hadn't seemed exceptionally well organized. There were powerful fighters, like the woman she killed during the Battle of the Rocky Hills, but the general management seemed somewhat loose.

That had worked in her favor thus far, and she could only hope it would continue to do so.

CHAPTER FORTY-ONE

Dorea carefully floated east toward the wooden hut her target resided in.

As far as she could tell, he was soundly sleeping, which would significantly help her. His construct somewhat impaired her ability to use magic within it, and she'd need even more time than usual to ensure the distraction was big enough.

Ever since the fight against the group of smilodons, she had been trying to find a new use for her Thunderclap.

It wasn't a spell yet, and given its heavy requirements, it might not become one soon, but the framework of it was complete, and she had thought it might become useful situationally.

That belief was proving to be correct. She finally reached the hut and hovered fifty feet above it, not daring to get closer in case she might get picked up by one of their lookouts.

Slowly and methodically, she started probing the crack beneath the door, finding it sufficient for her purposes.

With a gleeful smile that would have sent shivers down anyone's spine, Dorea started pushing more and more air in.

She had briefly considered suffocating him in his construct, but that would likely be noticed much more quickly as she'd need to create a vacuum in the middle of the encampment.

No, her current plan would do perfectly well.

Dorea spent half an hour condensing the air in a specific pattern next to the wood mage's bed, with great care and dedication.

The gaseous construct would, just like her Thunderclap, release a tremendous explosion of sound. Given its proximity to her target, she sincerely doubted he would survive.

The containment provided by his own wood would also enhance its effects. Like steam, the pressure would build up, forcing it apart at extremely high speeds.

To get that effect, all she'd need to do was plug the gap beneath the door she was using to push the necessary air in.

Once it went off, she'd need to move quickly, as the Mondeans realized they were under attack and started actively scanning inside the camp and not only outside.

The tricky part about it was not moving enough air to be noticeable but still keeping all that she already put in from waking the wood mage.

The distance certainly didn't help, but Dorea knuckled down with dogged determination.

She wiped the sweat from her forehead, having almost reached the critical mass. She could go over it and aim for a greater explosion, but then she couldn't be sure she wouldn't be hit by it, which would be counterproductive.

Finally, she stopped pulling in from the outside, satisfied with what she had accumulated. She took a few more minutes to ensure the mana was in the proper pattern and lifted the condensed marble above the bed.

She had almost expected the man to wake up at the last moment, alerted somehow to her attack, but he kept sleeping without a twitch. Not wanting to delay it any further, Dorea let go of her construct.

A thunderous bang resounded in the forest, startling animals for miles.

Birds squawked in fright as they took off from their perches, flapping around in confusion in great flocks. Innumerable critters and insects buzzed angrily. Great predators and small prey joined in a chorus of roars and brays.

In the Mondean encampment, chaos abounded. Where there had once been a wooden hut containing their secret weapon, now was a crater filled with debris from his construct, his body lying broken in the midst of it.

Alarms were raised immediately after as the men and women poured out of their tents like ants out of an anthill.

Shouts resounded as the leaders tried to restore some form of control. Questions were shouted, and orders were given as slowly the mages tried to identify whoever had attacked them.

Unfortunately for them, the bedlam prevented their efforts from working, as people ran around the camp, mixing and confusing their senses.

No army presented itself to face them, nor did any raiding party repeat the attack, slowly leading them to understand that whatever had happened had likely been the work of a small group, if not a singular person.

In the middle of it all, Dorea dropped down at the prisoners' enclosure, quickly noticing the now inert wood.

The only good thing about it being a wood mage is that their power is so con-nected to the concept of life that if he dies, his constructs also lose their strengths. No eternal building for you.

To the guards' credit, they noticed her only shortly after she had touched the ground, and they immediately rushed in, shouting for help as their sharp spears tried to pierce through the prisoners.

It was lucky, then, that Dorea had predicted such a thing. The air around their mouths was sucked away, leaving them to choke on nothing.

Desperately, the two men clutched at their throats, instinctively trying to remove a hand that wasn't there. She dispassionately let them for a few seconds before helping them along the way to the netherworld with a ring of water that squeezed down, crushing their larynxes.

Not wanting to waste any more time, Dorea crafted a large air platform and quickly placed her comrades on it.

As she jostled them, she expected some to wake up, but their eyes remained closed and their breaths even, signifying that something had been given to them to keep them docile.

Of course, they drugged them; how else could they expect to keep a group of mages prisoners otherwise? Stupid, I should have thought about it earlier.

Still, she was committed by then and couldn't leave them there. They had been lucky that no one had been killed so far, but if the Mondeans expected a rescue to be mounted, they might simply remove the problem entirely.

Dorea would have liked to have been able to place each person on an indi-vidual platform and lift them out in different patterns to avoid an attack on the larger one, which would break and drop everyone from a fatal height. Yet, she simply wasn't skilled enough to maneuver so many objects while ensuring their stability as she checked the ground to ensure no one spotted them.

Taking advantage of the chaos, Dorea started their ascent. With the clouds covering the moon and the stars, the only lights available were those of the torches at the ground level, and even then, there weren't many, as the Mondeans had wanted to keep a low profile.

Unfortunately, their escape didn't go unnoticed for long. The lookouts might have been concentrating their efforts on finding the elusive attacker outside the encampment, but the smarter members had started converging toward the pris-oners, both to ensure there was no jailbreak and to use them as hostages.

Instead, they found the two broken forms of the guards on the ground and the wooden construct without a ceiling.

One of the men looked up and, sensing something rapidly rising in the air, shot a bolt of lightning in its direction.

The flash briefly illuminated the night, showing that while he had missed, something had been there.

He shouted in alarm, a spark building at the tip of his finger. Immediately after, he dropped down, rolling to avoid being turned into a paste by a water bullet.

Damn, he has good instincts.

The fact that the man had managed to notice the attack being leveled against him, even though it was of a different element than his, meant that he either had an excellent battlefield awareness or, more likely, had somehow developed a way to sense extraneous magics.

That was an extremely dangerous capability, so Dorea redoubled her efforts to splatter him. A wobble in the platform holding the rescued prisoners alerted her to the fact that she simply wasn't in a position where she could engage in such a battle.

Therefore, she turned her efforts to providing covering fire as she restarted her ascent.

Quicker than she would have liked, more people joined in the man's efforts to bring her down. Spellfire started flashing in the sky, increasing the chaos of an already frenzied night.

Dorea felt more than one spell come too close for comfort, even as she put some distance between her and the camp.

When she saw people start to lift themselves up in the air, she decided that discretion had run its course and opened fire with all she had.

Lightning Spheres blasted enemy mages out of the air, and, given the increase in reserves she felt, she permanently took out at least a couple of them.

Still, her floating shields could only suffer so much battering, and they kept cracking after being hit, forcing her to focus once more on repairing them.

In her desperation, she started pushing them together, crafting a larger barrier to hide behind.

That gave the Mondeans something to focus their attacks on, and elemental blasts of all kinds rained upon her. The distance rendered most attacks weaker than they would have normally been, but moving so many people was still a massive effort while she held such a barrage back.

She instinctively melded the large shield with the two platforms, crafting a hollow sphere of compressed air.

This finally allowed her much more freedom, not having to manipulate so many different constructs simultaneously.

Now thinking more clearly, Dorea decided that the safety of her people needed to come first. While she would have liked—more than she wanted to admit—to stay behind and kill as many enemies as she could in a massive slugfest, she knew she couldn't possibly take on that many mages, especially when she had people she needed to protect.

Inspiration struck her, and with a grin, she spun her Air Boost around the massive sphere, blasting off into the distance.

She kept her frenzied pace up for almost an entire hour before she started feeling her reserves dwindle and was forced to touch down.

Looking around, Dorea found she had arrived closer to the spot where, weeks before, she had fought alongside the Heidel contingent against the huge Mondean woman.

The land still had scars of the fight, as trees had been felled and the ground was full of holes.

That might have been me . . . My bullets didn't work as well back then, but they certainly were enough to slap around some dumb idiots who thought they could charge a mage.

Refocusing on her charges, she unwound the sphere, making a mental note to try and replicate it in the future, and checked on her compatriots.

They hadn't been in particularly good shape before the turbulent flight, but now they were a sorry sight.

To her horror, Mark was missing a hand, blood sluggishly flowing out of the limb.

She rushed to his side with her heart beating madly in her chest and dug into her rucksack, looking for the poultices she had brought in case of battle.

Her sweaty, slippery fingers made finding the small jar all the more difficult, and she almost cried in relief when she felt it.

She immediately applied a thick wad of it on the stump, ripping a piece of gauze and tying it tightly.

Seeing the boy who looked so much like Rupert terribly injured under her watch brought back intense feelings. Her head pounded as she berated herself for losing track of her objective.

I just needed to get them out of that damn camp, and instead, I got drawn into a slugfest just because I thought I could take them all on. What a stupid idiot I am.

Finally, the blood stopped. The boy was deathly pale, though, and he'd need urgent medical care if it had been possible to move him safely. Unfortunately, they weren't in such a position.

Not only was the forest not safe at the moment since the Mondeans would be looking for them, but she wasn't sure she could transport him all the way to Whitecliff in such a way that he wouldn't be even more injured.

He might make it, but if he had been losing blood for the whole time she'd been flying around, there might already be nothing they could do.

Even if she abandoned the others and just took him, pushing Air Boost to its limits, she would take hours before she got close enough to get picked up by a patrol.

Also, she was exhausted by the battle and long flight. She simply didn't have the reserves necessary to make the trip. Especially if she wanted to still be there when the Mondeans inevitably attacked the Forest tribe.

It was a situation with no solution. She would simply have to pray to the Goddess that he'd survive the night and give him as much fluid as he could stomach.

In their early lessons, every mage had been taught by Voggo how to administer first aid and, in case it wasn't possible to move the wounded to the village, how to care for them.

Thus, Dorea relied heavily on those teachings as she looked in the woods for specific ingredients.

I might not have been trained as a shaman or a potioneer like Mom, but I have lived with them all my life. I can do this much.

She used her senses to identify the correct bushes, pushing them to the limit. The darkness didn't hinder her as she collected bilberries and willow bark. She conjured some water and pulped the ingredients into it, making sure to filter out the hard bits.

She then pushed the boy upright and, after opening his mouth with her hands, poured the liquid down his throat.

The brew was one she was taught would help with pain and inflammation, and since it contained water, it should replenish his liquids.

Of course, that would happen only if his system was still working well enough to absorb it, but there wasn't much else she could do about that.

Since his fate was in the hands of the Goddess, she left him propped up against a tree and went to check all the others.

A substantial amount of nicks and cuts were too fresh to not have been received during their escape, and she systematically treated them, using the little paste she had left sparingly, only on the worst injuries.

For the rest, she remade her earlier concoction and made them all drink it to help them along their road to recovery. Whatever the Mondeans had given to them to keep them down had to run its course sooner rather than later, as they were unlikely to want to lug them around when they could be made to walk on their own feet.

Either that or they never intended to wake them up.

But that's impossible; the women I overheard said that at least one would be given to the wood mage, which means they would need to be alive . . . I have to think positively. Otherwise, I'll never get out of this.

Dorea did her best not to fall into the hole of self-recrimination. Yes, she could have done better in defending her charges as they ran away, but maybe if she had focused only on defense, it would have goaded the Mondeans to attack even more; she'd simply never know.

And the fact that no one had died, even though Mark was severely injured, meant that she had achieved her objective of getting her people out of there.

There was no way she could have taken on the whole camp, and if she had left for Whitecliff to call for reinforcements, they simply wouldn't have made it back in time to catch them.

No, she had done all she could, and crying over her mistakes wouldn't fix anything. At least she had killed the wood mage . . .

Or have I? I don't remember any rush of power after I set off the Thunderclap. It's possible that he survived the blast and died later, during the chaos of the escape, but something tells me I would have known.

There was a difference in the types of elemental mana, and though she couldn't tell where one specific person's began and ended once she had absorbed it, she felt like she would have known if there was wood-aspected mana inside her.

Or maybe I was too far to absorb anything when he died? I keep forgetting that gathering mana is not an innate, automatic thing. I need to be there physically for it to happen.

That was a much better explanation. Of course, she'd never know until she saw the wood mage again.

Dorea wasn't one to relish in the act of killing, no matter how many times she had been forced to do it ever since the Wrath, but that was one person she wouldn't shed a tear for.

That reminded her that she was operating under a time constraint. If she wanted to be present to help when the Mondeans attacked—if they still did, but she didn't allow herself to think of such a rosy future—she needed to start moving soon.

She didn't know whether they'd still be able to locate the Forest village without the wood mage, but it was possible that they had already scouted it and were simply waiting at a distance for the opportune moment.

They might also simply wander around looking for it forever, but that felt more like wishful thinking.

She needed to settle the rescued mages, ensure they were safe even without her, and then rush back into the fray.

While she trusted the wards to hold for a while, she suspected not many of the Forest mages would be able to fight if they were breached. They might have their ancient spells, but that simply meant they didn't have to work as hard on developing their own skill.

Her planning was interrupted abruptly as she heard someone cough.

CHAPTER FORTY-TWO

The sound of coughing broke Dorea away from her contemplations. She jumped into action, rushing to Mel's side, helping the girl up, and pounding her back with a hand.

She finally stopped, gulping in large mouthfuls of air. Her unfocused eyes slowly regained their light as she slid down the tree Dorea had propped her up against.

"Careful now, take your time," the blonde whispered, conjuring a ball of water and offering it to the brunette.

"Wh-what's going on?" Mel asked fearfully.

Her expression crumpled as she regained her mental faculties, shivers shaking her frame.

Dorea immediately hugged her, trying her best to comfort the distraught mage. "You are safe now. I have rescued you all, and the wood mage has been dealt with."

She ignored the niggling voice telling her he might not have been finished after all. Even if he was still alive after what she had done to him, he wouldn't be in any condition to participate in the hostilities for a long time.

Her words were apparently all that Mel needed to finally break down. She gripped Dorea with surprising strength, desperately crying into her shoulder.

Whatever they had been through must have been horribly traumatizing, for someone like her to behave in such a way.

However much Dorea might not have gotten along with the girl, she knew her well enough to say that she had a core of steel, and to have been reduced to a crying wreck, the Mondeans must have treated her terribly.

They stayed there for a few minutes, the air mage crying her heart out as she released all the fear and pain she must have felt during her captivity.

Dorea felt somewhat awkward about it, since she hadn't been the best of friends with her, nor was she used to comforting others for so long, but she did her best to help her out, rubbing her back compassionately and muttering reassurances that she would be safe.

The moment was interrupted by the sound of shifting clothes as the others started waking up. Whatever the Mondeans had dosed them with must have been quite potent, as no one so much as made a peep during their flight, but it had evidently run its course.

The only one who still didn't move was Mark. The farmer's son was pale, and whatever energy his body had must have been spent trying to survive the loss of a limb and so much blood.

Dorea checked on him, grateful he was still breathing, before moving on to the others.

Tom, the friendly water mage, was the first to realize that they had been rescued, and as soon as he saw her, he started laughing in delight. "Yes! I knew it! I knew they wouldn't be able to get away with it!"

Dorea shook her head with a smile as he approached him. "How are you feeling? Everyone got banged up during the rescue, I'm sorry to say, but I've dealt with the worst of it."

His smile took on a more sinister look. "I'm fine. How many did you get?"

"At least five, amongst whom were the two guards. I've definitely injured the wood mage, but I'm not certain he's dead," she replied, immediately getting what he wanted to know.

"Good," was the only answer.

Tom was generally a pretty laid-back guy, but his latest misadventure seemed to put some backbone into him.

Dorea grinned back toothily, not having minded at all.

Unfortunately, she couldn't stay in the clearing, chatting with everyone as they slowly woke up from their drugged state.

If Dorea wanted to participate in the coming battle, she needed to start moving as quickly as possible, especially because her reserves weren't as full as she would have liked, which meant she needed to run without Air Boost.

She explained this to Tom, who shook his head, chuckling. "I get it. You need to be there. Kill as many of those bastards as you can!"

He slowly got up and started checking on the others, calling on his water magic to help clean wounds she had deemed not immediately important.

He shooed her away, taking on the role of first aid provider and doing a better job than she would have.

Dorea made sure he knew of Mark's condition, which he agreed to monitor with a grim cast. Beyond that, there was nothing else she could do.

They decided that as people started feeling better, two would be sent back to Whitecliff to ask for help transporting the farmer's son and whoever else needed it.

No one looked in good enough condition to participate in the coming battle, and Dorea didn't bother asking them.

Everyone had gone through a horrible experience, and while it might have been cathartic to face their captors in an open field, they risked doing more harm than good.

No, Dorea would go by herself, as at least one person from Whitecliff needed to be present. Otherwise, they'd risk the whole alliance.

If they were victorious, she'd spin a story of how the mage contingent had already fought with the Mondeans and had therefore done their duty.

Chief Samos was a reasonable person, and she was sure she'd be able to explain the situation to him without having to lie too much, as getting caught could have even worse consequences.

The last thing Tom informed her of was that another group of mages was expected to arrive within hours, this time from the south. It was something the Mondeans had known about—and he had overheard before getting drugged—and they had decided to attack so soon to beat them there.

The Heidels had apparently decided that they, too, would send reinforcements. Dorea only hoped they would arrive in time.

She left the ragtag group behind shortly thereafter, blasting off with an Air Boost to gain ground.

Half an hour later, she stopped the spell, wary of wasting too much mana.

I need to get there with enough power in reserve to enter the battle immediately. Of course, it'd be better if the Mondeans hadn't attacked yet, but knowing my luck, I shouldn't expect it.

As she ran through the forest, Dorea thought back to the rescue operation. She had definitely made some mistakes, like wasting too much time in the hopes of scoring some hits once she was found out, and she had been very fortunate to have had the idea to approach the camp from the sky, as it had likely saved her from being discovered.

But there was one thing she had done right, which she wanted to explore further.

During the volley she exchanged with the enemy mages, her control had been strained to the limits. Although she was the best at it in Whitecliff, she was still only a new Journeyman mage, and her skill level didn't permit such feats.

But necessity is the mother of invention. It's such a simple thing, pushing together the air barrier and platforms to make a spherical shield. But it still worked much better than anything else.

Not only did it block all the attacks that reached her, though admittedly they were severely weakened by the distance, but it also gave her much more maneuverability as she flew.

She had been so used to the platforms that she hadn't considered the possibility of improving upon them.

Of course, the power and concentration required for the sphere of air were much greater than that of a single platform, but if she could refine the concept in a spell, she'd have a fantastic addition to her repertoire.

The forest passed her by quickly as she maintained a decent pace in her run.

Her breath was steady, and the fresh morning air prevented excessive sweating. She stopped once in a while to regain her energy and gulped down some conjured water, but she always kept moving toward the Forest village.

I can see several different ways in which I could take this. Even just using it to fly around without having to worry too much about stability seems amazing . . . Well, the moment I have some free time, I should start working on it.

Dorea was aware that her fellow mages didn't all share the pressing need she felt to constantly push herself forward. Already, some were content with what they had achieved.

The most they would do was gather together to practice or show off, like that time at the beach, but there was no serious drive behind it.

Others, like Jonah or Mark the Blue, kept pushing themselves, but they still generally stuck to their strengths. After his first foray into offensive magic with the wind hammer, her friend had stopped that line entirely.

I understand that it's actually more helpful to the village as a whole that he keeps getting better at sensing and utility spells, but I just don't get how he can be content with it when there is so much more to do.

Admittedly, she had started her journey focused on combat magic, but she had never disdained other branches.

Indeed, just staying in the Forest village and having the chance to study their wards had made her want to experiment with some herself.

In the end, Dorea was aware that not everyone could be like her and that spreading herself too thin might be counterproductive to her efforts to stay at the top of the power rankings. Still, she just enjoyed exploring magic too much.

All through her deep pondering, she had gotten closer and closer to her target. Dawn had broken, and the sunlight had changed the scenery surrounding her.

The previously dark and foreboding trees were now a vibrant green, housing happily singing birds and critters of all types.

The woods were waking up with all the accompanying sounds and smells. Flowers started opening as boars snuffled around for sustenance.

It would have been an idyllic view, if only she didn't know that the Mondeans were likely approaching her allies in the same forest.

If they haven't already. I must have spooked them yesterday, but the fact that I only took the prisoners with me and didn't have a greater force alone probably told them I was by myself. They'll likely want to strike before reinforcements can come.

Having finally regained enough mana to feel comfortable using it to speed up her path, Dorea spun Air Boost around herself and quickly cut through the vegetation.

It took her another hour before she started noticing that the noises around her had actually quieted down.

This would have been impossible during the day unless in two specific cases.

Either one of the great predators of the woods had come out, but she was nowhere near one of those monsters' territories, or humans were making themselves noticed.

Considering how close she had gotten to Tumbling Lake, which she now knew served as a staging point for the Forest tribe's patrols, as it was the largest clearing close to their village, she would bet on the second of the two.

Dorea stopped her spell and advance, taking a moment to psych herself up.

The eerie silence told her that something was going on, likely a battle. She wasn't close enough yet to hear its sounds or feel it with her mystical senses, but her instinct told her that was it. And she had learned to trust it.

She drank some more water, quickly relieved herself, and hid her rucksack in one of the trees. It would only weigh her down in a fight.

Dorea slapped herself a couple of times to get her head in the right state of mind, which was easy considering the slowly festering anger she had been feeling ever since she had confirmed her worst fears of her friends having been taken prisoners.

More than that, her emotions in general had been close to the surface for a while, and though it was something she found useful in situations such as these, she decided she would have to talk about it with Voggo again soon.

It was time for a checkup on her "condition" anyways, and deep within, she feared the two might be connected.

From the distance, sounds of battle started filtering in.

The forest was quite dense this far in and acted as an excellent insulator, meaning the fighting had to be close for her to hear it.

Dorea quickly moved toward the noise, swearing under her breath at the worst-case scenario becoming reality.

She had hoped to have enough time to at least warn the Forest people about the Mondean contingent's composition and to rest enough to refill her reserves, but she'd have to make do with two-thirds.

I have become spoiled. In my first fight, I had a fifth of what I have now, and I still managed. If I can get a couple of hits in on their mages before they notice me, I'll be able to replenish my mana.

Finally, she started sensing the battle. From what she could tell, the Mondeans were having a tougher time than anyone had expected as the Forest people worked in concert with their signature spells, to significant effect.

They might not be particularly bloodthirsty, but their mages acting in lockstep as they wielded elemental armors and shot magical arrows was something to behold.

Surprisingly, it seemed like the Heidel group had made it in time. A dozen of them were fighting on the fringes, mostly handling the nonmagical and the long-range fighters.

Still, even if they might be able to win by themselves, the losses she could feel were already heavy, and if the fighting continued like it had been, they would only accumulate further.

It would be a pyrrhic victory, and since the Mondeans had shown absolutely zero hesitation, even after their assaults were repeatedly broken, such a loss of life could still spell their doom.

Now, Dorea was well aware that for all her growth, she still wasn't powerful enough to change the course of the battle by herself.

That meant that a direct assault was out. She couldn't simply come in from the side and start blasting. There wouldn't be anyone covering her, and she'd be forced to retreat immediately if she didn't get killed instantly.

No, she needed to pick a few specific people she'd try to take out from a safe distance.

There is no great body of water in the range I can use. Tumbling Lake is unfortunately too far for me, and even if it were here, I'd need to wrestle control of it from too many sources.

The problem with her plan was that magic had a tendency to lose its cohesion and power the farther it was from the caster, which meant she couldn't simply sit back in the canopy and shoot everyone from there.

Pressed for time, she opted to try and replicate what had worked the last time.

With a grunt of effort, Dorea condensed a sphere of air around herself, using it as both a barrier and a method of transportation.

Once satisfied with its thickness, she rose up in the air more smoothly than when using simple platforms, confirming that she needed to invest more time to make this construct into a spell.

Having risen above the trees, she finally saw the battle with her own eyes.

It was, at once, more and less chaotic than the one fought at the Rocky Hills.

There was no wall for the enemy to assault, as the Forest people would risk their wards' destruction in a direct confrontation, but their ranks were tighter than Whitecliff's had been. Their usage of the same spells all over the line gave the whole thing a more professional look, even though she could tell their mages were generally weaker.

The Mondeans, on the other hand, fought as they always did: with wild abandon and low cunning. They had the basics down as they concentrated their magical attacks on the center while the sides were made up of warriors who harassed at close range.

But it was obvious that no great tactician was guiding them, as the ranks were loose and discipline crumbled the moment one warrior thought they might have a chance at landing a final blow, even if it meant abandoning their post.

In all of this chaos, Dorea was glad to find a complete lack of wood magic being flung around.

The man might have simply not been a frontline fighter, but with what she suspected his role was, it was doubtful he wouldn't have contributed to the fighting.

It was much more likely that he simply was too injured to participate if he was still alive. But considering how the Mondeans had found the wards somehow, she didn't hold much hope there.

Still, she had a job to do, and so she set her mind to it. Identifying targets was more challenging than expected, as the lines shifted around as they fought, but she finally spotted the man who had first noticed her last night.

His long shaggy hair was easily recognizable, and the pencil mustache gave him away.

Thus decided, she drifted closer to the fighting until she was almost above it.

Taking a moment to align her shot, Dorea cast a Lightning Sphere through her wind barrier, noticing that it luckily didn't impede her workings much.

The ball of crackling electricity shot through the air, its speed enough that no one had the time to notice it.

It hit the man next to her target.

Unluckily for him, it was in the spell's nature to explode messily, and his entire left side was removed from existence by white-hot arcs.

Knowing that she couldn't count on her position being safe much longer, Dorea shot several barrages of Exploding Water Bullets into the mass of Mondean fighters before hurriedly flying toward her allies.

Her spherical barrier held under the barrage that came her way long enough for a blindingly bright shield to appear behind her and catch most of the attacks.

She let go of the cracked mess that had become of her protection and joined the line of forest people, walking as casually as she could.

"I told you she hadn't abandoned us!" exclaimed a familiar voice.

Dorea turned and saw Jasper, smiling brightly at her in relief, standing next to Shaman Samos, whose hand was extended toward the shield that had saved her hide.

"She has some explaining to do later. But first, let's deal with these bastards," the man grunted.

CHAPTER FORTY-THREE

She has some explaining to do later. But first, let's deal with these bastards," the man grunted.

Dorea smirked at the shaman and winked at Jasper, before joining back into the fighting.

The battle here was different compared to her last one. She had noticed this earlier, but being on the battlefield gave her a better perspective.

Not only had there been a pervasive sense of desperation during the one fought at Whitecliff that was missing here, but the stakes, in general, were lower.

The Mondeans hadn't managed to break the Forest people's morale by bringing out the wood mage—thanks to her intervention—and as such, they had been faced with a fiercer defense than they had expected.

To be honest, rather than a battle, this is a skirmish. People just don't commit enough to it to kill the enemy, instead preferring to stay safe. A lot have already died, that's true, but the numbers are just that limited.

The crux of the matter, though, was that neither force was capable of a significant victory. While she wouldn't have minded if the Mondeans ground themselves into nothingness, she couldn't allow that to happen to her allies.

"We need to do something to break them!" she shouted toward the shaman as she shot another wave of Bullets into the enemy shields.

Although Samos might have been annoyed with her for disappearing on the eve of the fight without saying anything, the man was savvy enough to leave that for later. "I know, but I have been too busy with shielding to do anything about it."

Dorea cast her senses into the enemy lines, seeking anyone who might have stood out in power, but found only average mages.

The Mondean Gifted were generally older than those from Whitecliff, probably because they had so many men, that they could send away to fight those that wouldn't change the tide of battle in their campaign in the mountains.

That, however, meant that only the lieutenants were formidable fighters, and it seemed that either this group's was skilled in stealth, or, more likely, given what she had overheard the night before, he was a political pick.

No one with personal power would have allowed the wood mage to behave in such a way otherwise, which meant that the commander was not as powerful as the tall woman she had fought at the Battle of the Rocky Hills.

Having considered all of that, she replied, "I'll take over shielding. You prepare what you can and deal with them once and for all."

Without waiting for a response, she grunted with effort as she put up a compressed air barrier inspired by her newest mode of transportation.

The wall slowly rose from the ground, causing shouts of surprise all over the battlefield, cutting off most of the attacks from the enemy lines, and leaving only the most skilled ones to watch out for.

Sweat beaded on her forehead as the effort of holding back so much power started crushing her. Dorea gritted her teeth and redoubled her grip on the magic.

More and more spells hammered into it, and had she been the girl she was even just two weeks before, she would have dropped the barrier then and there.

Instead, she dragged every ounce of mana in her system, grateful once again for the weird condition that had allowed her to steadily refill her reserves by killing enemy mages.

Finally, after what had to be no more than thirty seconds but felt like hours, a shout from behind called her back to the real world. "Drop down!"

Instinctively knowing that she had to follow the order or risk her own life, Dorea allowed the barrier to unravel, falling to the ground with a sigh of relief.

Above her head, a blindingly bright beam of light pierced through the remains of her magic, dispersing them like mist on a warm morning.

It made no sound, but to Dorea, it roared with the force of a hundred smilodons. Her system was entirely empty at this point, but she could feel it vibrating in response to the sheer mass of power that passed by her.

The beam lasted five more seconds, its power seemingly endless, but eventually, it ended.

Absolute silence followed for a while afterward. No one dared to move, as if afraid they could be targeted next by the immense power that had just been used.

Logically, Dorea knew that what had just happened had to have been caused by Samos and that the shaman would never do anything of the sort to his own people, but there was an instinctual part of her that screamed to stay still, so that maybe the predator wouldn't notice her.

She hadn't felt this way since that day in the grasslands, when Chief Yaomi took it upon herself to show her how vast the world could be.

Back then, she hadn't been able to sense the power used directly, but even visually, it had impacted her. What had just happened was on par with the column of fire she had witnessed that day, which told her Master-level magic had been used.

But that's impossible. Samos is undoubtedly powerful and gifted, but he's no Master . . . Unless it wasn't him who powered such an attack?

Her contemplation would have to be left for later since she started being able to feel some movement again.

The small trickle of power she had regenerated was definitely not enough to do anything with, but it allowed her to start sensing mana, which told her a rout was ongoing.

Carefully lifting herself from the ground, she winced at the pins and needles she felt in her limbs but still forced herself up.

Looking up, Dorea stared slack-jawed at the chasm that had been created. A five-foot-deep tunnel had been carved into the earth for at least five hundred feet, obliterating anything that had once stood there.

The Mondeans had been concentrating their strength in the middle, and where the majority of mages once stood, now there was nothing.

The remaining warriors, who had stood at the flanks and taken glee in harassing the defenders, were running away for their lives, leaving behind their more injured compatriots without a glance.

However much Dorea might have liked to chase them down and ensure they wouldn't be able to hurt anyone else, the gaping void she felt inside told her that she had definitely reached her limits.

She wasn't anywhere near as injured as she had been after the last battle, which she counted as a win, but she would be lucky to stumble around without help.

Every drop of mana she had had been used up to defend the line long enough for Samos to cast whatever *that* had been, and she felt that she had more than done her part.

So concentrated she had been on the enemy that she was surprised when she felt two hands grab her by the armpits and lift her up.

Dorea let out a squawk of shock, not having sensed anyone getting that close, and stumbled to the side, only to be caught again. "Steady there, I can tell you are spent. The battle's over."

It was the shaman, whom she had been thinking about just now, and he looked particularly haggard. His face was sallow, and his eyes tired, as if he had not been allowed sleep for a week.

The change in his presence from just a few minutes before told her that there had been a price to pay for such a powerful piece of magic.

"Thank you for your help, Dorea, daughter of Dodro and Lilian. It has been invaluable for the safety of our tribe, and I won't forget it anytime soon," he said, bowing his head.

The blonde sputtered, not having expected such formalities in the middle of the battlefield, but looking around, she noticed that people had already relaxed. There was a group forming up of what she suspected were the fresher warriors, who'd likely try to hunt down the remains of the Mondean force, but the fighting was over.

She returned her gaze to the chief, noticing for the first time the golden-threaded glove he was wearing.

It softly shone with unnatural light that, to her eyes, was slowly dimming. Thin chains of the same clothlike material hung loosely from each finger, apparently linked to nothing.

"O-oh yeah. We're allies; it's what we are supposed to do," she finally remembered to reply.

The man gave her one last tired smile before turning around to leave. "We'll talk more later. Please hang around this time."

His parting shot was somewhat deserved, even though Dorea was sure he'd understand once she thoroughly explained the situation.

"How cool was that?! Super beam, right in their face!"

This time, she wasn't surprised by the intrusion. Jasper's excited face was more endearing than annoying, even though she couldn't help but wonder how they were all getting used to fighting and death so easily.

"It was very cool. I still can't believe he could do that."

The boy got a shifty look, which piqued her interest. It was apparent that more was going on, especially considering Samos's sudden haggard appearance and his weird glove. Still, the fact that Jasper appeared to know something about it meant that it was common knowledge in the village.

Or at least, it wasn't that much of a secret. She put on her best smile and batted her eyelashes. "You wouldn't happen to know anything about that, would you?"

The boy held firm for about two seconds before his resolve crumbled. "He pulled from the wards. That's all I can tell you, really!"

Aha! So I was right in thinking that a power source was hidden in the village. And the weird glove thingy is probably an artifact made to control that power. And it likely takes a price from the user, given his condition. Which would also explain why he hadn't used it immediately. It's not like they were about to be overrun from the beginning, so it might have been better to hold such a card to his chest.

"Thank you, Jasper, you are always very kind to me." She bent down and kissed him on the cheek as a reward, leaving him red in the face and flustered.

The poor boy evidently didn't know what to do with his feelings, so he mumbled a goodbye and left.

Dorea shook her head in amusement at his antics. She then slowly started making her way to where the triage was being set up.

Although she didn't feel anything wrong with herself beyond the extreme tiredness that came from exhausting one's reserves so utterly, she had been scolded enough times to know that a checkup was still necessary.

She passed by the Heidel contingent, who looked to have made it through the fighting intact, even though they all sported some kind of injury.

She didn't know any of them, but she still stopped to say hello, remembering Voggo's lesson about how small acts such as that could only help.

As she waited in line for her visit, she directed her gaze to the wall of trees that served as an anchor for the wards.

It was apparent that such a piece of magic would also be greatly useful to Whitecliff. If they could discover the secret of their power source and possibly replicate it, they'd bypass the problem that stopped the previous generation from setting up a permanent one.

Maybe there is something in Voggo's archive. Goddess knows there are enough manuscripts and scrolls in there. We should probably attempt to learn more that way before we resort to espionage . . .

The remainder of the cleanup was left to the noncombatants once they had ensured no enemy was left nearby.

The one big difference with her previous experience was the almost complete lack of prisoners. Sure, they had caught a few as they tried escaping into the forest, but the colossal attack that had ended the fighting had also ensured almost none of the enemies survived.

It was as if a giant had taken a plow to the land and dragged it to make a trough. Everything that had been in its path was simply not there anymore.

It was a stark reminder that the world was much larger than she was used to.

Dorea might have fancied herself to be a talented mage and that her growth had been particularly fast, but nothing in her repertoire could have lasted a single second against such an attack.

Even if she were to put all her power into the wind barrier and concentrate it in a much smaller area than she had done to protect the shaman and give him the time necessary to prepare his attack, her resistance would have been futile.

The more I grow, the more I realize how much more I have to learn. There are people with more power in their pinkies than I have in my whole body, several times over.

Coming back to Whitecliff was always a relief after an extended mission. Doing so after having had to fight against the Mondeans, as they once again tried to break into their lands, and save her compatriots from captivity, Dorea felt a considerable weight be taken off her shoulders.

She had known that nothing had happened to the village, especially since a delegation had arrived at the Forest village, guided by Mark the lead scout, who had assured her of it.

Still, seeing with her own eyes that things were well was different.

The village was bustling with activity. Construction and refurbishment of abandoned buildings were ongoing, as they had been ever since the Wrath. The arrival of refugee groups had only made it more frantic.

Whitecliff was slowly but surely expanding, and Dorea knew of several expecting couples, which meant the population would keep increasing.

The fields were now being tended to by a mixture of those mages who preferred not to have to fight and the many people who didn't have a job of their own after leaving their villages.

Production was expected to be enough for everyone, especially considering what they could forage and hunt in the forest.

Surprisingly enough, more than a few men had volunteered to go fishing, which meant that these days the village had a much more stable source of seafood than they used to.

The situation with the Mondeans in the north was unlikely to resolve itself anytime soon, especially since—if what she suspected was right—they were sending only the dregs to fight them.

It was difficult for Dorea to imagine having so many people at her disposal that you could knowingly send them to their death. Still, it was almost certain that those they had fought were simply people who had been absorbed into the tribe as they kept growing and expanding.

Mav, the man she helped heal in the forest, had told her the Mondeans had about two hundred mages at their disposal. That number probably referred to the original tribe and didn't reflect the current reality.

To have sent forty or so Gifted over the course of the last few months and not have felt their absence at all meant that the actual number they had was likely above a thousand.

Facing such a force directly was simply impossible. Even when put together, the three allies in the south would be able to do little to defend themselves.

We are very lucky they are so busy with their war of conquest in the mountains. If they ever manage to win it and turn their attentions here fully, we'll be done for.

A part of her bristled at the thought of not having a chance. Hadn't she overcome the odds again and again? Hadn't they repelled attack after attack?

But she knew the truth. They would need a miracle to help them survive in such a situation.

Miracles I cannot do. But we can start setting up better defenses, that's for sure.

Indeed, the battle at the Forest village had shown her how useful the different branches of magic could be.

It was evident that if Whitecliff wanted to maintain its independence for much longer, it'd need to heavily invest in its defenses. Since no Archmage was about to take residence in their village to protect them, they'd need to do so themselves.

Luckily, they already had a solid base. The wall that encircled the settlement could be easily repurposed as an anchor for wards, from what little she understood, and it was only a matter of powering it out and deciding on the correct matrices.

Well, it's unlikely to be that simple, but I know Voggo has some records of the way we should craft them, and if there is something I'm good at, it's experimentation.

The war wasn't over, and Dorea was certain the Mondeans would pop up again, but for the moment, she'd have some time to dedicate to herself. To growing stronger, to deepening her friendships.

It wasn't exactly how she had imagined her life would go, but Dorea wouldn't change it for the world.

About the Author

Persimmon is the author of the Sapiens series, originally released on Royal Road. He has written fantasy stories for more than a decade and more recently began to specialize in the gamelit and progression fantasy subgenres. His work centers on themes of magical experimentation and adventure as well as exploration of the human psyche.

DISCOVER
STORIES UNBOUND

PodiumAudio.com